TWELVE BOUND BY FATE

MN BENNET

Hardcover ISBN: 978-1-967397-15-0
Paperback ISBN: 978-1-967397-14-3
Ebook ISBN: 978-1-967397-13-6

Edited by Charlie Knight (CKnightWrites.com)
Paperback cover art by Miblart (miblart.com)
Hardback cover art by GraphicSoul (https://www.graphicsoulart.com)
Formatting by Mayonaka Designs (mayonakadesigns.com)

www.mnbennet.com/

To everyone who has followed me since I started publishing. Your belief and support has brought this beautiful series to life.

READERS BE ADVISED

You've returned for the fifth installment in the Branches of Past and Future series. We're so close to the end of this six-book series. I've included a list of content warnings on the following page for those interested, and I will say they are mostly the same as previous installments. However, there are some darker elements added to this book.

You may know by now from reading this series—or even my others—that I very much believe in HEA and HFN in all my works. It's something I strive to bring no matter how long winding the journey is. You may be sad at times, but I hope you'll have a good time too. I try my best to include fluff where I can, sweet romance, and some laugh out loud scenes. I can't wait for you to see what's in store for Dorian, Milo, the students, and all the other wonderful characters popping onto the page.

This book contains the following elements:

Foul language
Alcohol use
Blood and violence
Scenes of graphic sex between adults
Character deaths (on the page, graphic and violent)
Animal death (on the page)
Strong themes of grief and guilt
Depression, anxiety, and self-hatred (both mild and overwhelming)
Queerphobia
Manipulation
Mental and physical assault
Bullying
Torture

I hope you'll enjoy this installment as much as I did.

There is a codex in the back of the book
explaining the magic and world in a bit more
detail for anyone who is interested.

WARD
REJUVENATION
PRIMAL
PSYCHIC
HEX
ENCHANTMENT
AUGMENTATION
BESTIAL
COSMIC
ENTROPY
ALTERATION
ARCANE
TELEKINESIS
SENSORY
BANISHMENT
LEVITATION

CHAPTER ONE

THE sky erupted with magic, surging with the radiant force of Gladiatrix's overwhelming power. In an instant, she had channeled enough force to sizzle the atmosphere and make every molecule in a quarter-mile radius vibrate. Even as nothing more than manifested psychic energy, my being shook in her presence. The mere aura of her strength hit hard. Gladiatrix released her levitation and nosedived to the ground. Each second, she plummeted while harnessing telekinesis, which propelled her faster.

Wards scattered across the cloaked base glowed in preparation for the assault. Not a single one had an opportunity to trigger, to activate, to defend the secret hideout of the Celestial Coven. One superior punch shattered every defense, from the wards lining the air to the sigils etched onto the building walls to the enchantments hidden beneath the surface of the ground. Gladiatrix's telekinesis boomed in waves, continuously circulating the terrain and smothering any opposition.

```
Name: Alicia Lawrence
Branch: Alteration (Supreme Physicality)
```

It made my presence difficult to maintain. Not that I was needed for this mission. My role in the Global Guild was quite limited. Mainly, I only existed as a discretionary consultant due to Milo's insistence and the fact that I was the only person who could remotely track The True Witch and her Celestial Coven.

All the same, I needed to be here. We hadn't located any of their hideouts in almost a month. After a small breakthrough over the summer, where I pinpointed nearly twenty secret refuges that The True Witch relied upon, our findings quickly became scarce, and the coven of vile witches worked harder to cover their tracks.

Gladiatrix tilted her head in a way that suggested she heightened her senses. I tried not to pry too deeply into her thoughts when she went on missions such as this. Mostly because she was the only witch I knew who was immediately aware of my psychic presence if I linked my telepathy to her mind. All part of her incredibly superior casting capabilities. Also, I wasn't technically supposed to send manifestations of myself on these infiltration missions. The Global Guild maintained strict rules on how their members, associates, freelancers, et cetera, used magic in their name. So, I used it in my name instead. All the same, Gladiatrix had a penchant for rules and maintained an adamant attitude toward authority and blah, blah, blah. Hence, I kept a healthy distance, barely glimpsing her surface thoughts.

"No witches, no warlocks, just demonic energy." Gladiatrix clenched her fists. "Looks like it's another demon disposal."

In a flash, she bolted through the steel doors of the facility and barreled ahead faster than my psychic presence could keep up with. Zipping down empty hallways and past abandoned rooms, she reached the hidden basement chamber where a murky mind dwelled in the shadows.

I didn't know how much the Celestial Coven relied on demons in the past, but since releasing and detaining Theodore Whitlock, the coven has kept plenty of them at nearly all their hideouts. No matter how quickly Global Guild forces scouted and infiltrated, there were never any witches or clues. Only demons.

"Only one demon," Gladiatrix said with a bored sigh. "Shame. Looks like the Celestial Coven might be running low on resources."

"They have no need for large forces when aligned with the tremendous strength of my kind." A pale gray creature slinked from the shadows, smiling with a jagged row of sharpened fangs.

Vampire! I shivered. Oh, how I despised vampires. They were some of the deadliest of demons lurking in the world. Thankfully, this one didn't possess a host body or bother augmenting its monstrous features into something humanoid, which vampires were notorious for doing. Unlike most demons, they could blend entirely in human form aside from prominent fanged eyeteeth and glassy red eyes. This vampire maintained its true form, though. Elongated arms reached its knees, which bent backward like a feline. The short black body hair added a bit of color to the hauntingly pale and clammy flesh.

"Soon, you will face the wrath of my entire clan, and as such, you shall know—"

In a blink, Gladiatrix leapt ahead and punched her whole arm through the vampire's head. She cast banishment in waves, shattering flesh and bone and tar in tandem.

"Next time, bring the whole clan to start with and give me a real challenge." Gladiatrix withdrew her arm, and by the time she wiped away a few drops of tar, the entire body of the vampire had been banished.

She truly was a one-woman army.

It didn't take long for her to clear away the rubble and search the debris in the basement for clues on the Celestial Coven's movements. I wasn't sure why Gladiatrix analyzed every little detail like they'd missed something. They never did. And anything potentially helpful was usually obliterated by their demon thralls before said demons were destroyed by Gladiatrix. Or any of the other Global Guild forces sent to investigate. Though, usually when it was out of the country, like this location, they wanted to send Gladiatrix because the board running the guild had to ensure the world only saw their best at work.

Once her search turned up nothing but scrapped tech, junk enchantments, and broken gadgets, Gladiatrix made her way back to the surface without investigating the upper levels of the building. The Celestial Coven never utilized any of their base's buildings but instead relied on network passageways below. This one didn't have much in that regard, so we were back to square one.

"You should've waited for me, love," a British accent called out.

A man flew toward us. Well, toward Gladiatrix. He wore a suit quite possibly more elegant and intricate than any of the suits Milo had. It didn't help that he had a majestic cape fluttering behind him. And yes, Gladiatrix wore her golden cape, too, but this guy used telekinesis to make the fabric flow. He wore a starlit silver mask that matched the interior of his cape design and an emerald green top hat that matched his suit. He was a pale man, ghostly even to me, and I lacked much of any type of tan. There was something oddly familiar about this man, but I couldn't place it.

The flutter of butterflies from Gladiatrix almost brought the walls of her thoughts down. My guess was she had a thing for accents or charming masked men. In either case, I didn't investigate too closely. Instead, I allowed the few surface thoughts that buzzed around her to fulfill my piqued curiosity.

"I told you I didn't need any backup," Gladiatrix said. "They didn't even bother with a real defense this time."

The last few operations she'd infiltrated had over a dozen demons awaiting her arrival. They didn't fare much better than the single vampire, so either the Celestial Coven was running low on demons they could control through Theodore Whitlock, or they figured it was a waste of valuable resources to throw them at witches like Gladiatrix, who cut through the fodder instantly.

"It's not about backup," the masked British gentleman responded. "I want to confirm the Global Guild isn't overstepping on matters best handled internally."

"The Celestial Coven is a *global* threat, and you're one of many countries they're bouncing between right now," Gladiatrix replied. "If you want to whip out the bureaucratic red tape, be my guest, but I don't have time for a pissing contest on who has the authority here, *King* Liberty."

"I'd never invoke bureaucratic policy, shudder the thought." King Liberty had a full-body convulsion to emphasize his comment. "I merely wish to keep things transparent with the public, that which should be known, of course. We both know your guild has the same cloak-and-dagger tactics as our Royal Army."

That made sense. King Liberty was one of those vigilante-approved witches in the UK. One of the more famous monikers, too. They had quite a few of them since all casting remained under the full control of the Crown. While vigilantes were popular among the public, those masked witches always had to maintain government approval to avoid arrest.

Kind of a paradox to be sanctioned by the government so they could act outside of government rule. Then again, I still found it hilarious how the monarchies clung to their authority by creating magical monopolies on who could and couldn't cast, then loaning their royal armies to their governments. Not that America had a much better system with guilds and governments arguing over power and freedom.

I didn't know the full extent of the current King Liberty, but the title and mask he wore came with notoriety. There was a lot of magical world history to cram into a single semester of classes, but I always managed to cover the Rise of Free Witches in the United Kingdom, which eventually led to vigilante witches casting all across Europe. When the monarchy seized control of all casting rights in the UK, they privatized and militarized all magic use under their authority, which allowed a lot of royal families across the continent to maintain power in some fashion.

The original King Liberty appeared over a hundred and fifty years ago. He was the first witch to oppose the Crown and use his magic for the betterment of the people without taking a cut of profits for the royal family.

This didn't go unchallenged, and for the better part of a decade, the Crown attempted to capture King Liberty for making a mockery of their rulership. When the military eventually detained the first King Liberty, they publicly stripped him of his mask, revealing the third son of the ruling family. A prince who would never claim the crown, and they painted him as a petty villain as opposed to a vigilante hero. They tortured King Liberty into confessing to acts of treason, and then they had him drawn and quartered. They burned his remains and used all the magic and influence at their disposal to remove him from all family records and public knowledge. His name never survived the test of time, but his legend certainly did.

His death wasn't in vain, as it inspired a new witch to wear the mask of King Liberty. The second King Liberty went on to inspire a hundred more witches to don masks of their own and carry the mantle of liberation. Those hundred vigilantes inspired a thousand more, and for the better part of a century, Europe had to contend against forces with real public appeal until they finally legalized the collection of masked heroes.

The current King Liberty was the twenty-second or twenty-third to wear the mask; I could never recall off hand how many there'd been. And I had no idea if he was part of the royal family or merely a citizen—the rumors made national headlines on occasion, but his mask and hat were seeped in enchantments and warding magics that kept my telepathy from delving deep into his mind. Probably something all the masked witches invested in to keep magic from outing their identities. Technology already gave them a run for their anonymity as it was.

"Does this mean you'll be abandoning me?" King Liberty asked. His flirtatious tone reeled me from my thoughts, and his emotions oozed with desire. "I was rather enjoying your company."

"Be grateful the Celestial Coven hasn't dug in deeper roots." Gladiatrix ignored his minxy smile and turned her gaze elsewhere. Despite her best efforts, she couldn't hide the coy smile King Liberty's flirtatious banter brought out.

With Gladiatrix and King Liberty settling into awkward conversation, it seemed there was nothing useful here for me to glean, so I crept back into the shadows of the psychic plane and traversed the magical realm to quickly return to my core self back in Chicago. A trip from England to the US took damn near a day for anyone else, but as a telepath with no limitations on the range of my magic, I swept across thousands of miles in mere minutes.

If only my manifestations could do more than observe, then I might actually be a real threat to the Celestial Coven and The True Witch.

CHAPTER TWO

I AWOKE to the throbbing headache of memories sorting themselves out in the worst type of mental Tetris. It seemed Gladiatrix didn't find any luck with the latest facility I'd located, which meant I needed to find another trail of Theodore or his mother. Their presence had become harder to pinpoint as the months passed, and fewer of my manifestations came back with results.

That said, I had a more difficult battle ahead of me this morning. Ben had slipped into our room again, unable to sleep by himself, and wedged himself between Milo and me around midnight. Now, he lay on top of me, sprawled out and crushing my bladder. When Milo made it clear he wanted to keep Ben and raise him, ensuring the kid didn't slip through the cracks after enduring so many horrors, I agreed to help. In order to officially foster Ben together, we had to prove we were a serious couple, which meant moving in together. Since Milo had the bigger place—an entire damn penthouse—I sold my house and moved in here.

Ben wasn't the only one currently crushing me. Milo had also nestled in closely because he loved to cuddle and hog the bed. He'd cocooned himself in the blankets and pressed himself right against me, nearly rolling me off the side of the bed. If that wasn't enough, Charlie had curled up into a tight ball of orange fluff and slept on my neck. Oxygen be damned when he needed his cuddles and affection.

"Meow," Carlie cried, which could only mean I was late when it came to providing her breakfast.

I sighed, showing her the mountain of clingy men in my life that kept me trapped in bed. Carlie didn't care. She strutted across the bed and gently nudged my foot with her head. A warning that a bite would soon follow if I didn't move.

With a delicate wave, I coiled telekinesis around Milo, Ben, and Charlie. Carefully lifting them, I twisted my wrist ever so to guide them to the other side of the king-size mattress. I set Milo down first, then placed Ben beside him and planted Charlie in between Ben's arms. As expected, Ben held him close, and Charlie nuzzled right up for the sleepy attention.

A piercing pain shot through my foot, and I nearly yelped, waking everyone up.

"Dammit, cat," I quietly hissed, which merely provoked a judgmental glare from Carlie, whose tail swished back and forth, thumping hard on the bed as she awaited her meal.

I got up, poured food in her bowl—skipped Charlie's bowl because I'd be damned if Carlie ate it all while he slept—then made my way through my morning routine. Bathroom, shower, balcony for a smoke. Except, I'd stopped doing that. I stood close to the balcony door, muscle memories and cravings still strongly intact even after six and a half weeks without a cigarette. It didn't take living together for long before Milo's worries and Ben's badgering had worn me down. I turned away and returned to the kitchen to cook breakfast. Well, if microwaving the breakfast sandwich Milo had meal-prepped counted as cooking.

Seriously, he'd make all kinds of dishes, from full-course meals to easy on-the-go snacks. He even made a bunch of those non-crust peanut butter and jelly sandwiches for Ben to take to school in his lunchbox. Milo had suburban dad hat down to a T, where I was still trying to figure out my place in the world.

Since my telepathy had grown, I'd decided to use this new gift to track down the Celestial Coven. Not that I'd been very successful. And technically,

I worked at Cerberus Guild again, but mostly just to appease the red tape that required me to be an official guild member enchanter in order for the Global Guild to acquiesce to my services as a freelance investigator in their case. Not that they wanted my help or used my services a lot. Most of my days were spent floundering between one project or another. It was almost October, and I hadn't started the new school year yet.

There was an emptiness that came with not returning to Gemini Academy. I'd kept my magic close to my students' minds over the summer to ensure their safety, but when the end of August rolled around and I hadn't returned to work, I closed off my mind to them. I wasn't ready for their reactions, their feelings—if they had any about my absence—but now that we'd entered October, they'd officially begin their internships. I truly hoped Chanelle found them all something perfect. I'd pestered her damn near enough to guarantee it.

"Morning, my grumpy little storm cloud." Milo wrapped an arm around my stomach and pulled me in for a hug from behind.

"You could just say good morning like a normal person."

"Where's the fun in that, my pouty prince?"

I sulked, which only made him giggle and squeeze me tighter. With his free hand, he moved it up my side until he reached my shoulders.

All these months later, he still tended to brush his fingers against the nape of my neck before kissing me there. I supposed he'd grown accustomed to my long hair and hadn't adjusted to the new cut. I liked it, though. Less maintenance, which was never my strongest trait.

"You nervous about today?"

"Why would I be nervous?" I shook loose and went to pack Ben's lunch. It mostly consisted of assembling the various snacks and such Milo had prepped in advance.

Admittedly, I was a bit anxious about today. The internships were officially starting up. I'd see my students again. Everything they worked for at the academy led them to their internship, and depending on who they landed with, it could make or break their chances in the industry. Not only that, but I wasn't with them these past few weeks and wasn't able to make any last-minute preparations. Wasn't able to ensure they'd stayed strong and done everything possible to improve their odds. I wasn't there. I wasn't—

"What's for breakfast?" Ben asked, pulling me from my concerns and back to the morning routine where my mind needed to stay grounded.

He was still in his pajamas as he trudged through the kitchen to the small eat-in table we often used for snacks and quick meals, unlike the dining room, where we tried to maintain regular dinners. Well, twice a week, for sure. Our schedules were a bit hectic here.

I ran my fingers through Ben's messy blue hair, fixing it some. Since harnessing his magic nonstop for days on end, his blue warding glow seemed to have forever seeped into his hair follicles. I didn't really have an answer for it. Neither did his pediatrician when we took him for his checkups, but she suggested it was nothing to worry about.

"Did you brush your teeth, mister?"

"No." Ben shook his head. "They're all gonna fall out, anyway."

"Yeah, but you need good habits," I explained. "For when your grown-up teeth come in."

"No, I'll just get dentures like my nanna had. Seems easier."

Milo chuckled.

"*Tell him to brush his goddamn teeth,*" I thought at Milo, linking our minds.

"You still gotta brush 'em, lil dude," Milo explained with a reluctant sigh as I continued badgering him with my thoughts. "Even if you want dentures, you need good gum health. And also, if you don't brush your teeth, your tongue could get moldy and fall out."

Ben gasped. "Will it turn blue? Like the moldy cheese? Maybe it can match my hair."

"No," Milo said, struggling not to smile. "It'd probably be black mold."

"Cool!"

"Not cool," I corrected, giving Milo another glance.

"And Dorian won't let you eat dessert if you don't brush your teeth."

"Oh, that's all the way at dinner. I can brush them then."

"You know he's got a long, grumpy memory. Might not wanna risk it."

Ben huffed, then stomped toward the bathroom, announcing every step of his morning routine.

"Taking off the cap," he shouted. "Squeezing toothpaste. Turning on the water."

"Why must you always make me the villain?"

"Because I'm not built for being the mean parent."

"And I am?" I glowered.

"I mean, if the scowl fits." Milo gestured to my frowning face, which he'd envisioned in his thoughts, giving me a much angrier expression and horns.

"Asshole."

"Language." Milo nodded as Ben made his way back to the kitchen table.

I huffed, buried my craving for a cigarette, and joined them for breakfast. As much as I couldn't stand being around either of them most of the time, I couldn't imagine my life without Milo and Ben.

"Meow." Charlie headbutted my leg and chirped until I reached down and pet him.

I couldn't imagine life without my kitty cats either.

Despite the looming threat of unknowns roaming this world, I was quite content with my life and how it'd turned out.

CHAPTER THREE

MILO and I dropped Ben off at school and then drove to work. Together. I still hadn't wrapped my head around all of it. Today wouldn't help matters. I'd be swimming in teen angst all morning once they arrived.

"You excited?"

"To brace for hundreds of obnoxious teen minds?" I scoffed. "It's gonna be a headache."

Milo tsked. "You're excited. Bet you've even got a little countdown going on in your head."

He whipped up to the front of Cerberus Guild and let one of the newer acolytes valet his car into the parking garage.

"Such an appropriate use of company resources."

"Did you just call him a resource?" Milo gasped. "He's a person, you know."

"You treated him like a resource, parking your car. I was making commentary on how that wasn't appropriate."

"For shame." Milo mockingly shook his head in disapproval.

"Oh, go fuck yourself."

"Why would I do that when I've got you for that?" Milo wiggled his eyebrows. "Speaking of...our morning is pretty clear until the interns show up. Wanna head up to my office for a little fun?"

"Pass," I said. "I'm gonna wait here for the students."

"Suit yourself." He swaggered away, intentionally making his hips and ass all the more appealing with each step he took. *"Don't come crying to me this afternoon when you're craving my cock."*

"Asshat." I huffed.

Most enchanters, acolytes, and other employees went about their morning like it wasn't any different from any other day. Granted, a few minds scrambled with a checklist of tasks to complete before the interns arrived, but no one waited as anxiously as I did. They'd all grown used to the yearly routine of gaining an intern or two and treated it more like a chore than an honor.

I found myself excited, eager, and on the edge of my seat. Which was why I decided to stand and wait. Milo kept his thoughts guarded, but I knew he had the guild master's ear and knew who everyone had been assigned to. Part of me hoped I had a student I knew, someone I had taught. Another part of me was drowning in anxiety over the pressure of having an intern. I'd only just recently returned to guild life, and I wasn't sure if I was ready to ensure someone—or someones; I might've ended up with two or three interns—was ready for the industry.

Students began to trickle in at Cerberus Guild, small groups at first, all hesitant to be the first through the glass doors leading into the most prestigious company in all of Chicago.

It was amazing seeing my homeroom coven again, even from a distance. How they'd grown since their first day at Gemini Academy. Naturally, Kenzo was the first one through the front doors, and much to my surprise, he managed to drag two of his classmates with him.

```
Name: Kenzo Ito
Branch: Hex (Disruption)
```

Rankings didn't matter much now that they'd landed their internships. But I hoped they'd continue improving this year, even students like Kenzo, who maintained top placement his entire time at the academy.

"Whoa, this is way bigger than my parents' guild," Gael said; the spikes lining his face helped frame his smile.

```
Name: Gael Martinez
Branch: Augmentation (Spikes)
```

I expected Gael to walk in alongside Kenzo since his bossy boyfriend tended to drag him everywhere for studying or training. But the bright smile and wide green eyes from Caleb as he strolled in on Kenzo's other side was quite surprising.

```
Name: Caleb Huxley
Branch: N/A
```

I figured he would arrive on his first day with Katherine or literally any other classmate. But it seemed, despite Kenzo's demanding rigor and brutal discipline over their summer training, he hadn't run Caleb off. I nearly smiled, glossing through each of their surface thoughts and gleaning that they both held the memory of Kenzo's apology close. Caleb considered it a breakthrough and a sign of rebuilding something. Kenzo only recalled his shortcomings and analyzed ways he could improve upon a future apology, which he truly believed Caleb deserved. But right now, Kenzo believed the only thing Caleb deserved was beratement, and he went off about his sloppy form during their morning job, which happened to include the banishment of neighboring wisps.

That explained why Gael and Caleb's pale faces were so flushed; they basically ran a half-marathon this morning at Kenzo's insistence. The pair ignored Kenzo, nodding in unison as he explained where they each needed to improve for the future, especially if they wanted to stand out during their internships.

Since internships didn't require students to wear their academy uniforms, the boys showed up in their own clothes, and much to my dismay, they wore workout gear. Nice workout clothing. Fine fabric tanks and name-brand joggers, but still gym clothes all the same. Not what I'd have recommended. Kenzo badgered Caleb that it didn't matter what they wore, and apparently, Gael seconded it with his knowledge of how guild internships worked based on his family ties to Hydra Guild.

"Mr. Frost!" Gael waved, rushing past Kenzo and over to me.

"How are you—"

"I'm fantastic," Gael blurted, his thoughts racing faster than I could track, and the words poured out almost as quickly. "It's so great to see you. How've you been? I've got so much to tell you. Oh man, you wouldn't believe who our new homeroom instructor is. Mrs. Whitehurst. She basically runs all the homeroom covens, though. I guess that's part of her new job. Not like your new job, Mr. Frost. Oh, crap. Not mister. Sorry about that. It's Enchanter Frost now, right? That's so cool. What inspired you to get back into guild work? Did you know today's our first day as interns? Bet you'll be one of our enchanter mentors. Oh, that'll be so cool. Think you'll have one of us? Who would it be? Who would you want it to be? I bet you'd wanna mentor—"

"None of us," an obnoxious voice interjected.

Without even turning, I knew who'd arrived. The minxy chaotic energy was palpable. Plus, the mere presence of this irritating student brought on a migraine. Not just from me. Even Kenzo's thoughts turned to frustration as he and Caleb made their way over.

"I can't believe you hated us sooooooo much you literally quit teaching," Gael said with boisterous laughter accompanied by the cluck of his rooster. The pair wore matching vests. Vibrant orange vests, which accentuated King Clucks' feathers and complemented Gael's deep amber complexion. Gael's surface thoughts indicated he'd spent a lot of time planning to roll in here with the perfect outfit for himself and his familiar.

```
Name: Gael Rios-Vega
Branch: Bestial (Familiar)
```

"Ba-ba-bawk," King Clucks added—something rude, as it made Gael snicker.

"Yeah, how terrible was Kenzo?" Gael asked, implying he was the source of my fleeing the world of education.

I sighed. If only it were that simple. "You realize I wouldn't be your homeroom teacher. Third-year students work directly with—"

"Blah, blah, blah." Gael waved a dismissive hand. "Yeah, yeah, but you still bailed on us. I was gonna take your history elective, but since you hated us so much that you quit—"

"He didn't hate us," Gael said, standing closer to Gael and King Clucks.

"You didn't, Mr. Frosty?" Gael asked with a twinkle of mischief in his brown eyes. "I mean, Enchanter Frosty."

"No, I could never hate anyone."

"Bullshit," Kenzo's thoughts nearly rattled me as he went down a list of students and staff he assumed I must've hated as he found them quite vexing. Naturally, despite how irritating Kenzo himself was, he had keen observations. I wouldn't say I hated the folks he listed off, but I could live peacefully without seeing a great deal of them ever again.

"So, why did you leave?" Gael asked.

Before I could form a response—a vague non-truth—Gael, being the kindest person in the world, spared me the headache.

"I bet he couldn't imagine life in the classroom without us," he said, flexing his spiked biceps. "We were absolutely wonderful. Delightful. And inspiring. Watching us chase our dreams is definitely what motivated Enchanter Frost to dive back into the industry. Right? Am I right? I'm totally right. Right? Right?"

He wasn't that far off. My homeroom coven did push my desire to go back into the industry. Granted, it had more to do with averting a possible future of them all dying along with the rest of Chicago, but they didn't need to hear that part.

"As per usual, you're absolutely correct, Gael."

"See." Gael's sharklike teeth beamed. "We're awesome sauce."

Gael and his rooster squinted, surface thoughts bubbling with suspicion before he finally let his mind settle on one warning. *"Do what you want, Mr. Frosty, but don't stand in the way of my internship with my boy Enchanter Evergreen."*

I scoffed. As if Milo would ever take on an intern. He'd already shrugged off his duties with his former acolytes, leaving them to fend for themselves.

"Hey, it's Mr. Frost!" a familiar voice called out.

"And Gael," the same voice responded.

"And Gael with Kenzo," another voice said. "And Caleb."

"You owe me twenty," said the same voice. "I said he wouldn't kill him before the internships."

"No, I said that."

"No, I did."

"No, you didn't. I did!"

"Neither of you liars said it. Carter did."

I turned to see a cluster of identical copies of Jamius huddled together with books in their hand. One by one, their attention waned, and they drifted away from their original ringleader.

"Focus up, fellas." Jamius clapped his hands to get the attention of his eight copies walking alongside him; each drifted back into formation with their eyes fixed on a book and doing their best to ignore their desperate urge to chat with the other students in the lobby. He'd taken out his braids since the last time I'd seen him, allowing for a more natural afro.

```
Name: Jamius Watson
Branch: Alteration (Duplication)
```

It was nice to see Jamius take my advice on expanding his comprehension through his copies. He'd gone an extra step, ensuring they each read and retained intel on all the Cerberus Guild protocols, industry standards, and enchanter stats. When Jamius reabsorbed his duplicates, he retained the knowledge and information they acquired without him, meaning he could amplify his learning intake so long as he could make his copies cooperate. We'd never made it that far in class, so I rather liked seeing him pull it off now.

One by one, his copies handed Jamius a book and exploded into nothingness. As the crowd thinned, I saw a fiery redhead making her way inside.

"Hey, guys," Melanie waved her hand, adding a flair of fire in the process.

```
Name: Melanie Dawson
Branch: Primal (Fire)
```

"You see that, Mr. Frost?" Melanie asked, noting how smooth her control over flames had become.

"It's Enchanter Frosty," Gael corrected.

"Oopsie," Melanie said. "Did you see that Enchanter Fro—"

"Melanie, don't waste words on basic nobodies." Layla raised her clawed hand, then gestured as if to shoo me from her presence. "Not all enchanters are equal, and you should honestly only speak to those on track to be successful. Not the pity hires."

```
Name: Layla Smythe
Branch: Bestial (Therianthropy)
```

She didn't wear her typical oversized academy blazer and tiny skirt. Instead, Layla wore a form-fitting bubblegum pink dress with black lacing. Melanie's mind wandered to the price tag, indicating Layla's accessories for the dress cost more than half her wardrobe. In truth, Layla had gone all out for today, convincing her parents to purchase her a customized designer augmentation wardrobe.

Augmented clothing lines allowed witches who shifted their physical form, much like Layla, not to rip apart their outfits. It magically changed with them. But Layla couldn't wear some basic bitch outfit. No, she needed the best designers to work with enchantments meant to create their augmentation clothing lines. She literally hired her own clothing line from the elites.

Layla stood for a few more seconds alone in the lobby area with Melanie until a handful of girls from Gemini arrived. Layla eyed each of the girls up and down in attendance, ensuring all put their best on today. Somehow, in her mind, they were there to make a good impression that'd properly reflect Layla. Okay, that I didn't miss. With a smug smirk of satisfaction, Layla turned on her heel and led the way as the group followed behind her like some gang of popularity.

I allowed my telepathy to drift outside and away from the noisy cluster of so many teens inside the lobby.

Two of my students nearly bumped into each other as they arrived from opposite directions.

"Whoops," Tara said, twirling around Katherine.

The pair laughed and paused for a breath neither had taken since rushing to the guild.

Katherine brushed a hand through her recently straightened, long, dark brown hair. She did her best to keep it presentable, but ended up having to fly to Cerberus Guild since she spent so much of her morning getting ready. Everything took more time than expected, from her make-up to her sapphire blue heels, which she already regretted thanks to the pinch of her toes, all the way to her dress that she'd picked out of quite possibly a hundred outfits this morning. Katherine wanted this morning to be perfect.

"You brought your familiar?" she asked.

Tara nodded. "I think she's close to leaving her cocoon and didn't want her to be stuck at home all day if that happened."

I smirked, eyes flitting toward Gael, which made him quirk his pierced brow in confusion and curiosity until my expression shifted into a scowl, and he returned to his conversation with the others.

While I didn't know everything my students had been up to over the summer, I did know the main components, which involved Gael rescuing a caterpillar that inched its way toward Tara from the clutches of King Clucks' beak. Even without knowing, Gael sensed the magic stirring in the tiny hungry insect, and somehow, he convinced Tara to keep a watchful eye over the bug until her link blossomed a few days later, and she awakened yet another branch.

```
Name: Tara Whitlock
Branch: Ward (Sealing)
Branch: Cosmic (Shadows)
Branch: Arcane (Intangibility)
Branch: Primal (Icicles)
Branch: Psychic (Banshee's Wail)
Branch: Bestial (Familiar)
```

"I see I'm not the only one lugging around massive equipment." Tara eyed the grimoire strapped to Katherine's hip.

A huge book, twice the size of a standard grimoire, and barely contained in Katherine's customized holster. She unstrapped it and held it in her hands. Katherine walked alongside Tara, showing off her new grimoire. Well, her old grimoire, by the looks of the cracked, creased binding of the book.

"Fancy," Tara said. "Or what's the opposite of fancy? Vintage? Can grimoires be vintage?"

```
Name: Katherine Harris
Branch: Enchantment (Spell Craft)
```

"Yes and no." Katherine held the book close. "My mom suggested I come with something impressive for my internship, something that shows my mentor I'm ready for anything."

"And this book does this how?"

"It's a rarity. My family has a lot of one-of-a-kind and long-since forgotten grimoires," Katherine explained. "This one happens to predate the fall of magic. Apparently, the Harris women passed it down over the generations, and many of them tried to access the spells with no success during the Eras of Silence."

Eras of Silence. A reference to the hundreds of years, magic had died out. No one knew why, but magic had vanished for many years before returning. Some people knew. I had access to the memories of three witches, the Sisters

Three, who knew of life before the fall of magic, but their memories were so jumbled and guarded that I'd barely made sense of any of it. Hell, understanding Milo's visions was easier than making sense of those dead witches' memories.

"And your mom seriously let you bring that?" Tara's question drew my thoughts back to the present and away from the mission I had, the one where I would bring down the Celestial Coven.

A twinge of guilt hit me, merging with a memory Tara kept close to the surface of her thoughts. Brewing like a storm above her ocean of sorrow lay the revelation Enchanter Evergreen shared with her over the summer. I couldn't in good conscience let the Global Guild make moves against the Celestial Coven without sharing the very twisted truth with Tara.

Tara stared blankly at Milo, completely dumbfounded by the news of The True Witch, the woman who aligned herself with Theodore Whitlock, the witch who planned to conquer the world.

"Of course she couldn't have just abandoned me," Tara had said to Milo, eyes flitting to the screen which projected her father since he still remained out of the country for business, but in truth, I suspected he hid from Amara and her coven. "So, she wants to unleash Hell and thinks I'm the key to this plan?"

Milo had nodded. It pained me still that he'd held back certain details, but Tobias Whitlock and the Global Guild were firmly on the same page: Tara didn't need to know the full extent of her mother's power or how she believed her daughter was a goddess meant to rule over everything. It was deranged. But that whole Celestial Coven held fancies of godhood, deluding themselves into believing their witchcraft held some sacred, ancient secrets.

What would Tara do when she learned her mother was the immortal leader of a coven bent on destroying the world because they believed in the gods of old?

"This fucking family." Tara burst into laughter. "I swear."

"It's important to note that Theodore may not be working with her willingly."

"Of course not. She's planning to control the world, and he wants to burn it all down." Tara shrugged, then cut her gaze toward her father. "But I'm sure neither would be profitable to Whitlock Industries, so hopefully, our shareholders devise a perfect plan."

"This is serious, Tara," Tobias finally spoke up.

"You can tell me all about how serious it is the next time I see you." Tara closed the computer and smiled at Enchanter Evergreen. "If that sums everything up, I should get going. School's around the corner, and I've updated my casting permit yet again."

With that, Tara kept the sadness of the memory buried and out of reach. It didn't pain her because she didn't dwell. Worse, she ignored it.

I shook away the memories Tara held, focused my telepathy, and stayed grounded here and now. There wasn't much I could enjoy with the stress of The True Witch and her coven looming in the world, threatening everyone, but I'd be damned if that fear stole today from me. I wanted to be present, see my students' arrival, watch the looks on their faces as they were assigned mentors, and silently cheer for them and all their successes.

"When you land an internship with who I landed with, definitely." Katherine's smile blossomed, reeling me closer.

She truly felt on top of the world, her thoughts soaring with excitement for today. Mostly for herself and the hope she had to impress her mentor, but also as she made her way inside, her thoughts flitted with excitement for her peers, her friends, and even the students at Gemini she didn't recognize in the lobby.

Trailing outside, not too far from Katherine and Tara, was another pair I had looked forward to seeing again.

"Sup." Carter fist-bumped a friend of his from the tennis team with his free hand before being dragged away by Jennifer, who had her fingers interlocked with his other hand. "Whoa!"

Carter took dramatic tumbling steps beside his girlfriend, half playful and half serious, since Jennifer didn't let up until they escaped the growing crowd.

Carter waved farewell to his teammates, knowing he'd see them at the first and final game of the season. He'd heeded my warning last year and finally worked up the nerve to tell his coaches he had to step down from the team to focus on his internship. It wasn't anything they weren't used to. Third years almost never followed through on sports or extracurriculars. Their main focus had to be their internships, especially if they wanted to land in a guild.

```
Name: Carter Howe
Branch: Rejuvenation (Vitality)
```

Given his magic and the versatility he had with it, Carter had a lot of options. Hell, I'd write him a letter of recommendation myself, considering he saved my life. But it honestly all came down to whether he ended up with the right mentor this year. Cerberus didn't have the best rejuvenation witches, and I knew Chanelle mentioned they'd be outsourcing to other guilds to fit the right bill for their student body, but honestly, I only wanted the best for Carter. For all my students. Admittedly, I'd always have a soft spot for Carter above the others. After all, he was the only reason I was here to see and support everyone.

Once they'd gotten inside, Jennifer squeezed Carter's hand tighter, focusing on his emotions above all others.

```
Name: Jennifer Jung
Branch: Psychic (Empathic)
```

Given the whirlwind of thoughts that hit me with this cluster of excited and anxious students, I could only imagine the emotions she had to endure.

A sharp pain of familiar stress struck Jennifer, and she buried it. The emotional wavelength was from someone she knew, someone I knew, too.

I cocked my head as Jennifer and Carter made their way through the lobby. Working my telepathy past them, I made my way back outside yet again. A nervous mind anxiously stood alone and watched everyone else make their way inside. I stretched my telepathy so I could glimpse this familiar mind, and much to my surprise, I spotted Yaritza standing alone in a blue dress, digging her heel into the pavement and working up the strength to step inside and smile.

```
Name: Yaritza Vargas
Branch: Cosmic (Star Shower)
```

Rarely did Yaritza show anything other than excitement for things to come, life, a random event, or quite literally anything. I lingered by her as a phantom of psychic energy, trying to find the source of her nervousness. It didn't dwell on the surface of her thoughts, but it ate away at her all the same. The more I searched, the more I began to realize how little I knew Yaritza compared to some of my other students. She always seemed fine. Truly content, and like a fool, I check-marked her off my to-do list of those to concern myself with. She wasn't the only student I glossed past, ignoring pain that didn't immediately catch my attention.

There were a few homeroom coven students who'd slipped through the cracks, so I could favor others and prioritize their needs as I worried for their well-being.

I shuddered, guilty and consumed, and let my telepathy cling close to Yaritza as she finally found the courage to step inside. With a bubbly smile and an exaggerated wave, she greeted everyone around her. None would notice the depression etched into her soul. Even I barely felt the trace amounts as forced joy covered insecurities. Pain and stress that'd been rooted deep inside her for years. Depression I'd ignored because it never outshone the illusion she put on, even internally.

My shoulders hunched, shamefully retreating into myself in horror that I'd missed this for so long.

The room swelled with elation, twisting thoughts into a frenzy of excitement, and before long, I'd lost track of Yaritza's sorrow or much of anything aside from the buzzing energy at the sudden arrival of everyone's favorite enchanter.

Milo waved to the crowd of students, ushering them to follow him toward the front doors of the building.

"It's an honor to have you all here," Milo announced. "Every enchanter is eager to start working alongside you, to see the magics you've learned to harness, the skills you've mastered, and the wonder you'll bring to the industry."

Cheers of delight followed, and Milo paused, allowing the energy to simmer some before he continued.

"Join me outside. We could take the stairs or, like, a million elevator trips, but I think a group as classy as you all deserve to meet their mentors in style." Milo levitated, leading the way to the upper floors of the Cerberus Guild, where he'd had several windows removed and turned into entryways that'd quickly funnel in hundreds of eager teen witches flying around the building.

I groaned and made my way to the elevator. Insufferable.

Chapter Four

I KEPT my telepathy looped close to my students, allowing a meager manifestation to float by them throughout the open space of the offices. This kept my mind mostly calm in the presence of hundreds of eager thoughts and the busy bustle of the city. Seriously, since the expansion of my telepathy, things had become even more chaotic in my day-to-day.

They'd cleared out all the cubicles belonging to the acolytes to make room in this space for the interns' arrival. It'd all get sorted back soon enough, but Cerberus Guild likely wasn't used to hosting several hundred students for announcements such as this. The room was cramped and stuffy and filled with far too many people, from eager interns, annoyed acolytes, and bored enchanters.

Guild Master Campbell stepped up to the podium, introducing herself, the importance of guild work, and how honored she was to be a part of this process before graciously stepping aside and making way for the new coordinator.

Chanelle practically floated as she approached the podium. Much like Campbell, Chanelle came out in a sleek business suit. The vibrant yellow of her blazer and pantsuit accentuated her deep brown complexion, and the gold of her blouse framed the jewels around her neckline. Since stepping up into this position, Chanelle had done everything in her power to match the prestige of the elites she worked side-by-side with each day. Even if it seemed to eat into her meager budget. Comparatively, at least. She might've left the classroom, but she was still far too close to education to make any real money.

The crowd of students cheered her on with almost as much excitement for her arrival as they did for Milo's. I rolled my eyes. She'd never survive outside the classroom. She liked building student connections far too much. It was annoying how she treated them like friends. At least she didn't do it in a pushover way; she merely used some tragic technique to make kids feel like equals through connection and blah, blah, blah.

I took a tense breath and let go of the thoughts. I was no longer a teacher. It was like carving out huge chunks of my identity, but I needed to stop dwelling on who I was and focus on who I needed to be in order to stop the Celestial Coven.

"It's wonderful to see all your faces this morning," Chanelle said. "Most students will be meeting their enchanters here this morning, but a few of you will be going to another guild for your internship. The purpose isn't that we couldn't find a placement for you in these wonderful halls, but rather that we found a more suitable mentor elsewhere. We want what's best for your magic and potential. It's important to ensure that everyone is paired with a compatible enchanter."

"Oh, who cares about the speeches and bullshit," Gael said, tuning out Chanelle's speech. "I just want them to get to the part where I'm working with Evergreen."

Kenzo tsked. "As if, bird brain. A moron like you? Yeah, right."

"I happen to know I will be working with Evergreen," Gael said with smug satisfaction, followed by a confident cluck of his rooster.

Based on his buzzing thoughts, he seemed quite confident in the fact.

"Sure." Kenzo nodded mockingly.

"You don't believe me?"

"I believe you believe it, but I also believe you're an absolute idiot, so there's that."

"Oh yeah?" Gael dug through his book bag. "Would an absolute idiot get one of these?"

He held up a crinkled form.

"A waiver excusing the guild for any injuries you might have during your internship?" Kenzo skimmed the form, letting out a light chuckle. "They'd definitely give you one of those. Of course, Cerberus is worried you'll injure yourself. Extra layer of legal protection."

"It's not from Cerberus," Gael said.

I closed my eyes so I could focus purely on the sight of my manifestation, who glossed over the messy, stained form. It was a waiver of liability and far more detailed than the standard waiver that Gemini Academy had students sign for attendance or internships.

"Wait," Kenzo nearly gasped. "Global Guild sent you a waiver?"

"Yep." Gael had this arrogant smirk. "And there's only one enchanter at Cerberus I know of that works at the Global Guild. So, looks like I'll be teaming up alongside the best enchanter in the whole world, while you probably get assigned a custodian or some shit. Maybe they'll teach you how to clean up your bitch attitude."

Kenzo balled a fist, creating a small burst of gray static before allowing the rage to fizzle away with his pent-up magic. A dozen or so quickly fleeting images of Kenzo bashing in Gael's face flooded through the angry teen's mind before he composed himself.

"You're not the only one with a waiver." Carter strolled up, revealing a pristine form unlike Gael's stained pages.

"Wait, Evergreen wants to work with you, too?" Gael stared suspiciously.

"Ba-ba-bawk."

"You're right, King Clucks." Gael nodded. "*Totally, just bringing him on 'cause he helped Frosty way back when.*"

Wait, what? Did Milo seriously recruit Carter as an intern because he saved my life? And why the hell would he ever recruit Gael as an intern? Why would he recruit any of my students as an intern?

It didn't take long before they projected all the internships, and I searched for my students among the very crowded roster.

Mentor: Enchanter Evergreen
Intern: Gael Martinez

The way Gael's aura lit up, radiating bright orange, it nearly outshone the streaks of envy clouding the edges. His spikes shrank a bit when his peers eyed him. Normally, he enjoyed attention, not a spotlight hog, but definitely in a goofy extrovert way. However, the jealousy etched onto a lot of expressions made his stomach twist in knots, and in turn gave me sinking, sulking secondhand symptoms. His emotions and thoughts surged with insecurities, outweighing everyone else.

"Way to show everyone up, porcupine." Kenzo shoulder bumped Gael, stealing his focus from the gawking crowd, and making him sheepishly smile.

I took a deep breath. Suddenly, the stress and fear withered away. All it took to calm Gael was a simple gesture of support from Kenzo.

"I mean, I didn't really do anything to land the internship." Gael's shark-like teeth glistened as he fought to keep his smile.

"What the actual hell?" Gael shouted, accompanied by a loud cluck. "They clearly put the wrong last name."

"Um, pretty sure it's not a typo, dude." Gael pointed further on the board. "Found you with another Global Guild enchanter."

Mentor: Enchanter Diaz
Interns: Gael Rios-Vega; Tiffany Sparks; Wesley Monte

Gael sulked, dwelling on this horrid placement. Even Tiffany's brief smile didn't lift his spirits, though he mentally noted how the gesture must've meant they weren't fighting this week, so he'd try his luck at flirting later. Christ, that kid had a one-track mind.

No wonder he had to sign a Global Guild waiver. Gael hadn't been assigned to Milo, but instead the very famous Texas Daddy—ugh, how I loathed that stage name—since the enchanter had set up roots in Chicago until the Celestial Coven mission was resolved. One would think Gael could appreciate interning with an enchanter so famous.

Mentor: Enchanter Lawrence
Interns: Carter Howe; Vik Smythe; Zoya Khan

Wow. Carter beamed with delight at seeing he'd work under Gladiatrix, one of the world's most renowned enchanters, and the pinnacle of trans activists among industry witches.

His excitement was overshadowed by the elation swelling inside Katherine.

She spotted her name under Guild Master Campbell and buzzed with eagerness to learn everything about running a guild, but disappointment clung to her when she saw she'd have so many other top-tier students alongside her. She'd have to work incredibly hard to stand out and make a name for herself.

Mentor: Guild Master Campbell
Interns: Katherine Harris; Layla Smythe; Amani Williams;
Jennifer Jung; Tatiana Owens; Olivia Flores

Last semester, Katherine's internal drive to learn more about the role of a guild master encouraged me to broach the topic with Campbell. She seemed rather aloof at the prospect of mentoring a student despite my determined pitch, expressing how Katherine noticed how few women take on the mantle of guild master.

Glossing over Campbell's thoughts, it became clear she took that message to heart, even if she pretended to placate me with utter disinterest. Campbell researched the most adaptable female students at Gemini and handpicked an entourage of interns she'd teach how to run the industry one day.

I continued skimming through the names projected in search of my homeroom coven students. Correction, my former homeroom coven students. Even if I'd stayed at Gemini, even if I'd continued teaching, they wouldn't be my students anymore.

"Mel, sweetie, you need to request a transfer." The disgust in Layla's voice cut through the air. "Seriously, Kraken is second-rate, and while you're not impressive, at least you're not sloppy like the rest of your group."

With that, Layla sauntered off and abandoned her friend so her clique could continue exploring the who's who of Cerberus Guild.

Melanie clammed up and read the name of her mentor and fellow interns.

Mentor: Enchanter Ortiz
Interns: Jamius Watson; Melanie Dawson; Yaritza Vargas

That was rather surprising. Most Gemini Academy students had landed with Cerberus Guild enchanters, but Chanelle had outsourced more than a few other guilds to work with a small chunk of the student body.

"What a bitch," Yaritza said in regard to Layla's comment. "Hellrazer is top-tier. Way better than interning for some office snob."

"Interning for a guild master is the most prestigious opportunity anyone could ever ask for."

"Your boss isn't here," Yaritza said, rolling her eyes. "You're not getting any bonus points for sucking up. Besides, the only ones worth being jealous of are the people interning with actual Global Guild members. But, like, Hellrazer is close enough. He was offered a spot and turned it down. We're going to learn so much!"

While I wanted to believe Enchanter Ortiz's fire magic would be great for Melanie and okay for Yaritza, I didn't see any reason for Jamius to be teamed up with the enchanter. Unless, of course, he had stipulated he wanted interns who shared familiarity with one another, which was common practice among lazy enchanters. If I had it my way, Ortiz wouldn't have even made the cut to the 'desperate last resort' list of suitable enchanters.

It had nothing to do with the fact that he was Milo's ex and everything to do with the fact that the fool lived life based on all of Milo's bad qualities with none of the charm or good intentions to balance them out. Hellrazer was Chicago's bad boy who didn't bend the rules so much as burn them to cinders in order to make his cases. To be clear, he didn't reject an offer from the Global Guild ranks. According to Milo, they rescinded the offer because of his cavalier behavior.

Ugh. I needed to have a word with Chanelle about this placement. Clearly, she was overworked and just slapping assignments together.

"Is there a reason you didn't mention signing a waiver?" Kenzo asked. His agitation reeled my attention back to him and Gael instead of wandering through the sea of students processing their internships.

"Well, when you didn't get one, I worried you might be a little jealous." Gael grimaced. "Not that you'd need to be jealous. I mean, I was worried I'd be jealous of how not jealous you'd be about the whole thing."

Gael gulped, mind swirling in Spanish thoughts.

Kenzo scoffed. "As if I care. Just don't let that arrogant fool ruin your success with tacky lessons on how to be a fuckboy instead of helping you harness your magic."

I glared. Milo wasn't a fuckboy. Well, not anymore. And that was mostly just his image during the early days of his fame.

"At least my enchanter is somewhat competent." Kenzo eyed his mentor, Enchanter Novak, who, along with Milo's other acolytes, had recently been promoted. As such, the three of them would each only have one intern. "Branchless and Whitlock are screwed."

I turned to find their names all grouped together.

Mentor: Enchanter Novak
Intern: Kenzo Ito

Mentor: Enchanter Russo
Intern: Caleb Huxley

Mentor: Enchanter Reed
Intern: Tara Whitlock

While I found Milo's former acolytes mostly competent, I didn't believe any of them were ready for interns quite yet. Especially the students they'd been assigned. I mean, granted, Lena Novak was probably the only person who could handle Kenzo's beratement and dish it back in equal measure. But Caleb being assigned to Hayden? The ditzy witch who was never on time for his life and possessed two branches. What was he going to teach Caleb? How unfair life was, and how to be late to literally every event?

Ellie's personality was nice enough for a pushover, but even with her lock capability, I didn't know how suitable a match she'd be for Tara. Sure, she'd identified some of Tara's branch threads in the past, but like the rest of us, she couldn't make much sense of it. Personally, Tara should be assigned one of the Global Guild witches. Maybe Wadsworth. Actually, considering his history with her mother, that was a bad idea. Just the thought of Tara's mother out there, roaming the world, eluding the Global Guild, and seeking to steal Tara away to fulfill some mad agenda. It made me queasy. When would she make her move?

I continued searching names, noticing how conveniently Wadsworth's name was missing from the list of mentors despite Gladiatrix and Diaz both taking on interns since their mission had relocated them to the city.

Wadsworth wasn't the only name missing from the board. I scoured every single mentor, mostly from Cerberus Guild, a few from other guilds, but I couldn't find my name anywhere.

Chanelle used the high-pitched blare of the microphone to cut through the conversations. Once she'd settled some of the idle chat, she quickly returned to the podium.

"Now that everyone's had a chance to check out who their mentor is, I'd like you all to meet up with them," Chanelle announced. "Those of you working with other guilds have transportation awaiting you downstairs. Your mentors are eagerly awaiting your arrival."

I cut through the thick crowd of students, making my way toward Campbell to have a word with her about her oversight in leaving me off the mentor list. Seemingly, I was the only person at Cerberus Guild not mentoring a student.

Yaritza and Melanie brushed past me, each trying to quickly make their way to the elevator without being spotted. It didn't work. Minds perked up at their discreet exit.

"Have fun on your little bus ride." Layla smirked, gathering a laugh from her friends.

Ugh. How quickly she turned to mock Melanie now that she'd been grouped with Yaritza.

"Have fun with your Girl Boss secretary gig," Yaritza quickly retorted.

"Bet you'll learn all the best ways to file paperwork."

It was a strong clapback that actually managed to irritate Layla, not that she let it show as she rolled her eyes and directed her friends to find their mentors. Truthfully, every intern would be learning the joys of paperwork. It was a nice break for enchanters to pass off their administrative to-dos off to rookies and lighten their caseloads. They'd get field experience, too, but not as much as in years past. Too much red tape for injuries and an angry public. Most enchanters played it safe and kept their interns in the wings for observational tasks.

Students continued funneling through the room in search of their enchanters, clogging up space as everyone tried to have introductions here. Enchanters really were such fucking morons. They had no understanding of learning. Hundreds of students in one setting were not going to pay attention, comprehend, or even hear half the introductory directives.

"Where's the cowboy dude?" Gael asked with a pouty huff, joining several others who'd been assigned a Global Guild mentor over by Chanelle.

"Those of you working with Enchanter Diaz will be meeting with him in the lobby," she explained. "He's not big on crowds."

I rolled my eyes. Based on Diaz's distant thoughts, he wasn't big on punctuality either.

"What about those assigned to Gladiatrix?" Carter asked eagerly. "I mean, to Enchanter Lawrence."

"She's still traveling for business," Chanelle explained. "She's expected to arrive later this afternoon, so you'll be shadowing me for the morning."

Impressive. The fact that Gladiatrix just wrapped up a case in the UK and was going to fly across the entire ocean and half the country in a few hours. Her speed was unparalleled.

I made my way to Guild Master Campbell, who had a trail of eager interns following her. With a quick wave of her hand, one of her three personal assistants intercepted the girls and ushered them off in a different direction. They had a tailored orientation to attend to for their first day, and by the brief glossing on Campbell's thoughts, it seemed her assistants would be doing the heavy lifting on the mentoring side of things.

I ground my teeth at that. She couldn't even be bothered by the full expectations of mentoring, yet she blatantly disregarded me for the role. And I knew she'd done it intentionally based on the buzzing irritation wafting from her surface thoughts or the frantic need consuming the other two personal assistants attempting and failing to intercept me.

"Not dealing with either of you," I snapped as I stomped between them and barreled toward Campbell's office door. "We need a word."

"Based on your demeanor, I'd say several words." Her sigh of exhaustion was feigned, but the headache my presence created was genuine. "You two can join the orientation. I'll handle Enchanter Frost."

"Handle me?"

"Your concerns, obviously." Campbell huffed, then blocked the door of her office with tight steps into my space. "No, it wasn't a mistake. No, I don't care that you've got years of education. No, I'm not a spiteful bitch, despite the rumors. No, you can't change my mind. No, I don't care whose cock you're sucking. No, the Global Guild doesn't have an opinion or say in the matter. Plus, you're just a consultant. No, there's literally nothing you could say or do to take on the role of a mentor. All the spots are filled thanks to our wonderful liaison, Mrs. Whitehurst."

Campbell's thoughts continued spiraling through her vindictive speech again and again. The words etched into her mind, making it impossible for me to glimpse anything else.

"I have experience with—"

"With classroom instruction, yes, yes, yes. Wonderful. You're welcome to return, if you like." Campbell's thoughts danced with the idea of breaking my enchanter contract early, then cycled through the same repetitive "no" speech she'd concocted to block my telepathy.

"You can't seriously think I'm underqualified for this."

"I think you sweet-talked our top enchanter into weaseling you into an elite position at a highly coveted guild," Campbell said with an icy stare. "I also think you're too inexperienced to handle the seriousness of mentoring."

"You've got three enchanters who literally just got promoted a week ago," I said in reference to Milo's former acolytes. "They're mentoring."

"They've been working within Cerberus' protocol for some time now, they understand my expectations, and they can handle working alongside the most demanding enchanter. Surely, you realize just because you're screwing Milo, it doesn't mean you can get everything you want. You're not ready for mentoring."

"That so?" I glared, delving deeper into her mind.

Beyond the speech she'd looped in her thoughts lay phony insults about screwing my way into this position, about quitting guild life more than a decade ago, about being an incompetent teacher. She hurled any and every staged thought she could muster to keep me from glimpsing the truth of things.

"Milo told you not to make me a mentor?" I seethed.

Campbell stared wide-eyed and stunned. "Goddammit. Stay out of my head."

With that, she stormed into her office and slammed the door to ignite the wards. It sealed her mind from my magic, but I'd already learned the truth.

I sent my telepathy surging through the crowd, zipping between every festering thought until I linked to Milo. He was in mid-conversation with his new intern, Gael, when I assaulted his mind with demands for an explanation.

"*Why the fuck are you preventing me from mentoring?*" I thought. "*Who the hell gave you the right?*"

Milo smirked, holding a finger up to pause his chat with Gael while rolling his eyes back slightly to fake a vision. "*You did, Dorian. You told me point-blank you didn't want any distractions from your mission to find and eliminate the Celestial Coven. It is because of that we've kept you off all Cerberus cases so you can prioritize your Global Guild work.*"

"Are you fucking kidding me?" I snapped, my voice carrying loudly to those nearby, and my thoughts slamming a bit aggressively against Milo's mind. "*You should've told me. Should've said something. Anything.*"

"*I didn't want to hurt your feelings.*"

"*Too late.*" I turned to leave, to escape the guild flooded with excitement and reminders of all the students I used to work with day in and day out.

I wasn't needed here.

CHAPTER FIVE

I REMAINED icy toward Milo the entire week while he acted extra sweet, which only further pissed me off. That and his need to call it my "frosty" ways whenever someone noticed me being cold. Ben even clammed up some due to my petulant attitude, so I had to put my anger on hold while at home. I didn't want the kid suffering my wrath just because Milo was an absolute asshole. But at work, I remained distant.

Not that he or anyone noticed. They were all preoccupied with their new interns, with their overzealous acolytes trying to remain in the spotlight, with their constant flow of casework. I, on the other hand, had nothing to occupy my time. No cases. I couldn't even continue my Celestial Coven work until a manifestation found a new lead, and despite them scouring the entire world, it became harder and harder to track The True Witch, Theodore, or any crumb of a lead on those wicked witches.

So, I spent most of my days in the training chamber. Cerberus Guild had several nice workout facilities, and their training chamber allowed for isolated control over branch exercises, physical endurance, and root practice. Plus, thanks to state-of-the-art technology and top-tier magic, it was the quietest place in Chicago. The minds of the city hummed softly here. My tether to my manifestations went nearly silent.

I flew around the empty chamber, hurling waves of telekinesis at the enchantment targets. Only about half of them glowed with a precision strike, which meant my technique still lacked. Hell, maybe Milo and Campbell were right. If I still moved about with the root proficiency of a second-year student, then how could I hope to mentor anyone?

"You're still keeping too much focus in your core," Milo's chipper voice echoed into the chamber room. "It's altering your telekinetic blows."

"And if I lessen the weight in my core, then my levitation will flounder and my aim will be off," I responded with gritted teeth.

"Not if you harness the thread of that telekinetic blow and follow through to the end," Milo said. "Trust me, I know a thing or two about blows. Blowing. Blowies. Plus, my precision strikes are always on point."

With that, Milo twirled his fingers to send a stray strike of telekinesis throughout the chamber room and hit each and every target I'd missed. He didn't even put the same weight behind his strike, yet still managed to fully activate the enchantment markers and complete the training module.

"Shouldn't you be working on a case or something? With your intern?"

"I've got Gael doing some fieldwork recon for me."

"What?"

"Yeah." Milo shrugged. "There's a shipment of illegal enchantments coming in."

"You sent Gael to stake out an illegal shipment of goods?" I wobbled in the air, losing all focus on my roots as my telepathy searched for my former student.

"Relax, I told Cassidy he'd be there." Milo chuckled. "She's gonna conveniently grab him and have a conversation about how things really work in this city. Then we'll have a chat, and I'm going to explain the crime syndicate of Chicago. Figure it'll do him good to meet the lady running the undercity."

"What the hell is wrong with you?"

"Nothing. Just doing my mentoring gig."

I descended to the opposite side of the chamber room toward the small sparring section where I could practice my punches.

"I suppose you're not going to tell the actual authorities about Cassidy's illegal enchantment scams?" I punched the bag, picturing Cassidy's face, Milo's face, my face.

"It's not a scam. They're just knockoff medical spells. And since they're actually affordable, I figured more folks would benefit from the ill-gotten medication than they would lose out from Cassidy lining her pockets with profits."

I snarled, throwing another hard punch. Of course, he'd already thought it out. He always thought ten steps ahead.

"You're putting too much weight in your strikes," Milo said, swaggering on over uninvited. "I could show you what I mean, if you like."

"No thanks."

"Come on?" Milo grinned. "Stop taking out your anger on a silly punching bag when I'm offering you a much better target."

Cocky. Cocky little bastard was trying to goad me into an argument. A conversation. And through what?

"I'm not fighting you."

"It's not a fight." Milo tugged his tie, loosening it some. "It's training."

"I'll pass."

"Afraid you can't hit me?" Milo popped his hip, using the motion to telekinetically knock the punching bag into my face.

"Son of a bitch."

"And here I thought you always liked my mama."

"Ass."

"Come on." Milo gestured an invitation while raising his fists. "We can practice combat skills."

"Is that necessary?"

"Usually, Campbell mandates fitness evaluations for all her enchanters." Milo circled me, thoughts playfully musing with ideas of turning this fight into something flirty.

I glared, squaring up and readying myself. "Stop treating me like I'm some rookie."

"You kind of are." Milo threw a few jabs, which were easy enough to avoid. "You're new to your role as an enchanter."

He was leading me into a verbal trap and a physical one. The flurry of slow strikes was pushing me closer to the wall where Milo meant to pin me. And naturally, I walked right into the trap without thinking.

"I'm not new," I said, swinging a fist. "I'm just a little rusty."

Milo pivoted out of the way and managed to kick me in the stomach at the same time. "More than rusty. Sloppy. Which is fine. You're better than most of the enchanters here, but that's not enough for you."

"Why's that?" I swung another fist.

My hit didn't connect, but it got me back to the center of the mat and out of Milo's trick.

"Because you don't want to be great. You want to be perfect. You want to avoid the mistakes of the past." Milo's demeanor shifted, calm and somber. "Last time you faltered, met an unstoppable foe, you lost a piece of yourself. We both did. The difference is you walked away and shut out everyone and everything."

Milo's loneliness crept to the surface of his thoughts. It sent an uncomfortable rush of warmth through him, embarrassment and shame and guilt for all the moments of his past he'd believed he failed to prevent.

It gnawed at my insides, reminding me that no matter who I was now, I was still that broken man who grieved and lost myself to grief, abandoning Milo in the process.

He did well to bury his sorrow, even if forcefully, while letting his mind dart with obvious tactical blows. I weaved around his leading strikes and moved in with one of my own. My fist connected with his chin, and left Milo stunned for a moment.

"What happened with Finn will never happen again."

Part of me believed that comment would end this, would silence Milo into surrender, but the wily bastard smirked.

"You're right, because I won't let you split your focus." Milo grabbed ahold of my arm and flipped me over his head. The whoosh of his telekinesis hurled me all the faster, but thankfully softened the landing when Milo slammed me down. "You want to aim big, target the deadliest coven of witches that ever witched it up, fine by me. I trust you. I believe in you.

I need you. But I'll be damned if you take on more than you're ready for, if you distract yourself, guilt yourself, overwork yourself, and burn out."

Milo's mind jigsawed with blurry possibilities. Most of his visions still remained veiled from me, even if several thousand were locked away safely in the back of my head. All the same, Milo never did anything maliciously. If he opposed me taking on an intern, he had his reasons. He'd likely seen every possible outcome of my failure to balance enchanter work, Global Guild missions, and mentoring.

Why was I always so thick-headed? I never managed to take anything at face value. I always had to pick a fight, to prove a point, to challenge Milo.

"Plus, we both know you'd never be satisfied with mentoring one kid or three kids or twenty kids." Milo stared down at me, grinning his goofy fucking grin, revealing all the stress knotted inside him had washed away. "We both know you're going to use your telepathy to stalk your students and check in on them, so I made sure you had the time for that."

I scoffed. "I don't stalk."

"You totally do, babe. It's cute. I like it." Milo smirked. "And since you won't have to officially mentor, you can focus on any and all your kiddos. Then bitch about their mentors not doing things to your liking."

"Like how you sent Gael off on some solo venture his first week?" I glowered. "Absolutely horrible."

"Exactly, just like that." Milo pointed a finger, commending my scolding. He was the worst. "I want you to prioritize the Celestial Coven. I want you to help me bring them down, to prevent the visions they conjure, the horrors they seek to unleash, and then I want you to go back to your usual grumpy self without the weight of the world on your shoulders."

"Here, I figured you'd like someone carrying a bit of the weight with you."

"Look, my workout routine requires I carry the weight of the world all on my own." Milo flexed. "How else do you think I got this cut?"

"You're absurd." I playfully shoved him.

"Yeah? How absurd?" Milo nudged me with his shoulder, his thoughts dancing with taunting words, and a desire to continue our sparring session.

"You know, I can predict all your moves, right?"

"When'd you become a mind reader?" Milo batted his lashes, taunting and sweet and so annoying.

"I can read your thoughts, so I already know what you're—"

POP.

I blinked in stunned surprise. "You just slapped me."

"I thought you'd see it coming." Milo snickered, circling me. "All that talk, and your moves are still so slow."

"That didn't count." I braced my arms and studied his movements. If I hadn't goaded him, his thoughts would flow more freely, yet now he tiptoed between ideas, making it harder to anticipate his next move.

"Left side." Milo swung, true to his word, and nearly decked me.

I tumbled backward as I maneuvered out of the way, then was forced to crawl away from Milo's continued strikes. He didn't relent for a second.

"You wanna work with the best, then you better hold your own with us." Milo stomped his foot with swift kicks that were leading me back to the wall. "You're following my thoughts, but you're not reacting fast enough to do a damn thing with them."

"I just need a second…" I rolled to my side, escaping Milo's next blow meant to box me against the wall.

"You don't get a second." Milo lunged, wrapping his arm around my neck and pinning me to the ground. "It only takes one second to fall right into a trap. One false move. One sloppy evasion. One misstep."

"Fine." I struggled to break free, but Milo's grip tightened. "I yield, whatever."

"Not whatever." Milo bucked his hips against me, holding me down and in place. "You have tremendous capabilities with your telepathy. You're probably the strongest psychic in the world."

I tsked. I was powerful but not so arrogant as to think such things.

"But your telepathy only goes so far."

"I get it, if an enemy works around my magic, they can turn it into a weakness."

"No, well, yes, but also your body doesn't move as fast as your comprehension," Milo explained. "Predicting your opponent's moves does no good if you can't capitalize on it. Instead, focus on their body language, predict with instinct, not insight."

"And how do I go about that?" I attempted to wriggle loose, but Milo still held tight to my throat and weighed down on me with his full body.

"Fighting is a lot like fucking," Milo whispered, his breath tickling the back of my ear. "You just have to focus on your partner's needs."

Milo bucked, grinding his crotch against my ass.

"Only when you're fighting, you exploit those needs and break them." Milo's words danced on the nape of my neck, sending a quiver of anticipation coursing through me. "When you're fucking, you gotta put in the real work."

Milo kissed my neck, working his way to my shoulder before biting down.

I groaned, raising my ass to meet him.

"Ready to surrender this battle to me?" Milo teased, running his tongue along the back of my ear before nibbling on the lobe.

Between the ticklish jolt and his cockiness, I couldn't stifle the laugh that escaped my mouth.

"Oh, laughing in the face of defeat." Milo whipped me around and slammed my back onto the mat. "Guess I'm gonna have to really put in the work to bring you down."

I chuckled. "I already am."

"Not all of you." Milo grabbed my belt, unfastening my pants with a level of expertise I'd never master.

In the few seconds I spent shimmying to lower them past my hips and assist, he'd yanked them down to my ankles, slipped off my shoes, carefully tugged the bunched fabric past my heels, and tossed my jeans, boxers, and socks to the other side of the arena floor.

"Are you serious?" I smiled because I couldn't hide it even if I wanted to play coy. "What if someone…you know."

"Unlike you, I filled the proper requisition form securing this time for a private training session."

"And what kind of training session is this, exactly?"

"I call it the art of humility." Milo fished a hand into his pocket, retrieving a small bottle of lube. "If you're going to be a pro enchanter, you gotta learn to take a loss while keeping your head held high."

I let out something between a scoff and a snort, because his mind was flooded with dirty desires and kinks he wanted to try in this training chamber for god only knows how long.

Milo cast telekinesis to softly slide my shirt up, the phantom pressure of gentle hands touching me all the while as he lifted my shirt off. Once he'd removed the final layer of clothing I had, Milo used his magic to unbutton his dress shirt, seductive and also careful not to wrinkle the fine silk.

I rolled my eyes.

"What?" He shrugged. "Some of us care about our wardrobe."

"Uh-huh."

With that, Milo sent the shirt fluttering away and leaned forward to straddle his arms on either side of me. The tension held for a few seconds before he kissed me, quick and distracting, so distracting I lost track of his hands, which worked their way down my chest, my stomach, and were suddenly cupping my ass. The cool touch of the lube with the suddenness of Milo's fingertips pressing at my hole sent a shiver of surprise through me.

"Fuuuck," I moaned. "You just happened to have that on hand?"

Part of me wondered if he'd had a vision or merely a suspicion since we'd been too busy for intimacy, and my sour attitude hadn't helped matters.

"Always be prepared," Milo said, licking my shaft.

When he reached the head of my cock, he swirled his tongue around the tip while working his fist up and down the base and used two fingers of his other hand to work his way inside me.

His mouth felt too good to search for answers, to speak coherent sentences, to think of anything other than the tightness of his throat. I gripped his beautiful blond hair and shoved him further down, forcing him to gag, to take all of me. My dick vibrated with excitement as he choked and swallowed and kept taking every inch as I thrust my hips up into him, all the while still working his way inside me.

"Dammit." I released Milo, unable to focus, lost in the delirium brought on by his oral skills.

Milo didn't stop gagging, taking the full length of my cock. He worked faster, swallowing from tip to base again and again until my mind swirled beyond measure.

"Stop." I gripped the mat, clawing at anything for some semblance of balance. "I'm gonna, I'm gonna…"

If he kept this up, I'd explode any second into his mouth.

"Milo, I'm gonna—"

Just like that, he swallowed the entirety of my cock one final time, while pressing just enough pressure inside me. I erupted, releasing a huge load into Milo's mouth. So much so, I felt it drip from his lips and spill onto my pubes.

"Now that I've left you utterly defeated, I think it's time I claim my prize." Milo grabbed my ankles and turned them, controlling me and ushering me back onto my stomach.

He wasn't wrong. I'd gladly surrender myself to him and this silly little wrestling fight/fuck fetish he had floating through his surface thoughts. It hummed in his mind, arousing me all over again. Even if my dick was too tired to rise to full attention, it was semi-alert and ready for Milo.

He grabbed my hips, adjusting me ever so slightly while I buried my face into the mat and handed the reins over. Once he'd angled my ass to his liking, Milo gripped a hip with one hand while steadying his dick into me with the other.

"Oooouuu." I hunched a bit as the head pushed through.

But with an inch pressed inside, Milo moved his hand to the small of my back and forced me back into an arched position.

"Ready?"

I nodded with a groan.

Milo took slow thrusts, easing his way into me inch by inch until our skin slapped, and he'd plunged all the way to the base. I bit back a pained moan, having gone weeks without him inside me, and finding it quite the undertaking. Milo ran his hands up and down my back, gently massaging me while casting telekinesis to distract and comfort me. All the while, he remained still, allowing me a minute to adjust to the full girth of his cock.

"I'm ready," I whispered with a hoarse breath.

Despite the initial pain, I craved him. I hungered for Milo's release and for his pleasure to dance in my thoughts.

Milo turned my head to meet him and kissed me while he pumped into me. Each thrust came faster and harder, but our lips didn't part. When I moaned, when I winced, when I ached, the sound poured into Milo and fueled him to pound into me with more force, to kiss me with more fury, to take me and fuck me to his satisfaction.

Seconds turned into minutes, and I quivered beneath Milo, taking his swift thrusts again and again until he tired of this position and flipped me onto my back.

"I wanna see you," he said, gesturing for me to wrap my hands under my legs, as he repositioned and slammed inside me again.

I scrunched my face, growling at the suddenness of him pushing back into me. The delight of my expression lit up Milo's thoughts. His lust for me, his need to fuck me—it fed his carnal hunger and mine.

I lay there, taking every pump of his cock, lost in the ecstasy of Milo's arousal, his pleasure. It didn't take long for my cock to swell, and Milo ran his hand along my shaft, stroking me in sync with his own thrusts. His cock pulsed inside me, his thoughts muttered his closeness, his hand demanded I join him. Soon, my body vibrated and linked to him, closer and closer with each stroke.

"I'm gonna…"

"Not yet," Milo demanded, finding a new pace which he wanted to relish, to savor, to pump into me a few more times for the pleasure.

He traced his hand along my face, caressing my jawline and following until his fingers ran through my hair. Gripping a fistful of my short, brown locks, Milo pounded with authority while jerking my head closer to him. Our lips locked. My cock throbbed. His cock raged. Each slap of our bodies brought us closer until I couldn't take it anymore.

I moaned into Milo's mouth, begging without words for release. He bit my lower lip.

"Cum for me," he whispered.

That was all I needed to finish. He unloaded inside me, and I let out everywhere. Our stomachs, the mat, possibly a few spurts on my face. Or maybe it was sweat or possibly drool. I didn't know. I lay with Milo collapsed on top of me, unable and unwilling to move. All I wanted was to bask in the post-coital glow and the comfort of Milo's body pressed to mine.

CHAPTER SIX

OVER the next few days, I took Milo's suggestion to heart. I needed to prioritize my work on searching for the Celestial Coven, to give Gladiatrix a lead she could use to finally put an end to this organization. And I also needed to check on my students. I couldn't ignore them if I wanted. My telepathy wouldn't allow such things.

So, while I went about my day at Cerberus, working on paperwork and channeling magic for my manifestations to harness from a distance, I looped my telepathy around the city and followed closely to my students during their internships.

Currently, I found myself drawn to Yaritza as I'd gone far too long ignoring her pain. Unintentionally or not, I'd never noticed the deeply etched depression she masked.

Yaritza, Jamius, and Melanie followed close behind Enchanter Ortiz, who'd gone with simple patrol work since, like many guilds, cases had been slow as of late. Ortiz wore a leather jacket, no shirt, and ripped jeans with more holes than fabric. Supposedly, this stylistic wardrobe had to do with his primal branch burning hot at all times—even in the bitter chill of autumn weather. Personally, I figured he liked to add to his bad boy heartthrob image.

```
Name: Santos Ortiz
Branch: Primal (Fire)
```

Unlike Melanie, Ortiz could create and control flames. Additionally, his fire burned white and black, each possessing unique qualities. I'd wager they were more on the arcane degree than the primal, but his license claimed they were purely primal.

"It's always important to remain vigilant and public." Ortiz kept them on the main streets, casting small black flames on the alley streets, to lure in wisps and small fiends for him to banish.

Only, he didn't banish them. Instead, he allowed the fiends to feed upon his flames, absorbing the magic and swelling in size. Once they'd devoured the nearby magic, they consumed the lingering wisps, growing more in the process.

"Oh, I got it." Yaritza took a step forward, but Ortiz blocked her path. "Wait for it."

And in a matter of seconds, the fiend sniffed the barren street and lunged into busy traffic searching for a new bounty. Cars swerved, but thanks to well-timed telekinesis, Ortiz prevented a collision.

"The most important part of our job."

"Protecting people," Yaritza said.

Ortiz scoffed. "Hardly."

The fiend drew the attention of others, and soon they'd blocked off the entire road. Traffic came to a halt, and people squirmed uncomfortably in their cars as the fiends searched for magic to consume.

"In order for the public to be grateful to guilds, they have to see us in action." Enchanter Ortiz lunged ahead, abandoning his interns and demonstrating his public prowess. In a few swift blows, he hurled white flames at the fiends, lacing banishment into his deadlier white fire, while levitating with an extra boost from his black flames.

The fire was all for show. Completely unnecessary for casting against such small threats, but Ortiz wanted the public to clamor, to stare in awe, to see his majestic strength. And they did. People rolled down their windows to cheer him on, to applaud his valiant efforts. All completely oblivious to the fact he'd orchestrated this little inconvenience before resolving it.

I tsked, nearly drawn back to my mind on the other side of the city. I wished Enchanter Ortiz's behavior was an outlier of uncommon practices. Sadly, too many enchanters relied on these strategies to gain public notoriety.

"You see," Ortiz said, returning to his interns. "It's that small inconvenience that reminds people why they need guild involvement."

"But you could've stopped the fiends on the streets," Jamius said. "We could've filmed it. Shown everyone how important—"

"Banishment posts rarely go viral," Ortiz interrupted. "No. Citizens need to see firsthand how much we help them. They need to feel the threat looming near them. These reminders are good for everyone."

"How so?" Jamius raised a brow, skeptical but curious.

"If we help them without their knowledge, they just see us as overpaid slackers," Ortiz explained. "So, I do my part by allowing the threats to lurk a little closer than some would prefer. It's a healthy reminder that if they want to stay safe, they'll always vote pro guild and do their part to pay the way to keep our salaries competitive."

I rolled my eyes. Ortiz's obnoxious ideology on guild philosophy would definitely worm its way into my students' heads. Hopefully, they'd see through his shallow behavior given time.

"Normally, we wouldn't spend our days patrolling the same streets on repeat," Ortiz said. "But cases are always slower closer to the holidays. No one wants to waste money on demonic energy or warlocks when they have to budget for flights home, presents, decorations, and everything else. It'll pick up after Christmas."

Yaritza, Jamius, and Melanie grumbled, trying to imagine how boring it'd be following Ortiz on street patrols for the next few months with no real work.

"Could we maybe search another neighborhood?" Yaritza asked.

"Yeah," Jamius said. "The South Side has tons of fiends. Might even find some cases there."

"Yeah, right." Melanie rolled her eyes, making the typical assumption that folks on the South Side couldn't afford to hire a guild. She wasn't wrong, but mocking poverty wasn't a great look on her.

"Technically speaking, guilds take cases from anywhere in the city that we're hired; however, there are specific locations that the city pays us to protect on a regular basis," Enchanter Ortiz explained. "See, Kraken has always been active on the West side. We don't patrol the whole area—far too many guilds fighting for turf—but we run the suburbs, and trust me, they're grateful for our many hands always tending to their protection."

His mind fluttered with the imagery of an actual kraken's ten tentacles shielding the city. Even though an actual kraken would probably attempt to destroy the city because they were a gigantic and threatening demon.

He wasn't wrong about the city employing guilds to monitor specific regions within their jurisdiction. It was a difficult balance because they didn't want guilds to overstep on police protocol, but they didn't want to risk citizens when guild interference would be beneficial. They also didn't want to pay exorbitant guild fees for exceptional acts of labor, so guilds only intervened in high-tier cases when the city offered proper compensation or a wealthy client stepped in to handle the costs. Money was the only real way to handle any problem. Magic was just an added bonus of assistance.

My students followed Ortiz for another hour as he lured fiends into more direct view of people, then allowed his interns the opportunity to banish them for small praise.

"Oooooh." Ortiz came to an abrupt stop, showing his beeping phone. "Might have a case for you yet. The ole guild master only ever calls when we've got an emergency gig."

Ortiz answered his call, revealing a video that had over fifty members, according to the small notification bubble in the corner.

"I need all enchanters near Humboldt Park to assist," the guild master said. "There's a massive disturbance, and authorities are being overwhelmed. Likely a warlock threat, but suspect fiend interference being drawn to the high volume of magical casting."

"We'll handle it," Ortiz responded. "I'm eight blocks away."

"Be cautious," the guild master said. "By all reports, our enchanters on the scene have already been struck down. Stay vigilant. I'll be sending teams to secure the scene soon."

My mind buzzed with thoughts of enchanters from multiple guilds throughout Chicago being contacted by their guild master. The leader of Kraken Guild wasn't kidding about backup. Considering Kraken was notorious for being glory hogs, it was surprising to see them reaching out for assistance. Milo's influence, no doubt. He pushed for collaboration nonstop. It was nice to see the fruits of his labor paying off.

"Looks like you kiddos will finally get some action," Ortiz said with a wicked smirk. "Remember the rules. You don't interfere. You're support roles unless the situation demands otherwise. But?"

"But it won't because you're a legend," Yaritza, Jamius, and Melanie all said in unison. Even their eyerolls were synced. They found it frustrating that he coddled them—if one could call it that—but I was grateful his bravado wouldn't risk their lives.

"Scope the terrain, take out low-level fiends, help stragglers evacuate the area, and have a comprehensive report to offer any other enchanters reporting to the scene."

With that, Ortiz bolted down the block. He used his black flames to enhance his flight, turning the corner in a flash. My students barely had a chance to get off the ground before Ortiz's mind had reached the scene. Whatever he spotted stirred through him uncomfortably, but I remained latched to my students' minds as they flew toward the incident.

By the time Yaritza, Jamius, and Melanie arrived at the scene, there were black and white flames raging everywhere. Black fire clung to citizens, shielding them from flying debris, while white fire burned gigantic arms that continued swinging erratically through buildings, the asphalt of the road, and everything else in their path.

"Fuck me." Yaritza's fear latched onto my mind, making it difficult to focus.

Towering above her, above most of the buildings on the street, was a huge witch.

"What is that?" Jamius asked.

"Giant magic." Melanie gulped.

She wasn't entirely wrong. They had the answer. They'd each studied the various branches in my class. They'd learned the names of thousands of known branch magics. All they needed was a little push, a little guidance. It was rare, but we'd covered this magic.

"This is an alteration branch," Yaritza said, recalling the type with a little suggestive whisper on my end. "Like Jamius' magic."

"This is nothing like mine," he added. "This is sizemorphic."

Sizemorphic magic allowed individuals to alter their bodies into larger or smaller proportions. The question was, did this witch have access to both capabilities or merely the enlargement portion?

"These damn flames," the witch roared.

His bellowing shout lessened as his body shrank, and much to my surprise, so did his clothing. His outfit must've been enchanted, which meant he wasn't some random criminal on a spree, but someone with funds. Someone with enough training to quickly compose himself and dodge nearby enchanters that swooped in to attack him in his smaller stature. It didn't work. Soon, he stood barely taller than Enchanter Ortiz, who didn't relent with his flames.

"Just because the target is smaller doesn't mean I'll be letting up." Ortiz waved his hands, hurling the massive array of white fire at the sizemorphic witch. It was enough to engulf the entire block, yet Ortiz honed the flames to strike the witch alone. "I'm about to show you why they call me Hellrazer!"

Part of me wondered if he planned to char the witch to cinders when I remembered Enchanter Ortiz's black and white flames had unique qualities he could manipulate. Likely, he'd use the white fire to conjure a prison that'd hold the sizemorphic witch in place, preventing his escape.

"You dare challenge the Celestial Coven." The sizemorphic witch seethed a venomous breath.

I trembled. They were here. Why? After all these months of avoiding us, dodging my telepathy, they'd returned. Taking rapid breaths, I tried to compose myself, to collect my thoughts, to scan the thoughts of the entire city. If this witch had come, did that mean the rest of the Celestial Coven had arrived, too? Did Theodore return with a legion of demons at his beck and call? Was The True Witch here?

"Witches of your caliber can never hold their own against my glory," the sizemorphic witch said. "I am Winston Cobalt, the alteration branch of the Celestial Coven. The true coven, the divine coven, the righteous coven. I lead the path to the glory of gods, serving as their vanguard. I come to announce your city's demise. To usher in a rebirth of this sad world."

"Oh, shut up," Ortiz shouted. "So you can change your size. Big deal. I'll burn you to ashes whether you're the size of a gnat or a skyscraper."

"I control more than my size." Winston smirked. "I control all matter of this world."

With a wave of telekinesis, Winston wrapped his magic around Ortiz's white flames, and in a blink, the fire vanished.

"How?" Ortiz searched the area, finding his fire hadn't vanished. The pulse of his flames called to him, still bent to his control, yet they were nowhere to be seen.

"Such a simple gift you were born with." Winston snapped his fingers. "The gods have no need for fools such as you."

The white flames exploded in front of Enchanter Ortiz, knocking him back and crashing through a wall.

Dammit. I shivered, caught in the wake of my frightened students who tried to make sense of the casting.

Other enchanters reported to the scene, each hurling their own attacks, but their magics vanished just as quickly as Ortiz's had, only to reappear and take out the witches who'd cast the strike.

"I can alter myself and all nonorganic materials," he explained. "You're wasting your time attempting to strike me down."

Even though Winston required a form of contact to alter the size of objects, it seemed he could extend his touch through the proxy of his telekinesis. Rare and damn near impossible for most witches. The level of concentration and channeling required to slip his branch into his root and merge them. That was well beyond proficient. Expertise on a level I should definitely have come to expect from a Celestial Coven witch.

This would be perfect for a floral witch, using primal control over plants to take down Winston Cobalt, but the way he continued manipulating his size while tearing through the street, then shrinking in size to counter any enchanters' attempted strike. None of them could compete with this witch.

I needed to stop him. A Celestial Coven witch dared to show their face here, and now, I'd remind them all why they spent the last several months on the run. Channeling my telepathy, I hurled the psychic energy at him, preparing to break his mind before he harmed anyone else.

Nothing.

The faintest glimmer of his surface thoughts revealed themselves, but even those were foggy, blurred, and difficult to comprehend.

It was those enchantments tattooed on his skin. Like the other Celestial Coven witches, he had many of them, likely meant to shield him from magics like mine. Still, I managed to override them when dealing with The True Witch and The Sisters Three. It was the close proximity. Even with my branch expanding in such tremendous force, if I wanted to override his protections and stop him, then I needed to get closer.

I focused my thoughts on the scene and back at my body in Cerberus Guild. Without delay, I bolted from the offices and flew from the building. If I dampened my telepathy and focused on my roots, I could fly there quicker, but unfortunately, my mind synced to the fear consuming my students.

They hid from the battle, watching enchanters get slammed to the ground, beaten without mercy, and bloodied at every attempt to stop Winston Cobalt.

"*We're going to die,*" Yaritza thought, her panic linking to mine, her fear growing as it fed off her depression, her anxiety, her doubt.

It was too much. I blinked away her terror, but I couldn't see anything except shadows. The blue sky turned fuzzy, and my flight floundered. I wobbled, barely able to focus as Yaritza's fear consumed me. I had to stop it. Stop her.

"*You need to calm down.*" I ground my teeth, focusing less on my own anxiousness for their survival, and more on a soothing tone that'd ease Yaritza away from her panic attack.

"Mr. Frost?" Yaritza asked.

Jamius and Melanie stared, visibly confused.

"*Yes,*" I thought. "*I'm arriving at the scene soon. Along with other enchanters.*"

"You are?" Yaritza asked, then turned to her friends. "Enchanter Frost is on the way. He's bringing help."

"*I need you all to fall back to a more secure location.*" Their current hiding spot wouldn't last much longer. The nearby cars had already been destroyed, and soon the rocky debris they hid behind would be too.

"We can't move." Yaritza shook her head. "If we do, he'll get us."

"*Not if you hide,*" I thought. "*All I want you to do is focus on scattered shots that'll obscure your movements. You and Melanie have the firepower to blind Winston's field of vision.*"

"Right." Yaritza swallowed hard, but a lump of fear remained.

"*Have Jamius cast every remaining duplicate he has to act as a buffer, a diversion.*"

"Right." Yaritza nodded. "*Jamius' duplicates are organic. The size manipulation won't work on them.*"

"*Then, you three get to safety.*" I flew through the skies of Chicago, locking my telepathy on Yaritza and propelling myself as quickly as possible. With so much focus fixed on my students and moving faster, the minds of damn near everyone else fell silent. "*Milo and the others are almost there. You'll be fine. You just need to get away and hold out for a few minutes.*"

It wasn't entirely a lie. Milo and other enchanters were likely very close; the buzzing minds of enchanters converged from every direction onto our point. And I was even closer. A few minutes from now, I'd arrive at the scene. It didn't matter if that witch had a thousand enchantments to shield himself from my telepathy. Once I made physical contact, I'd drop him as quickly as I did The Sisters Three.

"*This is all a good idea, but…*" Yaritza's mind popped with numbers and measurements at a dizzying rate. "I have a better idea."

"You have an idea?" Jamius croaked, turning back to Yaritza, who'd finally calmed down enough to think.

"He decreased his size so he could speed up the effects of his magic on other objects," Yaritza explained. "So, we need to make him bigger. Based on what I've seen, once he exceeds ten meters in stature, his casting significantly decreases. Probably a few seconds' lag for every meter in size multiplied by the distance of the object he's shrinking. Or enlarging—but we don't need to worry about that since he wouldn't enlarge something targeting him."

"What are you talking about?" Melanie asked.

Dammit. I pushed myself faster. Yaritza wasn't sticking with my plan. She was plotting a counterstrike.

"Jamius, you're gonna use your copies to engage and enrage."

"Meaning?"

"Taunt him till he grows."

"That I can do." Jamius nodded. "How big do you want him?"

Melanie snorted. "Oh, come on. That's a little funny. A little dirty."

"We could all die, and you're making dick jokes?" Yaritza shook her head. "You've been hanging out with Gael too much."

Melanie blushed, her thoughts fizzling toward the class clown she missed. Christ. She could very well die, and all her mind did was fixate on how she missed hooking up with the world's most irritating person.

No. They wouldn't die. None of them. I refused to let something so horrible happen. I needed to move faster.

"Melanie, I need you to take hold of Enchanter Ortiz's stray flames," Yaritza said. "Do you think you can make them bigger?"

She chuckled again, then finally composed herself. "If I mixed in a bit of standard fire, but it won't hold long. His fire's finicky."

"Exactly," Yaritza said, recalling a slight delay in the alteration of the flames compared to other enchanter strikes. "It's harder for Winston to manipulate. We can use that to our advantage."

"So, what is this big plan of yours?" Jamius asked.

"You're gonna make him grow, that'll slow down his size manipulation ability. He won't worry about staying smaller since he's already dealt with Enchanter Ortiz and the other first responders. Melanie is then gonna hit him with as much blinding firepower as she can. By the time he removes the flames, I'm going to hit him with a star shower unlike any other."

"Won't he just shrink it like everything else?"

"This will be huge," Yaritza explained. "Based on the size and distance correlation, if my measurements are precise, it'll be too big for him to stop in time."

Melanie and Jamius both stared skeptically.

"Trust me, I know my numbers."

And she did. Yaritza regularly counted out her pebbles, scattered rocks in the auxiliary gym when we trained, and anywhere she found herself in the city. It seemed that checking her surroundings to ensure she had full access to her branch became second nature to her. That, and her joy for math, which she didn't brag about much to anyone. Not even herself, hence why it rarely rose to the surface of her mind.

"Alrighty, let's do this." Jamius summoned every duplicate he could muster and sent them into the fray.

Despite their best efforts, their taunting did little to force Winston's hand. He had the advantage in telekinesis and physical combat. Every time his duplicates moved in close, Winston propelled them, destroyed them, or took his time slapping them around.

"I could move in with my flames," Melanie suggested, a bit queasy watching the many copies of Jamius get pummeled while the sadistic witch cackled at the fraught fight.

"No." Yaritza shook her head. "You have to focus on obscuring his vision. Jamius, make this work."

He groaned. "I'm trying."

"Try harder," Yaritza said with a stern confidence I'd never seen in her before.

"Fine." Jamius kicked his feet a bit and grumbled as thoughts of embarrassment filled his head. "But not a word from either of you. Ever."

"Huh?" They cocked their heads.

"I have another technique, but I swear to god if y'all tell anyone, I will kill you."

They each mimed zipping their lips.

Jamius smacked his cheeks a few times and then clapped his hands.

Each of his duplicates exploded. They reformed at half the size and twice the number. Twelve copies became twenty-four. Jamius clapped his hands again, cutting their size down even more, and made forty-eight. Then he repeated the process again and again until he had nearly eight hundred duplicates, each no bigger than his hand.

"Is this a joke?" Winston roared with laughter. "Going to strike me down with an army of tiny tyrants?"

"It ain't the size that counts, buddy," a high-pitched squeal came from one of the duplicates. "It's how you use it."

"Yeah, you oversized bitch!" another copy shouted.

"Charge!" a mousy squeak of a shout came from a copy declaring himself the general of this army.

They rushed Winston from every direction, easily flying through the air since, at their size, they didn't require much magic to levitate. Annoying bug bites for certain, but it worked. Winston swelled with rage, growing large enough to swat a hundred away at a time. He stomped throughout the streets back and forth until he'd massacred the majority of Jamius' miniature army. The original Jamius lay half-conscious and dreary from splitting his magic into so many versions of himself. Even smaller duplicates carried a heavy casting cost.

"Melanie, now."

She nodded and drew upon all the stray black and white flames on the block. She spiraled vibrant orange flames around them to keep Ortiz's erratic fire under her control, then sent waves at Winston. He struck out with telekinesis, shrinking the flames each time she hurled a section his way, but she kept the bulk of her fire high and blinding in an attempt to hide Yaritza's actions.

Yaritza dug her hands into the broken asphalt of the street and searched for the minerals within her control. Once she'd identified them through channeling, she called every speck of dust, every tiny pebble, every broken rock to her. Hundreds of them floated above her head, swirling into a massive boulder.

"Try stopping my meteor shower strike," Yaritza shouted with fury from all her repressed fears and frustration.

She unleashed a flaming boulder that could easily destroy the entire block. Hell, the entire neighborhood if it built enough force. But it didn't. Winston struck out with telekinesis and began shrinking the attack. As predicted, his large size slowed down his ability, and he couldn't compensate fast enough. Soon, the boulder was barreling on top of him, and he tried to physically overpower the attack, gripping it with pure telekinesis and gigantic arms.

"You might be able to handle one giant meteor, but can you handle a thousand burning comets?" Yaritza snapped her fingers, and every rock she'd gathered burst in a flurry of furious flames.

The attack made it impossible to see, to hear, to sense anything other than the cacophony of explosions. I snapped my link of telepathy and soared faster, still hearing the bursts, and knowing I'd nearly arrived.

Debris and smoke made it difficult to navigate. I spotted Yaritza doubled over and wheezing.

"You little bitch." Winston limped toward her. "You think...you think some pathetic no-name with a worthless branch like yours can stop me?"

Yaritza shuddered, stunned by the resilience of this witch. The Celestial Coven was on an entirely different level from other witches. But it didn't matter.

I descended, planting a hand on Winston's shoulder. "Stay the fuck away from my students."

Just like that, I bypassed the enchantments cloaking his mind and shattered it into pieces. Not irreparable, as I'd certainly like to delve into his thoughts and unravel all his secrets, but enough to keep him from putting up any resistance.

Winston's face fell flat, devoid of expression, and he collapsed to the ground in defeat.

"How'd you..." Yaritza stammered.

"I didn't do anything," I replied. "That was all you. You and your team.

I just came in and finished him, something I wouldn't have done without your brilliant plan."

Yaritza sighed, releasing a part of the voices in her head that always whispered she wasn't good enough. They wouldn't vanish after one success, but this battle had changed her, proved to her she belonged in this industry, and showed her how to believe in herself.

"I was pretty amazing." Yaritza smiled big and bright, much like I'd grown used to over the last few years.

It was a spectacular sight.

CHAPTER SEVEN

IT DIDN'T take long for the Global Guild to respond in waves, properly detain Winston Cobalt, and remove him from the area. Their first responders tended to citizens, cleaned up the area, and dealt with the bulk of the incident before most reporters arrived.

I followed Yaritza, Jamius, and Melanie to the hospital, where they were seen alongside their enchanter mentor, Santos Ortiz. Thankfully, most of their injuries were superficial.

After telepathically eavesdropping on their well-being, I responded to Milo's text and made my way to the Global Guild detainment facility. They didn't have an official location of operation, so this prison-like building remained cloaked from unwanted eyes and hidden from all forms of magic. Since the location constantly shifted, I had to follow a specialized GPS coordinate that'd undoubtedly expire within twenty-four hours as they continued moving throughout the city.

Much to my surprise, Gladiatrix was there with her interns. That much I expected. However, I didn't think she'd be so brazen as to hold a press conference a mere hundred feet from the cloaked facility.

Still, with a name as renowned as hers, she couldn't simply drop back into Chicago without some official statement. The press demanded answers, and as the fourth-highest-ranked witch in the world, it was her job to steer them to an appropriate response that didn't compromise the case.

"Does your return indicate a return of the Celestial Coven to Chicago?"

"Why weren't you at the incident today?"

"Did King Liberty reveal his identity to you?"

"Is this strike the first of many to come?"

"Are the rumors true about your involvement with King Liberty?"

"Will other high-ranking Global Guild members be arriving in Chicago?"

"How does the Global Guild intend to secure the situation?"

"What inspired you to become an enchanter mentor?"

"Will you be publicly introducing your interns?"

"Can they handle the expectations required of a Global Guild witch?"

Carter maintained a soft smile and positive demeanor. According to his surface thoughts, Gladiatrix had prepared all her interns for the bombardment of questions she usually received during press conferences. Carter sat between Gladiatrix's other two interns. Vik's face remained red the entire time, despite the calming affirmations they continued repeating in their head over and over. It didn't matter. A crowd this big made them anxious.

```
Name: Vik Smythe
Branch: Arcane (Copycat)
```

Personally, I hoped working with someone like Gladiatrix would help Vik with their anxiety.

Sitting on Carter's other side was a young woman with a dark olive complexion. I'd never had her in any of my classes. Honestly, I didn't know much about Zoya other than the glimmer of details that sat on Carter's surface thoughts. She was apparently an active member of the Gemini Pride Club.

```
Name: Zoya Khan
Branch: Alteration (Speed)
```

She probably possessed the closest branch to Gladiatrix, even if her physical power was limited to speed and reflex.

"Do you think it's a valuable use of Global Guild time and resources to take on interns?" asked Clint Johnson, a reporter from everyone's favorite conservative station who only believed in the value of magic when certain witches carried the torch.

Gladiatrix wasn't one of the witches this reporter approved of, and keeping his heinous surface thoughts out of my head was no easy task.

"Global Guild witches take on acolytes all the time," Gladiatrix responded. "It's important to train the next generation of enchanters. And as someone who was never afforded an internship during my time at an academy, I take the privilege of mentoring quite seriously."

Geez. I didn't realize there were academies out there that flagrantly disregarded their obligations and sent students into the industry without proper training. It was even more impressive to see how far Gladiatrix had risen independently.

"A follow-up, if you'll indulge me," Johnson said, diving right into his next question without missing a beat. "Did you choose your interns specifically because they're trans?"

My chest warmed, and my muscles tensed. The anxiety Vik held latched onto me, occupied by Carter and Zoya's, too. None of them hid their identities and wore their queerness with pride, but it stung to see this reporter immediately spin their placement as nothing more than a stunt by Gladiatrix.

"And if I did?" She didn't even dignify his absurd question with a full response.

"I understand you might feel it's important to diversify, but if you're picking a team of all trans interns, is that really diverse?"

"I assure you it is," Gladiatrix replied with a smile. "I find it sad that I have to dignify this type of questioning, especially when only twelve percent of trans witches are licensed in America."

"They're a small community." Johnson shrugged. "One that continues to grow based on certain influences but—"

"No, twelve percent of trans witches have a license to practice their magic," Gladiatrix corrected. "For such a small community, it is quite disheartening to see such a discrepancy in licensing."

"Of course, of course. You want to give back to your community, naturally," Johnson said, his thoughts twisting to the in-depth research he'd done for this press conference. "But is this the best use of Global Guild resources?"

"Are you calling me a resource?"

"I merely mean to state that as one of the top ten witches in the world, it's imperative that you—"

"In America," Gladiatrix corrected. "The Global Guild doesn't currently accept applications from witches who were born outside the United States."

"Of course," Johnson said through gritted teeth. "I only wish to examine if these students—and this has nothing to do with them being trans, that's you making it an issue, not me—but I worry they may not be qualified for this internship. Surely, there are other students with better credentials."

"I chose them specifically for their branches," Gladiatrix answered. "They are the most adaptable to my skillset and will benefit the most from my tutelage. And yes, I am making this a trans issue. As the first trans woman to rank in the Global Guild, I don't wish to be the last."

"Fine, sure, okay. But none of these students even made the top fifty at their academy." Johnson gestured to Carter, Vik, and Zoya, then kept his finger pointed at her the longest. "And this young *lady* was last ranked 558 at her academy. Surely, there were better candidates for someone of your caliber."

Gladiatrix kept her smile despite every desire to lunge forward and smack this reporter with enough force it'd quite literally send him to the moon.

"Gemini is one of the most elite academies in the country. It constantly ranks in the top one thousand and has even graced the top hundred in the nation on more than one occasion," Gladiatrix explained. "To be ranked 558 is to be one of 600 highly qualified students at the most competitive academy in the state. I assure you, every single student at Gemini is more than qualified to work as an intern or acolyte for any Global Guild member."

There was more to the story, to Zoya's story, but that wasn't Gladiatrix's to share. Zoya might've only barely passed her courses at Gemini, struggling to keep up with the others, but she faced more obstacles than many of her peers. Unlike Carter, whose parents accepted him immediately, or Vik, whose family remained mostly indifferent to their identity, Zoya faced extreme challenges. When she came out to her parents, they disowned her, and in order to maintain her placement at Gemini, Zoya had to legally emancipate herself, house herself, clothe herself, and feed herself. She worked full-time and attended classes. She trained nonstop. So while her record reflected she'd barely scraped by, her mind buzzed with a thousand obstacles only a handful of other students experienced as well.

"I was once ranked pretty low in the Global Guild," Gladiatrix said. "I sat at 427 for two years."

The crowd quieted.

"Some called my placement a stunt. Some speculated the Global Guild only wished to diversify their rankings." Gladiatrix glared at Johnson, recalling several articles he'd written about her, and bashing the Global Guild for pandering. "I proved them all wrong and moved up to the top ten. Some still believe it's merely a gimmick. I don't concern myself with their doubt. I prove them wrong every day by protecting this world from unspeakable threats."

"One more—"

PORN. Gay *fucking* porn.

It was certainly a vile abuse of my telepathy, but I absolutely sent Johnson images of naked men. It was surprisingly not that difficult to hijack his thought process with a bombardment of abs, ass, and cock. After an awkward thirty seconds of stunned silence, the reporter eased off and did everything to fixate on barely legal girls to reaffirm his masculinity. Fines be damned. I sent a psychic pulse to give him the worst migraine of his life. Definitely against the law, but it'd be worth a suspended license to shut that prick up.

The rest of the press conference went well for the most part. Few reporters wanted to pile on after the shit show demonstration Johnson had made.

"Hell of a press conference," I said when Gladiatrix and her interns made their way inside.

"Not even close to Hell," she replied with a half-smile. "That was kid gloves compared to some of the outlandish things I've had to shrug off with a perky little attitude and thank you to boot."

"Should they be in here?" I pointed to the interns.

"Wow, Mr. Frost. You don't think we're qualified either?" Carter asked with an aloof attitude, even if he resented some of the comments from before. He played it off well enough. Grabbing his chest, he feigned offense. "You wound me."

"I just mean because this facility is highly classified and even I have to get approval each time I show up."

"They won't be leaving the lobby," Gladiatrix replied. "Plus, the Global Guild has wards blocking them from disclosing classified intel."

I quirked a brow. "Is that legal?"

"They signed the waivers. I'm going to go with yes." And with that, Gladiatrix led the way deeper into the detainment chambers.

We arrived at a central office where Enchanter Wadsworth spent almost all his time. Here, he monitored details on the Celestial Coven, dictated patrol movements, and observed the other witches from the coven already detained.

He stood, propped up by his oxygen tank that he used more as a walker than for its intended purpose.

```
Name: Samual Wadsworth
Branch: Rejuvenation (Healing)
```

Milo stood beside him, ignoring the wafting smoke from Wadsworth's chain-smoking. Christ, how I missed cigarettes sometimes. Especially when I stepped through their perfectly foul aroma with just the right hint of soothing satisfaction. How could a smell ease the tension in my muscles? I shook away the desire and focused on Wadsworth's heavy wheezing. I didn't need that in my life. Not when I had Ben and Milo.

"This attack is no coincidence," Wadsworth said, lighting up another cigarette with the embers of his first. "Obviously, The True Witch is making her move and once again targeting Chicago for whatever reason."

"We know the reason," Milo said. "In part. It may be time to reach out to Tara Whitlock, put Global Guild protection on her."

My breathing hitched.

"No," Wadsworth said. "I've informed Tobias, questioned him as well, and while I find him irritating, I believe he has his daughter's best interest at heart."

"While he weathers the storm overseas?" Milo asked with an eyeroll.

Tobias Whitlock did leave Tara with an elite protective detail. Nearly fifty witches with military expertise that put them on par with some of the best enchanters.

"Why don't we focus on the witch we have detained?" Wadsworth said, shooting me a sour frown. "Maybe this one can actually be useful for once."

"I'm sorry," Milo said. "How many operations have you located in the last three months?"

"Lot of good it's done us." Wadsworth huffed.

Milo gave me a sympathetic shrug. "*I tried.*"

"I'm not worried. He's an ass to everyone," I said, cutting my gaze to the old man. "Even himself."

"Parlor tricks from a half-rate psychic." Wadsworth glared. "Hopefully, you can unravel something from this witch, since you haven't managed anything with the others."

Ugh. The grumpy old prick still resented the fact that I couldn't glean anything from Grim or Lazarus.

"When you find a way to raise the dead or piece together dust, I'll get right on it," I said with some snippy snark. "Until then, they don't have thoughts to read."

"Yada, yada. Excuses."

They weren't excuses. Lazarus had zero thoughts. No brain activity. No pulse either. I wasn't sure how he triggered his resurrection, but he knew not to come back to life while detained in our custody. As for Grim, his bones were smashed into such tiny pieces that most of him was dust, and his thoughts were even more fragmented than his body. We might've captured two pillars of the Celestial Coven, but there wasn't a damn thing we could do with them. I had access to The Sisters Three's memories, but they were jumbled and coded and arranged out of sequence. Organizing thousands of years' worth of memories wasn't a simple task. I might've defeated the wicked bitches, but they certainly got the last laugh, scrambling their memories.

"Look, just let me examine Winston," I said. "I'll get you intel."

"No," Wadsworth said. "I'm not sending you in until our divination witches find and locate any traps his mind might be armed with."

Good call. I'd walked into an enchantment trap of the mind before, and it hurt like fuck.

"Come back tomorrow, be useful, and see if you live up to the hype your dumb boyfriend never shuts the fuck up about." Wadsworth waved us off, but kept Gladiatrix close to discuss guild matters.

As we left, I retrieved my phone to add 'analyze evil witch's memories' to my to-do list.

"Oh, dammit."

"What's wrong?" Milo asked.

"I just realized my new caseload means I'll have to cancel as a chaperone for tomorrow's field trip," I replied. "Unless, of course, Winston is nice enough to unravel his thoughts for me without resistance."

"All part of the enchanter gig." Milo smiled. "Ben will understand."

"Will he? I worry. He was excited about me chaperoning. He hasn't really made any friends yet. He keeps to himself most days, and I don't know, I just thought—"

"How about I go? I can move my cases around tomorrow."

"You sure?"

"Yeah. Plus, who doesn't love the zoo?"

"They're not going to the zoo."

"Yes, they are. Ben's been talking about the animals all week."

"They're going to Familiar Rescue Haven."

Milo's smile fell away as his mind registered the name. It wasn't a field trip I would've planned for a bunch of elementary students, but I supposed there was some healthy benefit to showing them the less sunny side of life. Although I definitely didn't want to be there for all the questions the kids would have about death.

Chicago ran the only shelter in the state for familiars who lost their witch partner. Since their familiar bond couldn't relink with a new witch, they were often abandoned by the grieving family. More so out of necessity than cruelty. The fees for a familiar were pricey, and without their witch partner, their magic became finicky. Hence, why so few havens were properly funded to take on animals with magic. That and some were quite exotic, which meant more expensive to house and feed.

"So, then it's settled." Milo squeezed my shoulders. "I'll be the chaperone and you'll be the mighty enchanter."

His mind whirled with ideas on the reversal of our roles.

"You're still an enchanter. You're just making time for Ben, whereas I'm abandoning him."

"Ouch. You make working sound so cruel. Bettering the future. Keeping everyone safe. Stopping witch extremists. None of that sounds like abandonment to me."

"Yeah, yeah."

With that, Milo dragged me out of the Global Guild detainment facility, and we went home. It was impossible to relax. I found my telepathy returning to the detainment facility, unable to breach the protective barriers put in place, but already jumping at the opportunity for work. It made sleep difficult.

The Celestial Coven was making their move. The True Witch was making her move. Theodore Whitlock was making his move. I had to outsmart them all, stop them in their tracks, and bring an end to this vile group.

CHAPTER EIGHT

I SLUGGISHLY prepared to return and examine Winston's mind while Milo and Ben prepared for the field trip. Ben didn't even miss my absence; he was too wound up about all the animals they had on their roster. His teacher had shared the website and gave them a project before and after the field trip. Ben had made a pamphlet of all the animals he could squeeze onto the paper, along with a sentence about each one. Some of his words were bigger than his actual drawings. We needed to work more on his penmanship.

"Have fun," I said as they raced out of the house.

After finishing my coffee, I returned to the Global Guild detainment facility and sat alone in the secured room where they held Winston.

Thanks to my mind shatter, he remained unconscious. They kept him strapped to a bed surrounded by enchantments all the same. Despite all that, a small patrol of guards remained close, ready in case Winston attempted anything.

I dove into his mind, searching for names and faces of other members of the Celestial Coven. I searched for intel on The True Witch. I hunted down information about their hideouts. Anything and everything Winston kept locked in his memories.

"There we go." I stepped through the muck of his inner core, a place in ruins. That was my doing. I had no idea how the witch originally envisioned his mind, but I'd shattered such representations, leaving floating debris in every direction.

His mind was rocky islands filled with broken memories. I merely needed to find the correct pieces and stitch them back together.

I telekinetically dragged two zigzagged hunks of rock closer to one another, preparing to reunite the memories. A silhouette of a woman in a witch's hat stood tall on one rock while a blurry version of Winston stood on the other.

"This must be your recruitment." I felt the truth in that. An itch from the cloaked memory, the whispers right on the edge of his thoughts, but I couldn't put the rocks together. "Dammit."

Just beneath the memory lay a broken sigil. A hidden trap missed by the divination squad.

"Oh, come on." I huffed.

I grabbed hold of other broken memories locked on rocky debris, only to find more shattered traps waiting to be activated. It turned out that the witches Wadsworth sent to disarm any pesky enchantments only found active ones. There were still plenty of traps awaiting someone to trigger them. These broken sigils weren't nullified when shattered. They had parameters in place to reactivate when pieced together.

"So, Amara planned for my investigation."

Of course she did.

Great. Instead of delving into Winston's mind to find answers, I had the pleasure of spending the next several hours locating and disarming all the traps the divination squad missed.

By the time I'd finished scouring every fragment of his mind for threats, I only had time to delve into one memory.

Electricity surged through me, knocking me out of Winston's head.

"Son of a bitch." I snarled.

That prick used his sizemorphic ability to shrink down some of the traps so that I wouldn't detect them. Dealing with broken sigils was one thing, but now I had to go through his entire mind again, searching more thoroughly.

"Wadsworth be damned," I said to the guards stationed on either side of me. "I'll find him some intel tomorrow."

With that, I exited the cloaked detainment facility. Either their security measures had improved, or my magic was truly drained because all traces of thoughts vanished entirely the second I left. No faint whispers. Just utter silence. The noisy city confirmed it was the Global Guild warding that'd improved.

I barely kept my eyes open on the drive home. Delving deep into Winston's thoughts, evading those traps, searching for intel, all while maintaining my telepathy throughout Chicago and channeling magic into the threads that extended to my manifestations across the world. It was grueling. Not that I uncovered much of anything.

All I wanted to do when I got home was pass out and sync with Milo's thoughts to help keep the rest of the world at bay for a few hours. His mind was buzzing from the field trip. Ben's mind was lost on all the animals they'd seen. I would've liked to join them. It was nice that Milo got to step in and do the whole chaperone thing, but admittedly, I looked forward to the trip. Less so for the learning opportunity on familiar havens and more so at the chance of a little nostalgia for all the ridiculous field trips Gemini organized over the years.

"Hey, hey, hey." Milo immediately greeted me at the door, taking my jacket and sort of trapping me in the foyer. "How was your interrogation?"

"It wasn't an interrogation. More of a one-sided investigation," I explained. "I've got Winston locked in a daydream of destruction. The creep's content slaughtering imaginary people, and it makes it easier to search his past without interference."

"Clever. God, you're so clever." Milo smiled, though there was a tight pull at his cheeks. A tiny nervous tremble. "You're the smartest man I know. Brilliant really. And kind. Considerate. Loving."

"What the fuck did you do?" I slapped a hand on Milo's forehead, delving right past his lyrical distraction, and found his blatant secret floating at the top of his thoughts. "You son of a bitch."

"It's not my fault," Milo pleaded. "You weren't there. You don't understand how difficult—"

"It's not hard to say no." I glared. "You're gonna be hearing it a lot from me in the future."

Milo gulped. "I'm sorry. But I think you're going to love Sheamus."

"Absolutely not. Take him back."

"Oh, no." Milo shook his head. "That'd break Ben's heart. I'm not a monster. You tell him no."

"And be the villain, yet again." I dragged myself further into the penthouse and found Ben playing in the living room with his new dog.

A black and gray Pitbull with a floppy right ear sat next to Ben, wagging his tail back and forth. A jagged scar ran down the dog's face, going from his missing left ear down to his strong jaw. It kept his left eye closed and showed the patchy fur that'd never grown back.

"Did you even consider how Charlie or Carlie would react?"

"I did," Milo said. "The vet tech said Sheamus worked exceptionally well with other animals. Apparently, it's a quality many familiars possess."

Right on cue, Charlie ran into the room and nuzzled against my leg before abandoning me to cuddle up with this damn dog. Carlie, on the other hand, merely lay on the couch, curiously observing. Neither seemed to have a problem with the new addition. Of course, I had to be the jerk in the situation.

"Dorian," Ben shouted, finally noticing my arrival. "This is Sheamus. He's an American Pit Bull Terri-w-er. Isn't he the cutest?"

I nodded.

"Did you know three out of ten familiars become untethered?"

"No, I didn't."

"Did you know untethered means they lost their witch partner?"

"I inferred as much." I fought off a sour frown. Ben had a whole slew of statistics planned to divulge. Apparently, Milo had prepared him, and Ben paid very close attention during the field trip. If I said no now, I'd be an absolute monster.

"Only one out of ten untethered familiars gets fostered or adopted." Ben hugged Sheamus' neck, holding the dog close as the old hound licked Ben's face. "We're like brothers."

Oh, dammit. I rolled my eyes up. That was a dirty tactic. Bringing up Ben's foster status, how he'd lost his family, how we gave him a second chance. Milo and Ben were brilliant and vile.

"Look what cool tricks he can do." Ben held out his arms, and the dog barked, casting telekinesis which hurled Ben into the air, sending him flying around the living room.

That answered part of the question on why so few untethered familiars were adopted. Most people could barely afford a license to cover their magic practice, but to pay fees for a familiar that couldn't bond with another witch? Unlikely.

Thankfully, Milo had those absurdly high vaulted ceilings, but still not what I wanted for a six-year-old.

"Well, that's a safe little trick." I turned to Milo, who kept his blue eyes locked on Ben.

"No worries." Milo's fingers moved ever so slightly. At least he was latching his telekinesis onto Ben, too. "Remember, Sheamus. None of that unless me or Dorian are home, right?"

The dog sat at attention and nodded.

Okay, at least if they had to adopt a pet, they picked a familiar. They were almost as smart as the average person, which made them smarter than most people in general.

I plopped onto the couch and watched Ben play with Sheamus and Charlie for another hour or so, all while he rambled about the things he learned at the familiar haven. While I knew the haven worked to find homes for familiars who'd lost their witch partners, I didn't realize they did same-day adoptions.

Milo tensed when he caught my gaze shifting back to him. Of course they let him do a same-day adoption.

"Anything for Enchanter fucking Evergreen, huh?"

Milo grinned. *"I mean, can you blame them?"*

I rolled my eyes.

"But you should've seen how overcrowded the haven was. They were maxed

out on kennels; they're undersupplied on toys and equipment. All their funds go to food and magical warding and habitats. Just be glad Ben didn't want the cheetah or viper or giraffe. Where would Lenny the giraffe have fit? I didn't expect Ben to fall in love with the pup. But look how happy he is. It means a lot for him to have another friend."

I sighed. *"Fine. We can keep the dog."*

Sheamus looked back at me the moment I sent the thought to Milo. He gave me a very gruff 'as if I was leaving' expression. I shook it away. Too many years dealing with King Clucks. It wasn't like this dog could read my mind. Then the little bastard tilted his head like he planned to prove me wrong. This was what annoyed me about animals. I couldn't read their minds, understand them, know for certain just how much they did or didn't know.

"I'm going to take a shower," I said. "Mind making sure Ben gets ready for bed?"

"Absolutely." Milo smiled.

With that, I unwound while Milo, Ben, and the dog goofed around for the better part of the evening before bedtime rituals started up.

Sleep came surprisingly easy. The one benefit to the new dog was that Ben cuddled up to him right away and passed out in his own bed for a change. I was so drained that I dozed off quickly, and thanks to Milo's presence, I synced to his thoughts. They blocked out the city, silencing everyone nearby.

Milo's mind danced in memories, swam through fantasies, and drifted between visions. Eventually, the beauty of Milo's subconscious faded as the weight of the world he carried returned. Too often, he was burdened by visions, by nightmares, but the shadows that soon swirled around us were unfamiliar to me.

A young version of Milo, not much older than Ben, appeared in the darkness. It stretched out infinitely, reminding me of the horrors from the chimera's inner core. There was something demonic and unsettling about this nightmare. Soon, humanoid shadows sprang forth from the depths of the bleak black void surrounding us.

"No," Milo's high-pitched voice cried out.

I wanted to soothe this version of him, wanted to shake him free of this nightmare, but I lay asleep and locked in this fiendish hell.

One by one, they emerged from the shadows with piercing red eyes. Ten horrifying figures, each locked onto Milo. Each taking steps toward him, carrying a menacing weight of unspeakable terror in their wake. I couldn't place it, couldn't form the words to describe it, but I knew these unseen entities held truly devastating force. They would end the world. They would ruin everything.

Milo gasped, springing forward in the bed.

His jostling movement shook me free from my own slumber. I sat up, pressing a hand to his chest. His heart pounded, his skin was clammy, and his face was covered in a sheen of sweat.

"Are you okay?"

"Just a nightmare."

"I saw. What was that?"

"An OG vision," Milo said with a shudder. "Pretty sure it doesn't exist anymore; you know some possibilities just aren't possible. But it resurfaces occasionally."

"I thought your branch didn't kick in until middle school."

"Mostly," Milo said with a shrug. "Some triggered earlier. Well, you know. Your branch was weird during those early years, too."

I thought back to my imaginary friend who'd basically been a manifestation of a persona meant to serve as a buffer for the exhausting noises of the world. Now, he mostly checked in on Ben when he needed, which thankfully had become less and less with each passing day.

"What was the vision of?"

"You saw it. Beats the hell out of me."

"Hell being the operative word," I said, gently rubbing my hand over Milo's chest. "Did you get demonic vibes from it?"

I couldn't put it in clearer words than that, couldn't form much of a concrete explanation in my head, but the sensation held this eerie, demonic pulse. Maybe it had to do with how much of the vision remained veiled.

Branch magic struggled against demons, and they often showed resistance to it. Many of Milo's visions had been warped in the past due to demonic influence.

"Don't know, don't care." Milo slid back under the covers and pulled me along. "It's an expired vision. Don't we have current problems to focus on?"

"That we do." I scooted against Milo, playing the small spoon and letting him wrap me up in a hug. "Speaking of, you wouldn't believe how incompetent Wadsworth's divination team was. I have half a mind to say something."

"You know he'd just blame it on the fact they're"—Milo cleared his throat and made his voice surly—"phony psychics who don't belong in the angry old American guild I founded. Back in my day, psychics weren't even a branch. They were a twig."

I chuckled. "Dammit. You're right."

"Always am. It's my phony psychic gift." Milo nuzzled my neck. "But I do want to hear all about your day. Don't leave out one incompetent detail."

I lay in Milo's arms, wide awake and sharing my day with him into the late hours of the night.

CHAPTER NINE

SINCE the Celestial Coven wouldn't be so quickly undone, I spent all my working hours disarming more hidden traps inside Winston Cobalt's inner core. Eventually, I managed to find some not-so-useful memories on fragmented missions he'd taken part in, but only through blurry images, faded whispers, and eerie sensations crawling up my spine. This mind remained too jumbled, too bound for me to make full sense of it yet.

What I did manage to piece together was that it turned out the Celestial Coven incited warfare in nations through subtle nudging, pushing places onto the precipice of war when it benefited them. There were also memories of Winston's childhood floating about, but knowing whether or not he had a tough life wouldn't change what I needed to do.

I needed to break open his mind, shatter all the unnecessary pieces, and find intel on the Celestial Coven's movements. So, I worked and tinkered and toiled away for hours and days at a time. All the while, to keep my mind sharp, I allowed my telepathy to wander the city. It trailed my former homeroom coven students, tracking their progress during their internships.

Yaritza, Jamius, and Melanie were the first minds I found myself drawn to. They were most displeased with the direction their internship had taken. While Enchanter Ortiz recovered, he prioritized his guild paperwork, which meant his interns spent their days locked away in his office sorting case files, running around to get signatures, and organizing a chaotic system that made Milo's mess look half decent.

It put me at ease. They'd done impressive work, and now they could bask in the bureaucracy for a bit before returning to the field.

"What kind of actual garbage is this?" Gael's voice rang so loudly, I found my telepathy drawn to his tantrum on the other side of the city.

King Clucks crowed with disapproval while Gael studied a weird ball connected to a chain and eyed his mentor, whose smile he found grating.

Enchanter Diaz towered over Gael, standing tall above all his interns at 6'6. Despite Gael's attitude, Diaz didn't let it shake his smile, though his bear, Priscilla, obviously didn't care for the comment. She snarled, swatting a paw at the air.

```
Name: Emiliano Diaz
Branch: Bestial (Familiar)
```

"It's called a meteor hammer," Diaz said with his thick southern drawl. "They're quite fascinating weapons. A personal favorite of mine."

"Fine, let's trade," Gael insisted.

"Well, when you decide to pay the fees for a license to wield an enchanted weapon, you can pick it, but since I'm gracious enough to foot the bill for you three, perhaps you can be grateful."

"Wow." Gael stared slack-jawed for a moment. "Talk about emotional manipulation. Guilting me for something I never asked for. Expecting gratitude for a so-called gift. I see through your games."

Gael's tactless commentary continued even as the bear glared in his direction. In fact, King Clucks joined in with a puffed chest as if the tiny bird could do a thing against a thousand-pound beast.

The audacity.

"I gotta agree with Gael," Tiffany said, partially in truth. She hated giving Gael credit, mainly because the pair was in their ex's mode and had no casual conversations about dating again. The two were off and on depending on the day of the week. "I wanted something cool, like a sword. Instead, I get a staff? What am I? Five?"

Her beaver grunted.

```
Name: Tiffany Sparks
Branch: Bestial (Familiar)
```

"Exactly," Tiffany continued, twirling a blonde pigtail with one hand and the staff with her other. "This is some basic, boring bitch stuff right here. I wanna cut a fool, not thwack them."

"I don't know." Wesley shrugged, holding his batons while talking to his familiar, swimming inside a small fishbowl. "Moo-Moo and I like our weapons."

```
Name: Wesley Monte
Branch: Bestial (Familiar)
```

It was a yellow fish with white spots and odd little horns on its head. The most interesting—or disturbing—part was how the fish kept the portable aquarium enclosure afloat through precise telekinesis.

"Of course you do, you got batons," Gael said. "I should have batons but with razor blades."

Wesley grimaced and stepped away from Gael, while his fish familiar floated alongside him. Wesley had a deep, dark brown complexion, complemented by the bright yellow suit he wore. Not only did it match his familiar's yellow tone, but it also made him stand out in comparison to his fellow interns who didn't dress so formally. Gael wore jeans and a shirt, while Tiffany kept it casual with an oversized blouse and miniskirt. Apparently, Wesley's familiar continued pressuring him to dress to impress.

Based on his surface thoughts, it was easy enough to determine the familiar was a cowfish—hence the absurd name, no doubt. A truly bizarre-looking ocean animal. It never ceased to impress me the strange beasts that'd latch themselves to a witch. I bet it was a hassle having to constantly acquire saltwater and maintain aquariums for the fish, but at least it could telekinetically move its own fishbowl around.

Suddenly, Ben's dog, Sheamus, didn't seem like such a headache.

"Just so we're clear, a meteor hammer is one of the coolest and most complex weapons in the world," Diaz said, gesturing to Gael's weapon.

"It's a ball on a chain. What, am I practicing for marriage?" Gael started twirling round and round with little regard for his surroundings. "How complicated can—"

A sudden whoosh sent the metal ball crashing into the back of Gael's head.

Tiffany stood tensely with her hands raised in front of her face. "Sorry, sorry, sorry. It almost hit me."

"It did hit me," Gael screamed.

It was clear he picked his interns based on their branch magic, but he underestimated how challenging Gael would be as an intern. If I had to guess, I'd say he wanted to prepare these students in a way that the world never did for him. Diaz had lost his familiar partner twice. Once as a child and again as an acolyte. It was a horror he carried with him on every mission with his bear, Priscilla. While he'd healed a lot over the years, the loss and grief would never leave his heart.

"That's it, I'd like to file a formal complaint with your superior." Gael tossed the meteor hammer onto the ground. "This is unacceptable."

Diaz quirked a brow.

Most of Gael's petulant behavior came from the massive chip he still had on his shoulder because Milo hadn't picked him as an intern. In his mind, Gael believed Diaz ruined it, interfered, and was nothing but a knockoff version of his favorite enchanter. It didn't seem to matter to Gael that Diaz had ten more years' worth of industry experience or a higher ranking in the Global Guild. It didn't matter that his branch and behavior were perfectly suited for Gael. Nope. All he cared about was the fact that he despised Enchanter Diaz and would let him know it at every opportunity.

"I clearly need a new mentor." Gael folded his arms and huffed. "I suppose, under these circumstances, I can settle for, say, switching to Enchanter

Evergreen's team. I hear he still has openings."

"No." Diaz shook his head. "Evergreen's all filled up."

"No," Gael corrected. "He only has one intern. Transfer me immediately."

"If you don't want to be my intern, I can't make you." Diaz shrugged with a sad sigh, beleaguered and intentionally dramatized. "I suppose I'll let Mrs. Whitehurst know you've decided to quit the program and complete your studies without the internship portion."

"Wait, what?" Gael widened his eyes. "No. Absolutely, not. I never said that."

"I mean, if you don't want to stay, there's no alternative," Diaz said. "All mentors have been assigned. Maybe they can find you someone else who is willing to take on an intern who quits after just the first week, but I don't know. Quite the gamble. I don't believe in gambling, though."

"Ba-ba-bawk."

"Shut up, Clucks, we're not betting my future just because you like gambling." Gael shot his familiar an icy stare. After a brief moment of contemplation and utter fear, Gael faked a bright smile. "Upon further reflection, I suppose I can stick it out."

He picked up his meteor hammer off the ground and carefully twirled it. Diaz shot Gael a huge grin. Maybe the enchanter knew more about handling mischievous class clowns than I realized.

I chuckled a bit as I worked and allowed my telepathy to drift elsewhere.

While working in the Global Guild facility, the operations teleported to a new location. It regularly changed coordinates at an unspecified time and an undetermined place in Chicago. Making it unpredictable helped keep threats from tracking it. That said, the sudden shift twisted my telepathy around. It remained outstretched through the entire city, but with my location suddenly altered, I ended up bombarded by thoughts.

"Fuck," I hissed, searching for something to ground me.

Milo.

Gah, his mind always had such a soothing wavelength. It kept me afloat. It steered me away from the chaos. It brought me peace during turbulence. Currently, he was being absolutely ridiculous. Instead of working on any of his cases, he'd dragged his intern with him for some photo op.

They each wore matching gray suits, though Gael had his jacket and shirt specially tailored to be sleeveless, while augmenting the location of most of his spikes to his hands and arms. It gave him a much more threatening appearance, keeping his spikes larger and more centralized on his limbs and face. It also helped that he was a few inches taller than Milo, who was six-foot-two himself.

Gael's shark-like teeth beamed despite the cameraman repeatedly instructing him to tone down the smile.

"Sorry." Gael grinned, big and goofy and still buzzing with enthusiasm.

He remained awestruck working alongside his idol, truly believing the majestic and marvelous Enchanter Evergreen lived up to the hype. He was everything Gael aspired to become.

I groaned. "*You need to burst Gael's bubble before he collapses from fawning over your obnoxious ass.*"

Milo snorted. "*Rude.*"

Despite my intrusion, Milo quickly composed himself and gestured for the cameraman to pause. He turned and squared Gael's shoulders, carefully avoiding the large, protruding spikes.

"All right, it's time to bring the smolder." Milo shifted his expression, adding a sultry gaze and a minxy smile. "Tone down the joy, and pretend you've got to keep that excitement a secret. Anyone who finds out will steal it. And we're here to steal hearts, not have ours stolen."

Gael giggled a bit.

"*Okay, I gotta ask: Why pick Gael as your intern?*" I asked, searching for an answer among Milo's surface thoughts. "*Surely, you're not that in need of an ego boost that you need a fanboy clocking in every day.*"

"You know, Gael, I chose to work with you because I see a lot of potential," Milo answered. "I know it's easy to become starstruck. I've been there.

I still get there some days."

"Because of all the Global Guild witches?" Gael asked. "I heard you had a meeting with the top ten. Like all of them."

"They'll spread rumors about anything," Milo replied, yet he kept his thoughts on the subject veiled all the same.

I scrunched my face. Had he met with the top ten witches in America? Having Gladiatrix on the case was surely enough. Besides, I didn't think the top three witches worked any cases outside of presidential requests. The True Witch was dangerous, but she wasn't 'draw the attention of the nation's leaders' dangerous.

"Not everyone can see the good in not-so-good people," Milo said, reminding Gael of his recent slipup where he'd been caught sleuthing on Milo's behalf. Still a wicked mission plan for Milo and not one I fully grasped.

"I am sorry about the recon assignment." Gael grimaced, emotions almost as frantic as when he had to sit down and eat with Cassidy Gardner until Milo's arrival.

"Not at all," Milo said. "Cassidy was always going to catch you. Winning her over with charm, however, was unexpected. That's just how impressive you are."

"Oh." Gael blinked in shock.

"There's a light in you, Gael. A joy and belief that I know will carry so many people through hard times. You have the potential to be a beacon of hope for Chicago."

"Really?" Gael's brown eyes watered a bit, stunned by Milo's words.

"Yes, and in order to do that, you have to stop being in awe of those around you and start behaving like the presence of power you are. Live up to your potential and show me the Enchanter Martinez who I've seen protecting this city."

Gael beamed, then quickly composed himself and returned to the photo op, following Milo's lead. He spent the rest of the session studying Milo, imitating his actions and poses, and maintaining steady professional composure.

"You didn't answer my question," I thought. *"Did you pick Gael for his benefit or for someone else's?"*

"Excuse me?" Milo quirked a brow, then tilted his head ever so slightly to make the expression appear intentional for the camera.

"Between Gael Rios-Vega, Kenzo, and Caleb, I can already see them working harder because they feel they missed an opportunity—"

"They are each blessed by the enchanters they're working with." Milo gripped his suit jacket firmly, shifting his pose.

"I'm just curious. Maybe you thought Gael could spark their potentials by working with you."

"You think I'd compromise his future outcomes for someone else's? Preposterous." Milo shook his head disapprovingly. *"I never rely on the trolley problem for my moralistic compass. I divert the train and teach it new life skills, so it'll stay off the tracks."*

"That doesn't make any goddamn sense."

"Not much of what I do does." Milo turned back-to-back with Gael, each folding their arms and standing tall. *"Still, it all works out in the end."*

"You and your happy endings." I tsked.

"Hey, if you're a good boy, I'll give you a happy ending later tonight." Milo sent a slew of dirty thoughts my way. Wave after wave of kinks that sent my blood rushing from my head to my other head.

"You're becoming a distraction." I severed my link before Milo could retort with something slick and focused my telepathy back to analyzing the Celestial Coven witch in our custody.

Despite all my progress, I still had to be wary of traps and tricks placed by The True Witch. It didn't matter. I'd unravel everything and bring an end to her.

The Global Guild facility must've relocated close to Cerberus Guild because the familiar minds of those who worked there practically walked right into my head. Their thoughts were like noisy feet stomping in an upstairs apartment.

I allowed their thoughts in, letting them ground me and keep the rest of the city at bay.

Katherine clutched a stack of papers to her chest, nostrils flaring as she bit back her frustration. Once again, Layla and Amani had banded together to cut Katherine off and finish their paperwork tasks before running downstairs to fetch Guild Master Campbell a coffee from the incoming cart.

"Oops." Layla brushed by Katherine with a hard shove.

"Sorry." Amani knocked into Katherine, too, adding a bit of telekinesis, which sent the papers scattering to the floor.

```
Name: Amani Williams
Branch: Psychic (Glamour)
```

Campbell kept her interns busy, and she spent most of the time treating them like glorified assistants. Which in turn lightened the heavy workload Campbell's three PAs already had.

While Layla and Amani thrived in the menial tasks, seeing the purpose—or what they believed to be purpose since the girls often put the girls in their clique through the ringer for petty tasks and errands before moving them up some social ladder I couldn't be bothered to learn a goddamn thing about—Katherine struggled to find joy or meaning in this trivial labor. Nothing she did helped harness her magics, nothing she did taught her the inner workings of the industry, nothing she did seemed like a step toward leadership.

Part of me wanted to link Katherine's mind to Layla's, offering a glimmer of insight into the mindsets of mean girls. Since, according to Layla's logic, everything Campbell did fell in line with her expectations of a mean girl flourishing into a girlboss.

Katherine knelt to pick up the papers, and Jennifer skirted over to assist. Unlike Katherine, Jennifer didn't see this as an opportunity so much as something she merely needed to endure. Honestly, Jennifer probably had the healthiest outlook of all my homeroom coven students.

Katherine picked up her papers and watched Campbell make her way through the office, using her words more proficiently than the swirl of pink mist she emitted to direct her staff. Curiosity percolated in Katherine's mind, wondering ways she could mimic that magical versatility, and wondering how Campbell managed to use her rejuvenation magic for day-to-day tasks.

Some would argue that Campbell's branch was actually classified as an arcane style, which in most instances would've afforded her a leg up in the industry. However, given the speculations that her arcane magic was a mixture of rejuvenation and entropy energy, she officially applied for a rejuvenation branch to squash such theories. Somehow, she convinced the board assigning her license that the caustic burn of her mist fell within the rejuvenating parameters. Anything to avoid a career-ending branch association with the entropy magics.

"Tia, Katherine, come along." Campbell waved them over, using one of her assistants as a sign language translator for Tia since she didn't want the academy-assigned translator underfoot in her office.

"Yes, Guild Master Campbell," Katherine said, almost questioningly with curiosity as they followed her to her next meeting.

It didn't take long for Layla and Amani to intercept Campbell. Layla politely handed off the coffee and strutted beside the guild master, while Amani boldly pushed herself between Campbell and Katherine, giving a glare that'd intimidate most, but Katherine wouldn't back down when she'd somehow gained. She unfastened her grimoire, the frayed, bulky book, and clutched it close to her chest.

I quirked my brow, mentally tagging along and attempting to understand the bizarre move. Before her thoughts revealed anything, Katherine's actions demonstrated her goal. She used the book as an excuse to brace herself and bulldozed right into Amani, shoulder bumping her—practically tackling her fellow intern—and then bypassed Layla with the same ferocity.

A mistake that nearly knocked her into Campbell, but even as she pivoted, the coffee in Campbell's hand was knocked from her grip.

Katherine froze, mortified.

"Got it." Layla swooped in quickly, telekinetically catching the coffee cup and hot liquid inside, then delicately moving it back to Campbell's grasp. "Some people can be so clumsy. Certainly, not the impression you'd want to make in an important meeting."

"Thank you, Layla." Campbell sipped her drink, eyes smiling before turning sour and shooting daggers at the helpful intern. "But don't presume to know what impressions I intend to make during my meetings. Go file something or scare one of the useless acolytes into thinking your position holds some type of merit. I don't need you for this meeting."

Layla shivered, keeping the dread that flooded her veins hidden with a blank expression. "Of course, Guild Master Campbell."

"Goodbye." Campbell shooed Layla and Amani away before tilting her head to direct Katherine and Tia ahead.

Once out of sight from Campbell's attention, Layla glared. Her mind swirled with so many obscenities for her fellow interns that I could barely hear any other thoughts.

After Campbell stepped inside her office with the girls and closed her door, the minds of everyone else quieted. The wards shielding her privacy definitely dampened my telepathy, but didn't block it. My branch had grown far too powerful for standard cloaks and barriers.

"And who do we have here?" Cassidy Gardner asked, sending a heat of irritation coursing through me. So much so, it almost reeled my mind back to the Global Guild detainment center where I worked, but curiosity and concern kept me locked onto the meeting.

By day, Cassidy ran the prolific nightclub Gwendolyn's Guns & Gals, but by night, she funneled illegal enchantments throughout the city, having inherited her family's crime organization. Campbell setting aside time to meet with the crime lord could only mean Cassidy had finally gained enough clout to be considered a viable contributor for guild funding.

I recoiled. The idea of her working as a board member, a private donor, or an elite client each made my stomach twist into knots. It was bad enough that Milo turned to her on occasion when working on his investigations.

"Please, sit." Campbell gestured to Katherine and Tia, directing them to join the meeting as opposed to merely standing on the outskirts.

Katherine loosened her nervous grip on her grimoire and went to put it back in the holster on her hip.

"A tome that old must have quite a few fascinating outlawed spells." Cassidy's eyes lit up with intrigue.

"There could be some written text not permitted for practice, but I assure you there's nothing outlawed in spell craft literature, merely the—"

"Summoning of unsanctioned spells," Cassidy interjected. "Yes, I have quite an understanding of the enchantment doctrine of authority and usage. They'd have you believe their chokehold on casting is firm, but I've found the grip is rather loose."

"Says everyone right before the noose tightens." Campbell smirked, sipping her coffee.

"And you, what enchantment magic do you possess?" Cassidy turned her attention to Tia, who flicked her gaze between Cassidy's lips and the assistant signing.

Tia signed her response and then squeezed the necklace that tracked her spell-casting progress, as opposed to the newly acquired Cast-9-Watch every other student received.

```
Name: Tatiana Owens
Branch: Enchantment (Invocation)
```

I smirked. That tiny little jab was directed toward Campbell, as Tia learned working as her intern, the guild master held a tight leash on all the funding that passed through Gemini Academy. It meant every other student got the new tech to track their casting progress, while Tia needed to make do with her legally required accommodation because the board of officials couldn't possibly pay to update her technology.

"She says that her branch is related to the enchantment class, yes," the assistant translated for Tia, already avoiding the commentary meant to take a crack at Campbell. "And she says that her specific enchantment branch is invocation, which allows—"

"Allows her to speak spells into existence." Cassidy waved dismissively, not requiring the definition of the magic, but finding Tia's ability to sign spells fascinating as, like most of us, the only invocation enchantment magic she'd seen came from vocal language users.

"Just translate what she says," Campbell said, eyeing her assistant. "No need to express she's the one saying it. We won't mistake any commentary for your personal insight since you have none at this meeting or, quite frankly, ever."

Damn. I couldn't tell if that was supportive or cutting. On the one hand, she elevated Tia's voice in this meeting. On the other hand, she just announced her PA of five years had nothing of value to say.

"Based on my line of work, some people are better just seen, and nothing else." Cassidy smiled, placating as if the only work she involved herself in was in relation to the burlesque shows her elegant club put on. If that were remotely true, Campbell wouldn't have a sit-down meeting with the undercity boss.

It might've escaped Katherine and Tia's understanding, but I very much knew why Campbell invited those two into the meeting while excluding the other girls. They possessed enchantment branches, and Cassidy ran an illegal enchantment ring, selling black market spells to the common folk who couldn't afford government-issued magical assistance or legal practicing rights.

I rolled my eyes as Milo's thoughts on the subject infiltrated my own. He vehemently believed Cassidy cared for people and sold these products to help those who couldn't afford other options. In his mind, she was some type of Robin Hood-style witch out to help the masses. But I saw Cassidy for who she was: a social climbing, money-hungry mob boss who exploited the desperate and poor to build a throne on their pain and anguish in the undercity of Chicago, which she sought to rule. Milo had to see her as the lesser of evils, given the many horrors his magic showed him every day, and the friendship he still carried for Cassidy from their time together at Gemini Academy.

"Now, before we dive into business," Cassidy said, retrieving a small napkin-sized enchantment from her purse. "I'd like to ensure complete discretion."

"I assure you, we have plenty of privacy." Campbell gestured to her useless wards lining the walls.

"Humor me, will you?" Cassidy asked, handing off the napkin to Tia. "Perhaps one of your interns could activate the spell."

Campbell nodded for Tia to begin.

"A little extra protection never hurt anything," Cassidy said with a smug chuckle.

I tsked. Paranoid much.

The moment Tia finished signing the spell, a burst of energy knocked my mind from the room. It hit with such force that my telepathic projection hovered outside the goddamn Cerberus building.

Whatever, I had work to complete anyway.

Carter's anxiety pulled me through the sea of minds. At first, I worried that the horrors of his trauma, the trauma of my near death that he'd averted, were resurfacing. I could only imagine someone of Gladiatrix's level had dragged her interns onto harsh missions they weren't ready for. But much to my surprise, Carter's anxiety came in the form of a makeup artist telling him her life story while she applied products he normally avoided.

On either side of him sat Zoya and Vik, who also remained statuesque as a professional applied makeup.

"Now that we're almost done with the makeup test, we can hopefully move on to your casework for the day," a member of Gladiatrix's entourage said. "Ideally, we'll finish early so we can examine and reevaluate where your team needs improvement."

Technically speaking, they were assigned specially to Carter, Vik, and Zoya's entourage. Sort of a starter pack of success for the young interns and for this up-and-coming personal assistant who craved working for the elite enchanters so they could bask in that radiant secondhand fame.

"Can you stop calling this a case?" Carter huffed.

It wasn't an actual case that had Carter's mind whirling with anxiety. Nope. It was the practice questions for an upcoming interview he had. Gladiatrix's entourage of industry experts went to work preparing a social media rollout for Carter, Vik, and Zoya. Each would do some test posts, audience engagement, and a few live videos to gauge where their strengths and weaknesses were.

While Carter loved the spotlight and dreamed big for most of his life, actually living it as a reality scared the ever-living fuck out of him.

He'd much rather be slaying demons alongside Gladiatrix, instead of handling all the PR she navigated with finesse.

"Why couldn't we join Gladiatrix?" Carter asked, keeping his eyes rolled up to the ceiling as the makeup artist drew subtle liner under his blue eyes.

"Yeah," Vik said, concurring purely out of their fear of public speaking—which included talking on camera alone in a room. "Shouldn't we prioritize actually working on cases?"

"Interviews, press, and the spotlight are as important," Zoya commented, fluffing her dark brown hair to enhance the bounce of the curls the stylist had added. "If not more important, since saving lives only matters if people know about it."

Carter and Vik made uncomfortable expressions.

"Don't look at me like that." Zoya puckered her lips, double-checking the shade to her complexion. "You only want to be professional enchanters because they're in the spotlight, making it look heroic. They do this because they prioritize their public image. And if you want to make changes in the industry, you have to be in the industry. Loved by the industry."

"I suppose you're right." Carter shrugged. "Can't win the game if you don't play."

"Of course I'm right." Zoya zipped to the other side of the room and smiled. "I'm always right. Except when I vote. Then I'm left."

"I still think we'd gain more experience working on a case than talking to a camera about the case we aren't even on." Vik sank into their chair, making it difficult for their makeup artist to continue.

Gladiatrix had abandoned her interns with her entourage while she fought a demon overseas. Apparently, a massive hydra with more than a hundred heads and nearly the size of the Eiffel Tower had washed up on the shores of France and began attacking with unfathomable demonic energy.

It didn't take long to scroll through my phone and find articles on the incident. According to some reports, this was a world-ending assault, while more reputable sources claimed the threat had been highly exaggerated, hardly requiring Global Guild intervention.

Even without a manifestation attached, I knew the reason she'd gone there. She was a mere short flight from King Liberty's base of operations, and despite her best efforts to hide it from others and herself, the attraction she had for the masked vigilante was palpable when in his presence. I wagered she'd decided to handle this so-called global threat more so for an opportunity to flirt with her international crush than she had to bolster her international acclaim, despite what her entourage suggested.

"All right." Carter clapped his hands, drawing my attention from myself momentarily and back to my telepathy, which observed him. "Let's get this show started."

"Do we have to?" Vik cringed, already dreading a camera on their face.

"Relax," Zoya said, fluffing her dark brown curls. "If you get overwhelmed, just follow my lead."

With that, Zoya zipped ahead with her super speed and practiced poses in the staged room the entourage had acquired.

Multitasking had taken on a whole new level thanks to the upgrade in my branch. I did my best to continue searching through Winston's memories while putting away my phone and also placing Carter on the back burner of my thoughts.

As I tiptoed through Winston's mind, I found the grayscale of his thoughts alarming. Familiar to another mind I'd delved into before. Only, Winston didn't see the world in black and white. There weren't absolutes clawing at his developing psyche to hide away childhood traumas. No. It was more like the color, the depth, the emotion in his mind had been drained away. Perhaps a failsafe of the Celestial Coven or an illusion meant to lure psychics into a trap.

In either case, I remained on guard, anchoring my mind far outside the cell of the Global Guild. In fact, I let my telepathy drift far and wide across Chicago until it found the familiar mind from before.

"These dumb fuckers can't ever show up on time. How am I ever supposed to get anything done when I have to wait on these morons?" Kenzo scowled at his mentor, making it crystal clear he resented her for saddling him with such chumps.

His irritation would keep me grounded and alert. And while Kenzo's inner core still held strong to his black and white mentality, his absolutes meant to shield him from pain, there were areas of color blossoming. Orange cheer that'd invaded his daily thoughts thanks to his exhausting boyfriend. The one currently texting him good morning with way too many emojis. Still, Kenzo welcomed the distraction and replied. If only to distract from the fact that his fellow interns were running late.

There were also shades of gray growing where Kenzo had locked away his childhood memories. Gray everywhere a memory of Caleb stood. It seemed the pair had finally moved beyond their animosity. Well, beyond Kenzo's animosity. He'd buried his anger for Caleb and made quick work of closing the rift between them.

"Hey." Caleb waved, flying ahead of his mentor and cutting the street corner to meet Kenzo. "Sorry we're late. You wouldn't believe—"

"Don't give me whatever dumbass excuse Hayden's come up with today," Lena quickly interrupted. Her harsh glare intimidated Caleb more than any of Kenzo's menacing expressions, so he quickly clammed up. "I swear, he should've never been promoted to enchanter."

I scoffed. As if she were anywhere near ready herself.

```
Name: Lena Novak
Branch: Arcane (Bubble Burst)
```

Jamie's sister had grown since the loss of her brother, and I didn't merely mean in maturity. Her muscle definition had become quite noticeable, so much so that Milo begged her to change her stage name to Muscle Mommy, to which she threatened to throw him out a window. Still, I didn't think she was ready for the intensity of enchanter work or the mentoring role that came with it. Though while Kenzo found it grueling to be stuck with a team of enchanters opposed to one, I very much respected how Milo advocated that his former acolytes needed to be teamed together.

I chose to believe Milo did that because he wanted to look out for everyone's well-being; however, as Hayden turned the corner and flew down the street with a trail of glitter shimmering his path, the belief dissipated. Hayden's thoughts were abuzz with his romantic entanglements of last night, and it took all my power to bury the floating images of Lena and Ellie's naked bodies in his mind. Ugh. His thoughts were as annoying as his glittery magics.

```
Name: Hayden Russo
Branch: Cosmic (Teleportation)
Branch: Cosmic (Glitter)
```

While Milo denied it again and again, I had a sinking suspicion he'd always planned for Lena, Ellie, and Hayden to work as his acolytes, sort of as his own way of reliving our glory years. The tragic throuple who lost their footing when taking on too much guild work. The three meant to be, who lost one along the way, and then each other for more than a decade. Though that was mostly my fault. Like most things. Still, Milo's attempts to baby his former acolytes and steer them onto a happy pathway were rather obvious, even if he hid the actual thoughts themselves.

"You guys wouldn't believe what happened," Hayden let out an exasperated breath as he brushed his long bangs out of his face, bracing for Lena's rage and Ellie's disbelief when he realized one of them was missing. "Wait a second. I'm not the last one here. Today's not my fault."

"It is your fault," Lena said. "You're clearly infectious."

"Oooooh, maybe my smile's infectious too." Hayden went to playfully boop Lena until a bubble burst on his hand, burning him just enough to remind the young man that while she enjoyed rolling in bed with him, she didn't do PDA or touching of any kind in a public setting. "Or not."

"Can we just get started?" Kenzo folded his arms.

"I don't know why you're in such a rush," Lena said with a snide smile. "You that eager to take observation notes?"

Kenzo glared.

Lena's approach was very much to my liking. Despite Kenzo's vocal protests and loud beratement, his mentor didn't concede to his demands. In fact, she kept him on the sidelines in any and all cases they worked. She bullied Hayden and Ellie into doing the same with their interns. Basically, everyone here worked for Lena Novak, and Lena believed interns shouldn't step into combat until they understood all the basics of guild work.

Ideally, this would be how all internships worked. Sadly, most enchanters overestimated their interns' skills, deluded themselves into thinking they could react fast enough to assist in any situation, and were, quite frankly, idiots with no understanding of educational practices.

"What I wouldn't give to have a different mentor." Kenzo eyed up Caleb, who had his face buried in a book. "You know, while we're sitting here playing secretary, others get to actually face off against Celestial witches."

"*A* Celestial witch," Caleb replied, still reading. "And didn't they all land in the hospital? Alongside like forty enchanters?"

"Forty-three," Kenzo corrected. "And that's only because they're weaklings."

Kenzo's mind whirled with his interpretation of how Yaritza, Jamius, and Melanie fought against Winston Cobalt. Despite his mental flair for the dramatics, his theories weren't far off. Kenzo had a mind for strategic combat, seeing the moves everyone around him would make, and since he knew his homeroom coven members so well, he gauged a pretty accurate assessment of what they did in the battle.

Even though Yaritza had never demonstrated her giant star shower strike, Kenzo predicted it. He also hypothesized Melanie could control the black and white flames of her mentor, and he suspected Jamius would reveal his secret duplication technique soon enough. Honestly, Kenzo had a better grasp of his peers' magical abilities than I did. Which was utterly depressing on my part.

"Oh, there's Tara." Caleb pointed.

Enchanter Reed and Tara flew side-by-side, their long blonde locks blowing furiously through the wind as they raced down the street.

"So sorry we're late," Enchanter Reed said, telekinetically waving over coffee and donuts to everyone. "But I got snacks and caffeine."

```
Name: Ellie Reed
Branch: Ward (Skeleton Key)
```

"It's my fault," Tara said, levitating behind her while holding her small glass container that housed her familiar. "My father's back in the country…"

Kenzo's anger spiked momentarily, and I was reminded how he often swallowed the lump of disgust he held for the Whitlocks most days. Despite his fury and hatred for Tobias and Theodore Whitlock, he didn't let that anger extend to Tara. Instead, he snatched a bear claw out of Caleb's hand and chomped down on the sweet treat as a way of biting his tongue.

"I tried slipping out, but his PR team had me cornered and stripped and dressed for an impromptu interview this morning." Tara huffed. "Showing off how the family is a united front."

"I tried to drag her out of there, but somehow I ended up in the interview," Ellie said with a low chuckle. "I'm gonna be in Enchanter Weekly."

"Oh, that's awesome," Hayden and Caleb practically said in unison.

"You've barely been an enchanter for a week." Kenzo scoffed.

Lena smacked him on the back of the head, and the pair snarled at each other.

"Before I forget, I need to text Gael." Tara pulled out her phone while Caleb approached, studying her familiar and searching for a way to spark conversation.

He'd always found himself drawn to Tara, intrigued by her many branches, yet somehow that admiration he held also made it difficult to befriend her. Personally, I thought he had a bit of envy he hadn't quite sorted out. Understandable, considering every year Tara seemed to gain more and more branches while Caleb remained branchless.

"How's Gael?"

"Fine," Tara replied, still texting. "Less so when he finds out I'm dragging him to a stuffy gala."

"Oh?" Caleb asked, his green eyes wide with curiosity.

"My father likes Gael, so…"

"I knew he had terrible taste," Kenzo said, "but I didn't realize it was absolute shit."

Tara rolled her eyes, ignoring Kenzo's remark.

"Why does he like Gael?" Caleb asked, a bit confused. "I mean, Gael's nice enough, I suppose, but he's kind of…"

"An obnoxious asshat who never shuts the fuck up," Kenzo said.

Caleb shrugged, reluctantly agreeing.

"Gael's sweet," Tara replied. "Plus, my father has a soft spot for witches with familiars."

Really? That was odd. Tobias was an elitist snob and a walking douche-bag. Most folks didn't think highly of the bestial branch in general, but witches with familiars often received criticism for being weaker and relying on a beast. That was why Enchanter Diaz was the only witch in the Global Guild with a familiar—because he was a tenacious Texan who didn't stop at the dozen or so rejections they issued his applications. Ugh. Milo's fascination with the man had worn off on me, leaving me filled with random trivia on the giant fool.

"Also, let's be real," Tara said, sipping her hot chocolate. "He thinks Gael's fuck boy ways will fix me."

"Fix you?" Caleb quirked a brow.

"He thinks Gael's trying to sleep with me and that it'll help me find a suitable relationship and have lots of Whitlock babies."

"Oh." Caleb tensed at the awkwardness of Tara's cavalier attitude toward her father's ignorance of her sexuality.

But to no surprise, Tobias Whitlock was an idiot. Gael had many perverse thoughts—I often found myself trying to block out his crude imagination on a daily basis. That said, he never once saw Tara as anything other than a friend. Gael was an annoying pervert, but he respected people's boundaries and didn't try to flirt away someone's preferences. He didn't even make advances when someone said no. The ocean was big, and he didn't care what the fish caught looked like; so long as they said yes, he seemed content.

Plus, teenagers were fucking stupid, and too many of them found Gael's annoying antics charming.

Winston's body shuddered, convulsing instinctively. Even with so many of his active thoughts suppressed to his subconscious, the witch still felt me rummaging through his mind, and now that I'd stumbled onto something that could threaten his precious coven, he resisted my hold.

As much as I wanted to stick with them, to follow their morning, and use their minds to keep me grounded, I had no choice but to delve deeper into Winston's memories.

I'd finally unraveled the traps in this sector, pieced together the shattered thoughts, and had a memory of The True Witch right before my eyes.

Severing my connection with my students, I coiled as much of my telepathy back into myself as I could. Mountains of psychic energy still floated across the city, but the bulk radiated within me. I needed it as a buffer, a shield, a weapon to fend off the ferocity of any potential threats the Celestial Coven had in store. I'd learned all too well that letting my guard down for even an instant could be the death of me and everyone else.

CHAPTER TEN

I FOLLOWED the thread of the memory, launching myself deep within the moment while keeping a manifestation of myself at the ready, positioned in the inner core, and the main base of my magic locked outside Winston's mind where I stood.

It was imperative that I didn't mistake this opportunity for good fortune. The Celestial Coven thrived on traps, and I needed to ensure I didn't walk directly into one.

A blonde woman with a tan strutted toward Winston. Toward this memory of Winston in a getup, easily from something I might've found in a catalogue highlighting the nuclear family of the 1950s. It was nauseating to look at them both, yet informative all the same. Winston was a bit younger in appearance than how he looked now, but maybe by a sliver of a few years. And that could just be his current clean-shaven face and fresh haircut in comparison. That and the suit he had in the memory made him seem older.

"Have you considered our proposal?" the woman asked.

Winston slowed his aging, much like the pillars of the Celestial Coven. I thought it was a requirement of the four main members, but perhaps they encouraged immortality for all their coven members. In which case, that meant the possibility of more ancient magics at play.

"I seek to speak with your True Witch, not some lacky."

"We are no lackies." The blonde planted her hands on her hips, but there was a sway in her body that jerked ever so slightly in the opposite direction.

It was like she was being yanked by strings in every which way. A familiar sight.

"Respect us or—"

"You'll break my mind like so many others?" Winston grinned. "Yes, I'll admit, you lot have some serious psychic power, but it doesn't answer any of my questions."

Psychic supremacy. This was The Sisters Three, possessing a different witch from the one I'd banished them from when they attacked.

"What are you, exactly?" Winston asked, trying to make sense of the odd pluralization The Sisters Three used in reference to themselves. "What is *she*?"

"The True Witch is a god," they replied. "As are we."

"You say that, and the pitch is appealing, but I'm no gullible fool." Winston crossed his arms. "These enchantment enhancements, they're the source of your godhood? What happens when the charge they hold runs dry?"

"Our resources never run dry," The Sisters Three said in unison. "We are gods. Ascended beyond compare, but the world in its current state is too small to hold all our glory. We need to open it back up, return all the magic to this realm."

"So you keep saying, which is an easy enough lie to offer when lacking the power you claim to possess."

"We possess more power than any witch," The Sisters Three voice turned stern and echoed in Winston's mind. "But let us show you the glory of revolution, the tides of time we turned, the liberation of magic we seek."

Winston required evidence, proof of power, before he'd invest anything into this coven. Why The Sisters Three found themselves compelled to convince this witch, I wouldn't understand. He was powerful, but not to the same degree as the others. Perhaps all members of the Celestial Coven pale in comparison to the tremendous force the four pillars possessed. One could hope.

I braced for the impending flashes of visions, of history, the psychic witches etched into Winston's mind. They didn't merely show him their history; they seared it into his mind. I turned my head, studying the walls of Winston's inner core, looking deep into the crevices and finding the scars marred throughout his mind.

The entire story unfolded from this memory, and I traced the images hidden in his mind.

"We gather here today to liberate magic for all," Amara spoke to a crowd, dressed in a tunic. Her speech continued, echoing in a foreign language I didn't comprehend. "We will no longer bow to the greedy gods. We will show that godhood is for all, not merely the few blessed by circumstance."

It came with a delay, but the words were translated. An effort made by The Sisters Three, undoubtedly.

Amara appeared the same as she did now, but the creases around her eyes were deeper. There were calluses on her hands and cuts on her feet. Her clothing was speckled with dirt and grime. Her skin was worn and tired. But she held herself with strength, the same strength I'd seen with her calm composure thousands of years later.

There was something off about this memory, this moment. The crowd, the words, and the design all seemed genuine and false simultaneously. The reality was stitched together, and I could see the faint scarring of the lies. But why lie?

"Because this isn't Amara's life," I whispered.

She was much older than The Sisters Three. Predating them to such a point, they didn't have any idea. I recall that much when I scoured their minds before killing them.

"How astute," The Sisters Three said, stepping out of the strings of this memory and circling me like the vultures they were.

I half-expected them to spring out of the body they possessed from memory and attack me as a unified trio.

"Can't attack," the light-lilted voice said. "Not enough power," said the raspy-voiced sister. "Seems you ended us," said the stern voice, adding a sour glare from the face they shared in the body they'd stolen.

"Then how are you here?"

"We are but a fragment," the stern voice explained. "The tiniest of specs trickling in the recesses of our coven. A safety measure."

The same as how Finn had broken off a piece of his magic and locked it away inside my mind. The same way another piece had been broken off and trapped inside the mind of the chimera.

"If you think you can challenge me—"

The Sisters Three cackled. "Challenge you? No, no, no. You killed us fair and square. With little effort too, if the recollection dancing on the surface is truth and not conjecture."

"Then what the fuck are you doing?"

"You wish to see the truth, learn the history." They pointed at me, tracing the air. "Our memories are too broken to examine, huh?"

I didn't respond, merely glowered, and channeled psychic energy.

"The memory is true, but we don't know all the details. Amara was born long before our time, when the gods were cruel and selfish. Not like us. We want to give back to all. Those who came before only sought to rule. Rule without raining down gifts to their lessers. We give to all. Sacrifice so the world can have magic."

"Aside from the Greek backdrop, what's Amara supposed to be doing in this moment of history?"

"She's opening the Gate to Hell," The Sisters Three responded casually as if that were some random tidbit. "The gods hoarded power, locking away magic for themselves. By opening the gate, Amara unleashed magic for everyone."

"You're lying."

If Amara had done that, the world would be overrun with demons.

"It was," The Sisters Three said, not hiding their weak link to my thoughts. "Those demons raged through the world, unleashed in mass, and desperate for magic."

Images of golden silhouettes fighting off shadows from every direction flowed through my mind.

"The gods of old were overrun by the demon hordes. Demons and devils danced on the corpses of the old gods, the false gods, the dead gods."

Gold silhouettes fizzled out one by one, devoured by the gnawing shadows, replaced by splatters of blood until it pooled in every direction.

"I was born in an era where demons stormed across the lands." The Sisters Three steered me from the sea of blood. "My village was surrounded by harpy hunting grounds. The neighboring city made regular sacrifices to the krakens of the sea and the minotaur who burrowed tunnels through the streets. Demons dwelled everywhere, insatiable in their need for magic."

They made it seem as if all the myths and legends that we now knew to be demons actually walked side by side with people.

"They did. They hunted and devoured the best of the witches, consuming our magic and raining down chaos upon the earth." The Sisters Three's voice got soft—almost somber. "Magic finally belonged to us all, but Amara couldn't protect the world when it was infested with demons. So she founded the Celestial Coven. She sealed the Gate to Hell—banishing every demon once again but locking away all of the magic along with it."

Flashes of Amara, The Sisters Three, Lazarus, and Grim chanting a spell as the rest of their coven fought off hordes of demons played in my mind. One by one, their members were slaughtered until demons surrounded the four pillars. A bright light sprang from each of their eyes, burning away the demonic energy in every direction.

"In order to save the world, we had to strip it of the cancerous magic that lured demons in such destructive stampedes."

That was how magic vanished. The era of nothing, where we lost our connection entirely. That was because of the Celestial Coven.

The lights surrounding Amara and the other pillars curved and looped around them, wrapping each of them in a cocoon of magic before vanishing altogether.

"We fell into the astral realms between worlds, we slept and we cast protections until eventually the world was ready."

"Ready for what?"

"For when we finally returned," The Sisters Three said. "When we finally awoke after the centuries of slumber, we brought magic with us, magic for all with no need for demons to roam. The Gate of Hell remained sealed, but when we returned, we cracked the outer layer of the dimension just enough to give everyone a taste of magic."

"A taste?"

"Come now, surely you know that a tree requires more than four roots," they said. "A tree thrives with thousands of roots. We all had access to infinite strength. The number of branches now pales in comparison to what was. The strength of those branches was mightier than even your best witches of today."

The idea of more than four roots, hundreds or possibly thousands of them. It seemed absurd.

"We have so much more potential, all of us," they said. "We're meant to be gods."

"Gods? The audacity, the stupidity, the fanatical belief is pathetic."

"An expected response from a small mind with a sliver of power."

"A sliver that slaughtered you three with ease."

"And think what you could be when The True Witch achieves her goal," they said. "Imagine life after she properly completes her ritual. Godhood for all. Death but a fleeting, distant thing. Those lost souls, the infinite number, will be but a short visit away. We will all have the potential to traverse the universe in all its infinite glory."

"You're a delusional fool," I snapped. "And I won't let Amara or her coven force Tara into some terrible—"

"Terrible? Nonsense." The Sisters Three scoffed. "Tara is the goddess of all. She will rule everything, everyone, everywhere. She will grant us the universe."

"You can't be serious."

"Yes," they said. "The True Witch bore three children aligned with the stars above, casting rituals of old for promises of new."

"Three?" I quirked a brow.

"One as a sacrifice to the gods of old who sleep eternal," The Sisters Three said. "One to rule the demons of Hell. And one to reign over everything. Theodore and the abomination were brought into this world to ensure Tara had all she required for greatness."

"Abomination?"

"The sacrifice." The Sisters Three spoke with a venomous disgust. "A branchless thing."

"Branchless?"

"Their mere existence is blasphemous."

"I think I understand now." I held back the need to recoil at their hateful emotions oozing in Winston's mind. "You've been quite helpful. More so as a fragment than you ever were as broken memories in storage."

"We can divulge so much more."

"That won't be necessary." I retrieved their shattered, gnarled memories from my inner core and released them to the ether of the world. "There is nothing to be found there, only threads offering you a foothold in life."

"Nonsense," they said. "We are far too weak to be more than a whisper."

"If that were true, you wouldn't be so forthcoming."

"You doubt our words?" The Sisters Three feigned offense. "Gods never lie. Our words are destiny, prophecy, law."

"I believe what you shared holds truth to it," I said, channeling my magic. "But I believe there are pieces you left out. Omitted to mislead me, mislead Milo."

They tsked. "That clairvoyant is nothing to us."

"And you are nothing to him, to anyone." I clenched my fist, locking The Sisters Three in place. "It needs to remain that way. What is dead and gone should stay dead and gone."

"But wait, you have a chance to make amends for your actions."

I snorted. "Amends?"

"For standing against the gods, for opposing us," The Sisters Three said with a pathetic pleading of desperation. "We can ensure The True Witch allows you into this new world, the world fueled by infinite magic unlike any our dimension has held."

I isolated their fragment of being from the rest of Winston's mind, ensuring not a trace slipped by and tucked itself away.

"I'll pass." I crushed them beneath the pressure of my telepathy. "And when I encounter the remaining members of the Celestial Coven, I'll be sure to find the fragments you tucked away there, too."

I sent this piece of The Sisters Three to their death, destroying the fleeting magic.

It became clear that Amara had to die, too. If she would sacrifice one of her children for being branchless, if she'd lock another up until he obeyed her fanatical plan, then what would she do if Tara refused her? The True Witch was despicable, and I needed to end her and her Celestial Coven. Permanently.

CHAPTER ELEVEN

I CONTINUED scouring the world for leads on the Celestial Coven, sending out waves of manifestations to search for any possible clue. Since I hadn't had much luck on my own, I allowed a manifestation to trail alongside Gladiatrix, who'd found herself in London yet again. For a woman assigned to Chicago, she found every excuse in the book to fly across the ocean and help out the UK witches.

Granted, this particular visit might've been warranted. Maybe.

Long, sharp claws slashed at my translucent form, and I instinctively leapt back. Glowing red eyes studied where I'd been a moment ago.

Demons really did have a knack for tracking magic, anything to feed their insatiable hunger. Perhaps this one sensed my manifestation in the atmosphere. It wouldn't matter. The magic used to project myself in this way remained incorporeal for a reason. It prevented me from intervening physically, but it also protected my psychic forms from damage, which would inevitably injure my core self.

Gladiatrix lunged through the horde of vampires infesting the streets of London. She hacked through dozens at a time, swinging powerful fists fueled by a combination of her unmatched strength and waves of banishment. One by one, the vampires erupted, exploding demonic energy in every direction.

Following her trail, King Liberty raced to quickly remove the fiends and wisps that formed from the leftover energy. Another masked vigilante accompanied him, banishing demonic energy too. Her fiery red curls were knotted into a long braid that went well past her waist and whirled wildly as she zipped through the streets, flying close behind Gladiatrix.

These vigilante witches were top-notch, and still, they struggled to keep up with Gladiatrix. Admittedly, I stopped chasing after her, allowing my telepathy to flow through the streets of London. Bystanders who caught glimpses of the Global Guild witch filled my vision, helping me determine her next movements. Somewhere around forty or so vampires, I lost track of how many demons she'd slaughtered.

Once every ounce of demonic energy had been purged, Gladiatrix finally stopped moving. She stood in front of a large clock tower and caught her breath. Most wouldn't notice, but I'd trailed alongside her for months now, and I could spot the subtle signs of exhaustion she kept hidden behind a strong stance and confident face.

"Well, she's something for sure," the redheaded woman said with a thick Scottish accent.

She wore a mask similar to King Liberty, except the facial expression had a dramatically giant smile and clownish makeup. It was further accentuated by the jester hat on her head.

Queen of Jesters! That was her name. The mask was scarier than it was funny. There were too many vigilante witches to recall them all, but it seemed the most famous came out to work alongside Gladiatrix, which made sense. If America sent one of its best and brightest, then Britain wanted to highlight some of their best as well.

Though the Queen of Jesters wasn't a favorite of the Crown. The original one came into place around the 1940s when the royal family realized the people wanted easier ways to become licensed. You know, instead of signing over their life and service to the royal family. So, those in charge proposed entertainment licenses for witches with magic that could be used to perform for the royal family and other elites, as opposed to serving in their private army.

Thus, Queen of Jesters was born, a mockery of the offering the royal family gave. The original Queen of Jesters possessed a cosmic branch that created explosive colors, sort of like fireworks, which she used to prank every noble's party for the better part of a decade until the license policy was expanded so the people wouldn't have to simply serve as soldiers or clowns for the royal family.

"I can't sense any demonic energy in the city," Queen of Jesters said with a whistle. "Not a trace of demon or wisp."

"You two did most of the thorough cleaning," Gladiatrix said. "I just slapped around soap suds."

"If you say so," Queen of Jesters replied. "But I say we take you on tour, clean up the whole nation."

"You'd have to get the Global Guild to sign off first."

"Goddamn bureaucrats," Queen of Jesters replied with a shameful tsk. "They ruin everything."

"They offer as much as they deprive," King Liberty said, nodding with gratitude at Gladiatrix. "We appreciate them bypassing the red tape so you could offer assistance."

"Always." There was a softness in Gladiatrix's voice. A nervousness in the word that slipped from her lips. "Vampires can be a headache. Trust me, we've had a spike in the states, too."

"Really?" King Liberty asked quizzically. "They've been all over Europe, bouncing country to country faster than nations can rally their forces."

"Springing from one major city to the next, night after night," Queen of Jesters added.

"And just vampires?" Gladiatrix asked.

"Yeah, which is odd," King Liberty replied. "London doesn't get many demons in general, but the fact that they're banding together, and doing so with such extreme coordination, is bothersome."

"Well, it's not really coordinating," Queen of Jesters said. "They're all vampires, of course, they work together."

"Demons in general are typically isolated hunters," Gladiatrix corrected.

"And vampires are notorious for being more solitary than other demons,"

King Liberty said. "They're the sharks of the demon world."

"Aren't all demons sharks?" Queen of Jesters laughed.

"Yes, but vampires are among the deadliest."

It reminded me of the only other time demons had banded together for a major assault—under the chimera's leadership.

He was long since dead, thanks to my Doppler self, but there was one other individual who could strike such alliances.

"Welp, as much fun as this has been"—Queen of Jesters curtsied dramatically—"I should be taking my leave."

"A pleasure, always." King Liberty nodded.

"And an honor to make your acquaintance." Queen of Jesters shook Gladiatrix's hand. "I've never been fond of the Global Guild, but I suppose some of their members are worth a bit of gratitude."

"Well, thank you." Gladiatrix gently shook the vigilante witch's hand and tipped her head politely.

King Liberty waited for his fellow witch to take her leave before he casually moved in closer to Gladiatrix, leaving very little space between the two.

"Now that she's gone, we can have a bit of fun," he said with a bright smile. "I thought perhaps you'd like to see a bit of the town."

"I've seen plenty," Gladiatrix teased. "I quite literally ran circles around it for the better part of the night."

"Yes, but you haven't experienced London. And the city at night is something quite beautiful to behold. Almost as beautiful as you."

She considered it momentarily. Her time with King Liberty sent a shiver of excitement through her, coursing with a surge of anticipation and a dizzying delirium as she debated.

"You're cute," she answered. "But I don't do DL relationships."

"Oh? You wish to go public, my sweet?" King Liberty tilted his head, shooting Gladiatrix a minxy smile that made the powerful witch weak in the knees.

I very much understood the struggle of saying no to a sweet man who used his charm in the best and most obnoxious ways.

"I'd gladly hold your hand for all to see."

"King Liberty might, but I want a man brave enough to hold my hand without his mask." Gladiatrix's mind whirled with his identity. The name she couldn't call him hung on her lips, the face only she got to see, and only when no one else was around.

Temptation brought me closer to her thoughts, attempting to learn who King Liberty was underneath the mask, but when Gladiatrix clenched her fists, I backed away. It was doubtful she knew I was here, but given her enhanced senses, I didn't want to get some lecture on my eavesdropping.

King Liberty frowned, and his mind swirled with the politics surrounding his position. Damn. His thoughts must've been rampant with worry since his mind was mostly shielded from my telepathy thanks to the protective wards stitched into his costume.

It was a bizarre thing to have front row seats to their most private conversation and only grasp about a quarter of what was left unsaid between them.

"In order to honor King Liberty and the freedom the people of this nation deserve, I don't get to be brave or public." He cast his eyes downward, unable to meet Gladiatrix's gaze. "You deserve everything. You deserve a man who will give you everything. But I can only give what little is left from carrying the mantle."

"And sadly, I understand your position." Gladiatrix kissed King Liberty lightly, savoring the soft press of his lips and the gentle lick of his tongue. "But I can't give you my heart or feelings or my time if all you can offer is the leftover pieces of King Liberty's life."

"Wait, Alicia—"

With that, Gladiatrix vanished in a blurred bolt of speed. Flying or running across the ocean, I could barely track her presence. Her frustrated and heartbroken thoughts echoed in waves before fully dispersing now that she'd left.

Now that Gladiatrix was gone, there was nothing anchoring my manifestation. I floated aimlessly through the streets of London, gaining a crisper sense of the nearby minds now that all the demonic energy had been purged.

I wandered on the edges of the psychic plane where I'd quickly travel back to my core self. There was nothing in London any longer. No demons. No leads. No Celestial Coven.

"..."

Wordless thoughts whispered.

"..."

They called out.

"..."

They taunted me.

A chill ran through me; a familiar and frightening voice whispered in the darkness. Haunting and unreal. It couldn't be real. Still, if even the faintest chance existed, I needed to move forward.

Flying through the streets, I trailed the eerie thrum until I reached an abandoned building. An empty block, more like it. Few minds dwelled nearby, but the one at the center whispered a wicked hello.

Could he sense me? Was this some type of trap set by the Celestial Coven?

I froze, collecting myself, because I needed to investigate, to get answers. Even if this was a trap, a trick, it wouldn't harm me. Not in this fragmented state of being. Besides, the chances of this being real were slim. All this could be some British psychopath with a similar horror to their thoughts. It might not be the most horrifying man I'd ever had the displeasure of meeting.

When I managed to compose myself, I floated into the dank building and made my way through the rundown rooms until I reached a dark cellar. Fuck me. Of course, I'd have to go into the depths of the dark.

Light flickered at the bottom of the staircase. I followed the lights, spotting hundreds of candles illuminating a red pentagram that I desperately hoped had been drawn in paint and not the alternative.

Knelt on the floor in the center of the pentagram was Theodore Whitlock. He kept his eyes firmly shut as he held his hands in front of his chest, channeling magic. A smile crept onto his face.

"*Well, well, well,*" he thought. "*If it isn't my favorite psychic.*"

Chapter Twelve

THE psychopathy of his madness, his hatefulness, had lessened since last we met. Certainly, he was holding his true thoughts back, the vile tone of his crazed rage. But I wouldn't complain since it often sent a bone-piercing rattle through my mind.

He wore clean clothes, unlike the last time I stumbled upon him. Though this outfit was a simple loose-fitting shirt and plain breezy pants. Nothing like Theodore's style. His hair had grown longer, stringy and dingy, but it must've been by choice since he kept his face clean-shaven. His wrists were shackled with thick chainlike bracelets that had carved warding symbols. A similar collar was around his neck, and the warding symbols glowed with warning.

"*Careful, friend.*" Theodore's haunting blue eyes searched the room for my presence. "*These enchantments don't just detect my casting. If you're not cautious, they'll know you found me.*"

I backstepped, skirting the wall of the cellar. It did the trick. All but one symbol stopped glowing. That single symbol must've sensed Theodore's casting. Not that it prevented him from channeling.

"*Those goodie witches really did a number on the area.*" Theodore's mind scoured the city, searching for something as he channeled his magic. "*Miles *and miles away, my friends delay."*

He chuckled to himself, still scanning the room, still searching for me as if he'd ever see my intangible phantom form. I recoiled when his eyes landed on me. He couldn't see me. I knew this, but I believed, perhaps, to some extent, that he sensed me. Sensed my subtle psychic presence as he worked.

"Come out, come out, wherever you are," he said, not to me. No, he reserved his thoughts to speak with me. This comment was directed at the demonic energy he funneled into the cellar where he worked. "I beseech you, demon dogs. Do my bidding."

Wisps illuminated the room, their flashing white lights smacking into each other until those flickers turned into black ooze. Slime and filth that bubbled and popped with blistering heat. Fiends swelled around the pentagram, each roaring and clawing at one another, devouring each other until only one remained. It grew and blossomed and erupted into a new demon.

A vampire.

Was Theodore specifically summoning vampires? Did his power allow him the precision to control the type of demon ascended? And why vampires? Was it truly just because of their strength and ferocity?

The demon's elongated arms stretched wide, testing the perimeters of movement undoubtedly. There was musing and rage in those glassy red eyes that locked onto Theodore. This vampire was a pale yellow and had dark patches of golden body hair. Its claws were as bright as sunshine, and its teeth snapped as the vampire leapt forward.

"Foolish." Theodore held a hand up, compelling the demon to behave.

It resisted Theodore's grip, digging its clawed feet into the pentagram and tearing through the concrete flooring to reach the warlock.

"You waste your time, demon." Theodore snapped his fingers.

The vampire wailed, bones shattered, its knees buckled, and the beast bowed before Theodore.

"I control hundreds of you at a time with ease. Did you honestly believe you could resist my absolute authority?" Theodore smirked. "I am the demon prince, the Heretic of Hell."

"You are just another collared beast," the vampire hissed. "We may be bound by your leash, but I see the strings on you."

"The Celestial Coven prefers tame, scheduled chaos," Theodore said, confiding this to me, not the vampire who held no true understanding of the situation.

"I could snip those strings," the vampire insisted, a pleading expression on an otherwise mangled face of jagged teeth and frown lines.

"Free me?" Theodore laughed. "You think I'm trapped? Oh, no, friend."

He snapped his fingers, turning out the light in the vampire's eyes. Its expression went blank, and the demon obediently walked out of the cellar and crept upstairs.

"I'm as free as a bird."

According to his thoughts, the ones that leapt out joyfully around the room, searching for me, Theodore really didn't see himself as confined. Much like his time behind bars, Theodore patiently waited for an opportunity.

"*And what opportunity are you waiting for now?*"

"*You, my sweet psychic.*" Theodore tilted his head, locking his haunting blue eyes onto me. "*You're here to bring down the Celestial Coven, I presume.*"

"*And The True Witch,*" I added. "*Your mother.*"

Theodore sighed, long, dramatic, and bored.

"*She's so much more than that.*"

"*Yes, an ancient witch who opened the Gate of Hell so she could free magic to all, then somehow removed it from everyone?*"

"*You've been studying.*" Theodore adjusted his position, sitting forward on his hands and knees. "*Just don't buy into the propaganda too much. Liberation of magic may be the goal, but control and authority and order always remain high on Mother's to-do list.*"

He slinked ahead, crawling to the outermost part of the pentagram. As his fingers tiptoed on the edge of his confined space, the wards on his shackled wrist glowed.

"*What I wouldn't give for a little bit of human contact.*" Theodore looked up at me, giving the phoniest of puppy-dog stares.

"*Maybe you should ask your mommy for a hug.*"

A wicked smirk grew on his face. "*You're different, Dorian. Even the pulse of your telepathy holds more certainty, more strength.*"

"*What is the Celestial Coven planning?*"

"*I'll tell you everything for a kiss.*" Theodore leaned to the edge of the pentagram.

"*Not happening.*"

"*Sigh.*" Theodore flailed, holding his arms out and collapsing onto his back with as much drama as he could muster. "*Suppose it's for the best, though. I'd prefer our first kiss to be special. When it's just me and you and Evergreen in a pool of his own blood.*"

Flashes of red filled his mind. Milo's corpse lay before him. Theodore danced in bloody rain, and when he reached me, our lips met. Only, I still had long hair in his mind. I buried his sadistic fantasies. It made my skin crawl and my stomach queasy.

"We can revisit our romance after you defeat the Celestial Coven," Theodore said, breaking the silence of his thoughts.

"*When is the Celestial Coven going to strike, and where?*"

"Where else?" Theodore quirked a brow. "Chicago, of course. Anything to take away my joy. That, and she wants poor, tragic Tara."

"*She truly believes Tara is a god?*"

Theodore scoffed. "A god of incompetence. Seriously, the whole chosen one thing is so overrated. I should've slit her throat years ago."

There was no hesitation in his words, no malice either. It was just a fact. He could and would live without Tara. Killing her wasn't on his agenda; his desperate desires were things like burning Chicago to the ground or slaughtering his father. But he'd gladly kill his sister to remove any inconvenience she'd bring.

"*You're a fucking monster.*"

"Why thank you." Theodore batted his lashes. "I try my best."

"*Why is the Celestial Coven always summoning vampires instead of other demons?*"

"They're stronger than most." Theodore shrugged. "Good at blending, too."

"*They aren't the strongest, though, and none of yours have been blending whatsoever.*"

"True." Theodore hummed a bit, moving his fingers to cast dancing shadows with the flicker of candlelight. "They're also the best and strongest when it comes to possession."

I trembled.

"I could be fishing, though," Theodore said. "Mother tells me nothing. It's like she doesn't trust me just because I refuse to bend to her will."

A flicker of a memory danced on the surface of his thoughts, where he attempted to break free from the cell his mother locked him in. He used a bone from one of his friends' corpses—the three warlocks who were killed as punishment for Theodore's misbehavior—to fashion a makeshift blade. He stabbed The True Witch in the shoulder and bit down on another witch accompanying her. He nearly ripped out the other witch's throat before The True Witch confined him.

As quickly as the joyful musing blossomed, it wilted away to nothingness just as fast.

"All I do know is she's searching for the best and brightest among the vampires I summon."

"*Why?*"

Theodore shrugged. "Presumably because Chicago is crawling with powerful witches and annoying bitches."

I glowered.

"I thought it was funny," Theodore teased. "The point is, Mother only wants the best and brightest among the vampires I summon."

"*I didn't realize you could control the specific type of demon you summon.*"

"I can't, but they learn after a while," Theodore explained. "When I control the demonic energy, building it up to summon a demon, if anything other than a vampire crosses through, I'm to banish it immediately."

"*I see.*" I cleared my mind, preparing to take an immediate leave. "*How long will you be here?*"

"She never keeps me in one place more than a night," Theodore said. "And no, I don't have any ideas where I'll be moved next. Not even sure where I am now."

"*London.*"

Theodore scoffed. "At least I'm not missing anything exciting. I've always found the masked vigilantes who act too cool for fame so much more irksome than the annoying enchanters clamoring for attention."

I wanted to pinpoint this location, to offer it to the Global Guild. And I still could, but by the time I connected with my core self, Theodore would be gone. The trail would be cold again.

"You know, if you want to know where I'll end up next, you could always tag along."

Doubtful. Last time, The True Witch sensed my presence and expelled me immediately.

"And if you're worried about mother's little traps sniffing you out, I know a way to hide under the radar."

"*Really?*" I crept closer, cautiously.

"*Dive on in, friend.*" Theodore held open his mind, revealing the gnarled tree of his twisted thoughts. "*I promise to play nice.*"

"*Not happening.*"

"Shame. I was hoping we could braid each other's hair while divulging all our secrets." Theodore flicked his gaze at me. "Maybe even play a round or two of Seven Minutes in Hell."

I'd learned all I could from Theodore, so I took my leave without so much as a goodbye. It was unlikely the Global Guild would gain much intel from this encounter, but perhaps they'd make some sense out of it. Mostly, I hoped this meeting would spark Milo's clairvoyance. His visions always worked best when in proximity to a threat, even by extension.

Expelling what remained of my manifestation's energy, I floated through the psychic plane and returned to my core self to share all I'd gathered.

CHAPTER THIRTEEN

AFTER telling Milo and the Global Guild everything I'd learned, they assembled a meeting with their top members. It was clear they'd be making a move on Chicago soon, and as such, Milo wanted to convince the Global Guild to send their best to assist. I had access to the facility, but not the virtual meeting itself.

Gladiatrix stood outside the meeting room, staring at her buzzing phone.

"Pompous Prince?" Milo asked, peering over her shoulder at the incoming call. "Is he actually one of the princes, or is that just a fun name?"

Gladiatrix shut off her phone and stuffed it into her bag. It was clear she didn't want to talk to King Liberty even if she desperately craved his company. And she certainly didn't want to disclose her feelings to the ever-annoying and bubbly Enchanter Evergreen. I couldn't blame her there. Milo's cheer could get nauseating.

"I use Grump-a-Saurus for that one." Milo pointed at me, then pulled out his phone. "See."

"Seriously?" I glared.

"What?" Milo shrugged. "Where's the lie?"

I huffed.

"See, grumpy." Milo smiled. "And dinosaur-like."

I rolled my eyes.

"So," Milo said, turning back to Gladiatrix. "Is he the prince? Everyone suspects the third son, but I have money on the second. Or, more likely that duke from…ah, what's it called…"

Following Gladiatrix into the meeting, Milo went on and on about his theories behind the masked King Liberty. Like many of the vigilante's fans, Milo followed all the trending theories and even a few of the fandom forums. King Liberty's identity was a big deal. Bigger than most of the masked vigilantes in the United Kingdom. His unmasking even came with a seven-figure reward from multiple news outlets.

The moniker of King Liberty always remained among the nobles in England, though that was mostly speculation, as only a handful of those who donned the mask had come out publicly after retiring. It was suspected that those in the royal family or of high nobility were meant to carry on King Liberty's cause as penance. A way to offer respect to the original prince who was executed for wearing the mask as the first incarnation of King Liberty, and a constant reminder that the wealthiest in the nation were meant to serve the people, not the other way around.

I sat outside the meeting, uninterested in completing any of my own work, and far too wound up from my brief encounter with Theodore Whitlock to focus. Of course, the meeting itself was completely sealed off from outsiders. Wadsworth stepped up the security measures, locking my telepathy out of earshot. Ironic since he thought so little of psychics.

After the meeting, Milo kept close to Gladiatrix. No smile or joy, just a very calm demeanor. It seemed that attending a meeting with the top ten Global Guild members had washed away Milo's usual charm.

"It'd be nice if you could encourage your international contacts to assist."

"You want me to call King Liberty for a case?" She grimaced.

"Just thinking about the best possible outcome." Milo feigned surrender, raising his hands up. "Not trying to interfere with anyone's love life."

Gladiatrix scoffed. "I have no idea what you mean."

"Of course, of course." Milo grinned. "I'm just a silly clairvoyant asking a magnificent enchanter if she'll do this one teensy favor."

"Go away." Gladiatrix pouted, then retrieved her phone as Milo stepped away.

I let my telepathy wander close to her as I stepped away with Milo.

"Wonderful to hear from you, love." King Liberty answered his phone on the first ring.

"This isn't a social call."

"In our line of work, it never is," he replied. "How can I be of service?"

"Do you think you can see if any of your fellow masked witches would be willing to cross the sea?"

"Hmm. Shocking to see the Global Guild actually accepting assistance from their global allies."

"Is that a yes or not?"

"I know a few witches who'd love to shake things up in your little guild. What's the mission?"

"The vampire problem seems to be escalating here as well."

As Milo and I made our way further through the facility, we bumped into Diaz and his familiar. She obviously had better things to do as she growled at Diaz and kept strolling by us.

"She's hangry," Diaz said with a chuckle. "But how are you hanging?"

"Fine." Milo shrugged.

"Fine? Pssht. Come on, you just had a meeting with the top ten enchanters of the Global Guild. You gotta be better than fine."

"It wasn't that big of a deal." Milo scratched the back of his head nervously.

"Not that big of a deal?" Diaz slapped his thighs in protest. "You been here less than a year, and you're meeting with top brass. Meanwhile, I've got a decade under my belt, and they still make me get special clearance to bring Priscilla into Global Guild facilities."

"Seriously?"

"Yeah, they don't believe in accommodating *pets*." Diaz rolled his eyes.

"Well, the meeting was mostly just me being told my theories weren't warranted, and just because I *think* I saw a possibility, they firmly assure me that I've misdiagnosed the potential futures."

"Did they try to explain to you how your own branch works?" Diaz asked. "Please tell me they tried it at least once."

The pair laughed.

Diaz slapped a hand on Milo's shoulder. It sent a shiver through Milo that spread to me like a furious flame. While Milo did well burying his arousal for Diaz, it surfaced fast and bright in his thoughts. And quite frankly, it didn't bother me. Attraction happened a lot, sometimes without the mind fully registering the thought. I'd remind Milo he could stare or fantasize. It wasn't like my eyes didn't wander on occasion. What mattered was that my heart and body stayed with Milo and that Milo's heart and body stayed with me, too.

"How are you liking the city?" Milo asked, putting on a silly southern accent not at all similar to Diaz's. "I know it's a big ole change from big ole Texas."

"Vanessa and the kids are still adjusting to the move."

"Sorry I made you drag your whole family up here."

"It does 'em good to get a little change in scenery. Plus, I can be with them day-to-day on this long-term mission as opposed to the constant traveling for casework and blowing back to the house once or twice a month." Diaz tipped his hat. "You did me a favor, friend."

"Well, glad to hear it."

"You know, it'd be an even bigger favor if you considered joining us for a date night."

"Oh?"

"*Absolutely not.*" I shot Milo a look.

He simply gave me a minxy grin. "What'd you have in mind?"

"Maybe a family night." Diaz shrugged. "Maybe get a sitter and hit the town. Vanessa and I haven't explored much since we got here."

"We'll think about it," I said.

Milo nodded, and we stared at Diaz silently for the longest thirty seconds.

"Thanks, babe," Milo said randomly. "So, we talked it over, and we'd love to hang out."

"Wait, really?" Diaz cocked his head.

"Telepathy," Milo replied.

"Gotta love that trick," Diaz said, turning on his heel. "I'll text you the details."

"See you soon." Milo waved.

"I hate you."

"I love you, too, sweetie."

CHAPTER FOURTEEN

BEN practically choked the life out of me when we stepped out of the car. He flat out refused to walk, begging for a lift. He wrapped his arms around my neck and squeezed his legs around my waist. By the time we reached the porch, his grip had sufficiently cut off my circulation.

I glowered at Milo, linking our minds. *"How did I let you convince me to do this?"*

"It'll be good for Ben. For you. For all of us." Milo shot me a boyish grin, hiding his eager anticipation for a night out.

Our hosts' surface thoughts went through a frenzy of to-dos while we waited for them to answer. I did my best to contain my frustration.

"Gonna get stuck that way," Ben said and made a face, mocking my frown.

I pressed my forehead against his. "Good. I like it this way."

He snorted, giddy and always enjoying my attitude for some reason. Then he clammed up, burying his face into my neck the instant the door opened.

Diaz grinned, wearing a particularly flashy gold and silver corset vest which popped all the brighter against his white jeans. Christ, he was expecting a wild night on the town. I didn't even need to delve into his thoughts for the eager ache of excitement to cling to me. He and Milo shared the same exhausting wavelengths.

"You must be Sheamus." Diaz greeted our dog first, tipping his cowboy hat to the hound. "Priscilla loves making friends."

Sheamus kept close to me, pressed against my leg. Not a sign of affection for me, but merely his need to express loyalty purely for Ben, whom the hound would likely keep close to all night. Ben, in turn, would hide with Sheamus, and they'd prove even more reluctant than I was on an outing, leaving poor Milo devastated by the household introverts he'd tethered himself to.

"I heard you worked the search and rescue patrols," Diaz said, continuing his one-sided conversation with Sheamus. "Priscilla and I did that back in Texas for a few years. I wanted her to get the right kind of training before we stepped into guild work together."

A fleeting, faint image of his two former familiars who'd been slain in combat flashed in Diaz's thoughts. His eyes watered ever so slightly before he chuckled and washed away the sadness.

"Bet you two will have some fantastic stories to exchange."

A distant snarl caught Sheamus' attention. His good ear perked up, and he cocked his head curiously. Surely, the bear must've said something of interest.

"Go have fun," Ben whispered, his face still half buried in my neck.

Sheamus sniffed the doorway, then cautiously shuffled inside, leaving one less attendant to worry myself with. Now, I'd just have to convince Ben to relax and give the evening a shot.

"Hey, hey, hey," a woman in a gold and white dress said, drifting over as she levitated herself and a small child who wriggled in her grip. "So glad to see you join us."

Oh my god, she wore a matching outfit to her husband. They were *that* couple. And I meant that in possibly the nicest way. It was revolting, mostly. Their minds were synchronized, blissful, and commutative. Even without words or magic, they knew exactly how their other half felt. Gross.

"What's going on here?" Diaz asked, grabbing hold of the child dressed in pink.

"Diego was trying to sneak the dessert tray," Diaz's wife said.

She was quite the opposite of him. Where he was tall and muscular, she was short and stout, barely reaching his chest. Her round, flabby stomach and thick thighs were nothing like the image Milo carried in his memories of the much younger burlesque dancer he'd met more than a decade ago. It seemed time had caught up with her, but she carried it well and quite confidently. So confidently, in fact, Milo's eyes drifted to her very noticeable cleavage before he averted his gaze.

"I wasn't trying to sneak anything," the kid said with a frosting-faced grin. "Just my favorite flavors."

"Oh, just your favorite flavors, huh?" Diaz asked.

"Had to check." Diego smiled, cheeks covered in specks of chocolate.

Based on his sugar high surface thoughts, he didn't discriminate when it came to sweets. They were all his favorites.

"None of that," Diaz said. "Best behavior, buddy."

"Yes, sir." Diego huffed and prepared for the gentle landing as his dad planted him on the floor. He straightened his composure as he stood between his parents. Then, he adjusted his hot pink tie and greeted us.

"I'm Vanessa," his mother said, extending a hand to shake.

I used my free hand to greet her and kept a secure grip on Ben, who clung to me.

"And this is—"

"Diego, pleasure of course," the small boy said with flair, bowing dramatically before smiling. His missing front teeth made his expression all the more ridiculous, but he clearly wanted to imitate his father's behavior. "Wow. How'd you get your hair that shade of blue?"

Ben turned just enough to look down at the mesmerized Diego.

"It's amazing. I want hair that cool. I could never." Diego's big brown eyes stared like saucers at Ben's sky-blue hair. "Your dads let you dye it? Whoa. So cool. I'd totally rock pink."

"It's natural," Ben said.

"Natural?" Diego asked, wide-eyed. "Not-uh. How?"

"I dunno know." Ben shrugged. "Trauma."

"Wow!" Diego hovered, unconsciously casting his levitation, almost pressing his face against Ben's, then he whirled around to his parents. "Can I have drauma? Pleeeeaaassse."

"Um, hmmmmm." Diaz tipped his hat toward his wife. "Maybe if you ask your mom real nicely."

"Nope, not until you're older," Vanessa said with a nervous laugh.

"Mooooom, come on." Diego landed on the ground and tugged on her dress. "His daddies let him have drauma."

"If you want trauma so badly, go bother your sister," Vanessa said quite sternly. "She'll gladly accommodate you."

Diego huffed, thoughts of his mean twin sister swirling with his day-dream fantasies, and as quickly as his attitude turned sour, it just as quickly returned to something jubilant and lost on a high of sugar.

"Wanna hang out in my room?" Diego asked. "I can show you all the cool stuff I got. And I can introduce you to Mr. Wobbles."

"Mister who?"

"Only the best guy in the world," Diego said with a bright smile.

"Imaginary friend," Vanessa mouthed.

"He's very independent and expresses his curiosities through imagination," Diaz whispered.

"Or you can hang with my folks and your dads." Diego shrugged. "Whatevers."

"They're not my dads." Ben wriggled loose, climbing down me like a tree he'd grown bored with. "They're my guardians, is all."

The clarification served Ben well, protecting him from feelings he didn't wish to process, to feel. Family meant something. He'd lost that, and the idea of a new one came with a struggle. There was a war inside his heart that raged, equal parts betrayal and fear of losing love all over again. In a way, I related. I grasped why Ben needed the distance, the barrier—much like his magic.

Still, the words stung. It mostly pinched at Milo's heart, but his pain invaded my emotions and reminded me how Ben still needed that layer of distance. He wanted a family, but mostly, he wanted his family. Sadly, they were all dead, from his parents to his aunts and uncles and cousins and grandparents and godparents and friends of friends of friends. That beautiful town his family had helped build ended up obliterated, taking all of them with it. Everyone Ben had ever trusted and loved and cared for had died.

Now, he had two guardians who he didn't want to want but desperately needed to make it through a day. Most of the time, he struggled with others. Much like myself. Unlike me, Ben had valid reasons to crave isolation. The pain of losing others would be too much for him to handle again.

"Have fun," Milo called out, but Ben and Diego ignored the sad plea. "They'll have fun. Lots of fun."

Milo smiled brightly, eager to enjoy his night even if his thoughts swam with concern for Ben. I hadn't realized, only seeing Milo's excitement for a date night, but he anticipated Ben remaining at our side. He wanted his little pack of introverts. Milo worried he didn't spend nearly enough time with Ben, with Sheamus, with me. Even if we worked in the same building.

"*You might've been able to get rid of them,*" I thought, lightly shoulder-bumping Milo as we made our way inside. "*But you're stuck with me, mister.*"

The smile on Milo's face grew. "*I wouldn't have it any other way.*"

Cheer returned to his mind, and he eagerly led me into Diaz and Vanessa's house.

"I think you're going to enjoy the evening we planned," Vanessa said, thoughts drifting to the festivities of the exotic night out.

I strained to give the thinnest of smiles, one which apparently appeared more menacing than cheerful, based on the perplexed expressions I got in return.

"Dorian's more of a night-in kind of guy." Milo slapped my back. "But trust me, he's gonna have a blast at Gwendolyn's. We occasionally frequent the place together."

I shot Milo a glare. By 'frequent together,' Milo meant that my telepathy latched onto his mind whenever he went there for an investigation into some case, seeking advice from the wicked crime lord, Cassidy Gardner. The same one who now wedged her way into official meetings with guild masters like Campbell.

Gwendolyn's Guns & Gals remained one of my least favorite places in the world. Cassidy annoyed me to no end, the club itself was noisy, and the illegal enchantment ring the city overlooked was vexing to say the least.

Diaz and his wife clawed at my mind, pulling me from my own aggravation, and toward their desperate hunger for an outing, new friends in an area they found themselves so isolated in. Diaz found himself buried in work, wrapping up things in Texas, prioritizing his mentoring here in Chicago, and focusing on Global Guild tasks. It stretched him thin, leaving very little breathing room for easy nights like this.

Vanessa found herself lost in Chicago. It hadn't been the grand welcome back she had envisioned after more than a decade away from the city. Most of the women she associated with either left the city too or drifted to a very different lifestyle than the one she'd chosen.

"You know, I used to work at Gwendolyn's," Vanessa said with a bit of swagger as she stepped into the kitchen. "It's how we met."

"Oh, I remember." Milo smirked, recalling the case he and Diaz had, the one that led to the burlesque club, the dance Vanessa didn't even pause when the boys broke out into a fight with the warlock they chased down.

Diaz and Milo shared a look, their thoughts twisting together into the same recollection. It was always interesting when minds did that. Most people didn't even realize when they shared a look, a fleeting second or two, their thoughts actually synced together, even unknowingly. The two basked in the memory of the battle and the burlesque show that they shockingly didn't interrupt.

Vanessa's graceful moves and unflinching attitude during the battle piqued Diaz's interest, and he vowed not to leave Chicago without at least one night out with the beautiful dancer.

"Milo and Millie were adorable," Vanessa said, recalling the pair profusely apologizing to her after her performance.

"Millie?" Milo raised his brows. "That rolls off the tongue nicely."

"A lot about me rolls off the tongue nicely," Diaz chuckled.

"Plus, he's only Emiliano when I'm angry," Vanessa said with a surly tone and a swagger in her step as she carried over a tray of drinks.

We chatted for about thirty minutes before the babysitter arrived, then prepared to head out.

Milo poked his head in Diego's room, where the boys were rummaging through every single toy the kid had.

"We're heading out, buddy."

"Okay," Ben said, not looking back.

"If you need us, let us know."

"Have fun."

"You too." Milo lingered at the door, waiting for acknowledgement.

Ben finally turned around, a little giggly. "Bye."

Milo smiled, nodding as he closed the door. "He's totally gonna miss us."

"He'll be a total disaster without us," I said with a deadpan expression.

"Absolutely, not." Milo's brow crinkled. "Ben's quite independent. He'll be completely fine."

"You're such an overprotective daddy."

"Oh, hush." Milo nudged my shoulder.

I grinned the entire drive downtown, high on Milo's anxious parent thoughts. Admittedly, I occasionally became insufferable with the whole parenting thing, too. It was a lot of work, and Ben had so much to process. I couldn't help but be proud of us. All three of us.

Once we got to Gwendolyn's Guns & Gals, Cassidy greeted our arrival with a stern scowl and a hand on her hip.

"I'll assume there won't be any outbursts this time around?" she asked, eyes locked onto Diaz.

"As long as nothing nefarious is going on in these parts, little miss." Diaz tipped his hat and grinned.

Cassidy gave a fake smile. "Everything's above board here."

"That's a stretch," I muttered.

Milo nudged me. *"Oh, be nice. We're trying to have a fun night out, right?"*

"Fine." I rolled my eyes.

"I do hope you all enjoy yourselves." Cassidy ushered us to a VIP table and had complimentary cocktails brought out before any of us had a chance to open a menu.

The lights dimmed, bringing a hush to the conversations around the club. When the spotlight hit a large, feathered fan, the burlesque show began. Music kicked in, slow and alluring, and the dancer revealed her long legs first, delicately kicking them outside the cover of her feathered fan. Gloved fingers danced against the fans' edge, and when she snatched the handle, the feathers were engulfed in flames.

Applause and cheers kicked in, and the music moved more quickly. As the dancer revealed herself, it became clear that the only clothing to her outfit were the heels on her feet and the gloves on her hands. Though one could barely tell based on the flow of her flames that kept her completely covered.

Milo's eyes lit up, enthralled by the dance, by the other woman accompanying her with a wave of water to hide her own blurry body. Our whole table was locked onto the show. Hell, the entire audience became rapt. I supposed it was entertaining. When the fire and water clashed, the dancers had only the smoke to cover themselves, which they did so with delicate casting of telekinesis.

By the end of the show, the most anyone had seen was their stomachs, thighs, and a bit of cleavage. The choreography was quite spectacular, how they intertwined their magics in such an elegant performance.

Each show that followed became somehow more spectacular, with even more exotic magics from the bestial witch with a tiger familiar accompanying her to the dancer who transformed into a thousand rose petals, flying from table to table, and offering a discreet show before returning to the stage.

Okay. Maybe Cassidy Gardner knew how to entertain people. Whatever. She picked good talent. She was still awful.

"So," Milo steered the table conversation as the set wrapped up. "What exactly got you working in burlesque?"

"Cassidy's exhausting," Vanessa said with a wince from the sharp bite of her cocktail. "But she pays her girls better than anyone else and actually looks out for us. It was honestly the only way I could afford the psychic cleanses for years."

"Psychic cleanses?" I quirked a brow.

"I have a rough branch, so I get the excess energy cleared out every few months or so."

"Wow." I sipped my drink. "What's your branch exactly?"

"Oh, it's a nightmare," Vanessa replied with a playful wave and a coy smile.

Based on the fleeting surface thoughts she quickly buried, she meant that quite literally. Some type of nightmarish psychic energy that latched onto the minds of those nearby and drowned them in horrors of her making. My guess was that she could never afford to attend an academy and thus never got adequate training in how to control her branch. Those who couldn't control magical outbursts usually ended up having enchantment charms locked on them, preventing any and all magical use.

Not to mention, psychic branches like ours tended to be a bit harder to reel in, so the fees that came with the government stepping in and curbing our magic weren't cheap.

But the fact that she paid for psychic cleanses on her own said a lot. I'd looked into them once about a decade ago. They were far more effective than dampener pills since they didn't include all the added side effects, but the cleanses only lasted a few months. Last time I looked into it, a single session cost ten grand. I couldn't fathom paying for two or three sessions in a year, and I was absolutely certain they'd only gotten more expensive over time.

Vanessa and Emiliano's minds synced, locking onto one of the dancers now making her rounds to the tables, greeting the audience. It seemed they all came out for a bit of Q&A, along with the tips that came from brief conversation.

"She's lovely," Vanessa said, leaning closer to her husband. "Want me to talk to her, or were you thinking more of a free pass?"

My face flushed as Vanessa's mind whirled with tantalizing thoughts of what she'd do to that young dancer with or without her husband's company.

Emiliano noticed my reaction and smirked. Leaning in close to his wife, he whispered something, and based on how his mind flashed with images of bedding Milo and me, I quickly gathered their silent chat.

"You know, if it's something you two would be interested in," Emiliano suggested, pausing for us to finish the thought.

Milo smirked. "Certainly, something to consider."

"Never a rush," Vanessa said, gently squeezing her husband's bicep. "We just thought it'd be nice to float the idea your way. We'll be in the city a few more months, it seems."

"Could be fun to play." Emiliano locked eyes with Milo, both drifting to a near-intimate encounter they almost had, an opportunity missed, but mutual pining still existed.

Admittedly, their arousal ignited my own.

"We'll definitely consider it." Milo eyed me, cautious but curious, and absolutely convinced he needed to offer up a polite no to Emiliano and Vanessa.

"Absolutely," I replied, nonchalant and much to Milo's surprise.

"Great." Emiliano grinned from ear to ear. "Maybe we can plan for something in a few weeks."

"Oh, after that big case of yours is all wrapped up." Vanessa strummed her fingers against one another. "That'd be quite the celebration."

"Most definitely." Milo smirked, cheeks twitching a bit nervously, still convinced I was being generous to the topic.

"Why wait?" I asked with a casual shrug, leaving the rest of the party perplexed. "You've got a babysitter already booked for a late night. We've got an empty penthouse."

"I mean, she did say we could add an overnight if needed," Vanessa said with a shrug.

As the shock wore off, Milo's mind linked to mine. *"Are you sure about this? Swinging is a bold step. I know it's not really your thing."*

"You act like I wasn't a part of our throuple." I eyed him, sending memories of our time with Finn coursing through his surface thoughts. He quivered as his mind sank into the enticing exploits we'd shared what seemed a lifetime ago. *"You think a prude would let you and Finn run an Eiffel Tower on them as often as I did?"*

Milo grinned, cheeks turning slightly red as his thoughts twisted with flashes of him and Finn railing me from either end, using me entirely, and making me satisfy their every need until their carnal lust had been satiated. Some nights, they'd tag team me until none of us could stand the next day.

"Just because I don't flaunt my desires in crude humor like you and the lumbering giant over there"—I flicked my gaze to Diaz—*"doesn't mean I don't enjoy a night of misadventure."*

"It's just a big ask." Milo pursed his lips. *"And from the rumors I hear, quite the big ask."*

I smiled at Diaz. *"Oh, I am very curious to see what this big ole cowboy brings to the table."*

He might've had an annoying sense of humor, but like Milo, there was a certain charm to Emiliano's antics. And he was quite cute to look at. I could easily enjoy a night with him and Milo, so long as it was just the night.

"I only have two stipulations," I said, setting my drink aside. "I don't like the idea of messy feelings, but guessing by the professionalism already stirring in both of your thoughts, that won't be an issue."

"And the second?" Vanessa asked.

"I don't want to do anything with you." I grimaced. "No offense—you're quite lovely. But women just, uh… Yeah, it's not my thing."

"Fair enough." Vanessa traced her finger along the rim of her cocktail glass. "Shame. You might be the cutest one here."

"No worries," I said with a nervous chuckle as my cheeks flushed, and pin prickles danced on my skin. "I'm sure these two will keep you plenty occupied."

I sat with everyone's thoughts spinning to sexual curiosities of where the night would lead, and despite my own nervousness, I found myself enveloped by the lust of the evening. I'd chase this high and follow it with Milo at my side.

CHAPTER FIFTEEN

ON the drive home, I called Ben to check in with him. I wanted to make sure he'd be all right spending the night with his new friend. Considering he gave me a quick "yup" before handing the phone back to the babysitter and returning to play, I figured he'd be okay for the evening.

"You have a printer, right?" Vanessa asked as we stepped into the penthouse, scrolling through her phone.

"Yeah," Milo said, leading her toward the hall and directing her to the third room on the left, where the home office was located.

Vanessa and Milo spent a few minutes in there while Emiliano silently stared at me, goofy grin fully intact. He sat in a chair opposite the couch I took. Every time I opened my mouth to speak, his surface thoughts flitted with ways to stuff my mouth. It made my cheeks burn when he envisioned my gagging protests and left me too flustered to have a conversation. So, we silently stared at each other, each envisioning the other naked, and all the things we could do with our bodies.

"All righty," Vanessa said, finally returning with a stack of papers. "Usually, we spend more time running through the contract and give the other party or parties in this instance a chance to sit with the terms before engaging in a bit of fun. But if everyone's okay dotting their Is and crossing their

Ts, we can dive right into the good stuff."

I quirked a brow. "A contract?"

"Oh, absolutely," Vanessa said, filling out a section for what she was open to exploring in the bedroom with Milo. Already, her mind whirled with so many ideas it didn't seem much was off the table. Though she did fill in a section about firm 'nos,' which included contact with me.

"Don't you worry this sort of ruins the spontaneity of sex?" I asked with a questioning shrug.

"Sex is so much more than spontaneity," Vanessa explained. "It's an expression of pleasure, an exploration of bodies, of desires, of trust."

"Honestly, knowing what to expect can build just as much anticipation and yearning as not knowing," Emiliano added. "Plus, knowing what your partners are unwilling to do removes awkward play."

"And allows us all to focus on the fun fucking."

"Fair enough," Milo said. "Well, you can put a nix on bottoming from me. I'm not feeling it tonight."

"Damn shame," Emiliano said with a wink. "Guess I'll have to hope your partner is open to being opened."

"Um, yeah," I replied. "Pretty vers myself."

"Nice to know." Emiliano winked again.

"Before you agree, Millie should disclose size and circumference."

"I'm about nine inches uncut." Emiliano cleared his throat, letting the pause break the tension before revealing the rest. "And roughly four and a half inches thick."

"Well, fuck me," Milo said with a slack jaw.

"I mean, if you've had a change of heart." Emiliano chuckled.

"Nope. I'm good topping." Milo stretched his mouth momentarily, wondering if he could even fit the enchanter orally.

I wondered the very same.

"Is that all right with you?" Emiliano asked.

I nodded.

"You know what they say." Emiliano smirked. "Everything's bigger in Texas."

"Not true, I assure you," Vanessa said, briefly reminiscing over a handful of their more underwhelming polyamorous trysts.

"Totally true," Emiliano mouthed.

"Go ahead and fill out what you'd absolutely like to do, what you're open to trying, and what you are not willing to do." Vanessa slid a few of the forms over, including the NDA neatly tucked between a few pages. "This ensures privacy for all parties. It's especially important for our Global Guild men. The organization is still a bit more conservative than I care for, so images are important, sadly."

"Oh, he's right there with us." Emiliano nodded toward me.

"I'm not." I shook my head. "More of a glorified consultant telepath tracker guy."

"You keep using your brain to search the whole world, and they'll definitely make you a full-fledged member."

"For sure," Vanessa said, half-focused on her forms. "Makes me grateful my psychic energy isn't that massive."

I grimaced at the idea of actually working full-time for the Global Guild. It was already a headache enough clocking into Cerberus.

Ignoring the commentary, I went to work reading over the non-disclosure and safe sex policy Vanessa and Emiliano abided by when inviting others into their bed. Well, our bed on this particular occasion. Apparently, there was a raw ride clause that required a confirmed test panel and the obvious waiting period for results. Safe play it was. I ticked the box.

They had a lot of options listed, such as kissing, oral, vaginal, anal, rimming, slapping, spit, rough play, choking, cuddling, and easily a hundred other things. Plus, there was a write-in section for anything not already listed. It was hard to believe there could be more sex play available. They seemed to have everything covered.

Anything not check-marked was considered off the table; however, there was a second section of absolute nos or triggering play that wouldn't be allowed. I filled out the vaginal sex and anything with Vanessa. Well, I left kissing there. I could manage that if she wanted.

"*She is all yours,*" I thought to Milo as he filled out his form.

"Oky doky." He grinned. *"But be aware you are sharing your partner."*

I chuckled. *"You wanna ride the cowboy?"*

"Nope, I wanna make that pony giddy up."

I snorted.

Vanessa and Emiliano eyed me, then each other. After a brief pause, Vanessa turned to me.

"We're not opposed to magic in the bedroom," she said. "In fact, it can add such a spectacular spark. That said, communication is key to a good night."

"If you are uncomfortable saying anything in front of us, that's completely valid," Emiliano added. "But it's an indication that this might not be for you two."

"Oh, the telepathy thing," I replied. "Sorry, it's just a habit to link to Milo. It's usually because I have something snarky to say. Not that I had snarky stuff about you two. It was sexual stuff. All good sexual. Like the best."

Vanessa and Emiliano stared.

I sighed. "Someone interrupt me, please."

"Dorian could link us all, if everyone's open to that," Milo suggested.

"Oh, definitely," I said.

"Well, well, well," Emiliano said. "I'd love to share my thoughts with you."

"Trust me." I linked all our minds. *"I've already enjoyed the show you two have been sharing."*

"Our live performances are so much better," Vanessa thought, handing her completed form over to Milo.

After a brief exchange, everyone reviewed papers, and it seemed they were open to almost everything aside from a few kinks that required a returning play partner. Not certain this would be more than a one-time thing for us. Then again, I didn't go into date night expecting to fuck the other couple.

I went to the bathroom, taking a few minutes to calm down and clean up before the festivities began. I wasn't the only one who took the chance to prepare for the night. When I returned to the living room, Vanessa was sitting beside Milo on the couch, leaving plenty of room for me to join.

"Shall we move this to the bedroom?" Vanessa asked, sliding a hand between Milo's thighs.

My chest burned, synced to his arousal and curiosity. Before I could react, Emiliano plopped on the couch beside me and turned my head to face him. He kissed me, soft and sweet, taking his time to test my response. When my tongue moved to meet his, he moved in rougher. In a matter of seconds, he had his arms wrapped around my waist, and he'd lifted me up effortlessly to straddle his thighs.

Fuck. I immediately began grinding against him, enthralled by his desires and entranced by Milo and Vanessa's. Their lips were smacking nearby, but it didn't take long for the sound to fade.

Emiliano ran his hands under my shirt, teasing my skin with his strong hands. He slid a hand in my slacks, cupping my ass, and controlling the thrust of my hips as I rode him.

"Let's get this party moving, sweetheart," Emiliano said with a wispy breath between kisses.

I nodded in response, and he lifted us both up off the couch, carrying me into the bedroom.

Milo had Vanessa sprawled out in a big, cushioned recliner by the corner of the room. She slowly undressed while Milo worshipped her exposed skin, planting delicate kisses on her chest, her arms, her stomach, and her thighs. When all that remained were her bra and panties, Milo tore at the red lace until it snapped. Then he went to work, going down on her.

Vanessa's moans of ecstasy drew my attention only momentarily. She lay back in the chair, her breath hitching as Milo worked his tongue inside her. With a graceful elegance, Vanessa extended her right leg, raising it high, then wrapping it around Milo's neck. She held him close, thrusting into him to control the oral.

Milo's devilish delight flowed through the bedroom, leaving me entranced by his excitement. Soon, his hands worked their way up Vanessa's stomach, adding a bit of authority as he took his time eating her out.

Emiliano tossed me onto the bed, ripping off his clothes and putting on quite the distracting show himself. He added a delicate pulse of telekinesis to unravel his corset, each string a mesmerizing show as he stripped before me. His tight white boxer briefs left little to the imagination. Christ, this man was a goddamn giant in every sense of the word, and I wanted to climb him. No, I wanted to buckle beneath his weight, feel every muscle of his authority control me.

"What are you waiting for, boy?"

Right. Titles, proper addressing, and occasional name-calling were on his list.

"Apologies, sir." I unbuttoned my shirt, stifling the shiver of delight that surged through me.

Calling him 'sir' thrilled Emiliano and, in turn, made me eager to be his obedient boy.

By the time I'd gotten my shirt off, Emiliano had completely stripped. He stood at the edge of the bed with his dick facing me.

"Get over here, boy."

I obeyed, moving over and sliding my legs off the bed. He was very tall, but our bed had a high lift, so I leaned forward, bending to meet his cock. It was semi-erect and fit in my mouth easily. I bobbed my head up and down, savoring the prickles of excitement that buzzed across my skin.

"On your knees." Emiliano gripped my hair, taking a step back and dragging me off the bed.

I spit out his cock, nervous I'd clench my teeth in the sudden movement. He slammed me down to my knees and grabbed his cock, slapping the spit-covered pole against my face. The throbbing erection grew to full length after a few smacks, and before I could move to take it in, he shoved it back into my mouth, immediately gagging me.

As I choked, Emiliano ordered me to hold it there. I obeyed, running my hands over his waist and then cupping his firm ass cheeks. He bucked, pushing his cock deeper into my throat. It was difficult to breathe, but my dick throbbed in response, loving how he controlled me. Emiliano held my hair firm and bobbed my head up and down his shaft.

When I finally broke away to suck in a desperate, deep breath, he slapped my face and pushed me back onto his cock.

"Polish my dick, boy."

His mind quickly flitted to our safe word, wondering if he'd hear it in his mind if I thought it.

"*Don't worry, sir.*" I took in as much of his cock as I possibly could, coughing and gagging and spitting up, but holding firm on keeping as much of the length deep in my throat as possible. "*I'm far from breaking.*"

He smiled down at me, savoring the warmth of my mouth. He caressed my neck, then pushed me back, pinning my head against the bed and angling himself to shove his thick dick down my throat with ease.

"Guess I'm gonna have to put in a bit of extra work, isn't that right, boy?"

I gurgled in response, which only further aroused him. He didn't want to hear my thoughts in the moment. He wanted to hear me gag on his cock.

"Don't worry, baby." Emiliano bucked harder; his thighs smacked against my face as he wedged his cock deeper. "I'm gonna loosen that throat up real nice."

Holding me in place, Emiliano spent several minutes face fucking me. I took the brutal pounding down my throat, begging with gagged pleas for him to finish. It thrilled him, made him ram against me faster and harder, choking me until his thrusts became erratic.

"I'm gonna cum." He groaned. "You want my load?"

I gurgled in response, my glossy eyes looking up at him pleadingly.

"Fucking take it." He slammed his dick down my throat, holding it there.

It twitched, and Emiliano moaned. Suddenly, a warm spurt hit the back of my throat, and he slipped his dick out, releasing a second spurt on my tongue, and unleashing the rest of his load onto my mouth and chin.

"Fuuuuuck." Emiliano rubbed the head of his cock against my face, smearing his load everywhere.

With the release, the world came back into sense, and I noticed Milo again. He had Vanessa in doggystyle, fucking her fast and rough, while he yanked her hair back. The pair was entranced in their own pleasures.

"On the bed." Emiliano snapped his fingers, ordering me up.

As I stood, he stopped me, running his fingers over my cum covered face, and bringing them to my mouth. I sucked his salty fingers clean, and this continued until he'd wiped away his load from my face.

"Good boy." Emiliano kissed me, savoring the swap of spit and cum in our locked lips.

Without warning, he shoved me back onto the bed and climbed over me. Using telekinesis, he spun me around, so I faced Milo and Vanessa's direction. When I looked up at them, he shoved my head down into the mattress and rested his big hand on the nape of my neck. The weight and force kept me obedient.

"Time for your reward." Emiliano kissed my shoulder, giving me light pecks as he worked his way down my back and reached my ass. Spreading my cheeks with his hands, Emiliano went to work licking my hole.

I shuddered, sinking into the pleasure of the warm bathing. Each stroke of his tongue left me hollowed out, replaced by a calm satisfaction. He'd poke into me, testing me, and return to sweet kisses before running his tongue along the length of my crack.

"Damn." I moaned, unable to stop shaking. I trembled at his thorough, precise work, basking in the ecstasy of this rim job.

I turned into puddy, letting the work fade away, barely registering Vanessa's breathy panting or whimpers of pleasure.

When Emiliano had finished working me over, he grabbed a bottle of lube and heavily readied my hole. He ripped open a wrapper, and he slipped on a condom.

"Ready for this?"

I nodded.

He slid in slowly, stretching me further than I'd ever experienced.

"Oooouurrgh." I groaned, clawing at the mattress to no avail.

"Relax," Emiliano teased with a sharp thrust.

"Oh, fuck."

"It's not even all in, baby." He slapped my ass, squeezing my cheek. "I can still see plenty of meat."

I moaned, biting back a whimper with each thrust as Emiliano pushed his thick cock all the way into the base. Once inside, he paused, letting it sit there for a minute.

"Don't worry, baby." He kissed my nape. "I'll let you adjust before I wreck you."

I shuddered, doing my best not to clench.

"That's it." Emiliano nibbled my earlobe. "Give yourself over to me."

"Yes, sir."

He pulled back and pounded back into me, grunting with a feral need to own me. When I groaned, he repeated the motion.

"You ready for me to tear that ass up, baby boy?"

I nodded, burying my face into the mattress and biting down as Emiliano took faster thrusts.

"Come on, let me hear you." He grabbed a fistful of hair, yanking my head up.

I panted, releasing wispy breaths as Emiliano fucked my ass faster and rougher each minute.

In the corner, Milo had stepped away from Vanessa, who lay on the chair, sheen with sweat, and basking in the euphoria of climax. Milo unsheathed the condom from his dick, still semi-erect after cumming. Vanessa played with herself, eyes locked on her husband. Her thoughts painted a clear picture of Emiliano's massive cock slamming in and out of my ass again and again, which only made me brace more, uncertain how I managed to take such a fucking monster dick.

"Get on over here, boy." Emiliano gripped my hips, altering my position slightly, but his words weren't for me. I was an object to be used, made for his satisfaction. No, in this instance, he spoke to Milo, who readily joined him.

I opened my mouth, accommodating Milo, who went to work using my throat for his pleasure. They spit-roasted me, moving in a similar ebb and flow to pound me from both ends.

"Yeehaw." Emiliano slapped both my ass cheeks, then ran his hands up my back, gently caressing my muscles before shoving my head further, gagging me on Milo's cock.

The two men took their time enjoying me, and I savored every second. Each brutal thrust brought me closer to climaxing. Every time Milo choked me on his dick, I leaked precum. Every time Emiliano rammed into me with a heavy groan, I twitched as he rubbed my spot. Again and again, they worked me over. Sufficiently gagged, I couldn't respond.

"*I'm gonna cum.*"

"Good." Emiliano popped my lower back, forcing me into a deeper arch. "Cum for me."

He pounded faster than before, making me whimper and slobber over Milo's cock. It brought all of us closer and closer. I burst, lost in the delirium of release. As Milo used my mouth, I relished it, unable to focus in this blissful state. He pulled out of my mouth, rubbing his hard cock against my face as he relished my groans of pleasure. Emiliano continued pounding my ass until he finally pulled out and slipped off his condom. The hot cum sprayed along my back.

I was too exhausted to move, to think. I simply lay there panting at the edge of the bed. Milo was still too frisky. He climbed onto the bed and began kissing Emiliano. Unable to move, I allowed Vanessa's eyes to be mine, viewing the two men through her eyes. She watched Milo straddle her husband, teasing him with the lightest brush between his cheeks. When Emiliano's eyes widened with excitement, Milo shook his head.

"Roll over," Milo ordered.

Emiliano obeyed, letting Milo adjust the man's body to his liking before rolling a condom over his dick, and pushing the head of his cock into Emiliano. The man growled, bracing for Milo's entry.

"Easy, baby." Milo ran his hand up Emiliano's curving spine and straightened him out.

I lay there basking in Milo's pleasures, lost in his satisfaction. When he finished fucking Emiliano deep into the bed, he slid over to me, wrapping me in a tight embrace. We cuddled on the bed beside Vanessa and Emiliano. It was an adventurous night, exploring carnal pleasures and tasting the bliss that came with curiosity.

CHAPTER SIXTEEN

THE high from our couple's date night followed me for the next few days, keeping me afloat. Milo had a bit of pep in his step, too, being extra flirty at home and even more ravenous for time alone than he had been before. It seemed this little outing jump-started our romance, too. Not that it was lacking, but I found myself a bit more than usual, trying to keep up with Milo's eager exploits.

Still, I relished the happiness in our lives and would chase that high for as long as possible. It kept me content during my long hours of work. Between searching for leads on the Celestial Coven across the globe and scouring Winston Cobalt's mind for functional memories, I had a tiresome schedule.

I also let my manifestations wander the city, keeping a close eye on my students. Their internships continued to blossom, and I only hoped for the best for them all.

Despite being half asleep myself, my telepathy latched onto Milo as he left early for work. I followed alongside him in blurry wonder as he got ready and flew to Cerberus.

In his office, Milo prepared for some morning workout and set out three mats. Much to my surprise, a yawning Hayden and an eager Caleb stepped inside.

"Good morning, Enchanter Evergreen," Caleb said with far too much enthusiasm for five in the morning.

"Coffee…" Hayden groaned, stepping over to the collection of fancy gadgets Milo had in his office, from a basic pot to a top-notch espresso machine.

These were not Cerberus standard, but a fringe benefit to Enchanter Evergreen being so highly sought after.

"You didn't make coffee." Hayden pouted, tapping the empty pot. "No caffeine. Wwwwwwwwhy?"

"You could've been here on time and made your own."

"Boo," Hayden whined. "I'm technically an hour and forty minutes early."

"And yet you're still twenty minutes late for our training."

Caleb muffled a laugh, surface thoughts revealing this was pretty typical. Since his Cerberus badge as an intern didn't work outside of standard office hours, he always had to wait on Enchanter Russo to swipe him in late.

"All righty," Milo said, rubbing his hands together. "Let's start with some basic stretches and get our breathing synced up."

Hayden grumbled, following Caleb and Milo's lead as they started a yoga routine. This was quite unexpected. Glossing through their minds, it seemed they did this three days a week since the internship began. According to Hayden's exhausted morning mind, he'd been doing this since Milo hired him as an acolyte.

"It's important to remember your breathing," Milo said, demonstrating the transition into the next pose. "Our breathing connects us to our roots. The stronger our connection, the more likely we'll feel the chamber click when casting."

"Right," Caleb said, jotting a mental note.

It turned out Milo had been working with Caleb and Hayden on perfecting their root magics. Despite not having a full grasp of a perfected root magic himself, Milo took the pair under his wing. It made sense he'd work with the pair. Caleb had already demonstrated perfected banishment, even if he lacked the ability to fully control it, and Hayden possessed infinity draw, which meant his magic technically didn't have a limit. Though his body certainly did, and it seemed he didn't do his best work this early.

Not that I could blame the guy. I wrapped myself tighter in my blanket, enjoying the comfort of sinking into my mattress, while Hayden suffered with those two morning guys chipperly making their way through their yoga routine.

Black tar erupted into a flurry of white wisps that funneled around the corner, attempting to escape the pulse of banishment surging through the streets.

"Sloppy as usual, branchless." Kenzo weaved past Caleb, smirk on his face, and gray static in his palm. "Leave it to me."

"Not happening." Caleb flew faster, too fast for the corner.

A bolt of static zapped him just enough to lessen his telekinesis and make it easier for Caleb to pivot. With a lock on the wisps, he banished the cluster and cleared the area of demonic energy.

"Not bad." Kenzo shrugged.

"You didn't have to help," Caleb said. "I had it under control."

"Yeah, I know. Just trying out that whole teamwork bullshit thing that Novak keeps running her mouth about."

"What've I said about reporting in before flying off?" Enchanter Novak shouted from above, scouting the sky for any wisps floating away.

"Oh, shut the fuck up," Kenzo shouted back. "You're not my mother, you clingy psycho."

"*Thank God for small miracles,*" Novak thought.

"See, that's what I mean." Caleb gestured. "It seems less like you wanna follow Novak's advice and more like you wanna, I dunno know…"

"You clearly think you know something." Kenzo furrowed his brow. "Spit it out, branchless."

"It just seems like you're being overprotective. Well, not that. Um… Overhelpful, maybe? Like you are—hmmm, I dunno know—making up for being not the nicest or most helpful person in the past, and now you're like helpful overdrive. Just a little bit. Not like a lot lot. But with the static, you altered my trajectory just enough so I could finish the case. And last week, you used your hex to enhance my banishment on that fiend, so I don't know. Just a random, silly, weird little kind of observation I made. Maybe. I might be wrong."

"Oh, shut up, branchless." Kenzo shoulder bumped Caleb, leading him to follow, so they could make their way back to their mentors. "You're definitely overthinking it."

He wasn't, though, and that sent a cold rush of anxiety coursing through Kenzo. All the years he'd spent resenting Caleb, bullying his former best friend, belittling him, breaking him—it'd finally come to a head, and somehow the boys resolved their differences. In doing so, it left a huge weight of guilt consuming Kenzo from the inside out. It didn't help that Caleb didn't have a chip on his shoulder for Kenzo's many hateful antics. Nope, Caleb was simply grateful to have his friend back. It drove Kenzo mad. He needed to rectify his wrongs, needed to help Caleb.

So, Kenzo completely overcompensated by making Caleb his personal training project, ensuring that his branchless best friend would succeed. It also meant, occasionally, Kenzo helped Caleb achieve a task. Always something small and innocuous in Kenzo's mind. He didn't want Caleb getting a big ego over sloppy moves, but he hadn't realized that Caleb had noticed Kenzo's helpful little assists.

When the boys reached the rest of their group, Enchanter Russo called Caleb over, and the pair led the others down a few streets.

"Where are we going?" Novak asked, faintly recognizing the neighborhood they passed through.

"You might remember a case we took on a few weeks back," Russo said. "I thought we could grab a bite."

The group made their way into a hole-in-the-wall pizza restaurant that typically saw its best clientele around midnight to three in the morning, catching the hungry drunks bar hopping or heading home.

Still, the place had amazing, giant slices of pizza. They ordered and crowded into one large booth opposite a few kids recording themselves on their phones. After a few minutes, the kids kept stealing glances at the booth and whispering to each other.

"You're Enchanter Russo, right?" one of the kids asked.

"He works with Enchanter Evergreen," another said.

Hayden ended up being dragged away, chatting with the kids while everyone else ate their slice of pizza. Within a few minutes, the kids had somehow convinced Hayden to join them in some terrible dance trend.

"Wait, wait, wait," Hayden said. "If we're doing this, I'm going to need my badass intern."

He waved over a reluctant Caleb, whose moves were stiff, but he had the routine memorized within their first practice run through.

After the kids finished up, they laughed, thanked Hayden and Caleb, then left the empty restaurant.

"Okay, but I should probably upload my own vid of that trend," Hayden insisted. "Think we can pull that off again?"

Caleb nodded with a big, goofy grin. "Definitely."

"You know what would make it even better?" Hayden's eyes widened with a ridiculous idea. "What if we all did the trend? Mentor and intern match up."

Somehow, the absurdity of this didn't bother the employees in the back, more fixated on their phones than the handful of dancing customers in their store. And the prospect seemed to intrigue Ellie and Tara, who immediately joined in. Neither of them moved as well as the boys. In fact, Ellie seemed to step on Hayden's feet more times than not, and Tara nearly headbutted Caleb twice.

"Come on, Kenny." Caleb waved him over.

"Pass."

"Lena, try it out." Hayden trotted over to the booth, extending a hand, which she ignored.

"It's fun," Ellie added. "You don't have to take everything so seriously."

Lena scoffed. "I don't."

Tara fluffed her hair, posing carefree in front of the phone. "I think they're afraid."

Kenzo slowly craned his neck, appearing like some angry owl. "Excuse me?"

"Nothing." Caleb flailed his hands back and forth.

"I mean, it makes sense," Tara continued. "A bully perfectionist obsessed with how you're perceived despite pretending not to care what others think of you."

I smirked. She was certainly leaning heavily into a basic diagnosis. I'd wager she was enrolled in the introduction to psychology course and found a new lease on life from it. A lot of third-year students focused mostly on elective courses to keep their academics lighter, and I'd endured lots of students over the years who believed they were board-certified psychologists after reading a few chapters of their textbook.

That said, she was spot on about Kenzo. Lena too. Neither of them knew how to have fun because they couldn't quantify it into a form of achievement.

"Hey," Lena called to Kenzo, handing him her phone. "You think you can keep up?"

"Please." Kenzo studied the video playing, then passed the phone back. "Just try not to break anything."

With that, the pair slipped out of the booth and joined the others for their silly little dance.

"Okay, okay, okay." Hayden popped a hip and sent a trickle of telekinesis to start recording on his phone. "Let's get this—"

And almost immediately, Kenzo and Lena broke out into the absurdly trending dance routine, but they seemed to add a few more elements to their movements. Kenzo dropped to the floor, ducking below Lena's leg as she swept it over his head and twirled into some type of pirouette. While Lena continued fluttering back and forth with swanlike grace, Kenzo dragged himself on the floor in this rhythmic, choreographed motion, following Lena's movements and imitating an advanced version of the dance trend.

Meanwhile, Hayden and Ellie stared with slack jaws while Caleb cheered and Tara rolled her eyes. Admittedly, it was quite the sight.

As the dance came to an end, Lena and Kenzo broke apart and joined the others in two separate groups.

"Eleven years of ballet, bitches," Lena said, taking an elegant bow and twirling away. "Did you really think your silly dance was gonna best me?"

"Learn something new every day, love." Hayden smiled, wowed by both his girlfriends. Ellie might've lacked the coordination for the dance, but her free spirit didn't stop her from having fun. Lena, on the other hand, surprised everyone by revealing a new talent that Hayden hoped they could see more of in the future.

Ellie and Hayden joined Lena back at the booth to finish their lunch while Hayden edited the video.

"I have to know how you did that," Caleb said as Kenzo used his friend as a prop to steady himself.

Kenzo held Caleb's shoulder with one arm and grabbed his foot, tucked behind him with his other hand. It helped him stretch his leg muscles.

"Haven't you realized by now that I'm amazing at everything I do?" Kenzo said with the smallest of smiles and a cutting gaze at Tara. "Unlike some people."

"You even turn joy into a competition," Tara said with a hint of sour pity.

"No, I take joy in competition," Kenzo corrected. "There's a difference."

"Okay." Tara's sarcasm was lost on no one.

What Kenzo neglected to mention was that he spent most days in Gael's room studying for hours at a time, and his goofy boyfriend loved all the silly dances. While Kenzo never appeared on any of Gael's socials aside from the occasional photo or brief video cameo, he did participate in almost all of Gael's dance routines. Apparently, it was Gael's study reward that he requested the most.

While this was not the best use of their internship hours, I was glad they were unwinding and learning to have fun with each other. Especially since Kenzo and Caleb had lost so much time over the years.

I worked from Cerberus, handling some of Milo's paperwork. How he convinced me to take on the menial task of filling out an endless stack of forms, I'd never understand. Okay, well, not true. Milo had pulled every string to get me back into enchanter work, vouched for my telepathy with the Global Guild, and kept Guild Master Campbell off my back when it came to taking on actual casework to "earn" my exorbitant salary. Seriously, even as a lowly paid enchanter at Cerberus, I made nearly three times what I pulled working in education.

Alas, my vision started to blur after reading over so many contracts, and my hand was killing me from signing and dating as the proxy for Enchanter Evergreen's signature.

By the time lunch rolled around, I was too exhausted to go out, so I went down to the Cerberus café, which had a pretty top-notch spread. I could see why so many enchanters and acolytes ate here.

As I stuffed my face with a burger and scarfed down the crinkle fries, my telepathy wandered the café. A lot of third-year students took their lunches here, chatting with their friends about their internships.

Nearby, both Gaels dined together, and I let my telepathy linger around them a bit longer than the others. It was nice seeing some of my former homeroom coven students, and it was even better to glean a bit more insight into how they were progressing in their internships. They both had interesting choices for their mentors, so I wanted to ensure Milo and Diaz weren't dropping the ball.

"And they just let you bring that anywhere you go?" Gael asked, scooting his chair back as Gael and King Clucks took turns passing the metallic ball of their meteor hammer weapon back and forth.

"Yep," Gael said, taking a bite of his salad. "I got a permit and everything. It's part of my internship, and I'm legally allowed to use it in any way I see fit."

"Ba-ba-bawk."

Gael's thoughts flitted to the actual clauses of his permit that King Clucks must've referenced, and then he spaced out, ignoring them altogether while twirling his weapon around their table.

"I don't see why your mentor needs y'all to carry an enchanted weapon."

"Because they're badass," Gael insisted, slowing the pace of his meteor hammer and putting it down for a moment. "Diaz ain't so bad. I mean, he's no Enchanter Evergreen, but he's still cooler than most of the duds around this place."

"I don't know." Gael shrugged. "I think everyone's got pretty awesome mentors."

Gael scoffed. "Please, most of them are doing kiddie cases with wisps and fiends. Might as well have stuck around the academy. Last week, we took down a warlock."

By *we*, his thoughts revealed Diaz and Priscilla engaged in the actual combat while Gael and his fellow interns secured civilians and cleared the area. Admittedly, that was a good call on Diaz's part.

"What about you and Evergreen?"

"Mostly just training stuff," Gael said. "He's been busy coordinating with the Global Guild."

Of course, still trying to convince them to send their best and most capable enchanters for the Celestial Coven's impending attack.

"Oh, but we have been working on a cool new technique."

"Really?" Gael quirked a brow. "Like what?"

"Well, you know how Mr. Frost, er, I guess Enchanter Frost now…"

"Yeah, yeah, yeah, Mr. Frosty, go on."

"Okay, so you know how he helped me learn how to move my spikes."

Gael nodded, noting how Gael would make a few larger spikes around his shoulders or calves to limit their placement. It'd even helped improve the damage to his wardrobe, keeping him from constantly having to replace or repair ripped clothes. But, of course, Gael's mind didn't fixate on the practical day-to-day uses this new skill had in Gael's life. Nope. Gael's one-track mind flitted with inappropriate perks.

"Bet that helps with all the make-out seshes."

Gael blushed, making the spikes around his pale cheeks all the whiter by comparison.

Then, Gael—being the most obnoxious person in the world had to go on. "And the ass slamming too. Although I bet Kenzo would like a little spiky ass slapping. OhMyGod, does he ever slap your spiky butt? Or do you slap his with a full-blown spiky palm? Oh, don't make a spiky palm, I just realized that could go terribly under solo circumstances, and…"

"Please stop talking," Gael muttered, ignoring the rambles of his annoying friend.

"I'm just being supportive." Gael grinned, batting his lashes playfully. "All kinks deserve appreciation."

"You realize this is why Kenzo doesn't like you."

"Nice way to phrase hates," Gael said, continuing his lewd gestures. "And like he needs a reason to hate anyone. If someone so much as breathes around him, they end up on his shitlist."

"Aaaaaanywaaaaay, back to my new technique." Gael covered his forearms in spikes and the top half of his face, bending them in such a way that it looked like a mask. The spikes were so thick in their coverage, they completely hid Gael's pale skin.

"Whoa. The masked porcupine!"

Gael's smile dropped away, and he blinked with a moody, flat expression.

"The spiky likey," Gael continued as King Clucks bawked. "Yeah, yeah. The bone blender. The landshark. The giant—"

"Cierra la puta boca."

Gael laughed. "We're just teasing. It's super cool, dude."

Despite the giggles and the rooster's weird wheezy laugh, Gael let it go and continued.

"Yeah, and Evergreen said if I keep working at it, eventually I'll be able to make a full suit of armor just from my spikes."

"Coooool." Gael grabbed his meteor hammer. "Wanna test how durable your armor is?"

The spikes lining Gael's face shrank a bit sheepishly. "Um, I'm gonna pass."

"I promise to aim right for your face." Gael started twirling his meteor hammer over his head. "I swear, I've gotten so good with this. I'm practically a pro."

"Yeah, not gonna happen."

"Come on, dude. My aim is perfect." And just like that, Gael swung a little too low and clipped a few trays at a nearby table, throwing food everywhere. "Sorry!"

"Cl-cl-cluck."

Yaritza, Jamius, and Melanie continued working under Enchanter Ortiz with a newfound respect for the man after he nearly died trying to face off against the Celestial Coven witch. However, they hadn't seen any action even half as exciting—or terrifying—since then.

While they might not have been thrilled by the prospect, I was grateful. They'd faced a threatening foe, shone brilliantly, and lived to learn from the experience. I'd be happy if the rest of their internship focused on banishing fiends and handling paperwork.

Today was particularly boring for the group as they'd been dragged to some stuffy Kraken Guild ceremony. Lots of posturing and speeches meant to convince patrons to dig deep for their donations.

It took place on the rooftop of the guild, basking in the starlight above with a beautiful view of the city.

The constant back-to-back speeches left little time for chitchat, and the group started to get antsy. It was a far more formal event than any had previously attended. Hopefully, they'd survive long enough to slip out unnoticed later in the evening.

Kraken's guild master made his way up to the stage, an older man who practically competed with Wadsworth on seniority. After prattling on about himself and the founding of Kraken, he invited Enchanter Ortiz up to the stage.

"It's nice to take a moment and congratulate those who not only protect this city but work to make Kraken a stronger guild," Ortiz said. "I'd like to give a huge shoutout to my interns. In years past, I've had some real duds."

He did not just say that. This fucking guy.

"Most of these academy kids have no idea what they're doing."

Seriously? It was like he had a whole speech on the incompetence of education, while refusing to admit his narcissistic mentoring style fundamentally failed his former charges.

"But I have to say, Yaritza Vargas, Jamius Watson, and Melanie Dawson are true shining stars." Ortiz beamed with pride, unleashing a fiery celebration to draw everyone's eyes to his interns sitting at a nearby table.

The three of them clammed up momentarily, then soaked in the attention and applause.

"Kraken is fortunate to be blessed by such skilled interns," Ortiz continued. "Not only are we honored to help them grow into successful graduates, but we of Kraken would like to extend a formal invitation to all three as acolytes next year."

Wow. That was a hell of an offer. Ortiz was an obnoxious tool, but he did work at one of the top ten guilds in the state. For each of them to receive this opportunity was massive. Even if they ended up applying elsewhere, they could land competitive offers from another guild.

While interns weren't officially offered salaries, some were given stipends in the form of food and housing, scholarship programs for colleges, and honorary bonuses, which were basically a yearly paycheck in the form of some grandstanding unofficial pay.

"I hope you'll all take a moment to congratulate each of my interns later this evening," Ortiz continued before turning the speech onto himself.

He rambled on about his selflessness a bit longer than necessary. That wasn't just my thinking, but the combined thoughts of several in attendance. When he did finally move his speech back to my students, he discussed their combined efforts in helping bring down one of the greatest threats this city had ever seen.

I rolled my eyes. Winston Cobalt was certainly dangerous and a member of the notorious Celestial Coven. That said, independently, I wouldn't consider the witch that big of a threat. Still, I silently joined in on the applause offered to Yaritza, Jamius, and Melanie as they were praised for their valiant efforts.

The day dragged, and even my telepathy was worn out as the moonlight fought against the bright city lights. A breeze trailed alongside Carter as he flew through the streets, allowing the current to lighten the trip.

It turned out that working under Gladiatrix involved a lot more than PR stunts. His muscles were jelly, making it difficult for him to channel both his levitation and telekinesis roots at the same time in order to fly. Still, his heart fluttered, and he pushed himself to reach the Cerberus facility before their evening closing.

Well, technically, the guild was 24/7 to ensure optimal proficiency and clientele satisfaction, but the official hours of operation went from seven to eight. Aside from the skeleton crew working overnight, the last of the staff exited the building. Among those final members was Guild Master Campbell, who hopped into the back of a town car and went home. Her assistants and interns were quick to follow now that the building had been closed for the evening.

Jennifer split off from the rest of the girls, unable to handle the conflicting emotions much longer. Despite the frustration chiseling away at her spirits, her eyes lit up when Carter delicately landed in front of her with his hands tucked behind his back. He looked quite awkward with a gym bag slung over his shoulder and against his hip, while keeping his arms behind himself.

"Date night," she said with a small sigh. "Which I am super excited for. Don't let my face fool you."

"Of course not, Emo Queen."

Jennifer tsked, playfully shoving Carter's shoulder. Playing into the push, he backstepped dramatically and flailed one of his arms at Jennifer. She was so caught up in his theatrics, she reached out and, instead of grabbing ahold of him, she was left holding the bouquet of black roses.

"Ooooooh." Jennifer sniffed the wicked flowers. "So sweet."

"Well, if you're looking for something sweet…" Carter revealed an oddly shaped box in his other hand.

Oh, Christ. It was a coffin-shaped box of chocolates. Jennifer squealed, delighted by the gesture. She opened the coffin lid and basked in the sight of all the skull head chocolates. Quite a disturbing display. Some had red jam smeared over them for a bloody surprise. Some had what I could only guess was lemon jelly meant to represent pus or something equally gross.

There were also spiders and fingers and bats with floppy wings in this ghoulish box of chocolates. The most unsightly part was watching Jennifer pop three pieces in her mouth at once, devouring them.

"Sorry," she said with a mouthful. "Missed lunch and my break and still somehow didn't come close to finishing my assignments today."

"No worries," Carter said with a grin. "Busy, busy, busy learning how to run this city."

Jennifer rolled her eyes, then popped a skull in her mouth. When she bit down, for the briefest of seconds, she envisioned Layla's head cracking beneath her teeth. It was of little comfort, but the gooey insides sent a rush through her.

"More like learning how to tolerate those who will be," Jennifer said, struggling to keep up with the other interns. "Want a piece?"

Carter shook his head, then opened his gym bag, revealing a smoothie of some type.

"Just gonna have this to load up for tonight."

"Uh, do you want to reschedule?" Jennifer asked, finding the grueling workload of their internships coupled with actual class work exhausting, since she wanted to finish strong academically.

Unlike most students, Jennifer planned on attending college while working at a guild as an intern. It wasn't that guild witches avoided higher education; it was more like we streamlined coursework with online degrees. The added education made it easier to negotiate salaries when getting bumped up from an acolyte to a paid enchanter.

Still, my administrative casting degree—basically a glorified diploma in magic comprehension—didn't do me much good when I left the guild life. Alas, it was the most popular degree for guild witches to obtain. It had a straightforward pathway, it was offered online by nearly every college program in the state, and guilds came to expect it since it provided fundamental applications for casework.

All the same, Jennifer wanted more. She had an interest in engineering, and if she wanted to balance the two goals, that meant she had to put in more studying in her third year than nearly all her peers. A lot of them focused on lighter coursework to make room for their heavy internship obligations. Not Jennifer, though.

"I don't mind rescheduling," Jennifer said, adding a twinge of guilt because part of her wanted to go study. But another part of her never wanted to open a book again.

"No, because if we reschedule, then we'll keep pushing back date night," Carter replied. "I was thinking a light stroll through the park, catch up, and then part ways."

"So I can study, and you can do your evening trainings?"

"Precisely." Carter smiled.

It turned out Gladiatrix had her interns put in even more work than I realized. These evening trainings were meant to help her interns find new applications to their magic casting that they hadn't previously unlocked. Even if she was out of the city working another mission, Gladiatrix had a whole team of support to fill in and work with her interns for the night.

Despite both their minds drifting elsewhere, they enjoyed the company of each other and the night lights of the park. It was nice to know neither Jennifer nor Carter had become deterred by their busy schedules. It was even nicer seeing them find time for each other, grow together, even if they spent most of their time apart.

Oftentimes, young love such as this would burn out and splinter close to graduation. I had no idea what the future held for these two, but I believed they'd make it work.

"Layla, play nice," Guild Master Campbell said, though her sly smirk suggested the opposite.

"Of course, guild master." Layla nodded, then returned to reprimanding the acolytes who filed their forms incorrectly.

Campbell's thoughts twisted through her complex agenda for the day, though she took a minute to admire Layla's ambitious attitude. It seemed Campbell had a soft spot for the mean girl whose cutting comments were more ruthless than her sharp claws.

"Tia, Katherine, a word." Campbell breezed by her assistants' desks, where her interns often worked too.

"Yes, guild master?" Katherine pushed the paperwork she had handled aside, giving Campbell her undivided attention.

"I have another meeting planned with Cassidy Gardner, and I'd really appreciate you both joining me again."

Tia smiled, eager at the prospect, while Katherine merely nodded with agreement.

"She quite enjoys your talents," Campbell continued. "I think she has a soft spot for enchantment branches."

I scoffed. She didn't think it. She knew it just like everyone in the industry knew Cassidy Gardner worked in selling and distributing illegal enchantments.

"The most important part of being a successful guild master is wooing powerful patrons," Campbell explained. "This ensures the guild has enough funding to act independently."

"Well, aren't guilds already independent?" Katherine asked.

"Yes and no," Campbell said. "Some guilds take on too much federal funding, which in turn makes them pawns to the state. Our guild strives to remain empowered enough to make our own decisions and never be forced to act on every mandate or directive simply out of fear of losing financial stability."

She was right and wrong. Honestly, neither system was ideal. After all, Tobias Whitlock funded many of the best guilds in the city for years and had them in a chokehold for his whims over anything else. So, it really came down to answering to government bureaucrats with a million layers of red tape or allowing elitist snobs to dictate their personal desires onto the guilds they funded. I didn't know a better system, but hopefully, one day someone would find it.

"You know, Cassidy was particularly intrigued by your grimoire," Campbell said, gesturing for Katherine to pull it out.

Katherine unbuckled the straps on her thigh holster and lifted up her weathered leather book.

"I was thinking perhaps you could let her get a peek at a few of those pages," Campbell said, reaching out to touch the grimoire. "I'm certain there's a few old spells in there that'd certainly appeal to her fancies."

"No," Katherine shouted.

It startled Campbell and Tia, sending a surge of surprise through me. Honestly, though, hearing Katherine raise her voice left me stunned. I'd never seen her have even a small outburst in homeroom or any of her classes.

But here she was, clutching her grimoire close to her chest and facing away from Campbell. Dread bubbled inside Katherine as she squeezed the ancient tome tightly.

"She can't have the book." Katherine became frazzled and flustered, so unlike her.

"Ooookay," Campbell said with confusion and a hint of frustration. "It wouldn't be to keep. Just a peek."

"No," Katherine snapped. "I said no."

"Fine," Campbell sighed.

"Sorry. It's just a family heirloom," Katherine explained. "Can't just let anyone flip through the pages. It's precious."

Katherine's mind whirled with protective thoughts for the pages of her new grimoire. Well, her old grimoire. An ancient book that held a powerful grip on her emotions. It was unlike Katherine. Part of me wondered if this was misdirected anxiety. I'd seen it plenty of times in the past with students during their internships.

Working under a guild master came with a lot of additional pressures, and Katherine didn't have the most accommodating mentor. I made a mental note to reach out to Chanelle about my concerns. Since she single-handedly oversaw the interns, I didn't want my concerns for Katherine slipping through the cracks. It was too easy to get overwhelmed when monitoring hundreds of students' progress simultaneously.

CHAPTER SEVENTEEN

SNOW came early this season, making the walk to school so much longer. Ben wanted to stop and play and enjoy every snowflake. And of course, he wouldn't let go of my hand the entire time, which meant dragging me from one end of the sidewalk to the other.

"Think we'll get any over break?"

"I don't know." I shrugged.

His winter break was still a few weeks out. Honestly, given how reserved he was over Thanksgiving, I figured the next holiday would be fairly the same. The only part of his break he seemed to enjoy was hanging out with Diego and Delia. That in itself was short-lived since Diaz took his family back to Texas for the holiday to celebrate with their extended family.

"I've never had snow on Christmas," he said, recalling his holidays in California. "That'd be cool."

"It'd be cold," I replied.

Ben scrunched his face and shot me a look. Apparently, my sense of humor was unacceptable.

Once I dropped him off at school, I made my way to the Global Guild facility with the intention of completing my debrief on Winston Cobalt. It'd taken weeks of preparation and precision work, but I'd finally pieced together all the necessary memories I needed and removed every lingering trap in his head.

Now, I just needed to go through Winston's mind, retrieve vital intel, and pass it off to the Global Guild.

When I got to the facility, passed through the several clearance checkpoints, and reached the cell holding Winston Cobalt, Chanelle was standing outside with a big plastic bag.

"What are you doing here?"

"Lunch." Chanelle lifted the bag. "I figured we could catch up."

"This is a highly secured area," I replied, looking at the posted guards who kept their attention trained elsewhere. "How'd you even get in here?"

"Oh, please." Chanelle gestured dismissively. "Come on? It's me. Find a list I can't get my name on."

"Wow." I ushered her to the nearby breakroom I'd occasionally use when I needed to rest away from Winston's headache of a mind.

"I haven't seen you in ages," Chanelle said, bringing in a large bag filled to the brim with plastic trays of sushi.

And not the grocery store stuff. She'd stopped at one of the nicest restaurants in town and gotten a little bite of everything to go.

"What is this?"

"I thought we could catch up." She handed me a tray made for two. "Got your favorite."

Whoa. She had too. I was never a fan of the fancy rolls with the crunchy bits or a ton of things smashed together with only a thin layer of seaweed to hold them. I much preferred the classic rolls. Give me the squishy octopus, the tangy eel, the chewy clam, or the super salty roe.

"Did you ask Milo about this?"

"About what?" She stared, confused.

"About my favorite sushi."

"No. You told me."

"I did?" I couldn't quite recall, but there were many instances where Chanelle badgered me incessantly until I disclosed whatever the hell she demanded I share with her. "Surprised you remember."

"I'm a good friend, unlike some people."

"Oh." I popped the tray open and grabbed a piece of eel, savoring the smoky teriyaki tang. "This is guilt sushi."

"Damn straight—minus the hetero bullshit." Chanelle pursed her lips, pouting, then grabbed a piece of her crunchy tempura roll.

"How am I a bad friend?"

"You've been having double dates without me," Chanelle said. "I'd like to join your new friend group."

"What friend group?" I dipped the wasabi in the soy sauce, stirring it until the spicy green paste mixed with the salty sauce.

"Diaz and his wife. Milo mentioned you guys have been hanging out."

"Like two or three times," I answered, dipping a piece of the octopus into my sauce concoction before taking a bite.

"Well, what makes them so great?" Chanelle asked. "If you're looking to play, you should be hanging with me and Kyle."

I choked on the sushi, coughing and wheezing when the spicy sauce caught in my throat.

"What?" Chanelle made a face. "We are killers at any board game. And card games, it's over. Hand us the gold."

"I'm sorry, what?"

In my mind, when she said 'play,' I immediately envisioned the wrong type of play. Recalling how I'd spent a good portion of one night playing with Diaz's balls, gargling them at his request.

"Your game nights," Chanelle answered. "Didn't you just have one with the kids?"

"Ooooooh." I nodded in agreement. "Yes, we did. Duh."

Considering we'd only fucked the couple on one outing, the memory still rose to the surface of my thoughts more often than it did the other three. At least, Milo didn't dwell on it much, and when we spent time with the couple, they didn't seem to think about it either. Not in the same manner as I did. Maybe it was because I didn't hook up much, but I did enjoy the gathering. Still, it made our regular playdates a little awkward for me—and suddenly grateful I was the only telepath in the room.

"Is it cause we don't have kids?" Chanelle asked quite bluntly.

"No," I answered. "It's because I don't plan anything. Milo does it all. I just get dragged places."

"I see." She nodded. "I'm harassing the wrong guy. I'll go pester him soon enough."

"Thank you." I half-smiled. "For the sushi and the annoying friendship."

"You're stuck with me, bitch." Chanelle pinched her chopsticks in the air like she was trapping me.

"I couldn't be any luckier."

We spent the better part of the hour catching up. I asked her how the Cerberus-Gemini merger was holding up. She divulged the difficulties guild members had when they lacked basic comprehension of educational necessities. We discussed the student internships. Yes, I made it clear that I telepathically eavesdropped on my students, ensuring their progress over the last few months was going well. She shared the many check-in benchmarks she required to make sure none of the nearly six hundred third-year students at Gemini Academy slipped through the cracks.

All in all, it was a nice chat. Even listening to her ramble on about random gossip between staff members I couldn't give a fuck about was fun. It was just nice catching up.

"I should be getting back to Cerberus." Chanelle grabbed her purse. "Lots and lots of paperwork. Ugh, why did no one tell me being in charge would suck the life out of my soul?"

"I thought you liked sucking."

"Yeah, when I'm doing it." Chanelle playfully shoved me. "Lunch was nice."

"Thank you for the treat."

"Of course. And when this whole Celestial Coven nonsense is behind us"—Chanelle gestured to the unconscious Winston tied down in the nearby room—"we'll have to do a couple's date night."

"Oh?"

"Yes, minus the kids. You'll need a babysitter." Chanelle chuckled. "I can work with them, but I don't care to entertain small minds in off hours."

"Ben's smarter than most of Cerberus' clients."

"Careful," Chanelle said with a sultry smirk. "You sound like a protective papa bear."

"I'm literally just stating a fact." I scoffed. "Benjiman's test scores are—"

"Yes, mommy dearest. Your angel is the best and brightest little one in all the heavens." Chanelle swaggered out of the room, waving a dramatic goodbye. "Ta-ta, love."

I went back to work, scouring Winston's memories and taking notes on the members of the Celestial Coven. Having finally unlocked full access to his memories and organized them enough to make use of them made this work much easier. As suspected, the Celestial Coven kept a member for each branch. However, they only ever kept one witch per branch at a time, which meant they'd never have more than twelve members in their coven.

A good sign for us. Since I'd removed The Sisters Three—and they hadn't replaced the psychic branch according to Winston—and two other pillars of the Celestial Coven were detained, Grim and Lazarus, that knocked their ranks down. Plus, we held Winston Cobalt in custody, too, leaving the Celestial Coven at eight witches in total. Excluding Theodore Whitlock, who they forced to do their bidding. And honestly, that made him the biggest threat. They'd fill their ranks with demons—vampires in particular, which would leave Chicago vulnerable.

I took meticulous notes on the names and branches of the other Celestial Coven members, intending to relay all Winston had on them to the Global Guild. It would make bringing them down much easier if we knew what to expect from their magic. Their powers were rarities, and it was no wonder The True Witch recruited them. I recalled the bone staff she wielded, filled with enchanted gems housing the branch magics of all their former fallen coven members. A powerful weapon that possessed so many rare magics before I destroyed it.

In the distance, something glimmered. I turned to find an antique mirror floating through the abyss of Winston's memories. Strange. Nothing had remained intact. Everything from his treasured thoughts to his most fleeting fantasies required my restoration.

"Hello, Dorian Frost." The True Witch materialized in the mirror, dressed the same as the last time I'd seen her, in a low-cut black dress that revealed her many enchantment tattoos. She tipped her witch's hat just enough to reveal her haunting green eyes.

"Finally showing yourself." I approached the mirror. "Afraid I'll learn something about you?"

"You assume this puppet knows anything about me." The True Witch sprang forward, hands pressed against the mirror, and spoke in her phony French accent—a delicate dialect she'd mastered centuries ago to hide her real origins. "You won't learn my story rooting through this mind."

"I've already heard pieces from your dead psychics," I replied. "Lies, I'm sure."

"They were never one to distort my tale."

"Yes, but I'm sure you spoon-fed them fabrications for centuries." My nostrils flared, holding back the fury I held for Amara.

"I'm many things, a liar is not one."

"Said every single liar in the history of time." I stepped toward the mirror. "I'm going to end you. Just as easily as I have your coven members who've crossed me."

Amara stared, lost in astonishment, then burst into laughter.

"Did you honestly believe I allowed one of mine to be captured?" She spoke as if we hadn't rightfully taken Grim and Lazarus from her already. As if I hadn't slain The Sisters Three. "Winston was a pawn. Vital in some respects, but mostly just a sacrificial lamb to help clear the board of a tricky knight."

"Meaning?"

"Your telepathy is profound, I'll grant you that." Amara smirked. "But with you occupied, I can cleanse this city and retrieve the goddess."

"Your daughter." I glared. "You think Tara would want you to harm her home? Her city?"

"A goddess must not be distracted by mortal connections. And quite frankly, the Global Guild and your pest of a clairvoyant need to learn that when you cross the Celestial Coven, we leave nothing but ashes in our wake."

"Enough of this." I reached out psychically, preparing to drag as much of her mind through this mirror trap of hers as I could. I'd shatter her mind and this trap into a thousand pieces.

"Break the glass," she whispered. "It was my plan all along, darling."

With that, she blew a kiss. The smooch cracked the glass, each sliver spread like a lake of ice, and suddenly, I found myself plummeting. As I fell deeper into Winston's mind, the glass exploded above, shards glowing with sigils containing psychic traps.

"Don't worry. I know not to underestimate you like before," Amara called out, unleashing a dozen black chains to pin me down and hold me in place.

I fought against them, only to find myself more tangled than I'd started. They clung to me like sticky webs, dragging me deeper into the recesses of Winston's broken subconscious. When I reached out with telepathy, the shards of glass thrummed, triggering psychic traps that knocked me back. There was nothing I could do until I broke these chains, until I disarmed these traps.

The True Witch had arrived with her Celestial Coven and locked me away before making their first move on the city.

I roared, raging against the bindings. Dammit. I had to do something. Anything.

CHAPTER EIGHTEEN

A COLD chill snapped the tether holding me to my core self. The surge of psychic energy across the city indicated that all the manifestations of myself wandering through Chicago had been cut off from our core self. That could only mean I'd stepped into some type of trap.

Still, before the complete cutoff, my core self sent me intel on the Celestial Coven. I could only presume all the currently summoned manifestations in the area received the same update. But why give us information on the Celestial Coven and not an answer on why our core self had been so suddenly isolated? It could only mean that the Celestial Coven was making their move.

Were they attacking the Global Guild station? I needed to rally the other manifestations and find our way to our core self before something dangerous happened.

"The next time I see Katherine, I'm going to gouge out that bitch's eyes." Layla fumed, pressing her hand to the red welt across her face. The contempt fueling her stole my attention.

"It's not that bad," Amani lied.

Jennifer trailed closely, hiding a smile behind her carefully pursed black lips. While she found the slap Katherine gave Layla completely justified, it didn't fit her friend's emotional wavelength. Jennifer had a good gauge for emotional outbursts when the levees broke and people acted out of character.

Katherine's emotions were bubbly moments before they turned blank. Jennifer couldn't pinpoint it, but there was a total disconnect. No malice, sadness, or hatred when she smacked Layla. Not that Layla didn't have it coming. She shouted at Katherine, telling her off for messing something up, and stood in Katherine's way. It wasn't blank. There was a slight spike in irritation as Layla inconvenienced Katherine, but then she just grabbed her grimoire and left.

I quirked a brow. That was bizarre behavior for Katherine, but right now, I needed to leave Cerberus Guild and find my way back to my core self over at the Global Guild station.

Layla and all the interns—excluding Katherine—stepped into Guild Master Campbell's office as she took another meeting with Cassidy Gardner. Campbell did a headcount on her five interns and crinkled her nose with frustration for the missing intern. Apparently, Cassidy held intrigue for Katherine and Tia, always ready to exploit enchantment witches.

With nothing urgent surfacing in Campbell's thoughts, I realized whatever had happened hadn't become widespread yet. As a top-tier guild master, she'd be one of the first to receive urgent updates.

I floated toward the window, preparing to take my leave, when an explosion of demonic energy surged through the building. It was suffocating. In this psychic state, the bombardment of toxic auras from fiends lashed out at my mind.

"What the fuck?" Campbell checked the alerts on her large screen monitor, revealing fiends of all sizes running through Cerberus.

She had cameras on every floor, some blotted out with tar, some struck with magic by enchanters defending themselves against the sudden onslaught.

"Secure yourselves, banish these fiends, and cleanse the building," Campbell said into a microphone. "We're going into full lockdown."

Shit.

Metallic barriers began to seal each window in Campbell's office. The wards on her walls glowed.

"*The audacity of attacking my guild head-on.*" Campbell glowered, quickly coordinating her enchanters and acolytes in the building. "*Less than half our forces are here, but I can clear this building myself if need be.*"

As the last window closed, a shadowy figure burst through the glass, and a behemoth of a man stood at the edge of the office.

His magic hit in waves. Few witches who channeled gave off such radiant power. He must've been one of the Celestial Coven witches. I searched my thoughts, the new ones thrown at me from my core self.

Jagged diamond slivers held the broken window open, preventing a full lockdown on Cerberus Guild.

I recognized that magic.

"Can't believe I'm stuck dealing with all the little girls, when there are real witches to fight against."

"*You all need to be incredibly careful,*" I linked my thoughts to Campbell and all her interns. It took nearly every ounce of magic in my manifestation to project what intel I had on this member of the Celestial Coven.

```
Name: James Bardot
Branch: Primal (Diamond)
```

Not only did Bardot possess a powerful primal magic, but physically, he stood at 6'7 with a frame twice that of Enchanter Diaz. In fact, Bardot resembled Diaz's bear familiar more than a human with his huge muscles.

"*Frost?*" Campbell raised a brow; contempt covered her face and filled her thoughts, but when it settled, she saw my eavesdropping nature as something adventitious. "*Link us all and we'll strategize around this arrogant ass.*"

"*I could do that,*" I thought with a sigh. "*If I weren't a manifestation of myself. My original is otherwise occupied at the moment.*"

I only hoped my core self would break loose from the trap the coven had set soon enough. With all my psychic energy restored, I could help in the field of combat.

"Typical men," Campbell said with a light laugh. "Utterly useless after three seconds."

Did she just make an impotence joke about me?

"I'll show you useless." Bardot hurled a pulse of telekinesis at Campbell, which she blocked with a subtle flick of her wrist.

Her fingers twirled and sent pink mist to intercept the telekinesis. Despite the invisible pulse of energy, Campbell locked onto the beats and used her branch to devour the strike.

```
Name: Amelia Campbell
Branch: Rejuvenation (Pink Mist)
```

"Like I said." Campbell waved her hand and sent more pink mist chasing after Bardot, who did nothing to evade or escape the attack.

The pink swirls formed a human shape, coiling tightly around every inch of Bardot's body. After a minute of containment, Campbell released her magic.

"We neutralize here, girls, not kill," Campbell said with a smirk. "When we can avoid it. The paperwork's a bitch."

"Just like you." Bardot laughed, revealing his body coated in a layer of diamond protection.

The shiny stones shifted and migrated until they'd formed a proper suit of armor, like something a knight would've worn.

"Your little smoke trick clearly can't compare to my indomitable diamond form."

"And here I thought a diamond was a girl's best friend."

"Because you're all materialistic bitches."

"And I've had enough of you and your tragically transparent misogyny." Campbell threw a ball of telekinetic energy. "Mommy not hug you enough?"

"Shut your mouth!"

Her strike collided with a counter of telekinesis from Bardot, but with her added emotional jab, she managed to overpower him and knock him back a bit.

In a matter of seconds, the pair hurled waves of magic at one another.

Campbell slipped in her pink mist when she could, forcing Bardot to pivot and add another buffer of telekinesis. All the same, when Campbell did break past the witch's walls of protection, his diamond armor proved invulnerable. Her strikes, which should've been enough to throw the man through her tenth-story window, barely pelted him.

"If you're going to throw your branch into the mix, I should add mine, too." Bardot flung jagged diamonds meant to impale targets.

Fuck.

He wasn't aiming for Campbell. She saw the glimmer of light each diamond gave off as their trajectory tilted just enough to hit her interns.

"Look out." Campbell threw a wave of telekinesis to knock the diamonds off course.

"Predictable." Bardot hit Jennifer, Tia, and Olivia with a pulse of telekinesis.

The girls slammed against the office wall, and their thoughts went silent. Each of their minds sank into unconsciousness.

With another pulse of telekinesis, he attempted to strike down Layla and Amani, but the pair flew through the air, cartwheeling to the ceiling. Using their advanced levitation control, they stayed grounded above with telekinesis at the ready.

"Cloak them and move out," Campbell said with a snap of her fingers that pointed to Jennifer, Tia, and Olivia.

```
Name: Amani Williams
Branch: Psychic (Glamour)
```

Amani cast her glamours over herself and Layla, then the other girls, before quickly evacuating them.

"*Shit*," Layla thought, slamming the door shut. "I need to clear away the fiends before you step out there."

"Understood," Amani whispered, still remaining concealed with her illusions.

Campbell scowled, but didn't have many options. The girls weren't safe outside the office until Layla banished the fiends on the floor. That said, it limited Campbell's combat maneuvers. She couldn't go too wild with bystanders.

"So, are you going to just sit there on your ass, or do you plan on helping?" Campbell asked Cassidy, who continued lounging at the table with her tea.

"You know my license doesn't cover combat," she said with a chuckle. "The fees—so expensive. But I suppose if you're willing to overlook it, I can lend a hand."

Campbell rolled her eyes.

"Fine, fine." Cassidy stood, straightening her bright yellow dress and adjusting the flourish of ruffles around her neckline. "You know, handsome, with a branch like that, I could make you a star."

"The undercity bitch." Bardot scoffed. "I was instructed to handle your lot after clearing out the guilds."

"Oh, sweetie, you think you can destroy all the guilds?" Campbell smiled. "You won't even make it out of my office."

Based on the horde of fiends unleashed throughout the building and the chaos of whirling minds outside, I suspected other members of the Celestial Coven struck other top-tier guilds across Chicago.

"Let's see how flawless those carats are." Cassidy leapt forward and swung a fist dead center in Bardot's chest.

```
Name: Cassidy Gardner
Branch: Alteration (Enhanced Strength)
```

Despite her slender frame and dainty demeanor, Cassidy held the same branch that many in her family possessed. Her strength wasn't quite at the level of Gladiatrix, but I recalled Cassidy leveling a few walls during her days at Gemini Academy when we were still teens.

"Oh, was that your best shot, little girl?" A single crack lined Bardot's chest, which he quickly repaired by summoning a new jagged coat of diamonds over his armor plating.

Cassidy glowered. Disgust oozed off her in waves for Bardot's condescending attitude and blatant revulsion for women. In fact, his hatred of women seemed to fuel his casting. I found it odd he'd align himself to take orders from someone like The True Witch, given how he loathed women in authority.

"Just getting started." Cassidy punched Bardot again, and again, and again. Each strike went for the crack on his chest, hammering away until she'd broken a solid chunk of his diamond armor.

Once she'd managed that, Cassidy dug her hands into the small opening and attempted to pry apart his armor.

"Enough of this." Bardot stabbed a diamond shard through Cassidy's thigh.

She screamed in shock and pain, buckling under the weight of exhaustion. It didn't take long for Bardot to exploit the opportunity. With a wave of his hand, he hurled Cassidy through the shattered window and sent her plummeting nearly twenty stories.

I remained locked here, worried for my students, for all the students in this building, but a part of my psychic energy trailed alongside Cassidy. Though I never cared for the woman, I hoped she had enough strength to channel her roots. She did. Barely. She'd nearly hit the pavement when she pivoted with her telekinesis and buffered her angled crash with enough levitation to prevent any additional severe injuries. But she wouldn't be rejoining the fight in her condition.

"Screw this." Campbell glared at the fuzzy portrait on her office wall, a clear sign of Amani's illusions at work to blend herself and the other girls like a chameleon. A small smile crept onto Campbell's face, the memory of Milo buying her that portrait as a gift for her position as the new official guild master. Milo had sworn the artist had special magical properties added to the artwork, ensuring it could never be replicated, copied, or stolen. Hence, why Amani's near-perfect illusion turned out fuzzy when mimicking the portrait. "Recall Layla and move out. Fiends be damned."

Campbell waved her arms round and round in front of herself, like stirring a massive cauldron. The spell work she created came in the form of her pink mist and powerful telekinesis.

The wave of telekinetic energy circled Bardot, carrying the pink mist until it surrounded the diamond-armored witch. Campbell used her telekinesis as a buffer to hold Bardot and her mist in place.

"Now, feel the true wrath of my branch." Campbell channeled her potent rejuvenation branch, twisting the mist into a toxic, necrotic sludge.

The light pink soured and thickened like a stew. Droplets splashed and sizzled against Bardot's diamond flesh. He ignored it, believing himself untouchable. As a diamond-wielding witch in the Celestial Coven, I understood why he believed such things. Still, Campbell had certainty in her thoughts as she twisted more pink mist into her telekinetic bubble containing Bardot.

A sharp pain pierced Bardot, shocking him so much that his thoughts became clear for a moment.

FEAR.

He'd never experienced someone truly breaking through his diamond armor. A few cracks here and there, but never something so potent. The pink mist clung to his armor, eating away the diamonds even as he summoned more to replenish the coating. It didn't matter. The more protection Bardot added, the faster Campbell's magic seemed to eat away at it. Disintegrating the diamonds until pink mist gnawed at Bardot's flesh.

Bardot panicked, punching the telekinetic barrier holding him in place. Again and again, he thrashed within, to no avail. His strikes were disorganized and chaotic. Every time he managed to make a ripple in one area, Campbell repaired it while Bardot struck another spot.

"Release me, witch bitch!"

"As soon as I see bone, you prick." Campbell blew more mist into the funneling whirlwind of telekinesis.

Bardot roared in pain as pink acid melted through his diamond armor bit by bit. Soon it'd reach his flesh. Everything went well until he turned his eyes to unscathed feet. The floor didn't have a telekinetic barrier, and the pink mist floated above by a few inches.

"*You need to seal the floor,*" I warned Campbell, but it was too late.

Bardot cracked the floor open with a single punch, projecting a dozen diamond shards like shrapnel. Adding a burst of his own telekinesis, Bardot broke through the floor and vanished.

"Dammit, I need to alter the chemical levels," Campbell thought. *"If my mist hits anyone below, it'll kill them. If they're lucky."*

The degree she'd shifted her pink mist was apparently undocumented and not within the acceptable perimeters of her license. She rarely resorted to such caustic measures, but supposedly the chemical strike was strong enough to drop demons in their tracks—something few branch magics could claim.

"You defeated him?" Layla asked, surprised and impressed, having returned to see an empty bubble of pink mist.

"Not exactly," Campbell said. "Did you clear the floor?"

"Yes, but the others are still flooded with fiends," Layla explained. "The enchanters and acolytes here are doing their part, but it's like the fiends are organized."

"Because they are," I thought at them. *"Chances are, Theodore Whitlock is in the city, orchestrating the fiend's movements. Your best bet is—"*

The floor between Layla and Campbell burst open, carrying a newly re-armored Bardot as he held a diamond sword in each hand. With a swift thrust, he impaled Campbell through her chest and stomach.

"Noooo!" Layla screamed so loudly that it turned into a furious roar of anguish as her therianthrope form overtook her.

```
Name: Layla Smythe
Branch: Bestial (Therianthropy)
```

The tiny girl snarled, her body twisted and transformed until she towered over the threatening witch. Rage. So much rage exploded from Layla. With all her strength and added telekinesis, she slammed into Bardot, throwing him back into a wall.

"Guild Master..." Layla's voice cracked and broke as she swept in to catch Campbell.

There was nothing to be done. Her heart had stopped. Her breathing had ended. Her eyes stared out at nothingness, unable to register Layla's feline face or blotchy tears.

"*This can't be it…*" Campbell's mind whirled into the darkness of death.

"*I'm so sorry,*" I called out, hoping to give her something, anything in these final moments.

These seconds, which ticked by slowly, painfully.

"*I was supposed to fix it…*" Campbell's mind turned faint, bleeding in and out. "*I worked so hard to make this industry better for everyone. I'm not finished. I still have—*"

And like too many others, she was dead and gone forever. Campbell's mind fell away. Her life unfinished.

"*You need to run,*" I thought at Layla and Amani. "*Get the others and run!*"

"You heard him," Layla growled, eyeing Amani before locking her furious gaze onto Bardot. "Get out of here."

"Oh no, little girls." Bardot recalled his bloody diamond blades and shifted his stance for combat. "I still got a lot of fight in me and think it'll be fun to blow off steam, carving you little bitches up."

Layla roared, lunging for Bardot. Her slashes were swift, but his diamond flesh remained unharmed. Layla's telekinetic strikes didn't work a second time, not with Bardot expecting them. Amani dragged the others out, holding three unconscious bodies with her own telekinesis, but Bardot threw a diamond blade to block the doorway.

"Stick around."

Layla snarled and tackled Bardot. With the full force of her body, she managed to pin him to the floor, but he quickly overpowered her. Bardot straddled Layla's therianthrope form, punching her over and over. Each hit chipped away at Layla's strength. Still, she continued clawing, biting, and snarling to no avail.

The beating continued until Layla's willpower shattered and she transformed back into her human state.

"I'm going to take my time with you." Bardot wrapped his diamond fingers around Layla's neck and tightened his grip.

Layla gasped, choking as Bardot strangled her. Despite her best efforts, Layla couldn't break the grip on her throat. Her face turned red. She flailed and fought, but her arms grew heavier with each passing second.

"*NO!*" I roared, hitting Bardot with as much psychic energy as possible.

"*The telepath?*" Bardot looked up momentarily. "*Figures. The True Witch said she'd kill you. How predictable she'd fail. Still, if your best shot is to make me feel bad, you clearly don't know me.*"

It wasn't enough to do anything. All I managed was to bypass his protective psychic wards, unraveling his thoughts. I didn't have enough magic at my disposal to shatter his mind, to break him before he killed Layla. I failed.

Clack. Snap. Crack.

Lightning. Fire. Ice. Gravel. Each element zipped through the office in a flurry of swift slaps.

Chanelle stood in the doorway with an electric whip in hand. She'd knocked both of Bardot's diamond swords out of the office and snatched Layla into her grasp.

```
Name: Chanelle Whitehurst
Branch: Arcane (Infinity Spectrum)
```

"Leave my students alone." The rage and sadness in Chanelle's eyes flooded her emotions.

Seeing her frightened students, taking in the destruction of the guild, and finding a dead Guild Master Campbell sent Chanelle into a flurry of anger.

Her mind fell into the deep depression of Jamie's death that once consumed her. With a slow, calming breath, Chanelle buried that sorrow and focused on the future.

"Fall back, girls." Chanelle stepped in front of them and braced herself for fighting against Bardot, the diamond witch who came to slaughter everyone within the walls of Cerberus Guild. "*I'll never let down another one of my students again.*"

CHAPTER NINETEEN

I WASN'T sure what my other fellow manifestations were dealing with, but the chaotic thoughts surging through the city made it clear the Celestial Coven had come. Unlike the other psychic extensions, I managed to make my way back to the Global Guild station where my core self worked.

Outside the facility, Enchanter Diaz and his interns patrolled. There was no urgency in their surface thoughts, meaning the chaos in the city hadn't spread everywhere. A calculated strike, precision. Even though my core self had been struck down somehow from within, it seemed no one had realized yet.

"Sort of offensive the Global Guild would only assign one of theirs to guard their sanctum."

A slender guy with dark brown skin slicked toward Diaz and his interns. I fought off a headache from the memories shoved into my thoughts before losing connection with my core self.

"Dammit," I whispered, before linking my thoughts to Diaz and his interns. "This is one of the Celestial Coven witches. You need to be extremely careful."

```
Name: Lambert Finch
Branch: Bestial (Hybridization)
```

I shared what little intel I had on Finch, but I didn't know much about the hybridization branch.

"*Frosty?*"

"Ba-ba-bawk."

"*That sounds like a dangerous branch.*"

"*We need to stay on guard, Duchess.*"

"I'm absolutely flattered the Celestial Coven would send a fellow bestial branch witch to face me," Diaz said with a cocky grin. "Priscilla and I can't wait to test our might against you."

The armored bear roared ferociously as Diaz pulled out his enchanted sword.

"Please, you familiar witches think you're of the same caliber as me?" Finch scoffed, disgust pouring off his tongue. "You lot insult the bestial branch."

Diaz groaned. "You're one of *those* bestial users."

"Let me and King Clucks at him." Gael twirled his meteor hammer, letting the heavy metallic ball whirl faster and faster, adding a bit more slack to the chain with each swing. "We can take this cocky lil bitch on our own."

"Cl-cluck."

"Don't be arrogant, Gael." Diaz shifted his stance. "You wouldn't wanna come off like this fool."

"You wanna see fools?" Finch scowled. "I'll show you what fools you lot are challenging me."

Finch's eyes turned a golden brown. His nails grew long and black. His teeth turned fanged. Muscles swelled across his body, making him inflate and rip through his shirt. His heels arched like a cat's. Fur covered patches of his body.

Flickers of his thoughts bled through his protective warding.

Eagle's vision. Elephant's smell. Tiger's claws. Crocodile's jaw. Great

White's fangs. Cat's reflexes. Gorilla's strength and adaptability. Worst of all, Inland Taipan Snake venom secreted on his claws.

"*You all need to be incredibly cautious.*" I shared what animal intel I could, and Diaz filled in the blanks on the few I hadn't noticed.

Apparently, he had a strong encyclopedic knowledge of different animals, spending his efforts searching for fellow bestial witches of all types and helping them thrive in the enchanter world.

Priscilla growled, shaking her head and tearing off her helmet.

"Girl, what's wrong?" Diaz turned to his familiar.

"Ba-ba-bawk!" King Clucks flapped his wings, fluttering and jumping away from Gael.

Duchess made a strange noise and thwacked her tail a few times before levitating in the air.

"Moo-Moo, chill out." Wesley attempted to settle his cowfish, who circled the tiny fishbowl enclosure at a dangerous speed, knocking water out in the process.

"It's a pheromone cocktail of my own creation," Finch explained. "There's a lot of tragic branches out there, but I've found familiar witches utterly worthless. You share your magic with an animal, reliant and pathetic. Without your beasts, you're nothing. This cocktail blurs their senses, drives them primal, and severs that telepathic link y'all share while they're in a feral state."

Priscilla roared, then turned to run away. She bulldozed into the street, casting telekinesis erratically at nearby cars.

"Shit," Diaz muttered. "*She's going to kill someone at this rate.*"

"Duchess, stop it." Tiffany tried to grab her levitating beaver, who chased after Wesley.

Not Wesley, but his fish familiar in the small fishbowl.

"Leave Moo-Moo alone!" Wesley screamed, running from Duchess, who gripped the teen's shirt with her tiny, grabby hands, gnawing on his clothes with her chattering teeth.

"I have to stop Priscilla." Diaz sheathed his sword and flew after his raging familiar.

"Pathetic jokes." Finch snickered. "I'll kill you lot when I finish my assignment. Save you the embarrassment of living with such failure."

"I'm no joke," Gael said, flying in front of Finch and blocking his path inside. "And we're no failures."

"We?" Finch laughed. "It's just you, boy. Your coven is busy chasing their stupid pets."

At that comment, Gael swung his meteor hammer, aiming the large metallic ball at Finch's head. But the witch's reflexes were superior, and he quickly pivoted out of the way.

"King Clucks isn't a pet."

"Ba-ba-bawk!" From out of nowhere, the rooster fluttered beside Finch, attempting to claw or peck the man, only to miss.

Finch snarled at the bird but unknowingly walked right into the path of the meteor hammer. It smacked him on the back of the head, flipping him around until he landed flat on his stomach.

"All those animal traits you copied, and you didn't think to mimic the genius prowess of a rooster?" Gael shook his head disapprovingly. "Big mistake."

```
Name: Gael Rios-Vega
Branch: Bestial (Familiar)
```

Finch leapt up, lunging for Gael with his venomous claws. Without an ounce of fear, Gael twirled to the side, evading the strike and lashing out with his meteor hammer.

Even as it missed, Gael's telekinesis carefully twisted the trajectory as Gael yanked and turned the angle of his weapon. Through precise aiming and added magic, he continued making brutal swings that'd knock Finch off balance.

As Finch adapted to Gael's attacks, he found himself facing the wrath of the world's most aggressive bird yet again. King Clucks sprang into combat, avoiding Gael's weapon and knocking Finch into the path of a strike every time.

Whenever the witch managed to dodge the hammer, a beak or claw sliced into him. Whenever he evaded King Clucks' fury, he found himself smacked with the meteor hammer. All the animal skills in the world didn't help. In fact, they worked against him. This hybridization ability allowed him to take on animal traits, but his thoughts turned feral the longer he used them. His hostility made it difficult for him to think, to focus, to counter.

"How is your damn bird immune to the pheromones?" Finch roared.

"He's not," Gael said with a smirk. "But if you think King Clucks, Peck-fender of the Unhatched Dozen, is only with me because of the familiar bond, then you don't know a goddamn thing about friendship."

"Cl-cl-cluck!" King Clucks kicked Finch into the path of the meteor hammer with a powerful addition of telekinesis.

The hammer smacked the witch directly in the face, flipping him back onto the ground. Gael swung the weapon a few times, building up as much momentum as possible, before adding his own telekinesis to the fold and slamming the meteor hammer directly onto Finch's chest.

He knocked the air out of Finch's lungs. He sent a searing pain coursing through Finch's body.

Finch snarled, chattered, and roared all at once. His skin turned scaly. His mind went feral. Wings sprouted from his back. Webbed flesh hung from his arms. Tails thrashed. Hundreds of tiny horns erupted from his head.

I had no idea how many animal traits he currently channeled, but it overrode his senses. Finch lunged at Gael, spitting an acidic sludge from his throat.

"Ba-ba." King Clucks flapped his wings, telekinetically knocking the spit off course.

"Thanks," Gael said, swinging his meteor hammer.

Finch rolled out his tongue, easily the length of Gael's weapon, and snatched it away. When he landed in front of Gael, he swiped at him with those venomous claws. No, more like talons now.

Gael darted out of Finch's path, barely avoiding the deadly swipe, and managed to retrieve his stolen weapon in the process.

"This is over." Finch gloated, gesturing to his own unblemished arm.

Gael looked to see a small cut on his forearm. Panic took hold. He'd been warned about the venomous cut. My breathing hitched, caught on the anxiety building inside Gael.

"It only takes a drop to kill a man in minutes."

Gael trembled, slowing the swing of his meteor hammer. I didn't know what to do for him. How to help. If there was even help for venom from an animal not native to this city, state, country. A snake's venom that killed with every bite.

"Then I better finish this fast," Gael said with a smirk. His cheeks twitched nervously, but he maintained his confidence, even if purely bravado. "Not a sentence I say often."

Gael waited for Finch to move in close again; this time, he was prepared to let the witch land a strike, so he could bind Finch with the meteor hammer. He was already poisoned, so he figured it couldn't get much worse.

He was wrong. If a drop had already made his legs wobble, what would a dose ten times that do?

Finch moved in close, about to slash Gael across the chest, when a watery portal opened above the pair.

"I don't think so." Carter leapt out and swung a fist direct center into Finch's gut.

It knocked the breath out of the villainous witch and sent him flying back several yards before he pivoted with a touch of telekinesis and the adaptability of his animal traits.

```
Name: Carter Howe
Branch: Rejuvenation (Vitality)
```

Carter stood tall in a defensive stance I'd seen Gladiatrix take on many times on her missions. It appeared Carter's mentor taught him more than how to compose himself for the media. She'd taught him how to channel his vitality just right so that he could swing a punch nearly as powerful as Gladiatrix's.

"It's too late," Gael said with a panicky wince. He dropped to his knees, hyperventilating as the venom from a single cut coursed through his bloodstream. "He poisoned me."

"What?" Carter dropped beside Gael, checking him over and finding the small nick on his forearm. "What kind of poison?"

"Deadly." Gael shrugged. "Snake venom. Don't remember the name, just that a single drop will kill me in minutes."

"Then we better purge it in seconds." Carter slapped a hand over Gael's cut and another on the boy's chest.

Carter's mind whirled with the anatomy of the human body he'd worked on memorizing since the day he saved my life. It was a beautiful sight, watching Carter blossom and grow from an event that once paralyzed him, from a trauma that haunted him for months. Now, he'd taken the fear he had when stitching together my slashed throat and used it to save lives with medical knowledge and a unique use of his rejuvenation branch.

With a dash of telekinesis, Carter altered the ebb and flow of Gael's blood, forcing the venom back to the open wound. Gael squirmed, uncomfortable and uncertain.

"It's almost done," Carter said with a soothing smile. "Just so you know, this is not the way to extract venom."

"Then why are you doing it this way?"

"Because with my vitality coursing through your veins, I'm giving you the edge against the toxins," Carter said, delicately adding a pulse of telekinesis to circulate the venom out of the cut. An added benefit to Carter's vitality magic was that it created a subtle glow to Gael's bloodstream, muscular system, and body in general. It wasn't something I saw, but something Carter fixated on as he worked. The dark droplets flowing through Gael's body represented the poison Carter still needed to extract. "And that's the last of it. You're welcome."

"Dude, I could kiss you."

"I have a girlfriend."

"I'll kiss her too, if you want." Gael grinned until Carter thunked him on the head.

"Why'd I just save your life?"

"Because I'm adorable."

"*Look out,*" I yelled.

"Mr. Frost?" Carter turned to find Finch lunging directly for him and Gael, claws drawn and fangs bared.

Another watery portal opened, and a blurred figure zipped through, kicking Finch off course. Before he could recover, another portal opened, and the blurred figure knocked into Finch again. This process continued until a dozen watery portals were opened and Finch had been struck a hundred different times.

"We got your back," Vik said, stepping from one of the portals they'd created.

I smiled, in awe of how well they'd mastered Jamie Novak's branch. They gave life to his memory every time they used his watery portals.

```
Name: Vik Smythe
Branch: Arcane (Copycat)
```

"Woohoo!" Zoya shouted, punching Finch across the face, before vanishing into a portal and reappearing with a cackle of delight as she kicked him in the back.

```
Name: Zoya Khan
Branch: Alteration (Speed)
```

Finch changed his erratic composure, stilling himself, even as Zoya continued leaping from portals faster than the eye could see, and striking him before vanishing again just as quickly.

Dammit, his senses were tracking her patterns.

"Gotcha," Finch hissed, turning to slash a blurred figure of Zoya as she came up behind him.

She altered her stance, attempting to dodge, but she was coming in too quickly. Gladiatrix had worked with her on ways to channel her speed to turn it into a heavy-hitter attack, but the precision of altering her momentum was still something they had to train.

"I don't think so." Vik fell through a portal and reappeared between Zoya and Finch. They punched Finch in the face, knocking him back with a blow twice as brutal as Carter's punch earlier.

Vik had made mastering Jamie's branch a personal mission of theirs; however, they'd been assigned to master Gladiatrix's branch while under her tutelage. Sure, Vik would never manage to mimic Gladiatrix's attack power one hundred percent, but they'd come closer than any other witch with their copycat magic.

"You fucking brats," Finch roared. "This ends now."

"I agree." Diaz leapt into the fray with his sword drawn. "Can't let these interns show me up, now, can I?"

Diaz jumped at Finch, sword aimed, and enchantments glowing. The pair clashed, Diaz moving faster than I'd ever seen before. His enchantments enhanced his reaction time, but they stalled Finch's reflexes, and after several careful slashes, Diaz brought Finch to his knees.

Finch's eyes turned glossy and returned to their normal brown. Smoke sizzled and wafted from his body, taking with it the animal traits that'd enhanced his skills.

Diaz hit Finch in the back of the head with the butt of his sword. When the witch keeled over and passed out, Diaz summoned rope from one of the symbols of his sword.

"Whoa, how'd you do that?" Gael asked, fully recovered from the venom scare.

"It's important to make sure your certified enchantment weapon is stocked with all the best supplies," Diaz explained as he hogtied Finch, restraining the Celestial Coven enemy. "Don't worry, I'll show you all the best enchantments to add to your weapon. If, of course, you decide to keep it when you enter the field."

"Oh, definitely," Gael said with glee.

After Diaz dealt with Finch, he messaged Global Guild superiors for his next move. Since the station he guarded wasn't set up for Finch, he didn't know if he had the authority to bring in the detained witch.

I contemplated reaching out to him, warning him that something had trapped my core self inside. But if other witches from the Celestial Coven arrived, I'd need to ensure Diaz held this line. It turned out he and his interns were quite capable.

"Woohoo," Gael yelled. "Impressive as hell, Texas Daddy."

"Thanks, kid." Diaz tipped his hat. "You and your familiar were pretty amazing yourselves. You two should be very proud."

Gael grinned. "You hear that, bestie? We're the frickin best."

"I mean, we pretty much saved the day," Zoya said, planting her hands on her hips. "But yeah, take all the credit."

"Gladly." Gael grinned, shooting her a wink, which of course made the girl blush.

I buried the memories that surfaced in each of their minds of the nights they spent getting to know each other.

"Not that I'm not grateful for your timely arrival, but what are you three doing here?" Diaz asked.

"Gladiatrix sent us here," Carter answered. "She's meeting with the others from the top ten before bringing them to this facility."

"Well, that was the plan," Vik added. "But if the Celestial Coven is here…"

"Then she's probably kicking their asses all over town," Zoya said.

"Those idiots picked the wrong time to attack Chicago," Gael said. "Isn't that right, buddy?"

Gael went to pick King Clucks up but faced the wrath of the bird's swift pecks.

"Ow, ow, ow…" Gael backed away. "Let's hope those pheromones wear off soon."

"Agreed." Diaz sighed.

"Hey, where's Priscilla?"

"Oh, no worries," Diaz said. "Even without our bond, I know her hangry face. I lured her into the nearby sushi place, told them to clear out, and left my card. Christ, Vanessa's gonna kill me."

"Yikes."

"Here's hoping the Global Guild covers it." Diaz chuckled.

Despite everything, it seemed they had things under control. I needed to move inside and find my core self. Hopefully, I could assist in whatever release from a trap my core self needed.

As I drifted inside, I found the typical wards were already stripped. A convenience for me, but bizarre that someone managed to remove every single protection without triggering a single alert.

"Child's play," Katherine said with a nasally huff as she snapped her fingers, forcing the next door open.

What the fuck was she doing here? And why was my student breaking into the Global Guild facility?

CHAPTER TWENTY

KATHERINE entered deeper into the Global Guild facility. I didn't understand why. Had she been sent here by Guild Master Campbell? Another manifestation of myself was at the guild; I usually kept an extension of my magic there, but I could only imagine how the guild was reacting to the Celestial Coven's arrival. Were they even aware yet? I hated being so disconnected from myself and extensions. I had no real clue what was happening around the city.

> Name: Katherine Harris
> Branch: Enchantment (Spell Craft)

"What are you doing, Katherine?" I linked my mind to hers, attempting to pry out an answer.

Sigils similar to those guarding the Celestial Coven formed around her surface thoughts, cloaking her mind.

"What the…"

"You managed to break off a piece of your psychic energy before The True Witch could detain you," Katherine said, waving a hand in my direction. "A pity."

The wave of magic meant to eat away my presence, shattering my manifested form, but I'd experienced this once before when Amara caught me spying. I dodged the strike, albeit barely, but decided to quietly follow Katherine for answers.

With that, she strode to the end of the room and deciphered the locking mechanism of enchantment securities within seconds. After bypassing the door protections, she was greeted by a dozen guards posted inside the facility.

"What are you doing in here?"

"No time for this," Katherine said, humming a strange tune, which conjured weird yellow musical notes. They were foul and nauseating, creating an eerie melody.

The guards used telekinesis to wave away the notes. Wards lining the walls glowed, prepared to unleash defensive measures. Then, everything went silent, except for the thrum of the vibrating notes. They exploded and cleared the room of any threats.

While these weren't ranked members within the Global Guild, each of the guards held high standing as guild enchanters before they were recruited by the Global Guild. To see them all collapse without putting up any resistance was baffling.

I hovered close to Katherine, attempting to gain some discreet insight into her thoughts, but they were guarded heavily by sigils similar to the ones every member of the Celestial Coven had within their minds.

Impossible.

If she'd had those sigils protecting her thoughts before, I'd have noticed them. Katherine's mind had always been open to others.

Was this Katherine? Was this some body double? No. It was her magical frequency, but this wasn't the Katherine I knew. Did she have some wicked doppler of her own making? Could Katherine's enchantment magic even create something such as that? Even if she were like me, mine was a psychic projection. This was Katherine in the flesh, full body, but her mind and personality seemed so cold from the girl I'd taught for years.

"Katherine?" Caleb's voice pulled my focus.

He stood in the next secured chamber of the Global Guild facility with

Enchanter Reed and Russo. Katherine ignored Caleb's curious tone and confused face, walking past him and toward a locked, vault-like door.

Hayden Russo blocked her path and waved.

"Sorry," he said with a grin. "That's a bit above your clearance."

"It's a bit above our clearance," Ellie added with an extra emphasis. "What are you doing here, hun?"

"Yeah, Katherine, is everything okay?" Caleb approached, trying to look Katherine in the eyes.

Katherine surveyed the room, tilting her head and locking her eyes on Ellie. "Why is your charge not with you?"

"My charge?"

"Your pupil."

"My intern?" Ellie responded with a giggle. "Um, Tara's fine, just running late. You'd think she was studying under Hayden."

"Hey," he protested. "I'm almost punctual half the time now."

"Lies," Ellie said with a raspy whisper.

Katherine sighed. Frustration bubbled from her surface thoughts, not matching the irritation I'd come to glean from the girl. Katherine's irritation almost immediately came accompanied by a twinge of guilt because, when people made her mad, she tried her best to see things from their perspective.

But not now. Now, Katherine merely oozed annoyance for the bubbly enchanters. She quickly muttered another spell. I went to warn them until her eyes rolled back. It became clear from the flutter of her lashes and the markings lining the air around that she was casting a divination spell.

What was she looking for?

"*There's something wrong with Katherine,*" I linked my thoughts to Ellie and Hayden.

"Enchanter Frost?" Ellie asked.

"Still here, huh?" Katherine tsked. "No matter."

Ignoring my presence, she turned to the door Hayden had blocked and raised her arms. Chanting a spell, Katherine's light brown skin glowed momentarily, her voice echoed, and her hair blew wildly, locked in the chaos of a high-tier spell.

"You need to stop her," I insisted. *"She's summoning something."*

That was about all I could make out from her chant.

"Lock." Ellie bound the enchantments Katherine cast.

```
Name: Ellie Reed
Branch: Ward (Skeleton Key)
```

"Silly, child." Katherine whistled the same tune as earlier, releasing pale yellow music notes.

Hayden's eyes drooped, but he teleported away, escaping the slumbering sounds. He even conjured a shimmering false trail for the melody to chase.

```
Name: Hayden Russo
Branch: Cosmic (Teleportation)
Branch: Cosmic (Glitter)
```

Except the notes vanished with him and reappeared at his next destination. Katherine managed to add some type of homing feature to her spell.

She was casting multiple high-tier spells in tandem without so much as breaking a sweat or even referencing her grimoire. I knew she was good, but that seemed so off. Everything about her, even her thoughts, had an altered flow to them. This wasn't Katherine. It couldn't be.

"Lock. Lock. Lock." Ellie attempted to bind the melody, but it reached her all the same.

Ellie and Hayden fell unconscious at Caleb's feet.

"Katherine, stop this."

She ignored him, returning to her summoning. I didn't know what to expect, but seeing the wall in front of her shatter and two glass cells being dragged directly in front of her wasn't what I anticipated. Katherine snapped her fingers, and the symbols keeping those glass cells sealed crumbled away. The glass cracked. Long weblike strands.

Inside each cell lay a pillar of the Celestial Coven. The dust of Grim's shattered bones and the rotten corpse of Lazarus.

She proceeded to walk closer to the fallen witches, ignoring Caleb's concern, his confusion.

"It's time," Katherine said. "You're required to retrieve the goddess."

More guards moved in, following the path of destruction Katherine's spell created when she ripped the cells through the building, tearing apart everything between her and the Celestial Coven members.

"Sleep," Katherine commanded, sending those damn musical notes to knock out the incoming forces.

A burst of energy struck a few notes, causing them to coil inward on themselves and implode. Caleb stared at the remaining music notes, attempting to strike with another blaze of perfected banishment.

```
Name: Caleb Huxley
Branch: N/A
```

"None of that." Katherine hit Caleb with a wave of telekinesis, slamming the boy into a nearby wall. "I'll deal with you in time, abomination."

The crunch of bones sent a shiver through me. Grim's dust swirled round and round as bones formed, then broke, and reformed. This process repeated itself over and over again until a skull cackled. Arms contorted, snatching stray rib bones and attaching them to a wriggling spine. What a bizarre sight, seeing a skeleton piece itself together one bone at a time.

When he'd assembled all the pieces, Grim held out his bony hands to Katherine.

"Make yourself and those damn enchantments useful," he snapped. "Summon me something to wear."

Katherine traced her finger in the air, writing out a spell, and then recited the words. She summoned a black robe for Grim. Obviously, wardrobe casting wasn't something innately in her repertoire. Though I found it strange she had so many high-tier spells to begin with. I studied her ancient grimoire, the one she'd acquired over the summer. It must've held these new spells.

The grimoire. Maybe there was something in it that sparked this bizarre change in Katherine. But could a spell gone awry really do all this? And why would a spellbook from her family's collection cause this?

"What took you so long?" Lazarus asked, stripping off his filthy clothes.

Katherine conjured him a pristine suit.

"Amara had a lot of moving pieces—"

"Do not speak her name as if you are our equal," Lazarus said with a venomous scowl, buttoning his dress shirt.

Katherine gave him an icy stare in return, but bit her tongue.

"Oh, give the girl… Eh, you're a girl, now, right?" Grim cocked his skull head in Katherine's direction. "Whatever, just give her a break. Look what she brought me."

Grim broke off two of his lower ribs, immediately regrowing them, but used the broken ribs to form a large bone scythe. With his new weapon, the reaper-like witch lunged at the unconscious guards, ripping them to pieces.

I recoiled.

He plucked a blue eye from one woman and a brown eye from a man. The bloody eyes floated in his empty sockets. Next, he carved open bodies, cackling as he ripped out organs. The sounds of squishy insides being rifled through made me queasy. Some organs he tossed aside with disinterest, while others he stuffed beneath his garbs.

"Finally," Grim said, taking a deep breath. "Feeling like myself again. I hate long naps."

"Can we commence?" Katherine asked. "The True Witch requires you two to retrieve the goddess."

"And what will you do?" Lazarus glared.

"I'll be bringing this one to The True Witch." Katherine gestured to Caleb, who lay there quietly, attempting to make sense of this terrifying situation.

"What is that boy to Amara?"

"Hmmm. Seems the oh-so-great one doesn't know everything. Shame." Katherine created a blue portal doorway behind Lazarus, then opened a white portal doorway underneath Caleb.

My heart jumped, flooded with Caleb's fear as he plummeted. Gone.

Where had Katherine taken him? She stepped over to her white portal and hopped in before I got any answers.

What the hell was happening? Why would Amara want Caleb? I thought she was after Tara. And what happened to Katherine? My mind raced with dreadful questions, concerns, confusion. I needed to find my core self and join this fight now.

"Let us be gone," Lazarus said, stepping through the blue portal.

"Yeah, yeah, yeah." Grim waved a dismissive hand. "Just let me adjust my lungs. They're sitting on my kidneys."

Grim sorted his newly procured organs around, tangling them below his ribcage. When he reached the portal door, a pop of gray static disrupted the wavelengths, and tiny bubbles exploded, sealing the portal before Grim could escape.

Kenzo and Lena stood strong, angry expressions directed at Grim and magics at the ready. Behind them, Gael stood with his spikes protruding in a defensive coating. Milo must've left him at the Global Guild facility while he retrieved the top ten enchanters.

I only hoped he got to them soon. We'd need those enchanters now that the Celestial Coven was moving on Chicago in full force.

"You're gonna tell me exactly what the hell just happened?" Kenzo fumed. "Why is know-it-all suddenly working with you lot, and where the hell did she take Caleb?"

CHAPTER TWENTY-ONE

"BREAK him apart," Lena declared, following her own advice by unleashing a bombardment of bubbles.

```
Name: Lena Novak
Branch: Arcane (Bubble Burst)
```

Grim swatted a few away with his scythe but ignored the vast majority. A big mistake on his part. They went to immediate work, popping against his bones. The sizzle caught Grim's attention, and the sharpened edge of his blade dulled some, facing the brunt of Lena's attack.

"Hey, ugly," Kenzo shouted, hurling a bolt of gray static. "I asked you a goddamn question."

```
Name: Kenzo Ito
Branch: Hex (Disruption)
```

"Don't know, don't care, don't squeal." Grim's teeth chattered, biting back laughter.

Kenzo's hex broke off Grim's arm.

"Seriously?" Grim controlled his arm and reattached it.

```
Name: Grim
Branch: Augmentation (Skeletal Manipulation)
```

I didn't need to disclose Grim's abilities to them, as every guild member at Cerberus had a full debrief on the pillars of the Celestial Coven. Though we didn't think they'd break free from detainment so easily.

"Let's see how you hold up when we rip all of your bones apart." Lena threw more bubbles at Grim.

"Oh, you mean like this?" Grim shattered his body into a hundred different pieces, using one hand to carry his scythe and another to carry his robe, while all his bones split apart and slipped between Lena's attack. "Cool trick, huh?"

Grim reformed his bones beside Ellie and Hayden's unconscious bodies. Lena hesitated.

"Do these two mean something to you?" Grim raised his scythe.

"Don't you dare touch them," Lena snapped.

"Hmmm." Grim's head spun around. "I do so love a good dare."

"Gotcha." Kenzo flew out from the side of Grim's direction, hitting the scythe with a massive bolt of hex magic. "Have fun piecing that back together."

Grim stared at his scythe; everything seemed in order.

"Ah, I see what you've done." Grim swung the scythe aimlessly. "You broke my connection to these bones. So be it."

Grim discarded his weapon.

Lena lunged forward, forcing Grim back with a massive bubble larger than his body. Grim flew away, distancing himself from Ellie and Hayden.

"Get them out of here," Lena demanded, popping her big bubble and sending a thousand surging toward Grim.

"You need backup," Kenzo insisted, hurling more hexing static between the openings of Lena's bubbles.

It prevented Grim from breaking apart to evade, and started boxing him into the corner.

"Now, dammit." Lena scowled.

"I got it." Gael levitated over to Ellie and Hayden, checking their vitals, and then telekinetically carrying them through the debris and into a saferoom down the hall.

"Think you can pay attention now?" Kenzo glared.

"Oh, fuck off, pipsqueak."

With that, Lena and Kenzo struck out with synchronized precision. Lena's bubbles continued causing caustic damage to Grim's bones, while Kenzo's static created an electrical cage.

"Step on through, asshole," Kenzo gloated. "I dare you."

"Well, I've never been one to turn down a dare." Grim's teeth chattered as he spoke. Not from fear, but anticipation. "You know, my control over my skeletal system is profound."

"It's something," Lena retorted. "Can't believe this one held his own against Gladiatrix."

"Don't be arrogant." Kenzo scoffed.

"In her defense, she held back quite a bit," Grim said, slipping off his black robe. "In my defense, so did I."

Lena's bubbles sizzled against Grim's skull, melting pieces away.

"I've been told my full strength can be erratic, and The True Witch prefers more delicate attacks." Grim's teeth cracked against each other, turning sharp and jagged. "But I won't tell her if you don't."

And just like that, Grim's bones expanded, growing larger and larger. His hand swatted away the bubbles with powerful telekinesis, sending them crashing into Kenzo's hexed cage.

"I don't think so." Kenzo swirled his strike around, countering to loop around Grim's hand.

Just as before, he managed to break the bones apart from the whole. Only now they reformed into a smaller skeleton. Several smaller skeletons.

"Soldiers, formation," Grim demanded with a chaotic cackle. "Kill them!"

His skeleton warriors leapt for Lena and Kenzo. Lena punched one with so much force that it shattered into a thousand pieces. But a second slashed her arm, ignoring her defensive bubble barrier. It ate away at the striking skeleton, but it didn't matter. A nerve had been sliced, and Lena's mobility had been hindered.

"They're pawns," Lena said.

"Caught that," Kenzo said, backflipping away from a deadly pair hacking and swiping for him. It didn't matter if he broke off pieces of them with hexing. They still gave pursuit.

Grim swelled, towering over Lena and Kenzo, and growing so gigantic his mere presence broke through the ceiling. Damn. He was channeling telekinesis from every direction of his body, causing a barrier effect. It'd keep Lena and Kenzo's strikes from landing unless they threw more force behind their blows. The tradeoff being that they wouldn't last as long.

Kenzo froze, taking in the sight of this gigantic skeleton.

The weight of his body must've been too much for Grim, even with his control. He tumbled forward, shifting his shape from a standard human skeletal system to some bizarre monstrosity. Each of his ribs transformed into talon-tipped feet like a centipede. His legs changed into clawed tails, which thrashed about, destroying more of the building.

Grim screeched, running about the facility, breaking through walls, and dodging Lena's heavy-handed bubble attacks. They pushed past Grim's telekinetic barrier but didn't phase his giant bones like once before.

He swatted at Lena with his giant arms, holding his body up with his clawed rib feet. One of those clawed feet nearly impaled Kenzo until Gael reappeared, tackling Kenzo.

Neither concerned themselves with Gael's spikes, since Kenzo made a habit of pricking himself and declaring it was nothing.

"Sorry," Kenzo wheezed.

A similar fear choked him up. The same fear from the night Peter Graham attacked the party and nearly killed Kenzo. The night Jamie Novak died. That night still haunted me too, but for much different reasons.

Kenzo buried his fear and focused on what he knew.

"He's just too big."

"You're lucky Gael's not here." Gael grinned suggestively.

"Take this seriously," Kenzo snapped. "This isn't a joke. He's massive and a threat and—"

"Excuse me? Aren't you the one constantly professing size doesn't matter when you pin me to the mat?" Gael quirked a brow, thoughts flitting to his many one-on-one trainings with Kenzo, where his boyfriend often bested him.

"That's different. Your technique is sloppy," Kenzo said. "And you're soft."

"My spikes have entered the chat, calling bullshit." Gael beamed, shark-like teeth easing Kenzo's nerves.

They each stood, and Kenzo told Gael to move back.

"Focus on distant strikes," he said. "And try to stay off his radar."

"As long as you do the same." Gael backed up, aiming his spikes at the skeleton soldiers.

"Let's see what kind of trouble my lovelies can cause." Grim gestured his giant hand toward the nearby street. "Go, my pretties. Slaughter the masses, purge the fat of this city."

Lena panicked, knowing she couldn't abandon this battle against Grim, but if she didn't give chase, those skeleton soldiers would kill civilians.

"*Diaz is nearby,*" I thought, linking my mind to Lena's. "*I'll warn him of the incoming threat.*"

I sent the warning, stretching what little magic I had as far as it'd go. Hopefully, his team had recovered by now and could handle those skeleton stragglers.

"*Nice tip.*" Lena sent a flurry of bubbles for Grim. "*And where exactly are you right now? Care to actually help, Enchanter?*"

"*Currently indisposed, but still doing my part,*" I replied. "*How about you save the backtalk and pay attention?*"

Lena frowned, annoyed and in complete agreement, which only further pissed her off.

In order to break past his protective barrier, Lena had to fly in close and hit with a potent flurry of bubbles. It worked a few times, but soon, Grim changed his form, adding defensive spikes wherever Lena hovered. They sprouted long and curled unnaturally, chasing after Lena until she fell back.

Kenzo continued lashing out with his gray static, attempting to disrupt the bone spikes protruding from Grim's giant limbs.

"*Focus less on countering him,*" I thought, linking to Kenzo's mind. "*Lena's got that covered.*"

"Frost?" Kenzo tsked, more annoyed than startled. "*Get out of my head. You're not my teacher anymore.*"

"*Maybe so, but I know your branch pretty well, and I know you could be doing a lot better than these bug bite disruptions.*"

Kenzo's scowl lessened, and the thought of casting a hex to get me out of his head only crossed his mind a few times. "*Well? I don't have all day.*"

"*We know your disruption can break apart magic or amplify it.*" I recalled several times in class when Kenzo used his hex in such a manner.

A small smile crept on his face as I shared images of Gael twirling round and round when Kenzo triggered his levitation root. When Layla screeched at the row of lockers, she telekinetically ripped off their hinges after a tiny telekinetic burst meant to knock someone over flew out of control. When Melanie set her own hair on fire because she was practicing her juggling instead of paying attention during a training session with Kenzo. All prime examples of Kenzo amplifying another person's magic instead of breaking it down.

"*Am I supposed to make his bones grow even bigger and hope he collapses from the weight?*" Kenzo growled. "*That's a useless fucking idea, Frost. No wonder they kicked you out of teaching.*"

"*First off, I took a sabbatical. Secondly, no, you dick.*" I huffed. "*You're only thinking of amplifying to cause harm. What if you aimed just enough amplification to assist?*"

Kenzo's eyes widened. "*Lena's precision cascade of bubbles. I could turn those thousands into millions and maximize their effectiveness.*"

"*Precisely.*"

"Not bad, Frost." Kenzo aimed his static at Lena's bubbles. "*I take back half the times I called you a dumbass.*"

"To be fair, you only ever thought it."

"True." Kenzo grinned. *"But we both know you heard me."*

"What are you doing?" Lena watched as static coiled around her attacks.

"Helping," Kenzo answered. "Pay attention."

Lena scowled before realizing her bubbles had multiplied. She fired off a few others, aiming for Kenzo's hexing static. A few swelled in size, others split into copies, and a few grew a thicker sheen to contain more acidic damage.

"About time, pipsqueak." Lena leapt into the fray of combat, belting Grim with her bubble magic and lunging for Kenzo's static strikes. Each one amped up her strength, making it impossible for Grim to catch her. At every turn, she broke off his spiked appendages, tore through his bone shields, shattered his extra limbs, and left a wake of destruction in her path.

"Enough of this." Grim roared, casting telekinesis from his mouth. It was such a powerful burst that several of his sharp teeth snapped off.

Lena managed to withstand the telekinetic strike and evade the jagged teeth projectiles, but in that slowed moment, Grim used one of his tails to throw her back.

As Lena flew back, propelled faster than she could pivot, Grim thrashed about, slamming his hands in every direction to destroy what remained of the facility.

Gael was caught directly in Grim's path. The behemoth aimed his open palm at Gael. His muscles were too sore to move. The strain in his body had caught up to him as he'd overexerted himself, using up nearly all his spikes.

"Gael!" Kenzo screamed, unleashing a massive bolt of white lightning.

It struck Gael before Grim's hand. Instantaneously, Gael's spikes protruded, twisting around each other, forming layers upon layers of armored protection. In a matter of seconds, Gael's trembling body transformed into a fully armored suit of spikes.

```
Name: Gael Martinez
Branch: Augmentation (Spikes)
```

His chest and back were covered in overlapping spikes flattened out. His forearms and calves were coated in small prickles. His shoulders held massive spike plating twisted into deadly curls. His head was protected by a mask of carefully adorned spikes. Two twisted into horns similar to those of a bull.

Grim's open palm slammed down onto Gael, but met fierce resistance. Spikes darted out, reinforcing Gael's stance as he fought against the hand twice his size.

"Aaaaahhh!" Gael roared, unleashing a flurry of spikes from his arms and chest.

Each one tore through Grim's hand, climbing up the giant skeleton, and impaling his bone arm until the spikes snapped the joints at the shoulder.

Kenzo stared in awe at Gael. His boyfriend fired off large spikes as explosive projectiles aimed at Grim's chest. They exploded, creating a thousand needles of destruction.

Grim shrieked, swinging his other arm at Gael. Instead of running, Gael hunkered down and refused to give an inch. With the reinforcements of his spikes and added pulse of telekinesis, Gael withstood the massive swing and sent Grim tumbling backward.

"You think that does anything?" Grim bellowed. "I'll repair myself in seconds and beat you to death."

"Not happening." Kenzo unleashed another bolt of lightning, but this one was black. It struck Grim's fallen arm and completely disintegrated it.

The arm shook, gathering the broken bits together, and slowly lifted itself off the ground in an attempt to return to Grim.

Kenzo's branch had evolved, grown to a whole new degree. With white static, he could perfectly amplify other magics. With the black static, he could completely shatter another magic. What incredible power.

"I've had enough of you," Kenzo shouted, firing off another bolt of black lightning.

It crackled and sizzled against Grim's body. He thrashed about, swinging and kicking erratically, but it didn't matter. Kenzo's targeted strike already took effect, shrinking the grim reaper witch back down to his standard size.

"You think I can't win this?" Grim's jaw chattered as he spoke. "I'm a pillar of the Celestial Coven. I'm unstoppable. I defied Death. I defiled Life.

I am depravity incarnate. I don't get defeated by some pathetic hex witch."

"Would you settle for a hex witch and his arcane mentor?" Lena asked, hovering behind Grim.

Before he could turn around, she fired off thousands of bubbles, each one eating away at Grim's bones, popping with acidic damage.

A white bolt struck one of the bubbles and then pinged between all the others, amplifying Lena's attack a hundred-fold.

Grim vanished entirely, leaving behind only a few dust particles that Lena's bubbles quickly went to work searching for and detaining. If the witch somehow survived this onslaught, he wouldn't escape.

But something told me Grim was gone. The last time he was broken down to this level, his thoughts were fragmented beyond deciphering. Now, the dust of his remains held a silent hum. A vacuum of being. Emptiness trying to find itself.

"How amazing!" Gael shouted. "We were so cool. Total badasses."

"You were okay," Lena said. "Mostly in my way."

"Please." Kenzo scoffed. "If anyone was in the way, it was you and your whining."

"Excuse me?"

"Leave my girlfriend alone," Kenzo whined, imitating Lena. "Leave my boyfriend alone. Wah."

"Oh, you want to talk about crying over boyfriends?" Lena asked, her stare pointedly locked on Kenzo's reddened face.

He hadn't cried, but his eyes did tear up for a second when he believed Gael was about to be crushed. It left his face a little splotchy.

"At least my boyfriend was useful in this battle." Kenzo folded his arms and turned his head away. "Sort of."

"Sort of?" Gael held out his arms, showcasing his full suit of armor. "Look at me. I was a baddie. A total king. You can't deny it!"

Kenzo kept his pouty expression, mainly because he got a silent giggle out of Gael flailing about for his attention. Lena went to check on Ellie and Hayden.

"*Thanks,*" Kenzo thought. "*For your lame idea, Frost. It was helpful or whatever.*"

I smiled. "*You're welcome.*"

Then I proceeded to drift away toward the presence of my core self. With all the other magics finally settling and the threat of the Celestial Coven diminished—at least here—I followed the pulse of my telepathy. My core self was nearby, resisting some type of trap. If I could interact and free myself, then I could enter this battle and put an end to the invasion.

CHAPTER TWENTY-TWO

CHANELLE continued rotating through her elements and cosmic energy, not finding anything that managed to cut through Bardot's diamond armor or keep him back for very long.

"*You need to retreat,*" I thought at her, having linked our minds. "*Your magic is good, but—*"

"*Good?*" Chanelle wheezed, exhausted from keeping herself and the students safe from diamond projectiles. "*My magic's the damn best. Versatile and deadly. Like all the best bi girls.*"

I huffed, ignoring her taking this lightly. Despite her positive attitude—for the students' benefit, no doubt—her body became sluggish the more this fight dragged on. While dodging projectiles wasn't easy, close combat was a non-starter for her, and Bardot kept trying to box her in.

"*Look, diamonds are damn near impossible to destroy,*" I thought. "*Your whip isn't the weapon that'll break that armor apart.*"

"*You're right,*" Chanelle pulled her whip back until it vanished. "*They can melt, though, can't they? Everything melts.*"

"*What are you planning?*"

"*What temp do you think? Like 10,000 degrees or some shit.*"

"*A little over 4,000,*" Jennifer thought, much to the mental murmurs of everyone's surprise. "*What? I pay attention in science class. And knowing when minerals melt is fascinating.*"

Now that she, Tia, and Olivia had woken back up, they had a solid defensive line. Layla and Amani guarded the door from encroaching fiends. They were drawn to the massive source of magic that Bardot and Chanelle released. Jennifer and Olivia channeled their psychic branches, enhancing my partial manifestation strength to create a telepathic link between everyone.

I wished they had a bit more magic at their disposal. Then I'd be able to connect to one of my other manifestations, reach Milo or another Global Guild member, or better yet, figure out what happened to my core self.

How I desperately wanted to find out where my core self was, but I couldn't abandon Chanelle during this battle.

"*Tia, you wouldn't happen to have an ice shield or something resistant to light and heat?*"

Tia cocked her head. "*I might be able to whip something up.*"

"*Sweetie, love the pun.*" Chanelle smirked.

Tia groaned at her choice of words.

"*What are you planning?*" I asked.

"*Something spectacular.*"

"Let's end this." Bardot summoned a great sword made of diamond, then conjured several diamond spikes to protrude from the blade like jagged branches. "I'm bored with your silly little whip trick."

"Oh?" Chanelle channeled her magic. "That's a first. Usually, my whip is quite entertaining. Never met a man who wanted me to wrap it up, unless I was wrapping him up."

"*Gross, Mrs. Whitehurst,*" Tia, Olivia, and Amani thought at the same time toward their homeroom teacher's suggestive commentary.

"Well, seems you're all out of steam with it anyway." Bardot pointed his blade at Chanelle, revealing the oversized length of his blade that filled half the office space.

"Honey, no." Chanelle created sparkling lights around her arms, weaving them like threads. "*Now, Tia.*"

Tia signed a complex enchantment, summoning webbed barriers made of ice and steel and black glowing energy. It cloaked the girls at the edge of the office.

"I prefer the whip for style, but my branch allows me to control primal and cosmic energy in any form I choose," Chanelle explained as the sparkling lights covered her entire body. "Your diamonds are strong, but this armor burns hotter than the stars above."

Chanelle had transformed her whip into a full-body suit of armor made of literal starlight. She was too bright to look directly at, even Bardot winced despite his diamond visor to filter the shine.

"You said something about ending this, right?" Chanelle barreled toward Bardot, and each step she took revealed a secondary element to her armor—a warped black train of a dress that flowed behind her.

When Chanelle reached Bardot, she swung a fist, missing him completely. It was a feint, one meant to cast a light pulse of telekinesis which flung her bizarre dress forward. The black train wrapped around the pair, locking them close together.

"*What are you doing?*"

Chanelle's train turned sticky and oozed around them like a horde of fiends bound together. No, like tar meant to bind them together. She made fabric out of literal tar to trap Bardot in place.

Chanelle hugged him.

"Get off me, you bitch." Bardot struck Chanelle with his free arm, wrestling to break her grip.

"Kill 'em with kindness, I always say." Chanelle tightened her grip, intensifying the heat of her armor until Bardot screamed.

It burned with such intensity that he stood immobilized, unable to continue his assault to break free. Chanelle's starlight burned so strong, it seared the enchantments shielding Bardot's thoughts.

His mind whirled in overdrive, lost in the agony that his receptors kept signaling. His diamond armor held strong for now, but it burned too hot for him to handle.

Even though the armor hadn't melted yet, the suit was too hot. It burned him from the inside out. Chanelle didn't relent—not until chunks of diamond fell away piece by piece, revealing red flesh, blistered flesh, burned flesh.

Bardot thrashed against the scalding tar, desperately dragging himself away from Chanelle's starlit armor, which now melted Bardot's broken diamond armor until the liquid bubbled and sizzled to nothingness.

Every desperate strike Bardot made did nothing to faze Chanelle. Her armor wasn't built to handle the heavy-handed blows, the erratic bursts of telekinesis, or the stray diamonds hurled as a means of escape. Still, Chanelle held out until every single diamond disappeared.

"You're finished." Chanelle panted, struggling to maintain her starlit armor, but holding the form strong until Bardot collapsed at her feet.

The broken behemoth writhed in agony, wincing with every breath.

Chanelle's starlit armor fell to pieces, shattering into a million specs of sparkly dust that fluttered out the window, caught on a breeze. It hurt to stand, hurt to breathe, hurt to smile, but Chanelle maintained her composure. She wanted the girls to see her walk away from this battle with her head held high because one day they might find themselves in a fight just as dangerous.

Like Milo, Chanelle believed in optimism and the effect it had on outcomes. Belief could win a battle just as much as talent. A lovely sentiment, though I disagreed.

Tia dropped her barrier, staring in awe at her teacher. Chanelle truly was the most badass educator I'd ever met. Why she picked this path over the guild life, I would never understand, but I was grateful every day knowing she had.

"Is it over?" Olivia asked.

"No," Layla said with disdain. "He's still alive."

"He's down for the count," Chanelle said. "This part is over."

"Still, there's all the fiends running around," Amani said.

"One thing at a time," Chanelle said, summoning a floral whip made of pink petals to detain Bardot.

I'd seen her summon the floral whip on several occasions, mostly made from a flurry of colorful petals, but not this time. Perhaps a nod to Campbell's magic, it seemed like something Chanelle would do. A small way to honor the fallen guild master. Using the pink pedals, Chanelle bound them around Bardot's arms and legs, extending the length of the whip until she'd looped them tight.

"You bitches," Bardot snarled. "I won't be brought down. I'm a god. A god ordained for greatness. I am a member of the Celestial Coven. You don't stop me. You're nothing!"

"Keep it up." Chanelle tightened the floral bindings. "I'll add some starlight to those roses."

"You think I'm afraid of you?" Bardot thrashed. "I'm not afraid of anything."

"You wanna know fear?" Jennifer tilted her head.

```
Name: Jennifer Jung
Branch: Psychic (Empathic)
```

"Don't engage," Chanelle said.

"No, he doesn't know fear." Jennifer channeled her empathy, siphoning as much fear from the building as she could, stealing it from the minds of everyone on the street, and pulling in the fear until a mass of dark blue energy hovered above her. "Let me introduce him to it."

A silhouette of a creature made of all white, representing Jennifer's empathy, carried the fear over to Bardot. The beast opened the man's mouth and shoved the fear unbound down his throat. He choked on terror, mind lost to the delirium of a thousand horrors he'd never noticed until this moment.

"That'll shut him up for a while." Jennifer stumbled, having severely overexerted herself.

"Good." Layla kicked the petrified Bardot. "The bastard deserves worse."

With that, Layla went over to Campbell's body, offering the fallen guild master a moment of silence, then moved the body over to a couch.

"I wish we could do something more for her," Chanelle whispered.

"We can clear her guild of these goddamned fiends," Layla said furiously, hiding the lump of sorrow in her throat. "She worked hard to make this the best guild in the state. Let's remind everyone that's still true."

Layla turned, channeling her claws and fueling them with banishment. Amani walked beside her; Jennifer forced herself up and joined them. Tia and Olivia followed too.

"*Well, Dorian?*" Chanelle thought, revealing her intrigue now that the dust here had mostly settled. "*What's going on around the city?*"

"*I honestly don't know,*" I thought.

"*Maybe you can tell Milo to get those top ten enchanters to do some of the heavy lifting,*" Chanelle thought. "*I know he was supposed to grab them today.*"

A hell of a time for the Celestial Coven to strike. I didn't know if it was hubris on The True Witch's part or if she truly believed she had enough strength to challenge the top ten enchanters when they'd all gathered together.

"*I'm sort of disconnected from myself at the moment,*" I explained.

"*Then you need to go resolve that,*" she thought. "*Don't worry. I'll secure Cerberus, and I'll watch over the girls.*"

I studied Layla and the others as they banished fiends. They didn't need protection. They were ready for all the hardships and horrors that came with the industry.

CHAPTER TWENTY-THREE

MILO soared through the city, ignoring the outbursts of destruction from nearby guilds and the pleas from enchanters fighting hordes of fiends in the streets. Instead, he focused on a looming threat that I couldn't make sense of. Even as a manifestation latched to his side, I barely kept up with the whirl of intel filling his mind.

I wanted to reach out, to tell him I'd been locked in a psychic trap. But when Milo reached his destination, I froze at the sight of the destruction.

The Global Tower, an embassy of magic authority, had been leveled. Not the entire building, but the top five stories now littered the ground with debris. Flames fluttered across the block. Ten sets of red eyes locked onto Milo as he slowly hovered toward the demons.

"She said the clairvoyant would show up," one of the demons spoke, sending an icy chill through my body.

This was no demon. This demon possessed a host. This was a devil. And he possessed the most frightening host imaginable. A muscular man with a slight tan and slicked-back blond hair.

Richard Kingston, the number one witch in the world. The strongest witch in the Global Guild. He was known as America's sentinel. America's vanguard. He was also occasionally referred to as America's dick, given his name and our nation's need to swing our metaphorical cock around in a measuring contest for authority.

These ten witches were the top ten members of the Global Guild. The greatest enchanters in America. The collection of power that'd finally agreed to gather so we could put an end to The True Witch and her Celestial Coven. And now… Now they all stood possessed by demons.

Gladiatrix and Wadsworth stared down Milo with their shimmering crimson eyes. Even as a fragment of psychic energy, the pulsating ferocity of their demonic energy made me recoil. How had the top ten guild witches in the world all been possessed by demons? The True Witch managed to subdue them all long enough for possession. A frightening thought.

And not just any demons, but a clan of vampires now poised as mighty devils with the strongest host bodies they could ever require. These might not be perfect hosts, like what the chimera craved when trying to possess my body, but each of these witches would contain their vampire demon long enough for it to wreak havoc upon the world.

Milo descended to the streets below, encouraging the devils to follow him by keeping his guard down. What kind of recklessness was he planning? As he landed on the street, he picked a spot not entirely covered by debris. The devils encircled him from every direction, glimmer of excitement in their eyes, and sadistic fanged smiles.

"I've trained for this possibility," Milo said quite casually, as if he weren't surrounded by ten foes with the superior advantage. Not that I doubted Milo's skills, but any one of these enchanters would push him past his limits. The idea that he believed he could hold his own against all ten simultaneously. The audacity.

Yet, he really did believe it. While I couldn't make full sense of his garbled visions, I believed he exaggerated on training for this precise possibility. The murkiest realities he feared only ever gave him inklings of ideas. Milo didn't know for certain what he needed to ready himself for, but he knew he needed to prepare for something foul and demonic—since they obscured their movements from magical detection. The irony of Milo preparing for a battle against demons because he couldn't predict the impending battle against demons wasn't lost on me.

"This was actually my first vision," Milo said with a smile, crossing one arm over the other to stretch his muscles. "It'll be nice to finally clear that one from the books. So to speak."

His first vision? I shuddered, taking in the sight of the ten sets of crimson eyes. This was the vision I'd seen in his nightmare. Milo said it was outdated, impossible. Of course he lied.

"You know, preparing for this actually kept me motivated during my training regimes." Milo bent his leg, lifting the foot behind him, so he could grab hold of it and stretch the muscles. He repeated the process with his other leg, then did a few squats. "Still, I never expected to face ten devils possessing the top ten witches in the Global Guild. This should make for quite the entertainment."

Milo's eyes flitted around the area, surveying bystanders, tracking the news helicopter, and the others recklessly livestreaming this impending battle. These people should be fleeing for their lives, not recording the scene.

"Time to show y'all why they call me The Inevitable Future." Milo smiled, big and confident, so much so that his bright blue eyes closed for a second. He stood before these threats without a care in the world, even if his thoughts surged in and out of visions, looping through endless scenarios.

"The hubris of psychics," Gladiatrix hissed. Correction, the demon possessing her body hissed. It seeped through every cell of her being, manifesting the raw radiance of a devil.

```
Name: Alicia Lawrence
Branch: Alteration (Supreme Physicality)
Rank: 4th
```

I trembled. These vampires were nothing like the chimera. They oozed with power either because they had too much to hide or simply didn't concern themselves with discretion. I'd never felt demonic energy on this level. Even looking in their direction made my skin crawl.

"Let us rid ourselves of this witch so we can feast upon the city," the demon possessing Wadsworth said. His tired, old body moving freely without the aches and pains of nearly a century and a half of pushing well past his limitations.

```
Name: Samual Wadsworth
Branch: Rejuvenation (Healing)
Rank: 8th
```

"Shall we begin?" Milo asked, lunging forward in a blink.

I'd never seen him move so quickly. I'd never seen anyone move so quickly. Even the devils were stunned, especially the ones possessing Gladiatrix and Wadsworth. Milo snatched the pair by their faces and then slammed them headfirst onto the ground.

The earth cracked, the devil's eyes glowed white, and a flurry of demonic energy erupted into nothingness.

What the hell was that?

"How'd you…" The devil possessing Enchanter Kingston stared wide-eyed at the unconscious Gladiatrix and Wadsworth.

Milo banished two devils at the same time. Their thoughts were faint, lost in the murkiness of slumber, but they were alive. The last time Milo banished a devil, he had to channel a hundred fellow witches to ensure the chimera's exorcism didn't kill Jamie Novak in the process.

"I told you; I've been preparing for this battle my entire life." Milo shifted his stance, raising his fists. "The only true way to face a devil is through your root magics, so I perfected mine."

What? Milo had perfected his banishment root. This whole time, he'd just been holding back, encouraging others to assist him. No, it was more than that. Milo moved at a blurred speed that would compete with Gladiatrix on her best day. That meant Milo lightened the weight of his body with levitation and propelled himself with telekinesis. He perfected those roots, too.

Had Milo really been holding himself back this entire time? He always proved he could handle the hardest of battles, but he often preferred outcomes that gathered alliances and grateful comrades who went on to achieve more heroics after their encounter. Still, did Milo believe that with his perfected roots, he could hold his own against the ten most powerful witches in the world?

"Enough of this," snapped the devil possessing Enchanter Barlowe. He was pale and sickly looking, though some of that could be attributed to the possession.

```
Name: Maximus Barlowe
Branch: Arcane (Heavenly Ice)
Rank: 3rd
```

The devil channeled Barlowe's branch, drawing the molecules of water and the refraction of light in the air to twist them into a unique type of ice under Barlowe's control. The arcane magic was a mix of primal, cosmic, and rejuvenation.

Before he could impale Milo with a dozen icy blades, Milo waved a hand to destroy the attack.

"Impossible," Barlowe's devil said.

"Perfected telekinesis can do wonders." Milo grinned, leaping forward to strike Barlowe with banishment.

"Not happening." A glittery flicker of light appeared beside Barlowe, and another devil snatched him up and teleported out of Milo's reach.

```
Name: Miguel Lopez
Branch: Cosmic (Shimmer)
Rank: 5th
```

Enchanter Lopez had a deep amber complexion and a similar build to Milo's. Even their jaws held the same clenched tension.

"Perfected roots or not, you can't maintain them for very long," said the devil possessing Enchanter Stone. "Wear the witch down, then feast upon him."

```
Name: Conrad Stone
Branch: Primal (Floral Divinity)
Rank: 2nd
```

The second-oldest member of the Global Guild and currently ranked second, while in his early fifties. Enchanter Stone, most commonly known as Nature's Champion, despite notoriously selling out to corporations and acting as their spokesperson. I shook away my personal disdain for the witch and focused on the devil using his body to hurl hundreds of thorned vines at Milo.

They burst before reaching Milo. Every vine, pedal, and leaf exploded into puffs of green mist before blowing away in the wind.

Holy hell. I just realized what Milo was doing with his perfected telekinesis. He was literally ripping apart their attacks cell by cell. He controlled every single one of them on a molecular level, dividing and destroying. If he did that to the devils themselves, he'd easily win this battle. He could shatter their host bodies, then banish them as they struggled to regain their senses without possession.

I tsked.

But Milo would never do something so callous. He tried to save everyone, which meant he'd drag this battle out, ensuring none of the top ten perished.

"Perfected or not, he can't cast if bound," the devil possessing Stone shouted, before conjuring a floral shield of thorny plants. "Rebecca, lock him down."

I scanned the field, finding Enchanter Robbins summoning golden chains from the earth below her.

```
Name: Rebecca Robbins
Branch: Ward (Benevolent Chains)
Rank: 7th
```

The perversion of not only stealing these witches' bodies but also referring to each other by the enchanter's names. It reminded me how demons and devils preferred to keep their true names secretive.

The stern, hateful expression on her face was so opposite from everything they showed on television. The glow of her chains glimmered against her rainbow-dyed pixie cut. She was an enchanter of positivity and progress, pushing for acceptance—at least that was what all my students would say anyway.

Robbins hurled golden chains at Milo, forcing him to retreat. Since they were made of warding magic, Milo couldn't counter them with telekinesis. Those chains sapped magic away, and if they shackled Milo, this battle would end.

The teleporting devil lunged for Milo, bouncing circles around him. It allowed the devil to strike Milo with several surprise attacks while also obscuring his vision. The bright shimmer of light was like an explosion of high beams again and again. Even I struggled from a safe distance.

"You know, I trained a teleporter," Milo said, snatching Miguel by the throat. "It's not easy predicting your movements, but even without realizing, you follow a pattern."

His time with Hayden had given him an edge with other teleporting witches. Milo tossed the devil into the path of the encroaching golden chains.

While he hadn't managed to banish the devil, he did force the one possessing Robbins to retract her warding chains. I assumed the devil couldn't simply turn off the ward power or hadn't learned how to control the chains with such precision. In either sense, it stalled her and the teleporter she'd trapped.

In the few seconds Milo took to catch his breath, two devils sprang out from either side of him. They weren't aiming for an attack, simply attempting to make contact with him.

Fuck. That was their attack.

He managed to avoid the first one, spinning around her and kicking her down into Stone's floral shield.

That was close. The witch in question was Enchanter Spade.

```
Name: Skylar Spade
Branch: Hex (Curse Contract)
Rank: 10th
```

Supposedly, she could create any rule so long as she spoke it into existence, but she had to make contact with the target she wished to summon a rule upon. Dammit. If that devil touched Milo, all she'd have to do was create a rule to prevent Milo from breathing, demand he drop dead that second, or any other type of hellish instant killing strike the enchanter herself would never utilize.

"Ooooh, fuck," Milo roared, knocking the other witch back.

He'd only grazed Milo with the lightest swipe.

```
Name: Trevor Ford
Branch: Rejuvenation (Sensory Lapse)
Rank: 6th
```

But with the ability to dull or enhance any senses or sensory receptors with contact, the light jab weighed heavily on Milo. Every muscle in his right arm burned. His nerves throbbed with agony, and Milo twitched, fighting to maintain his composure.

Another devil leapt into the fray, attempting to slash Milo's already injured arm. He sprang away from the angry blond, dodging the persistent attacks, but hurling chunks of debris with telekinesis to serve as coverage. It didn't work as the devil phased right through the rocks, continuing its pursuit.

```
Name: Lance Whitlock
Branch: Arcane (Intangibility)
Rank: 9th
```

Enchanter Whitlock was a distant cousin of Tara's, apparently quite distant, as her thoughts never lingered long on the man, even when classmates would ask questions. He was a legend in the Global Guild, but Tara never met the man. A real shame considering he possessed the same intangibility branch as her.

Milo continued dodging blows from Enchanter Whitlock, evading his attacks, while attempting to hit the witch, too. Unfortunately, every well-trained punch Milo threw went right through Whitlock's intangible body, only for him to re-corporealize a moment later and hit Milo.

"You can't defeat me, witch," the devil possessing Whitlock hissed. "I'm a god."

"Been hearing that a lot lately." Milo punched the devil through his head, missing completely, but managing to skirt away before the devil struck him.

"Face it, you're—" The devil froze midsentence with a pained look of shock on his face. "What did you…"

He roared in agony, slapping his head again and again, unable to ease the pain.

What did Milo do?

When the devil finally composed himself, he turned intangible again, allowing a small rock to fall from his head. It thudded on the ground, and the devil glared.

"Such a tiny thing caused this?"

"The way I wanna make a dick joke right now," Milo said, clotheslining the distracted devil.

Before the devil could compose itself, Milo threw telekinetic pulses to knock the devil off course and send it crashing hard into the ground.

"Enough of this," said the devil possessing Enchanter Kingston.

He stepped forward, unleashing white, feathered wings and summoning a glowing golden halo over his head.

```
Name: Richard Kingston
Branch: Alteration (Supreme Physicality)
Branch: Cosmic (Divine Halo)
Branch: Augmentation (Wings)
Rank: 1st
```

Personally, I believed the Christian presence of his branches played a bigger role in his ranking than his actual ability. It was profound how religion evolved, finding purpose in magic, and claiming God or whoever blessed the most faithful with great magics—and, of course, demons were naturally drawn to sin and the sinful.

I couldn't help but wonder how the pious would react to their devoted hero being possessed.

The Global Guild, like too many organizations, favored religious backgrounds and fair complexions more than talent—they'd only recently loosened their chokehold on conservative views. That said, Enchanter Kingston also possessed the same strength and speed as Gladiatrix. Milo would need to be on his guard since this devil wouldn't be fooled like the ones that had possessed Gladiatrix and Wadsworth.

"A devil in angel's clothing." Milo grinned. "How poetic."

"This ends now." Enchanter Kingston's wings flapped, and he vanished in a powerful gale.

The gust reeled Milo forward and swept him directly into Kingston's path. The devil reappeared in a blink, fist balled, and swinging a furious strike meant to knock Milo's head clean off.

"Aaargh!" Milo yelled in pain as he blocked the blow with his already injured right arm.

A crunch hit hard, followed by a thousand tiny cracks as every bone in Milo's arm broke.

The nerves in his arm were still in hyperdrive, raging with a fiery throb. When the realization that Kingston's fist had shattered the bones of Milo's forearm, his face turned ghostly white. Every thought in Milo's mind went silent. The pain bled through his entire body, and he nearly buckled right there.

To be struck by the strongest man on earth while his sensations for pain in his arm were elevated. How Milo managed to stand was beyond me. He truly was on a completely different level from anyone I'd ever encountered.

"Got you right where I want ya." Milo grimaced, slapping his left hand over Kingston's face.

The bright light of the halo created a caustic burn, singeing Milo's skin. That ridiculous halo was for more than just show. It protected Kingston from close combat strikes.

Not that it mattered. Milo's banishment kicked in in waves, repelling and neutralizing the magic of Kingston's halo. Even his wings diminished some, feathers crumbling to ashes as they were locked within Milo's perfected banishment.

"How's it feel, devil?" Milo tightened his grip on Kingston's face, digging his nails in deep. "All that power, and your possession means nothing in the end."

"Stop him!" Kingston roared.

The devils possessing Stone and Barlowe flew close, throwing plants and ice at Milo to no avail. His perfected banishment shattered all magical attacks, but because his focus was split on countering incoming magic, it slowed the exorcism of the devil possessing Richard Kingston.

The devil possessing Robbins attempted to bind Milo with her golden warding chains again, only this time, they rusted over instantly. The symbols cracked apart. The golden glow turned a deep copper brown. The chains themselves crumbled into ashes, propelled and destroyed by Milo's banishment in tandem with telekinesis.

"I'm in my perfected state," Milo declared, blue eyes shimmering with the purple glow of psychic energy. "As long as I channel all four roots simultaneously, you can't touch me."

"Let's see about that," the devil possessing Whitlock appeared from below, bringing two other devils with him.

The hex enchanter slapped a hand on Milo's chest. "Stop casting."

"Your commands require contact." Milo smirked, his body pulsing with a thin protective layer of levitation repulsion. The very magic in our cores that allowed us to float now coated Milo from head to toe, repelling threats.

The sensory enchanter slapped Milo, attempting to strike enhanced pain throughout, but Milo's cloak held strong.

"Wait your turn, you'll all be banished soon enough." With that, Milo sent a surge of telekinesis, propelling the devils away and leaving him alone with the devil possessing the number one enchanter. Milo applied more pressure, dropping the shrieking devil to his knees.

A high-pitched scream drew Milo's attention. Hovering high in the sky, a small child wriggled in terror, surrounded by a shimmer of light.

"You might be immune to our casting efforts, but these mortal fools aren't," said the devil possessing Enchanter Lopez. He held the child by the collar of their shirt with one hand and tapped his forehead with the other. "One thing I've learned, studying the mind of this feeble witch, is that enchanters such as yourself waste time and energy protecting the vulnerable."

Milo glared, still focusing his banishment on expelling the devil from Richard Kingston.

"Your species would be so much stronger if you all collectively culled the weak," the devil said, teleporting away, and leaving the small child to plummet.

Milo leapt into action, flying faster than he'd ever done before, and catching the child midair. It wasn't enough. A shimmer of light appeared, quickly followed by a man's scream. Milo spotted another bystander falling from a terrible height. He soared over, wrapping the man in a telekinetic grip.

Shimmers of light sparked from every direction, carrying a screaming person in their wake. Some of the bystanders snatched into the sky were able to levitate on their own accord, but many required Milo's intervention. He swept back and forth, catching innocent people before they plummeted to their deaths. As he held nearly thirty people in his telekinetic grasp, waves of magical strikes came from below.

Deadly plants erupted from the earth. Shards of jagged ice catapulted ahead. Golden chains bound the witches who tried to fly away on their own.

Milo did everything in his power to dodge the strikes, weaving not only himself, but everyone in his grasp. It took all he had to sweep through the sky, keeping every single person safe.

Kingston zipped through the air and hovered in front of Milo in a flash. His hand was clawed from the devil's vampiric nature slipping through. The hand was bloody, though. I blinked with confusion, mine and Milo's.

Blood trickled down Milo's face, making his vision splotchy. He'd been slashed across the face.

"Aren't you a tasty treat?" The devil licked his clawed fingers, then lunged for Milo and sank his fangs into Milo's neck.

I quivered, synced to Milo's aching body. A rush of heat swept over him, followed by an icy chill that left him drained. Milo's magic waned, giving way to the civilians he held telekinetically. His eyes rolled back, locked in Kingston's embrace as he gorged on Milo's blood.

There was nothing I could do. I couldn't help Milo. I couldn't interact. I couldn't reach my core self. All I could do was watch Milo's agonizing death.

The devil laughed, leaning back some and basking in the bloody mess he had made. "You were a fool to think you could defeat us on your own."

And in that instance, a fist struck Enchanter Kingston with such tremendous force that it sent him propelling to the ground and crashing through the street several hundred feet.

"He's not alone." Gladiatrix floated beside Milo, fury on her face and body tensed for combat.

CHAPTER TWENTY-FOUR

GLADIATRIX grabbed hold of the people Milo had lost a grip on, then used her telekinesis to send them all far enough to safely escape. As she descended to the streets with Milo, Wadsworth flew over and immediately went to work on Milo's arm, neck, and face.

"Damn, dumb kid." Wadsworth jerked Milo's arm, twisting it despite Milo's pained yelps and pleas. "Shut up. I have to examine the infection. That sensory bullshit can have long-term effects. Do you want to be in constant agony for the rest of your life?"

Milo shook his head.

"Then shut the fuck up and let me work." Wadsworth glowered. "Gladiatrix, can you handle them while I tend to this goddamn idiot? If I don't deal with these injuries now, they'll never heal right."

"Don't worry about—" Milo groaned when Wadsworth thumped his broken forearm.

"I can handle the top three." Gladiatrix shifted her stance. "But the others? I'm gonna need help on that one."

"Cocky," Wadsworth said. "I know you think they intentionally hold your ranking back, but the top three aren't to be quarreled with."

"Oh, I know." Gladiatrix smirked. "But I also know those devils can only harness about half of our magic while suppressing our consciousness. Plus, they don't possess any of our trained instincts."

"They have their own hellish instincts," Wadsworth said. "But alas, I can't handle the others. I'd need to take my Infinite State, which would mean no healing Enchanter Dumbass here."

"Hey," Milo whined. "I saved your lives. It was all part of my plan. Exorcise you two, hold off the other eight, you come into action, and the day is saved. Sort of. Still, lots of other moving pieces."

"Like I said, Enchanter Dumbass needs me." Wadsworth went to work healing Milo.

"That's okay," Gladiatrix said. "I brought my own backup."

"Which I accounted for, too," Milo insisted, revealing mental musings of the speedy flight plan he booked. "You're welcome."

Two masked witches flew from a distance, making their way closer until Gladiatrix had a clear sight of King Liberty and Queen of Jesters.

"You two made it just in time."

"You wouldn't believe the amount of demonic energy flowing through this city," Queen of Jesters said. "You sure you don't want us in the field with the others?"

It seemed quite a few vigilante witches had hopped the pond and come to aid Chicago.

"Nope." Gladiatrix nodded to the gathering devils. "I need you two to hold those five back, while I exorcise those three."

"Love, are those the top three witches in America?" King Liberty asked. "You know, I feel your ranking system is overrated, but that seems reckless."

"Just watch my back." Gladiatrix punched a fist into her palm. "While I knock these boys onto theirs."

With that, Gladiatrix lunged ahead and sprang into combat with the top three Global Guild witches. Her punches clashed with the devil possessing Enchanter Kingston. Her movements were erratic and sophisticated all at once, turning the plants Enchanter Stone summoned into the direct path of the ice strikes Enchanter Barlowe used. The battle turned chaotic and difficult to follow. Gladiatrix moved at a blurred speed similar to Milo's, only she never slowed down, making it impossible to track.

Her speed in this battle was nothing like what I'd previously witnessed. It was as if she unleashed her full strength all at once. The occasional snarl from a devil drew my eye, but by the time I glanced in that direction, they'd all vanished yet again.

"You heard the lady." King Liberty summoned a green shield around himself and a second around Milo and Wadsworth.

Several of the possessed enchanters struck out at King Liberty's shield. When their magics failed, they slashed with their clawed hands. Two devils even leapt for the barrier protecting Wadsworth as he healed Milo.

I jumped. They were trying to finish off Milo.

The initial panic in me settled. Nothing these devils did would break through King Liberty's barriers. He held the strongest classified warding magic in the world.

Many speculated King Liberty possessed two of the best warding magics. A blue barrier specifically designed to shield against mystical properties, and a yellow barrier created to absorb kinetic energy. Merging the two into the ultimate green shield that could handle all forms of physical or magical threats. Others proclaimed King Liberty, being of obvious royal blood—since many of the previous wearers of the mask alluded to noble standing, much like the very first incarnation—that this green barrier was an arcane branch.

In either case, King Liberty never confirmed suspicions, much like he never confirmed his identity. And despite being on the list of approved vigilantes in the UK, he technically didn't hold a license. None of the vigilante witches obtained licenses, not when their goal was to buck the system that repressed the masses by labeling, fining, and taxing a person for their inherent magical gifts.

"Do I get to go all out?" Queen of Jesters asked.

King Liberty sighed. "Yes. Have fun."

Queen of Jesters giggled, slamming her hands down into the broken gravel of the street. The debris clustered together, forming bizarrely shaped arms. The undisturbed part of the road cracked and broke loose, forming a strange torso. Suddenly, the behemoth human form made of concrete stood tall.

"It's alive," Queen of Jesters said with a cackle, looking up at her towering creation. "It's alive!"

"I swear to Christ she does that every time she makes one of those ragdolls," King Liberty muttered under his breath.

This ragdoll magic clearly allowed Queen of Jesters to manifest living attributes into nonorganic materials. Quite the unique branch. Useful too, as the ragdoll swung swift fists, making it almost impossible for the devils to dodge.

A pulse of psychic magic struck me from out of nowhere. Not nowhere. From me. My core self. The sudden pull snatched me from the battlefield, dragging me through the streets of Chicago and to the Global Guild facility. What the hell had happened here? It was completely destroyed.

Suddenly, the link pulling me back to my core self triggered an onslaught of memories. Every manifestation yelled at the funneling burst of collective memories. Our core self revealed the battle he'd endured, breaking apart thousands of psychic traps, and releasing himself from Amara's wicked telepath chains.

But with his memories came dozens more. Battles against the gigantic skeleton that destroyed the Global Guild facility, Katherine's strange infiltration, Milo's war against the top ten witches, Chanelle's incredible starlit armor, Carter's amazing rescue, Gael's brazen solo fight, the attack on Cerberus Guild, and the death of Guild Master Campbell.

Many more memories revealed themselves, showing the attack extended across the city, leaving nearly every enchanter occupied by either fiends, demons, or a witch from the Celestial Coven.

One by one, the manifestations faded until all that remained was our core self.

...

...

...

Now that I'd broken free from Amara's trap and collected all my stray magic across the city, I knew what I needed to do. I stumbled to my feet, exhausted from the sheer magnitude of the psychic trap meant to contain me, but I refused to rest. Not until I knew everyone was safe, not until I knew what happened to Caleb, not until I stopped The True Witch once and for all.

I released a few manifestations, imbuing them with an extra burst of magic, so our link wouldn't be severed this time. Sending one to Milo, I had to know his recovery went well, and I sent a few others to check on my students. I didn't know where to begin with Katherine and Caleb, so I put a blanket search across the city for their minds, hoping one of my manifestations would be close enough to rescue them.

I sent the last manifestation I summoned directly to Whitlock Estate, where I knew Amara would soon find herself. She wanted to take Tara, and that wasn't going to happen.

Chapter Twenty-Five

I BOLTED through the psychic plane, zipping across the city instantaneously to reach the Whitlock Estate. Their steel gates were flung open, their stone walls left bare without a single active ward. Floating onto the grounds, I found bloody grass leading to corpses scattered across the lawn.

Every elite bodyguard Tobias Whitlock had hired lay dead. From the deep slashes and bloody mess, it was clear Lazarus had made quick work of them. There wasn't much casting debris, meaning they barely had a chance to defend themselves before Lazarus hacked them down. More than thirty well-trained ex-military enchanter-level witches, and not one of them managed to derail this pillar of the Celestial Coven.

Sending the information to my core self through the link we shared, I pressed forward and made my way inside the mansion.

Much to my surprise, Tobias stood at the railing of the stairs, practically greeting Lazarus' arrival.

Tobias had aged a lot since the last time I saw him. Wrinkles deepened his stern expression. What little blond hair he had before had finally turned white or fallen out. His cheeks were sunken in, and his eyes were heavy with sleep deprivation. Whether the many legal cases against him had added to this fatigue or Theodore's escape, coupled with The True Witch's arrival, I couldn't discern.

The golden shield of Tobias' arcane branch already cloaked his thoughts and guarded against Lazarus' impending attack.

"The audacity of stepping into my home." Tobias grimaced. "Amara overreaches. When I send you back to her, she'll realize I have no time for her fanatical obsession."

"You speak of audacity yet utter a goddess's name as if your tongue has earned such a thing."

"My tongue has experienced far more than Amara's name, peasant." Tobias chuckled. "Oh, yes, she told me all about you, *Lazarus*. Your myth is far more entertaining than your true origins."

"You know nothing of me."

Tobias' piercing blue eyes held utter contempt, judgment, and so much superiority. I didn't even need to read his thoughts to feel the disgust in his expression.

"I know you were blessed with a brilliant branch." Tobias took a step down, closing the distance between himself and Lazarus in the foyer. "I know you used it to claw your way out of the gutters of your city, a city made of stone and mud and kings who didn't know the first thing about ruling."

Lazarus glared.

"I know after several thousand years of living, you've finally reached the pinnacle of your skills. You think yourself grand." Tobias shook his head disapprovingly. "You honed your magic for a millennium, and it is nothing compared to what I was born with. Brilliance isn't trained; it's inherited."

"I was only sent to retrieve the girl, but taking your head will be an added boon."

Tobias laughed. "Come then, peasant. Show me what you're made of."

The term cut deep, reminding Lazarus of the life he escaped, the years of servitude, the centuries of burying the inferiority complex that plagued him. Tobias shook Lazarus so deeply that his thoughts floated freely from frustration.

But flustered or not, Lazarus fixated on Tobias' branches.

```
Name: Tobias Whitlock
Branch: Arcane (Abjuration)
Branch: Cosmic (Shadows)
Branch: Bestial (Familiar)
```

Whoa. I had no idea Tobias possessed multiple branches or the fact that he, too, had a familiar. Was it another insect like Tara's?

Lazarus held his hands out flat, channeling his telekinesis so the swipes would cut deep like a blade. Without hesitation, Lazarus leapt at Tobias, attempting to slash the man's throat. A futile effort, met with a sharp clink as his hand struck a golden shield glowing at Tobias' neck.

"I thought Amara would prepare you for me," Tobias said, casting telekinesis to throw Lazarus back. "She swore the pillars were in a league of their own. I find the pillars of the Celestial Coven a bit overrated."

If only he realized Grim had joined The Sisters Three in death, he'd definitely gloat. More. He'd gloat more. Geez, it was difficult to root for Tobias' victory, knowing he achieved it by assuming everyone born poor was insignificant, and their achievements meant nothing. Still, I hoped he'd hold out against Lazarus until the Global Guild sent their reinforcements.

"Shall we end this, peasant?"

"Your shield will break long before my stamina wanes."

"We'll see about that." Tobias extended his arms, unleashing shadows across the mansion.

His control of them differed from Tara's. Whereas she usually summoned them as tendrils, he conjured his shadows in a massive wave of darkness. Only, they didn't cover much. They spread across the rooms, hiding the floor and reaching Lazarus' waist.

"I assume Amara has warned you what comes next."

"If you think I fear your beast, you're a—"

A giant fucking crocodile sprang up out of the shadows and snatched Lazarus by the torso before dragging him beneath the shadows.

Holy fucking hell. I trembled, floating higher up toward the ceiling. Yes,

I was incorporeal, but the idea of being this close to a crocodile was fucking terrifying. How the hell did Tobias have a crocodile? A goddamn giant crocodile. That was his familiar? It was a monstrosity. An apex predator of pure destruction.

The crocodile's tail rose above the shadows, thrashing about a bit, but then lowered again. Lazarus screamed and fought against the beast, but the shadows barely moved in response. It was like a silent black lake of death.

"Titus, behave," Tobias warned. "I told you to immobilize the witch, not kill him."

The crocodile's snout lifted above the shadows, and his jaw opened, revealing a bloody and worn Lazarus. He immediately flew away, landing on the ceiling with his back pressed to it. His bloody chest heaved as he took frightened, panting breaths. His eyes darted between the shadows where Titus now floated above in full view and to Tobias, who merely smiled at the alarmed enemy.

Hell. The crocodile's snout to the tip of its tail was easily twenty feet. Maybe more. The width was massive, unlike anything I'd seen in pictures or on television. I didn't know much about crocodiles other than that their bite was deadly; they kept growing with age, and they evolved over millions of years to be the perfect predator. Oh, and they were very fucking patient.

The way Titus' eyes locked onto Lazarus, I believed the crocodile was a second away from lunging into the air and snatching him up. After all, Titus was a familiar, so he was a goddamn crocodile with root magics.

"Usually, Titus gets to feast upon those foolish enough to cross me," Tobias explained. "But with your particular branch, I wouldn't want my old friend to get an upset stomach."

```
Name: Lazarus
Branch: Rejuvenation (Resurrection)
```

"No, no, no." Tobias waved his finger back and forth to emphasize his words. "I have something far grander in store for you."

Titus growled, a truly unsettling sight.

"Yes, retrieve him," Tobias said, dispelling his shadows.

Titus dropped down to the floor and thwacked his tail a few times. It created a pulse of telekinesis that dragged Lazarus back down. He thrashed against the pull, but the crocodile snarled and hissed, snapping his teeth. It seemed to create a stronger hold over Lazarus, even in a telekinetic form. Did the crocodile add his jaw strength to his telekinesis?

"Amara has had lots of dalliances with this one," Tobias spoke to his familiar as if they didn't hold Lazarus hostage. "It speaks volumes that after centuries of courtship, she never did commit to him."

Titus hissed in response.

"Yes, truly." Tobias chuckled, then turned to the frazzled and frightened Lazarus. "He was speaking on her promiscuity and your peasantry."

Lazarus glared, pretending to overcome his fear, but in reality, his mind swam in it.

"Although I find it truly hilarious that despite all Lazarus' achievements in his simple little eternity, Amara didn't seek him out for her ritual." Tobias turned his attention back to his crocodile. "No, he wasn't what she required. When Amara sought to bring a goddess into this world, she came for Whitlock stock."

Titus hissed in response.

"True. Our lineage does date back to before the fall of magic," Tobias replied. "Did you know that, peasant? You may've served one of my ancestors."

Lazarus resisted his telekinetic bindings, only for the crocodile to clamp his jaw and force Lazarus to become still.

"Okay, let us end this." Tobias retrieved a small metal case from his pocket, then cast his golden shield around Lazarus' body. "We'll see how much affection Amara holds for you when she comes for Tara."

Tobias opened the case and pulled out a piece of paper with an enchantment on it. Slapping the page onto Lazarus' chest, it unleashed hundreds of metallic threads that sprang around Lazarus' glowing body and bound the man in a cocoon of sorts.

"Remember, Titus, if Amara makes a true move for Tara beyond musings or hollow threats, slaughter her."

The crocodile growled in response.

With that, Tobias waved his hand and conjured his black lake of shadows for Titus to lurk beneath. He then made his way back upstairs, leaving the entire mansion set into a dreadful trap.

"*You see a trap because you assume Tobias is a threat.*" The doors swung open for Amara's grand entrance. "*Surprised?*"

I glared down at her, invisible to the eye, and now guarding my thoughts from her intrusion. She wore a white dress, low-cut and with blood-red draped sleeves.

"*It's not my branch,*" she thought, green eyes smiling. "*Just an enchantment to ready myself for unforeseen threats such as a pesky telepath breaking free from my trap and snooping where he doesn't belong.*"

Ignoring her, I turned to warn Tobias.

"Tobi, my love," Amara shouted, announcing her arrival and drawing Tobias back to the top of the staircase.

"You look wonderful, my dear," he said, golden shield at the ready.

"Of course I do." Amara shrugged playfully. "You look tired, Tobi. Not the sweet boyish fool I loved so."

"Do narcissists understand love?"

"I don't know." She shrugged again, running her fingers through the shadows. "I shall ask our son."

"I admire your resolve, your commitment, and I will always find your particular madness charming," Tobias said, making his way halfway down the stairs. "But I will not allow you to drag Tara into your madness."

"You speak as if you have a choice."

"If you want your pillar back, leave now." Tobias gestured to the cocooned Lazarus.

"Quite a powerful binding." Amara examined the threads of the cocoon. "But even the best magics fizzle out when the witch who cast them is drained or removed."

"That's why I paid for the enchantment, my dear." Tobias pointed to the piece of paper at the center of Lazarus' chest. "More refined than even what your enchantment prodigy can put together. Basically, if I die, it'll hold strong for the better part of a century. Maybe longer."

Amara giggled. "I've taken longer naps."

In that instance, the crocodile sprang from the shadows, barreling toward Amara, jaws wide open.

Amara raised her hands in response, fingers extended. Her telekinesis barely stopped the beast. The crocodile froze midair, thrashing about in response.

"Titus, such a pity. I always enjoyed your company." Amara frowned, then waved her arms in opposite directions.

The action ripped through the crocodile, snapping the animal's neck and tearing its body apart into large chunks tossed across the mansion.

"Do not look at me like that," Amara said to Tobias, not even facing his hateful stare. "You intended to let Titus kill me. Quite unkind."

The sadness in Tobias' heart sang so loudly, his emotions were crystal clear. Despite the protective golden barrier he had up, he couldn't cloak the deep sorrow that etched away his resolve. Memories of a small boy crept to the surface of Tobias' mind, revealing him more than fifty years ago, wandering in a swamp, alone and terrified. His suit was ruined, his face frantic, but he kept searching until he reached a hidden lake where Titus rested.

Unlike most familiars, Titus had demanded his human partner seek him out. Tobias had always respected his familiar for that.

"So, this is her?" Tara asked, cautiously revealing herself at the railing upstairs. "This is The True Witch?"

"Go back to your room."

"I can help."

"Let her stay." Amara smiled at Tara. "It is quite brave to step out here, an action of a goddess in the making."

"You're not ready for Amara."

"You act as if I've come to fight Tara." Amara shook her head. "She's my daughter, my savior, my goddess."

"Are you satisfied?" Tobias asked Tara. "She's more psychotic than your brother."

"I don't think Theo is psychotic," Amara mused. "I think he just has tantrums due to bad parenting. Not pointing any fingers."

"Says the woman who abandoned us," Tara said with a lump of fear and resentment stuck in her throat.

"I didn't abandon you." Amara tsked. "I prepared the world for your ascent. I ensured you would have the universe. I have paved the road to your eternal supremacy."

"Funny, all I remember asking for was a mom who loved me." Tara's eyes watered.

"Oh, Tara, I do love you," Amara said with feigned sweetness. "You'll see that when I get you away from your father."

"You're not taking her." Tobias' golden shield flickered.

Amara nodded to the crocodile's corpse. "You're not the only one who brought in a ringer, love."

Suddenly, a blue portal opened above Tara and her father. Theodore Whitlock descended, blades in hand, and a wicked smile on his face. Tobias' golden shield fell away entirely, and as it disappeared, so did one of the enchantment tattoos on Amara's chest.

"Hello, Father!" Theodore stabbed Tobias in the stomach with both blades and collapsed atop the man. "How long I've waited for this moment."

Tara screamed, unleashing shadow tendrils and icicles at her brother.

"None of that, my sweet." Amara waved a hand, summoning another blue portal beneath Tara's feet.

Shocked, she fell halfway through before triggering her levitation. Good. Now she just needed to...

The portal moved upward at Amara's discretion, sweeping Tara away.

No. No. NO!

"It is time to go, Theodore." Amara walked up the stairs, taking her time while Theodore carved his blades across his father's chest.

He dragged them slowly, meticulously, and used the weight of his body and telekinesis to keep the man pinned beneath him. When Tobias screamed, Theodore laughed. When Tobias cried out, Theodore laughed louder.

"Come, now."

"No," Theodore snapped. "I was promised—"

"Your father's death, which you have obtained." Amara flicked her wrist and snapped Tobias' neck. "I don't have time for your petty vengeances."

"You bitch." Theodore leapt up; bloody blades raised.

"We've discussed this language." Amara flicked her wrist again, dropping Theodore to his knees, forcing his head to bow, and his hands to release the blades. "You will be an obedient boy, or you'll go to your room until I say otherwise."

"Have fun opening Hell without me."

"Sweetie, I will break you long before I need you for that."

"Promises, promises," Theodore said through gritted teeth.

Amara opened a blue portal, ushering Theodore to go through it. This was it. This was the last I'd see of them. They'd grabbed Tara. They'd taken Caleb for some reason. They had a hold over Katherine somehow. I couldn't let it end like this.

There was only one solution. I severed the link to my core self and rushed into Theodore's mind.

"*Well, well, well.*" Theodore shivered as he stepped through the portal. "*If it isn't my favorite psychic, come to play.*"

CHAPTER TWENTY-SIX

AMARA breezed through the portal into a dark chamber with an ancient presence. The magic of this place radiated raw energy. Pillars adorned this room with crude pictographs of demons in odd stories of old, forgotten artwork. The floor was made of dirt and stone. The walls were rough and rigid like a cave, yet the ceiling was polished porcelain marble. Glowing sigils were carved across the ceiling, forming strange spells.

"*Where are we?*" I whispered in Theodore's head, hoping the question alone would spark an involuntary answer from him.

Unfortunately, Theodore's mind was far too trained, too controlled, to share revelations unintentionally.

He tilted his head, following Amara obediently. "*You could learn all about this place if you delve a bit deeper into my thoughts.*"

I ignored his offer. Sitting in Theodore's mind was like dancing on a spiderweb above a tar pit. One misstep and I'd go from in danger to dead.

Around the corner of a collection of pillars sat Caleb and Tara. They were locked within the confines of a pentagram similar to the one that held Theodore when I found him weeks back in London. Only this pentagram was held together by a pillar at each of the five points.

"Does this mean I get a reprieve from my timeout?" Theodore asked, a sadistic smile on his face at seeing his sister and the boy he had attempted to kill on their knees.

"Why have you brought this boy, Moire?" Amara asked.

I knew that name from the list of Celestial Coven members I'd identified.

```
Name: Moire
Branch: Enchantment (Spell Craft)
```

That explained who was puppeteering Katherine, but it still didn't explain how the enchantment witch hijacked Katherine's mind.

"Don't tell me you've grown attached to this girl's life." Amara chuckled.

"It is not this witch's life that intrigues me, but the presence of this boy's existence." Katherine gestured—correction, Moire gestured—to Caleb. "Recognize your sacrifice?"

What?

The confusion and fear of that question spiked anxiety in Caleb and Tara as well. It was difficult to fully glean their thoughts while hiding in Theodore's head. Unlike them, his mind held intrigue over anything else.

"Impossible," Amara said rather flippantly.

"I know the abomination's magical frequency," Moire said, dehumanizing Caleb's very existence. "Who do you think coordinated your arrangement with Hell?"

Amara stared into Caleb's frantic green eyes.

"How is the goddess to ascend if you don't fulfill your arrangement?" Moire asked, accusatory and demanding.

"I do not understand." Amara tilted her head, studying Caleb, taking in his every feature. "The old gods never showed displeasure with my sacrifice. They didn't call out and demand a correction."

"Why would they?" Moire snapped. "Your failure would be more entertaining. Our failure."

"So, this is my dead baby brother?" Theodore asked, cutting right to the question dancing in everyone's mind.

Caleb stared wide-eyed in stunned confusion. Tara went to speak, but her mind was a hurricane of questions.

I supposed Caleb looked somewhat like Theodore and Tara, but not that much. None of this made any sense.

"There is only one answer." Amara opened a blue portal, dragging a body through. "Tobi deceived me."

Tobias Whitlock's corpse collapsed on the ground in front of Amara.

"Dad," Tara spoke softly, choking up at the sight of his body splayed out.

"I always knew he was soft," Amara said. "But I had no idea he'd go to such lengths to fool me."

"And you wish to waste time clarifying with him?" Moire had a pointed expression, visibly annoyed with Amara.

"I do," Amara replied. "The more answers I have, the more likely I will be able to rectify this error with the old gods above and the demons below."

Moire huffed.

"Prepare the necessary spell," Amara commanded of Moire, who reluctantly flipped through the pages of her grimoire.

"What are you doing, old hag?" Theodore asked.

Amara responded by snapping her fingers and dropping Theodore to his knees. The crack of bone sent a sharp ache through me. Clearly, I connected too much too soon to Theodore's mind. I needed to be cautious, avoid sinking too deeply.

"This makes some sense, though," Amara said while Moire whispered a spell. "I believed the old gods simply worked slowly when cleansing the world of branchless tragedies. When in truth, they'd simply never received the proper tribute."

"Wait, what?" Caleb asked. "I'm the reason—"

"You're not the source of branchless witches," Amara clarified. "Their diseased presence is the price of keeping all of Hell out of this dimension. Sadly, with magic mostly cut off from our world, too many are born weak and worthless, such as yourself."

Amara's cutting comment dug deeper into Caleb than any mean word about branchless witches ever had. So much of this overwhelmed him, unable to wrap his head around being related to Tara, being an abomination meant for sacrifice, being adopted by a mother who left when he was four, raised by grandparents who lied to him his entire life. Unless they didn't know. Who knew? Was this true? How was it possible?

"You were merely meant to serve as a cure to the cancer those witches bring to our world," Amara continued. "Powerless, useless, broken things. You were supposed to put an end to that when gifted to Hell."

Caleb's face turned a stark, ghostly white. "Gifted to Hell?"

"Of course," Amara continued. "An abomination such as yourself was only brought into this world to descend into Hell. And as you descend, the goddess shall ascend."

"You're disgusting," Tara spoke with pure hatred for her mother and abject horror for Moire's actions.

The enchantment witch controlling Katherine used a knife to carve open Tobias' chest, then reached inside and pumped his heart, still chanting some spell.

"Don't you see, Tara? This thing is the source of your stagnant troubles." Amara described Caleb as a thing, delight in her venomous green eyes. "I believed your father's poor tutelage led to your slow understanding of your gifts. It is simply because the abomination still walks this world."

"Stop calling him that," Tara shouted, the effects of her Banshee's Wail cracked the air around her.

It wasn't enough to break her free from the pentagram trap, but perhaps if Tara applied more of her magic, she could overpower the confinement.

"You'll see." Amara smiled at Tara. "When we properly fulfill the ritual, the old gods will bestow their blessings on you, and your magic will amplify a thousand times over."

"I don't give a fuck about being your stupid goddess," Tara screamed, cracking another layer of the barrier containing her and Caleb.

"If you were stronger now, not held back by that thing you were forced to share a womb with, you could break this barrier now." Amara tapped her fingers along the cracks, more amused by Tara's efforts than concerned by the potential threat.

Caleb sank into himself, barely comprehending the unearthed revelations of his existence. Never in his life had he felt so truly useless, but knowing his breathing held back Tara, held back thousands more. It devastated him. For so long, Caleb had believed that if he worked hard, he could achieve so much. Now, he questioned every choice, every desire.

Katherine's eyes rolled to the back of her head as Moire chanted louder, running her bloody fingers over her face. The droplets moved of their own accord, following the guidance of this bizarre ritual, and formed bloody symbols across Katherine's cheeks.

"*This is necromancy,*" I whispered.

"*How dare she?*" Theodore's nostrils flared, contempt and fury ate away at him as he believed his father was being granted a second chance.

"*That's not how necromancy works,*" I clarified. "*There is no true resurrection, no second chance.*"

After losing Finn, I scoured the world a hundred times over researching ways to bring him back, to fight against my grief and avoid ever having to face the horrors of his absence.

Necromancy didn't bring the dead back to life, so much as it turned the corpse into a puppet for whatever memories were stored in the body. They were just animated, rotten flesh that could parrot old times.

In the countries where they'd legalized necromancy, people went to great lengths to resurrect their loved ones. They'd use rejuvenation magics to keep the corpses healthy and life-like; they'd use necromancy to keep as many memories as possible intact; they'd use enchantments to keep the memories from deteriorating. The longer a corpse rotted, the more memories faded away.

It was a foolish endeavor, the most desperate attempt to hold onto their lost loved ones. I couldn't fault them, having come close to considering the rituals and practices, but never having anywhere near the funds for such abominable magic.

Tobias' eyes glowed with a black hue, and his jaw cracked as he opened it wide to wheeze a pitiful breath of life into his corpse.

"Tobi, it seems you kept a secret from me."

"Many, my love," he gasped with a foul echo of something sinister crawling inside to help utter the words.

"You didn't kill the abomination."

"Tried," Tobias wheezed. "Theodore was far too crafty, surviving despite my best efforts to cleanse the world of his rot."

That cut deep inside the infected wounds of Theodore's soul. He'd always known his father despised him, but to see this resurrected corpse confuse the abomination Amara referenced as Theodore, purely because he knew his father found him utterly disgusting.

"I am referring to the Slave King of Hell," Amara snapped.

That horrifying moniker sent a shiver through Caleb. This title of king, of slave, of Hell itself belonged to him, and he had no idea what it meant. What it truly meant. Was he supposed to rule over the demons? Was he meant to serve beneath them? Would he reign or suffer if Amara completed this wretched ritual?

He wouldn't have to find out those answers. I'd kill her the instant an opportunity presented itself.

"*You and me both, friend.*" Theodore lifted his gaze to the ceiling, his haunting blue eyes turned a bit glossy, but any sadness that touched his heart vanished just as quickly.

"I couldn't sacrifice, Tate," Tobias' corpse spoke with a soft fondness. "He was my baby boy."

Amara scoffed. "You named it."

The vulnerability of his words and the lack of protection his mind held as a mere living corpse opened his thoughts to me. They were fragmented, already stained with bile and rot, but some came in crystal clear.

Flashes of an exhausted Amara, pained and crying as she delivered her children. A sweaty, exhausted mother holding her small babe, the infant who held her heart. She cradled baby Tara with a softness I'd never seen on the cruel witch's face.

However, when Tobias presented his baby boy, Caleb, she turned away, refusing to acknowledge him.

"I took him to the Gate of Hell," Tobias continued. "I followed the ritual as you commanded. When the envoy arrived, these demons stepped into our world, hatred and filth, and they dared to take my child."

Amara glowered.

"I banished them, then sealed the Gate."

"Leaving me none the wiser." Amara tsked. "And you hid him under my nose?"

"Found a branchless witch who wanted a child," Tobias said. "Came from a family of branchless witches. Provided an altered birth certificate with a new date. Kept him in Chicago. Good place to hide him. He was close enough to cloak if you came looking, far enough to avoid suspicion."

Caleb listened intently, haunted by more questions than answers. There were few things he remembered about his mother, but he very clearly recalled the day she left him.

"It's just not working out," Caleb's mother had said, tousling his hair. *"It's not you, it's me. I'm just not cut out for the mommy thing."*

Christ. The way Caleb's mother abandoned him came across like a bad breakup line. It'd never haunted him before, finding joy with grandparents who showered him with love. He'd also believed in offering people grace when they had shortcomings. The way he saw her abandonment as a shortcoming instead of a failure astonished me. But now he believed himself the cause of her leaving.

"Do you regret it?" Caleb asked, calling out to Tobias. "Not sacrificing me?"

My heart dropped, wanting desperately to call out to Caleb and reassure him here and now, but I only had one chance to surprise Amara. If I took a misstep now, losing the opportunity of an advantage, he and Tara would suffer for my error.

Caleb craved an answer from Tobias, knowing so little of the man, but understanding he possessed a cruel streak. He thought so little of branchless witches, he'd pushed Tara to her limits to master her many magics, and Caleb sank into this despair that maybe the world would've been better if he'd been given to Hell.

"Never," Tobias wheezed. "Tate is a Whitlock. Destined for greatness. I mostly watched from afar, careful and cautious."

It became clear from the memories soaked in this corpse that Tobias sent Tara to Gemini specifically because he learned of Caleb's interest in the academy. Had he pulled strings to get them assigned to the same homeroom coven?

"Tate did so well on his own," Tobias said with a crack of his jaw as his body struggled to function. "Perfected a root magic. Excelled in an academy surrounded by branches far superior. Never deterred. Barely required my help to get into Gemini, whereas Tara required a significant endowment for her acceptance."

Caleb was stunned to learn he hadn't earned his place in Gemini Academy. Tobias Whitlock had bought it.

That was a lie. Even if Tobias nudged, he must've done so incredibly discreetly. Caleb earned his place. He fought day in and day out to prove he deserved to attend Gemini.

I wanted to reach out and strangle that corpse, slap these memories back to wherever Tobias was rotting. How dare he diminish Caleb's hard work?

"I even took Amara's proxy for Theodore, found real use for the doctor."

"Kendall?" Amara asked with a small smile, probably reminiscing about how she had slaughtered the woman for leading Theodore astray. "You pushed for her branchless research to what end?"

"To give Tate a branch of his own one day," Tobias answered. "He is sophisticated, stellar without a branch, so I imagine he would do truly great things if gifted with the Whitlock inheritance of power. Magic which is rightfully—"

"Oh, shut the fuck up, Tobi." Amara severed the connection, lighting Tobias' corpse on fire, nearly burning Katherine in the process.

"Don't do that," Moire snapped. "You could've ignited me."

"Please, you'd just find a new body." Amara waved a dismissive hand.

Theodore flicked his attention onto Tara, who sat completely still, absorbing this revelation.

"*Well, well, well, tragic little Tara.*" He smirked.

"What will we do with the abomination?" Moire asked.

"Sacrifice it, of course," Amara answered. "I will wait for the right constellation and perform the ritual. Perhaps offer a few additional souls as compensation for Tobi's crass behavior. The delay, the deaths of the demon envoy. They will be grateful to finally have their rightful Slave King of Hell, but this will require a delicate touch."

"Enough of this bullshit," Tara shouted, shadows shattering her barrier.

That was what drew Theodore's gaze. He'd noticed his sister slip her shadows into the cracks of the barrier that hid the golden hue of her warding magic. Now that the barrier had burst, the golden glow of her sealing magic revealed itself on the symbols of the pentagram.

Simply amazing.

Tara had come so far with her branches.

"You leave me no choice, Mother." Tara stepped in front of Caleb, who was still kneeling on the ground in dismay and disbelief. "I will end your life here and now before I allow you to hurt Caleb or anyone else."

"Bold words from a broken goddess." Amara craned her neck, tilting her hat in the process, and taking in the sight of her daughter with pure pride. "Don't worry, my sweet. Mommy will fix you."

CHAPTER TWENTY-SEVEN

TARA didn't hesitate for a second, immediately buffering Caleb with a golden aura meant to shield him from damage, while she lunged ahead. Sinking into the floor with her intangibility magic, Tara all but vanished until she reappeared behind Amara with shadowed tendrils lashing out.

Amara spun around, defending herself with cosmic light. The two clashed again, light versus darkness. But Tara added an icy chill to her shadows, doing everything in her power to close the distance.

Her mind was steady, unafraid of the battle, of her mother, of unleashing the full extent of her branches. I'd never seen Tara move with such confidence.

"*You could help,*" I thought, pleading with Theodore.

He tugged at his enchanted collar. "*Never involve oneself in family squabbles, I always say.*"

"Moire, detain the goddess." Amara weaved around Tara's strikes, barely avoiding fatal blows.

Still, I expected Amara to put up a greater fight. Perhaps she held back because she didn't want to harm her daughter.

"*Doubtful,*" Theodore mused, plopping into a crisscross position to observe the fight. "*She's probably just drained from her brief battle with the top ten.*"

Theodore revealed flashes of Amara appearing before the top ten witches, detaining them all in her Oceanic Collapse magic before releasing the vampires to possess them. Christ, if she unleashed that onto Tara, this fight would end in seconds.

"Get the hell out of my friend's body!" Tara raged, hurling a flurry of shadow tendrils at Moire, aiming to restrain Katherine's body entirely.

Moire muttered a spell, and the shadows exploded into autumn leaves. They hit the ground and crumbled away to nothingness.

"Get out of Katherine!" Caleb swung a fist, full force, and stopped before colliding with Katherine's chest. "Now!"

Without hesitation or delay, he cast banishment. If only he realized she wasn't a demon possessing Katherine but another witch who'd somehow wedged her way into Katherine's mind.

Moire screeched, furious and in utter agony, nearly toppling over before Amara intervened and telekinetically threw Caleb back.

"Caleb," Katherine said in a fog.

"Shut up, girl." Moire slapped her hands on Katherine's temples and forced her back down into the depths of her own mind.

"Sloppy, Moire."

"It's not my fault," she hissed. "That abomination did something to my magic. Made it fuzzy for a moment."

That was it. He'd struck out with a perfected banishment. If he had more time to focus his casting on Moire, he'd definitely defeat her, but with Amara playing interference, that wouldn't happen.

I knew what needed to be done.

"*Don't go,*" Theodore whispered. "*Let's enjoy the show.*"

I abandoned his mind and raced toward Moire.

"*I'm going to get Katherine back. You two hold off Amara until I return.*" I linked to Caleb and Tara momentarily.

"*Mr. Frost?*" Tara thought. "*Are others on the way?*"

"*It's just me for now,*" I replied. "*We're going to have a hell of a fight, but I believe we can stop Amara together.*"

With that, I dropped into Katherine's mind, preventing Moire from assisting in the battle. I could only hope Caleb and Tara held their own until I returned.

The intrusion came with a strong pulse of telepathy. I might lack the strength to kick Moire out of Katherine's head with ease, but I certainly put a stop to her puppeteering. Outside, Katherine's body stood completely immobilized, and I wouldn't allow it to move again until Katherine took control over her autonomy once more.

Inside her inner core, I realized why Katherine and Caleb got along so well. They had the same mindset, using a library to sort their thoughts and memories. Very analytic.

While Caleb's library revolved around dates and magic types and pro-files of all the witches he studied, Katherine's focused more on the source of magic itself. Rows upon rows of books contained enchantment spells Katherine had learned over the years.

The library was divided into sections. Enchantment spells Katherine had learned from other witches, enchantment spells Katherine had created herself, magics that existed without an enchantment spell variation. Those would likely be the rare branches that held too many unique complexities to mimic, like Gladiatrix's branch. Sure, Katherine could and had created enchantments to enhance her strength and speed, but it was unlikely that anyone could create a spell to match such unparalleled power.

I made my way through this massive library, searching for hints of Katherine's consciousness and traces of lingering memories, but finding nothing except barren aisles.

There were two minds in here—three, including myself—but aside from the faintest of touches, I couldn't locate either of them.

"That's it," I muttered. "Location spell."

Outside the mind, I was just a telepath, but inside the mind, my magic could do quite literally whatever I willed it to do. If I wanted to cast divination, then suddenly my branch allowed for such things.

Conjuring a collection of twinkling lights, I ordered them to guide me to Katherine. They scrambled in every direction, searching between the shelves and far behind in the shadows of Katherine's mind.

"Find her consciousness," I clarified. "I want to see Katherine, not her thoughts or memories. Her being."

The flurry of lights returned, circling around me again and again until they carried a small picture book.

Oh, fuck me.

I grabbed the book, read through it, and found it resembled a story about Katherine. She was the type who tucked her memories into stories. Well, she didn't choose it. Most people had no idea how their inner core worked. It just functioned for them.

Flipping through the pages, I read about the stick figure version of Katherine who always smiled and cheered and prayed for the best of everyone around her.

"Seriously?" I flipped through the pages, waiting for an opportunity.

The twinkling lights blinked, and I knew now was my chance. I jumped into the picture book, falling further into Katherine's mind, and navigating my way through a chamber of memories.

This book was one of many tales, each leading to the same minefield of memories. A collection of her past pushed together in a bizarre style. Her mind was difficult to navigate, but I found myself led to a recent memory.

The lights of my spell guided me to a moment between Katherine and her mother.

"This book is rather special to our family," Katherine's mother explained.

Her red hair was stringy, and her face was exceptionally pale. More so than I'd seen during parent-teacher conferences. Exhaustion weighed heavily on her eyes, and her lips were pulled into a tight, rigid smile.

"I want you to have this grimoire." Her hands trembled a bit, nervously clutching the ancient grimoire Katherine received for her internship.

"She doesn't want to share it," a young voice said.

I turned to find a small version of Katherine observing her own thoughts, her own memories. How astounding.

"If I paid attention, real attention, I would've seen the effects the grimoire had on my mommy." Katherine jotted notes in a pink unicorn-themed notebook. "All I thought about was how cool it'd be."

She was lost in her own mind, reverted to a childish form of herself.

"What happened to you?"

"The book," she replied, pausing the memory right before her mother handed her—the teen version of Katherine—the grimoire. "I accepted it, greedily read the spells, and gave over my body to this witch."

"How?"

"A spell triggered purely by reading the words." The young Katherine kicked her feet against the ground. "Such a rookie mistake."

"It wasn't a mistake," I said. "You couldn't have known."

"I should've."

I knelt down to meet Katherine at eye level. "I know you're frightened. I know you've been through so much already."

"I'm not scared." The small girl clutched her notebook, using it as a shield over her chest.

"It's okay to be scared," I said. "Fear can protect us from rushing into something dangerous. And fear is proof we have something to live for."

Katherine averted her gaze, thoughts twirling around the many memories outside this storybook I'd fallen into.

"I need your help," I said. "Help me fight off the witch keeping you from living your life."

"The magic is too strong." Katherine trembled. "The spell craft enchantments are at a level I didn't even know was possible."

"I'll let you in on a little secret, inside the mind, belief is the strongest magic." I stood back up. "Psychics know that more than anyone else, but I promise if you believe in your magic, it won't falter."

She hesitated, mind cautiously considering, but finally, the belief trickled through her little by little.

Katherine grew back into herself, transforming from the small, frightened child into the brave young woman I'd taught for the last several years.

"Impressive," a raspy voice called out from the shadows.

"It's her." Katherine trembled.

"I'm here with you." I planted a hand on her shoulder, easing the fear building inside Katherine.

Her knees quaked, but she finally steadied herself.

"How sweet," the raspy voice called out. "I thought my trap would be enough to detain you, telepath."

Moire stepped out of the shadows, revealing herself. Only she presented herself as an older version of Katherine. She wore an elegant dress, something Victorian style with a gothic touch. The dress itself was strapless, exposing her shoulders and cleavage. Her light brown skin was covered in tattooed symbols.

"Mortal bodies are dull, but I do what I can with their limiting attributes." Moire ran her fingers through her long black hair that fell well past her waist.

"Let's kick her the hell out of your head."

CHAPTER TWENTY-EIGHT

"THIS mind is saturated in my magic," Moire declared. "Here, I reign supreme."

"You should know better than most, constructing those futile telepath traps that when it comes to the mind, I am the one who reigns."

"Hubris will be your downfall." Moire summoned tentacles of fire, ice, and electricity. Each element blazed with power.

"Putting your hands on my student will be your downfall." I waved a hand, conjuring a gust to smother the protective tentacles. "Katherine, this is your mind. Anything you will into belief will aid you. Trust your magic, trust yourself."

"Right." She nodded nervously, still shaken by having her autonomy stripped away by this vicious witch.

"The girl was but a tool, one with a potent enchantment branch, but I've brought down witches ten times her level."

"You haven't faced anyone of my level." Katherine took a shaky breath and whispered a spell, summoning the same elemental tentacles as Moire. "Just as you were in my head, I was in yours."

"Learn much did you?"

"Memorized every wicked spell, from the foulest constructs to the most deadly of assaults." Katherine waved her arms in Moire's direction, commanding her elemental tentacles to lash out.

As Moire leapt away, I stomped my foot onto the ground, willing the earth to reach out and stop her. Clawed hands made of mud and gravel grabbed at the witch, each one slowing Moire's escape, stalling her evasion.

Water and fire collided, coiling around the witch in a steamy explosion, followed by a dozen other elemental bombardments. Katherine didn't relent for a second, channeling more magic into the spell and binding Moire within a hundred elemental tentacles.

"You two truly believe that will be enough to stop a witch of the Celestial Coven," Moire said from behind us.

I whipped around, only to get struck back with a powerful pulse of telekinesis.

"You read my spells, girl." Moire breathed a piece of twine between her fingers, extending her hands far apart to show the length of the thread. "But you have no understanding of spell craft magic. We are creation itself. The greatest of all magics. It is I alone who keeps the Celestial Coven safe from threats; it is I who conjures the necessary craftsmanship these witches require to be the supreme deities they aspire to be once more."

Katherine clapped her hands, creating a gray spark between her palms. It darted ahead, sizzling along the thread Moire held until the magic in her spell fizzled out. Did Katherine just use a spell to copy Kenzo's branch? She must've done that without his permission because no way was Kenzo going to sit down and assist Katherine in that spell.

"I will admit, you have some top-tier spells," Katherine said with a smile. "More elite than anything I've ever laid my eyes on. It took me weeks to decipher the codex you used in your grimoire. And when I finally did, I still couldn't comprehend the levels of some of your creations."

Spell craft allowed an enchantment witch to write their own spells, speak them into existence, but a witch only had so much magic to channel. Katherine's mind whispered ideas to exploit Moire's energy, drain her, and bring her down.

"You really believe she's at her limit?" I linked our minds.

"Nowhere close," Katherine replied. *"But I learned something about her while she was controlling me."*

"What's that?"

"I just need you to distract her long enough for me to regain control of my body."

Of course, even with Katherine's mind made her own again, her body was still entranced by Moire's grasp.

"I'll kick her out of your head."

"No." Katherine glared at Moire. *"I don't want her getting away."*

Perhaps Moire's body was far away, tucked somewhere safe. If I expelled her now, Katherine would be free, but the witch would have the advantage of an ambush. With Tara and Caleb already fighting against Amara, I couldn't risk letting Moire escape to counterstrike later.

"Okay." I cracked my neck. *"What do you need me to do?"*

"Hold the bitch back while I work on a new spell." Katherine dropped to her knees, immediately going to work, tracing symbols into the dirt.

"Oh, little one, I'm tempted to let you write out whatever sad spell you think will offer you victory." Moire sauntered toward us. "The devastation when you realize you're up against someone far superior to you will be delicious."

"How about you focus on me?" I said, teleporting behind Moire and swinging a fist.

Before I connected, she created a green shield, protecting herself.

"Nice barrier." I commanded the shield to bend inward, wrapping around Moire and slowly crushing her. "Anything you can do, I can manipulate. You might have a million spells, but I have a billion bizarre thoughts."

Moire screamed, creating a skull-crushing headache that shook my focus. Once free, she flew away, hurling fireballs at me. I smacked them back toward her, commanding they take on a lion's form. The fiery cats lunged for Moire, roaring furiously with the full intention of tearing open the witch's jugular.

But Moire hissed a spell, calling forth rain clouds. The lions roared as they were engulfed by a watery death. The droplets splashed down on me, harmless at first, but almost instantly followed by a painful pinch.

"Fucking hell." I brushed away the watery monsters.

Moire had used a spell to make it rain spiders. Spiders made of goddamn water. The more I destroyed, telekinetically waved away, the more that gathered into larger water spiders. Soon, a dozen spiders half my size surrounded me.

I willed myself to relax, ignoring the chittering hisses of these watery monstrosities. Ben's constant curious comments popped into my head. Ever since his trip to the animal shelter, since getting that damn dog, he's been obsessed with all things animals. The kid would probably end up a veterinarian or zookeeper or running his own haven for untethered familiars.

Unable to remember the exact origins of the predator, I focused less on specifics and more on sheer force. If Moire wanted to create water spiders, then I'd create a horde of electrical wasps. Ben mentioned they hunted spiders to feed their young. He also mentioned they're vicious.

My manifested magical attack buzzed through Katherine's mind, tearing apart the spiders until nothing remained. I directed the horde to strike Moire.

Thousands upon thousands stung the witch, sparks of electricity stunned her, and soon she screamed an anguished defeat, consumed by the wrath of the wasp horde.

"Are you done with the dramatics?" I asked, listening intently to where she might reveal herself.

"I thought you'd enjoy the flair." She leapt from my shadow, a blade in her hand.

I spun around, catching her arm, but tumbling backward. We crashed onto the ground and rolled around, each fighting desperately to avoid the blade's edge.

"You do so enjoy murdering my coven."

I fought against the blade, panicking as the tip pressed to my neck. Dying in the mind wasn't a true death, but it might as well be. As a manifested extension, if I died here, I wouldn't be able to help. I wouldn't be able to protect my students. I wouldn't be able to end this coven.

"You killed my best friend," Moire screamed, tracing the blade's tip along my scar.

How poetic, planning to end me the way I'd damn near died at Theodore's hands.

"Sorry about your psychic witches," I groaned, bending Moire's hand and forcing the blade away. "But they put their hands on Milo; there was no coming back for them after that."

And while the Global Guild, along with every other government agency, wanted to detain the Celestial Coven witches if possible, I would never go back and change my decision. I stood by it, proudly, knowing those horrid sisters deserved to be sent to their deaths, if only to free the unwilling mind of their host body, and prevent a thousand more to follow in such a cruel fate.

"The Sisters Three?" Moire scoffed. "You think I give a damn about those petty witches."

I crinkled my brow, perplexed and also exhausted, fighting to keep Moire off me.

"I speak of my sister, my daughter, my creation." Moire lifted the blade high, snatching it free from my grasp. "You killed her like she meant nothing."

A flash of my battle at Gemini Academy appeared on the surface of Moire's mind, completely unguarded. The anguish of losing her loved one struck when I ripped the bone staff magic from Amara. I shattered it, releasing the many souls bound to it.

"One of the fallen members of the coven," I said, out of breath. "When I released them, you lost your loved one."

"No, you fool." Moire laughed lightly. "Those fragments held no memories, only magic."

"She's speaking of the staff itself," Katherine said, standing up again, and holding her hands in a weird position, almost as if she held an invisible object. "The staff was sentient, much like Moire has become over the centuries."

"What?" I blinked, more confused by every passing word.

"That ends now." Katherine pulled her hands apart in a ripping motion. Moire screamed, her body shredding apart before me.

"What the hell?"

"She's the grimoire," Katherine explained, continuing her tearing actions. "Now that I have control over my body again, I'm ripping her apart one spell at a time."

Moire's bloody and broken body began falling apart like paper sent through the shredder.

She wasn't a witch with enchantment magic. Moire was the enchantment magic, a sentient spell gone awry. And the skull staff that Amara once wielded was Moire's creation, an attempt to breathe life into another spell, conjure a living being out of magical energy.

I forced myself up, furious and disgusted by this creature. She reminded me far too much of my doppler, the stray persona that nearly ruined my life.

"I will not be defeated." Moire's severed limbs and broken bits fell away, leaving only a string of symbols that took on the form of a giant beast.

"I've had enough of sentient magic to last ten lifetimes," I said, unleashing as much telepathy as I could spare to shatter the enraged consciousness of this living grimoire.

"I am the most powerful witch in the world," Moire screeched, bleeding ink and shattering nearby memories.

They wouldn't be gone permanently, so long as I had a chance to mend Katherine's mind later, but if Moire kept this up, she'd leave Katherine a broken shell.

"Enough of this." I used all the magic at my disposal to contain Moire's wrath.

"I created more spells than any enchantment witch before me," Moire roared. "I offered the Celestial Coven greatness. I am far more than any pillar. I am the knowledge itself. Unstoppable."

"How's that superiority taste?" Katherine asked, holding a flame between her hands. "Is it as delicious as you thought?"

I created a buffer long enough for Katherine to chant a new spell, one which lit Moire ablaze. As the grimoire burned outside, Moire burned in here. Soon her beastly form crumbled to cinders and floating ash.

"Get the hell out of my head," Katherine wheezed, fully exhausted, but standing triumphant against a member of the Celestial Coven.

"Good job," I said with a small smile and a nod of approval. "You were amazing, Katherine."

"I wouldn't have been able to do this without your help, Mr.—er, Enchanter Frost."

"Either is fine," I said. "Now, let's go help the others."

"Right." Katherine nodded. "I might have the perfect spell to give them an edge against The True Witch."

"Good." I carried my consciousness toward the surface of Katherine's mind, prepared to do all I could to assist in Amara's defeat.

When Katherine fully awoke, she stared at the burned grimoire, torn and scorched pages scattered all around her. All signs of Moire's consciousness had vanished. Definitely a cruel fate, but she didn't leave us much choice in the matter. I wasn't about to let an evil grimoire shatter Katherine's mind and leave her body a living puppet.

"No," Katherine whispered in absolute horror.

Her petrified expression nearly locked me in place, lost in her fear. I turned to see Caleb and Tara defeated and unconscious at Amara's feet.

"We're too late."

CHAPTER TWENTY-NINE

"WHAT *do we do?"* Katherine trembled, knees ready to buckle any second. "I can't fight her on my own. I can't—"

"You aren't alone." I kept my manifested form linked to her mind, conserving as much of my remaining strength as possible.

My hope was that, with Moire gone, it'd limit Amara's access to those tattooed spells she always utilized.

"I can get past her guard," I thought. *"I'll shatter her mind while you trap her."*

"She's got a dozen different protection spells at the ready." Katherine eyed Amara's tattooed chest and shoulders. *"No way I break through all of them in one go."*

"They might be on the fritz since Moire is gone."

"Doubtful." Katherine shook her head. *"These are prepared spells. The magic and energy to create them are already in place. They literally only require a simple activation trigger."*

"Dammit."

"With Moire gone, The True Witch might not get new spells anytime soon, but she still has full access to everything else."

"Then I'll go in and shatter her mind—what parts I can." I prepared to

leap out of Katherine's head. *"While I hold her back, you grab Caleb and Tara and get as far away from this place as possible."*

Amara turned her gaze toward us, piercing green eyes falling to the burned grimoire.

"Impressive, little girl." Amara smirked, no sign of sadness or empathy for her fallen coven mate. "Few can hold their own against such a titan of knowledge."

Katherine took a step back, frightened and suddenly struggling to recall any spell she'd ever memorized.

"Did you do this all on your own?" Amara asked, taking strong strides toward us. Her heels clicked against the cave floor. "Or did a pesky telepath assist you?"

Her eyes glowed momentarily, casting some spell likely meant to locate me.

"He seems to be everywhere," Amara said with a chuckle. "Like an omnipotent gnat, always there to irritate me."

Amara flicked her wrist, opening a blue portal behind Katherine.

"Shame about Moire. She'll be difficult to replace." Amara waved her hand, telekinetically throwing Katherine into the portal. "If you survive the destruction I have planned for your city, little girl, I will find you and extend an invitation. The Celestial Coven could use a strong enchantment witch."

Katherine fell through the doorway, engulfed by blistering blue lights, and a whoosh that rattled with the force of an earthquake. This was not the calm travel of before. It seemed the doorway required Amara's presence to keep the portal safe. Katherine crashed against the walls of the portal several times, shouting in pain, but unable to control her movements in this place.

When she finally fell through, she returned to Whitlock Estate, where Tobias and his familiar Titus lay dead on the floor beside her.

The portal doorway must've been preprogrammed, not offering Amara much choice in the matter.

"No," Katherine cried. "It can't end like this."

"There's nothing we can do."

"I'm not losing them, not because I..." Katherine choked on her words, but not her thoughts. Blame bounced in her head, guilt quickly consuming her. "I can fix this. I know I can. I'll fix this. I have to fix this."

She chanted a spell, creating blue sparks from where we fell out. Each verse ate away at what little magic she had left, making her vision blurry and her body numb. Still, she continued chanting, attempting to reopen the portal.

"*Stop,*" I insisted. "*Even if you open the portal, you can't keep it open for long.*"

"Long enough to step through." Katherine ground her teeth, channeling more magic into the sparks of the sealed portal.

"*And what if your spell fails halfway back?*" I asked. "*You could end up lost in some astral plane of existence.*"

Katherine ignored me.

"*What happens if you make it to the other side?*" I asked. "*The True Witch will not spare you a second time.*"

"I can't leave Caleb," Katherine cried. "Do you have any idea what she plans to do to him?"

"*I do.*"

"She's going to sacrifice him to demons," Katherine sobbed. "Open the Gate of Hell and throw him into it."

"*We'll stop her.*"

Amara mentioned requiring a constellation, something preordained for the ritual. She wouldn't kill him now. We had time to save him, to save Tara.

"This is all my fault." Katherine fell to her knees, magic completely drained, and emotions overwhelmed. "If I had never opened that book, never fallen for such a stupid trick, then Moire wouldn't have gotten in my head. If she hadn't gotten into my head, I would've been able to help. Instead, she used me to capture Caleb, to unleash horrible witches and spells onto the city. I caused this."

"*You didn't cause any of this,*" I said, reminded of my own guilt for every shortcoming I blamed myself for over the years. "*You are seventeen years old. You are an intern. You are not responsible for the actions of the Celestial Coven.*"

"I have to do something…"

"*And you will,*" I said. "*We all will. Soon. We need to regroup and come up with a plan, and then we'll strike back in full force. This isn't over. Amara won't harm Caleb. I refuse to allow it. We'll stop her once and for all.*"

Even as I spoke these words and pushed all the belief I had out into the world, doubt crept into my mind.

"*I have to go, Katherine. My magic is almost completely gone, but when I connect with my core self, I'll send help to get you.*"

Katherine finally took in her surroundings, realizing the horrid place she'd landed. Wiping away her tears, she sniveled and did her best to stay strong.

It broke my heart seeing Katherine so devastated, knowing I'd failed so horribly. Even as the last fragments of magic holding my manifested form together crumbled away, I couldn't shake free from the guilt that followed me back to my core self.

I stood beside Wadsworth, connecting with these new memories and seeing how much had unfolded after sending a manifestation to the Whitlock Estate. If I'd gone there myself, perhaps it would've made a difference. Instead, I flew to Milo's side, watching Wadsworth work while there wasn't a goddamn thing for me to do here.

Even now, they loaded Milo into an ambulance, and I stood by uselessly.

I should've gone to the Whitlocks myself. Sending a manifestation was so fucking stupid. Now Tara and Caleb were captured. Amara had all the pieces she wanted. Her goddess, her knight, and her sacrifice.

Composing myself as best I could, I informed the nearby Global Guild reps about the incident at the Whitlock Estate, sending them to retrieve Katherine, and hopefully any possible clues on a lead. Then I flew to the hospital where they'd taken Milo and the top ten Global Guild members, now that that battle had finally concluded with all the devils being exorcised.

As the dust settled, the city had survived, but at what cost? Pain and devastation radiated throughout Chicago, minds suffering with the anguish of loss, of death. The Celestial Coven came in full force and nearly destroyed us, yet their only goal was to grab Tara. They'd laid waste to our guilds and defeated the top ten witches of America with ease.

I had no idea what came next, but I wasn't ready for it. I had to be ready. There were too many lives at stake for me to fail again.

CHAPTER THIRTY

THE city mourned in a way I'd never experienced. Grief had a stranglehold on so many minds, it locked me in their sorrow. I found myself spiraling, every breath a reminder of the sadness I fought after losing Finn.

After the Celestial Coven's attack, no one felt safe any longer. They'd struck with a handful of witches, several enthralled demons, and a horde of fiends. Chicago braced for the next assault, unsure how we'd fare a second time.

Thirty-eight enchanters had laid down their lives defending this city. Four guild masters died protecting their people. The minds of Cerberus cried out, devastated by Campbell's loss. A strict woman, certainly, but one who'd earned the respect of her enchanters but refused to settle, to compromise, to accept defeat. She died victorious, even if she never saw the end of that battle.

I spent my days at the hospital during Milo's recovery. Wadsworth's magic had worked wonders to prevent long-term nerve damage or the need for surgery, but Milo's injuries still required intensive care.

He grieved the most during these somber days. This was no victory; his battle held no successes in his mind. Protecting the city from ten devils didn't matter to him because knowing so many others died defending Chicago meant he'd failed elsewhere. Milo burdened himself with planning for the best possible outcomes, yet this battle had turned into an absolute failure.

Death at every corner. Tara and Caleb abducted. Amara one step closer to unveiling her world-shattering plan.

Grief consumed me from everywhere during these first few days. I clung to the saddest minds, the familiar minds, the minds of those I cared for the most. If I had to suffer this sadness, I would at least know how they fared.

Kenzo's rage was unbridled. All his rage went into a punching bag, enhanced by protective wards so the thing wouldn't break when struck with telekinesis or branch magics. The soothing aura of Gael's presence did nothing to elevate the hatred in Kenzo's heart. Day in and day out, Kenzo trained, planned, calculated, and thought back to every mistake he'd made.

Success? He saw none.

Unlocking a new aspect of his branch meant nothing because he couldn't control it. More to the point, he couldn't bask in this achievement knowing that he'd failed Caleb. He didn't know why they'd abducted his best friend; he only knew that Caleb was gone.

Every time Kenzo struck the punching bag, his thoughts fluttered back to something mean he'd said to Caleb. All he could remember was years of cruel teasing, heartless words, and bullying he'd never make amends for now. Kenzo grieved inside, sad and broken, but on the outside, he raged.

Gray static sizzled along the punching bag's protective wards, keeping the training tool intact.

"Goddammit." Kenzo spun through the air and kicked the punching bag with enough force to snap the tether holding it in place.

That hadn't been his goal. No, his goal was to use his black hex magic to completely disarm the punching bag. Then he'd use his white hex magic to amplify his magic and destroy the training tool.

Kenzo believed he couldn't do a single thing right. He panted, weary and exhausted, but refusing to stop. Only failures rested. Kenzo had spent enough time being a failure.

I believed a great deal of his newfound enhancement to his magic came from an emotional drive. His need to protect Gael sparked the release of hex magic to its greatest form. Now, instead of embracing his emotions, he worked to bury them, leaving only room for rage and self-hatred.

After things settled, calmed as best they could, I would reach out to Kenzo and help him train. I owed him that much. After all, so much of this failure rested on my shoulders. I should've stopped Amara when she attacked Gemini Academy. I should've tracked her down over the last few months and ended her. I should've been prepared for her assault on Chicago.

Kenzo didn't need to blame himself for Caleb's abduction. That blame fell to me.

Guilt consumed Yaritza over the last few days. Kraken Guild had been attacked by a few demons and so many fiends when the Celestial Coven struck. What had seemed like a truly devastating attack in the moment had turned out to be one of the lighter assaults.

Yaritza, Jamius, and Melanie had managed to take out a demon on their own. An ogre thrashing about the halls of Kraken. While their mentor raged against a demon of his own, they defended their enchanters back, and successfully did what so few could accomplish.

It should've been something for Yaritza to bask in, to brag about, but as the city mourned, her success felt ill-timed. It hurt to look back at the incident with pride, to see her role in it diminished because of the ultimate outcome.

She wasn't the only mind to feel this way. And she should've been proud of her accomplishments. While the city still suffered, it suffered less because of her success. I hoped she'd see that in time, understand that, and take pride in her accomplishment.

Wadsworth didn't give a damn about the devastating defeat. All he concerned himself with was tracking down The True Witch, following any lead, no matter how small. As he sucked a deep inhale of his cigarette, I found myself entranced by the aroma.

There was something so soothing about the first inhale after a hard day, something so satisfying about exhaling all my worries, and watching them waft in the air.

The harsh cough that followed Wadsworth's next deep inhale reeled me back in, reminding me why I let go of the habit. I didn't care about polluting my lungs, rotting my body, but the people I cared most about certainly did. Milo and Ben wouldn't want me smoking, and thus, I pushed the craving aside.

Taking in Wadsworth as a person, I realized that he was my life unfulfilled. He obsessed over tracking down The True Witch so much so that he pushed everyone in his life aside, buried his desires, and lost himself to this mission. I had to stop Amara, help save my students, but I couldn't lose myself in the process.

It'd taken damn near a lifetime to finally accept happiness. I couldn't sacrifice it all for a mission.

"Are you listening to a goddamn thing I'm saying, you stupid fucking telepath?"

I glowered in response, half-tempted to show him the full extent of my stupid telepathy.

"Yes," I said with a huff. "You want me to facilitate a meeting with Caleb's grandparents."

"No, moron." Wadsworth coughed, struggling to catch his breath, and I didn't hold mine in hopes he'd find the air he so desperately needed. "I...I already arranged the meeting. You are to use your telepathy to gather any necessary information."

"I doubt they know anything."

"There's only one way to find out." Wadsworth took off into the air, demanding that I follow.

Despite his frail body and constant state of exhaustion, his casting remained top-tier, and he flew through the streets at incredible speed. I struggled to keep up.

When we arrived at Caleb's home, I followed Wadsworth to the door, where he announced our arrival with a heavy knock.

The elderly Mrs. Huxley answered the door. She didn't recognize me, either, because my appearance had changed since the last parent-teacher conference or simply because she never expected her grandson's former homeroom teacher to knock on her door.

That, or perhaps she was simply lost in her worries. Mrs. Huxley's mind was in a frazzled state, lost in her grief for Caleb's disappearance, in her confusion as to why he was abducted, and not satisfied by the lack of clarification the Global Guild offered.

For the briefest of seconds, she let her spirits lift when she realized who Enchanter Wadsworth was.

"Did you find him?" she asked, a longing in her weary eyes.

"Apologies," Wadsworth said, clearing his throat. "We haven't, but I hoped perhaps you could speak with me, and we might learn more about Caleb and why this came about."

"What could we possibly tell you?" A stern, agitated voice called out from behind Mrs. Huxley.

Her husband stomped to the door, practically barring our entrance. He'd transformed all his worries into rage, directing them at the incompetence of the Global Guild. I couldn't rightfully argue against his anger. It was well placed. The Global Guild had failed. I had failed.

"Please," Wadsworth insisted. "Every tiny detail makes a difference."

That statement was meant to convince Caleb's grandparents, but was directed toward me. As they led us inside, Wadsworth's thoughts screamed at me to do my goddamn telepathic job and learn what I could from their minds.

It meant diving in deeper than normal. I wouldn't have to traipse through their inner cores, but I would need to delve past their surface thoughts, rooting through the in-between spaces. That kind of snooping was occasionally noticed, so I'd need to be cautious.

The cramped house was cluttered with children's toys and strewn about laundry. It made sitting in the living room very uncomfortable. Plus, it was clear they had pets. Cats, for certain, considering the palpable odor from the dirty litterbox.

Between their grief and general exhaustion, it seemed Caleb's grandparents had fallen behind on their home. They were in desperate need of retirement, but were forced to continue working so they could support themselves and their grandson. By the looks of things, more than just their grandson.

Most of their thoughts were hazy, muddled, and buried in decades of fogged-over memories. Not at all unusual considering their age. Still, their minds weren't guarded, and the fact that neither had any training with magic, it didn't seem they noticed my heavy-footed entrance as I dove into their minds.

They didn't know anything about Caleb's secret adoption, about The True Witch, or the Celestial Coven—and I certainly didn't want to be the one to inform them. All they knew was their daughter had a son, and she loved being a mother until the stress caught up to her.

Caleb's grandmother recalled the way her daughter retreated into herself in the weeks leading up to her walking out. Perhaps Caleb's mother struggled with the secret arrangement. Perhaps she expected more from Tobias Whitlock. Perhaps she simply became overwhelmed with motherhood.

It seemed all their children had these difficulties. Mr. and Mrs. Huxley had four children of their own. Caleb's mother, who left him at their doorstep when he was four, ran as far from Chicago as she could get.

Last they heard, she was in California, but that was nine years ago. She'd only reached out for a deposit on a place. During the twenty-minute call, she never once asked about Caleb, and when she realized her parents couldn't help her, the contact stopped altogether.

Christ. She was a real fucking prize. Tobias couldn't have found a real home for Caleb? All those connections, and he left Caleb here.

I swallowed hard at that, averting my gaze from the somber eyes staring back at me as Wadsworth remained calm and procedural. Caleb's grandparents were good people, they just didn't know much, aspire to much, or have much to offer. Still, they did their best to support Caleb's dreams.

They were just extremely worn down by time and obligations.

The mess in the house was contributed to by three other children currently at school. Apparently, Caleb helped around the house, from cleaning and cooking to babysitting. Working too—I remembered Caleb often took odd jobs to help cover bills and medications his grandparents needed.

As for their other three children, they were no help. It seemed Caleb's cousins were left with the grandparents after their mother was incarcerated, and from what I gathered, any father figures shared a similar fate or simply didn't exist in the kids' lives. Caleb's uncle only ever came around when he needed money or something to steal. And his one aunt who'd clawed her way out of the South Side had moved to the suburbs just outside the city and completely wrote off her family. Not that I could blame her, but I did pity the grandkids suffering from drama they never had a hand in.

I'd always known Caleb worked harder than most students, but I had no idea just how many things he juggled outside of his academics and magic training. Work, chores, children, elderly grandparents, deadbeat relatives, a shitty neighborhood, and a thousand other things he'd taken on from a young age and never complained about.

"We're not going to find any leads here." I shot Wadsworth a look, ensuring he paid attention to the thoughts I sent his way.

While I hadn't come any closer to finding Caleb or Tara, I wouldn't be deterred. I would do whatever it took to make sure they got a chance to live outside the dark shadow of The True Witch's fanatical obsession.

An angry depression whispered to me from afar. The spike of annoyance was a familiar wavelength, but the sadness clawing at every waking thought didn't resonate with what I'd experienced. Layla's mind, even in her worst state, never lacked confidence. She'd grown attached to Campbell in her short time as her intern, and watching the guild master die, knowing there was nothing she could do to prevent it—that struck Layla with more force than any attack.

"I'm leaving a tray out here for you," Vik called from the other side of Layla's door.

They'd stopped by a lot to check in on Layla, which she found utterly aggravating. In fact, Vik's little stops were the only time Layla dragged herself from depressed self-pity and into a mild state of aggravation.

Layla growled, indicating Vik need not cling to the door. Reluctantly, they left their cousin alone, fully intending to stop by later to check in. It seemed Layla's parents were out of the country, and as the only child in her family still living at home, that meant she had no one during this time.

No one except Vik.

Well, that wasn't entirely true.

Layla listened to the patter of Vik's steps become faint as they departed, but a familiar smell drew her attention. Levitating outside Layla's window was Amani. She held a bag with Layla's favorite snack and a tray container with two lattes.

Grudgingly, Layla dragged herself out of bed and opened the window. While several snide quips popped into her head, Layla merely blinked an annoyed response. Amani didn't speak. She simply handed her best friend the bag and climbed inside.

The pair sat on Layla's bed and ate their egg bites and blueberry bread in silence. Layla took a few sips of her drink, but didn't want the sad haze she'd felt all day to wash away, so she set the latte aside.

"I'm fine." Layla climbed under her covers and turned away from Amani.

"I know." Amani lay on top of the blanket but scooted closer to her friend. "Maybe I'm not."

Delicately, Amani placed a hand on Layla's shoulder, gently squeezing as her friend fought back tears. Layla rested a clawed hand on Amani's and let herself become enveloped by her sadness.

My mind wandered to the outskirts of the Whitlock Estate, drawn to the person ignoring his sadness in favor of chaos.

The barred gates weren't a bother for Gael or King Clucks as they levitated over the stone wall. Without delay, Gael went to a PIN pad station and typed in a passcode, clearly disarming any alarm protocols from triggering. All the employees patrolling these grounds might be gone or dead, but the border of the home was still lined with wards and enchantments meant to defend the property or alert authorities.

I was a bit perplexed that Tara had trusted Gael with literal security details, but I suppose I never fully understood their friendship.

Gael didn't walk with the same swagger, his thoughts didn't carry curious mischief, and he didn't chat with his familiar during the trek to the mansion. Once inside, they bypassed the home alarms and lingered in the entryway.

The police had secured the house after the attack, and authorities had removed the corpses, but left behind many bloodstains.

Fear spiked through Gael, wondering if any of this belonged to Tara. Had she been harmed before she was taken? Had she fought? Had she been afraid? Had she been alone?

Gael's eyes watered, thoughts clouded with concerns. King Clucks flapped his wings, hopping onto Gael's shoulder, and soothing the worries away as best a bird could.

The pair took their time through the mansion, navigating the massive floor plan with ease. Gael had a memory in nearly every room, from studying to playing games to dragging Tara around her own estate in demand of a silly tour.

Making his way upstairs, Gael approached Tara's bedroom and lingered in the doorway. He half-expected her to pop out, smile on her face, sunlight in her blue eyes, but there was no trace of Tara here. Not entirely, anyway.

Gael's presence became clear as he strode to the other side of the bedroom and retrieved a small glass terrarium that housed Tara's cocooned familiar. So much had happened, and I forgot about her new branch, about her familiar going through a silent growth spurt.

After he grabbed the tank, Gael departed with haste, unable to bear another second in Tara's home without her.

As difficult as it was, the somber minds of my students kept me grounded in the days that passed. So many people were lost in their grief, devastated by the destruction, and I found solace in keeping a watchful eye over those I cared about. It also helped pass the hours as Milo slept, recovering after his fateful battle against the top ten enchanters in the world.

CHAPTER THIRTY-ONE

BEN squirmed in the backseat, fidgeting the entire drive to the hospital. It helped that he had Sheamus nearby, keeping him calm every time Ben's anxiety spiked. I still wasn't the biggest fan of the old hound, mainly because I ended up with most of the walking duties. Especially with Milo's recovery.

Thankfully, we were here to bring Milo home. I wanted to do this alone, have Ben see Milo happy and healthy—even if he faked it a little—but Ben insisted. When I spoke with his therapist, she suggested this would be good for Ben. Something about working through previous traumas and learning the dangers of magic weren't always fatal. Or something like that. Honestly, I tuned the woman out most days. She rambled on about philosophy and intentions and blah, blah, blah.

I only agreed to the therapy because Milo insisted, and it seemed like the right move for Ben's well-being. That didn't mean I needed some so-called professional offering unsolicited advice about my emotional state, too. These sessions were just for Ben, not for me.

"All righty," I said, pulling into a parking spot on the fourth floor of the hospital parking garage. "Let's get going."

Dread flooded my mind, making my veins run cold. I wobbled as I stepped out of the car, struggling to compose myself and shake off this fear oozing from Ben.

"I'll just wait," Ben mumbled.

"No," I said, opening the passenger door. "We're going inside."

"I can wait here."

"No, Ben." I unfastened him from his car seat. "Milo is waiting on us."

"Then hurry up." Ben tried to fasten himself in again.

"Ben, come on." I went to unfasten him yet again.

"No," Ben screamed, snatching his seatbelt.

"Benjiman," I snapped. "We're not doing this."

Sheamus barked. Ben cried. The parking garage turned into an overstimulated emotional rollercoaster with a tiny breakdown.

Running my hands through my hair, I yanked hard to bite back a scream. Anything to distract myself from the turmoil crawling under my skin. I wanted a cigarette. Needed a cigarette. Needed to cry, to rage, to roar, but I couldn't. Not right now.

Ben had his fit, letting the tears flow heavily as he let the overwhelming sadness pour out. Children never had a good grip on their emotional state, and Ben's had been ricocheted every which way in the last year, so I understood. Still, it sucked having to be the adult, be the strong grown-up, and maintain my composure while Ben released sadness.

I stood there, letting Ben have a tantrum, until he wore himself out. Sheamus whimpered a bit, tail wagging with frantic concern. As Ben calmed down, Sheamus rested his head on the boy's lap.

"Are you feeling better?"

"No." Ben sniveled.

"Me either." I unfastened Ben from his car seat and lifted him out.

When I tried to set him down, he clung to me.

"Nooo," Ben whined.

"Fine." I repositioned him against my hip, gaining a better grip on Ben, then I snapped my fingers, directing Sheamus to hop out of the car.

Sheamus stood close to me, cautious not to stray far as we entered the hospital. I double-checked my wallet, ensuring I had Sheamus' familiar waiver, because I wasn't in the mood for anyone's bullshit about me bringing a dog into the hospital. There were already a few minds giving me sour thoughts with their unwanted opinions.

They felt it was inappropriate to bring a beast into the hospital. They assumed I was a bestial witch, something that came with many other assumptions about my lifestyle. Christ, I knew people had weighted opinions about every branch of magic, but lately, I found myself encumbered by the hate bestial witches received.

When we reached Milo's floor, our minds synced, and I swore he sensed my approach. It was as if my mere psychic touch was enough to alert him to my presence.

Milo stepped out of his room, ignoring the nurse insisting he sit in his wheelchair. I released a bated breath, at ease seeing him well and eager to return home. Admittedly, he looked silly in the short-sleeved undershirt and sweats I'd brought him. But Milo wasn't going to sneak away in one of his trademark suits, rushing off to save the day. While I couldn't guarantee he wouldn't have tried to escape solo, I figured keeping him in casual clothes lowered the probability. After all, he preferred to save the day in style.

Milo smiled, completely carefree, and eager to get out of the hospital. While he'd mostly recovered under Wadsworth's care, the doctors insisted on keeping a close eye on Milo's healed injuries. Most rejuvenation came with limited capabilities, and severe injuries like those Milo had obtained had a tendency to open back up. Thankfully, Wadsworth's arrogance came with a plethora of expertise, and his rejuvenation didn't falter.

Still, Wadsworth could only do so much considering the severity of Milo's injuries. Two scars ran along Milo's face. The first slash mark went over Milo's nose on an angle, with a sharp cut over his cheek. The second slash mark followed the same angle with a jagged cut along Milo's right eye.

Milo's bright smile and genuine joy helped me bury my fears, my concerns. Those big, beautiful blue eyes smiled, too, and I was grateful Wadsworth had preserved Milo's vision.

Ben tensed, breathing hastening as he absorbed Milo's appearance.

"Your arm…" Ben choked up, staring at the many scars running up Milo's right arm.

Enchanter Kingston's punch had shattered every bone in Milo's arm, torn through flesh, and created severe nerve damage. While the bones had been mended and the nerve damage had mostly been repaired, a lot of the skin held the memories of the damage Milo had taken.

"Looks worse than it feels, buddy." Milo reached out, extending his hand to Ben, who hesitated for a moment.

Soon, his trepidation fell away, and he walked over with his arms held out. Milo, in turn, picked him up.

I resisted the idea, but Milo insisted. He held Ben with his formerly injured arm, showing the young boy that nothing was wrong.

"Your face." Ben ran his fingers over Milo's scars, processing the damage, trying his best to sort his confused and anxious thoughts.

"I like 'em," Milo said with a big grin.

"Please don't make light of these injuries."

"I'd never." Milo shot me a look. *"But scars are sexy."*

"Seriously?"

Milo's gaze lingered on my neck, staring at my scar. The one that'd nearly ended my life, the one that brought Milo and me back together. Okay, maybe scars weren't the worst thing.

After speaking with the doctors and searching their minds for reassurance on all my follow-up questions, I left with Milo, Ben, and Sheamus. By the time we reached the car, Milo was winded. He hid it well, but the fatigue ran off him in waves.

I fastened Ben into his seat and ushered Sheamus into the back seat. Then, I turned to Milo and pressed a hand on his shoulder.

Part of me wanted to steady him, another part of me wanted to shake him, throttle him.

"I know, I owe you a long conversation," Milo said with a solemn smile. "A lot happened, a lot I didn't fully anticipate."

He meant Caleb's kidnapping. He'd prepared for Tara's abduction and tried his best to ensure the Global Guild would prevent Amara from taking her divine goddess to be. Still, so much unraveled in ways no one could've prepared for, not even the world's best clairvoyant.

The weight of death cracked Milo's heart. I didn't want to pick a battle with him, knowing he silently grieved Campbell's loss, mourned the deaths of the other enchanters who put their lives on the line for Chicago.

"You could've told me about the top ten," I said. "About your perfected roots. About—"

"Tell a worrywart like you that I planned to fight the top ten Global Guild witches?" Milo laughed it off, giving me a sassy scoff. "Please, you would've worried me into the grave."

"Jerk."

"You love it."

"I do." I pressed my forehead against his. "But I'm not the only one who worries about you now."

I let my gaze drift in Ben's direction, whose focus had shifted to Sheamus.

"I know." Milo's bottom lip trembled momentarily. "I'll do better."

"I love you." I kissed him soft and sweet, just enough to steady his nerves.

It wasn't a long kiss. More of a peck, something to express my affection. How I'd changed, lost in this love for Milo.

"Love you, too." Milo kissed me back, savoring the taste of my mouth.

We took shallow breaths, holding this moment alone in the parking garage for a minute. I let everyone else's thoughts in the city wash away, locking my mind onto Milo's entirely. He was my everything.

There was so much more we needed to discuss, things that'd happened, battles to come, but for now, I wanted to take my family home.

I took my time driving, allowing Milo to relax in the passenger seat. The rest did him good, letting his muscles ease and his mind wander between sleepy half-thoughts. I indulged in his soothing thoughts, allowing Milo's comfort to ease my concerns. Milo was my everything, and having him back kept me grounded in these terrible times.

Ben's mood had lifted by the time we got inside the penthouse. He ran through the living room, screaming as Sheamus playfully chased him. The pair made a game of it, lost in silly thoughts and completely distracted from his earlier fears.

"All right, settle down," I said.

"Let them have a little fun." Milo gently nudged me, pressing his shoulder against mine.

The briefest contact filled me with butterflies.

"You know," Ben said, hugging Sheamus' neck and giggling as the dog licked his face. "You and Sheamus can be scar buddies."

Sheamus' patchy fur and missing left ear sent a shiver through me. It wasn't the injury or appearance itself, so much as the pain this old hound had endured. As protective as Sheamus had become over Ben, I could only imagine how hard the dog fought to protect his former familiar bonded witch.

Those injuries were a painful, permanent reminder of the battle the dog lost in saving his partner's life.

"Oh, definitely." Milo knelt down, pressing his face against Sheamus' so the scarred sides were prominent. "Look at us twinning."

Ben giggled, holding his arms out so he could fly. Sheamus barked, casting telekinesis meant to lift his favorite human. Milo smiled, helping to steady Ben's flight around the living room. Charlie chirped, running over to join in the fun. Carlie meowed, annoyed by the ruckus. I basked in the happiness of our home.

This family I'd built meant everything to me. I loved them all more and more every single day.

Chapter Thirty-Two

THE coming days didn't offer much of a reprieve. Many funerals were scheduled, many vigils were held, many tears were shed, and so much hope was lost.

When I arrived at Guild Master Campbell's funeral, the overcast clouds gave way, ushering in a heavy rain. It masked some of the sorrow on familiar faces. Layla continued grieving, hit hard by the death. The death of her mentor, her inspiration. A death she couldn't prevent despite her best efforts.

She looked weary without her typical confident expression. Her eyes were splotchy. For the first time since I'd met her, Layla didn't have her hair styled in her cute little pigtails. Instead, she let her long brown hair hang lifelessly, catching in the rain as she sank with her feelings.

I wanted to comfort her, but I had nothing to offer. Death hollowed me out too much, and any advice I had on the subject would likely be detrimental. My only hope was that Layla didn't cling to this pain for years.

Before I reached Milo, another mind often filled with anger called out. Kenzo. He'd come here to offer his respects, yet his heart and mind were a thousand miles away. Anguished thoughts twisting in on themselves ate away at him. Guilt consumed him. Each breath he took stung. Nothing reassured him, eased the pain.

Caleb had been abducted, and Kenzo was flooded with worry.

He wasn't the only mind stuck on Caleb's loss, Tara's loss. They'd been taken from us, from the city, and held captive by a psychotic witch.

My telepathy spanned the length of the funeral, hit with the anguish from thousands of thoughts. Everyone from Cerberus had come. Nearly everyone. One mind far away hadn't made it out the front door before grief consumed her. Here, though, so many came to show their respects. Cerberus members, students, other guild masters, enchanters, civilians, investors, and many others, all of whom considered Campbell a friend and ally.

But far on the other side of the city, my telepathy snaked through the busy streets until I reached Katherine's home. She lay on her bed, dressed in black, but unable to pull herself together. She sobbed, too devastated by her role in things. The possession ate away at her, haunting her with memories of Moire's cruel actions. Guilt flooded her every fleeting thought, convinced she could've helped Caleb and Tara if only she'd done better. Been better.

She wasn't at fault.

I only hoped she saw that soon enough.

Making my way around the edges of the crowd, I carefully pressed through the sea of black. Milo stood silently, mourning Campbell. His solemn expression made the scars on his face all the more prominent. Those jagged slash marks haunted me. He was fine, healed, but they were a constant reminder of the battles he'd always find himself entering.

The ten most powerful witches in the Global Guild opposed him, and he jumped into the fray without a moment of hesitation. But the pride he had for that fight was lost on him here and now.

I endured the thoughts of everyone around us because Milo needed the peace to quietly grieve Campbell's loss. Latching my telepathy to Milo, sinking into his mind fully, would offer a reprieve I desperately craved in this abyss of anguish. But I couldn't burden Milo right now. I needed to stand tall, offer myself as a pillar of support when he needed it.

During the sermon, a small spark of joy steered my magic. It was mixed with a twinge of guilt, but mostly relief. A few rows back, Lena stood between Hayden and Ellie, taking in the kind words and ceremonial verses meant to offer Campbell a final farewell.

Lena had already experienced a tremendous loss when Jamie was taken from her, taken from this world. There weren't many left in her life that she cared for. She'd distanced herself from her family. She rarely associated with colleagues, Hayden and Ellie being the exception. And as she took in the service, Lena counted her blessings that she hadn't lost either of the loves of her life.

While I didn't care much for the trio as individuals. They mostly annoyed me, Lena with her sourpuss attitude, Ellie with her constant niceties, and Hayden with her ditzy aloofness. They were a vexing throuple. Still, I silently sent a wish for the very same thing Lena hoped for. May Lena, Ellie, and Hayden never experience the pain of losing one another.

I loved Milo and Finn just as deeply as Lena loved her partners. Losing Finn… I would never fully recover from it, but I was happy to finally allow myself to be happy again. May no one have to endure the grueling journey of grief I dragged myself through.

After the funeral wrapped up, lines formed for the crowd to funnel through and offer their final respects to Guild Master Campbell as she was lowered into the ground. Drop some dirt, a rose, or a pink ribbon—options galore for Campbell. Whether the ribbon represented the cancer she'd survived or a symbolic nod to her branch, I didn't ask. Many in the crowd speculated one or the other.

Milo lingered particularly long at Campbell's grave, a rose in his shaky hand. Unable to bear the moment, he cast his gaze up to the rain, letting the water splash against his face and mix with the tears he hid.

This would be the only moment Milo allowed himself to mourn, to lose himself in the sadness of death. Enchanter Evergreen never let loss slow him down, never let grief prevent him from bringing joy to the world. He'd lock away his many memories of Campbell somewhere deep in his mind, pulling them out when he needed to recall the fondness they shared.

She was a boss he loved annoying. A friend he loved consoling. An ex he loved to tease. Campbell meant the world to Milo. His mind flitted through blurry visions as he took in the rainfall. One by one, Milo tucked those possibilities away, locking them up to never be seen again.

I imagined those possible futures were of Campbell in another life, one where she wasn't cut down in the heat of battle. Whatever possible futures Milo saw of a world where Campbell still lived, it brought momentary relief. The tiniest of smiles crept on his face before he composed himself with a stoic expression.

Milo dropped a rose and whispered a final farewell to Guild Master Amelia Campbell.

I kept my distance from Milo, offering him solitude. It was so rare for him to have a moment to himself. After all, Enchanter Evergreen had a huge fandom, one that would surely grow now that he'd cemented himself as a prodigy of the perfected root magics. Still, everyone in attendance offered him space, most lost in their own grief.

Lena pulled herself away from her partners, catching my attention. She joined a somber Kenzo and shared a word with him. I didn't eavesdrop, finding Kenzo's guilt particularly difficult to handle right now. But whatever was shared offered a brief respite to the pain carved in Kenzo's heart.

Milo really did know what he was doing when suggesting that pairing. Lena needed an intern who would remind her of Jamie, even in the smallest of ways. And Kenzo needed a mentor who didn't find him the least bit intimidating but still wanted the best outcome for his future.

As Milo and I made our way out of the cemetery, Cassidy Gardner swaggered through the crowd. She took swift steps full of purpose, walking with only the faintest hint of a limp from the thigh injury she'd endured. Security circled her, their thoughts vigilant on those nearby, even though there was no threat to be found.

Perhaps the attack she suffered at Cerberus had her more on guard.

"Can we talk, Milo?" Cassidy squeezed the handle of her umbrella tightly, offering the slightest tilt to shield Milo from the downpour, and just enough so the slosh would splash harder against me. "Privately."

I glowered but bit my tongue. Milo had already lost someone dear to him. I didn't want to pick at his friendship with Cassidy. Even if I despised her every breath.

"I'm just going to share whatever you say with him later," Milo said with a forced grin. Thoughts of turning on his charm were instinctual, even as he grieved. "Hell, it's Dorian. He'll probably eavesdrop with that pesky telepathy you despise."

"It's not the telepathy I despise." Cassidy fixed her gaze on me, making it clear we shared mutual disdain for one another.

"What can I do for you, Cass?"

"It's about what I can do for you," she replied. "As I understand it, that diamond fucker has been detained. Locked in a deeper hole than just about anyone can get to."

Bardot, the witch who killed Campbell. He wasn't the only Celestial Coven witch detained after the attack. Bardot, Finch, and even Cobalt—who remained immobilized after I shattered his mind months back—were all taken into custody. Lazarus' bound body within an impenetrable enchantment was collected as well, along with the remnants of Grim's shattered bones. I explained he was an empty vessel, but the authorities didn't care.

Whoever they were superseded Global Guild control and determined the Celestial Coven to be an active terrorist threat, thus removing them in some covert and classified action. I wasn't even certain if Wadsworth himself knew where those fallen members of the Celestial Coven had been taken.

"If you're worried about him getting out, I assure—"

"Perish the thought." Cassidy pursed her lips. "From what I understand, where he landed is worse than death. A fitting fate."

I glimpsed the edges of Cassidy's mind, attempting to pry a location from her thoughts. Static cloaked the images, some type of enchantment shield. Not her doing. Living in Chicago, I knew the touch of Cassidy Gardner's illegal enchantments. They floated around everywhere for the right price.

No, it was as if the intel itself came with a hexed ward to protect the knowledge. That was high-level magic casting if I'd ever experienced it. There was no amount of sleuthing that could pry that information from someone. It all came from clearance and influence. Who knew Cassidy had government connections that ran so high? Higher than Milo.

"I just wanted you to know my resources are at your disposal," Cassidy said, stepping in closer to Milo. "Every single one of them. No, need to plead or get sentimental."

"That's quite gracious."

"I know." Cassidy tilted her head, tightening her eyes on Milo. "I'll help you find and eliminate what remains of this Celestial Coven and their trashy True Witch."

"Why the assistance?" I asked.

"They killed a friend of mine." Cassidy flicked her attention back to Campbell's gravesite. "They also seem determined to destroy my city."

"And we couldn't have that now, could we?" I scoffed.

"Certainly not," she replied, turning her attention back to Milo.

"Thank you, Cassidy." Milo gave her a half-hug, holding the embrace longer than she was comfortable with.

Still, her thoughts contended to accept the hug, understanding Milo was a softie.

"I have resources your Global Guild doesn't," Cassidy continued, finally freeing herself from Milo. "They wouldn't wanna get their hands dirty."

"And you do?" I asked.

"I get the best manicures in town," Cassidy said with a smile. "I don't mind breaking a nail from time to time."

"I will consider your offer," Milo said.

"You do that, darling." With that, Cassidy turned on her heel, escorted by an entourage of security.

As Cassidy left, the crowd thinned, and I followed Milo back to the parking lot.

Milo leaned against my shoulder, pressing his head against mine. "*Thank you.*"

I didn't reply, merely slowed my pace so Milo could rest against me.

"It means a lot you were here," he whispered. "That you're always here."

"I'm not going anywhere." I turned, facing toward him as we approached the car. "I promise you."

"*I love you.*" Milo leaned in, kissing me gently.

"*I love you, too.*" I kissed him back, pouring my heart into his mind, letting the rhythmic beat fill our thoughts as our lips smacked.

CHAPTER THIRTY-THREE

I FLIPPED through the channels, looking for Beverly Cleverly Live, America's number one talk show based in New York. Anyone who was anyone hoped to land a seat on Ms. Cleverly's couch.

"But now the Global Guild—"

I paused, having flicked right past *that* channel. You know the channel. The one with news anchors who have the intellectual nuance of a fucking thimble. The station with reporters who praise the hate of the world and claim victimhood every single time their audience wasn't centered on all matters.

What I needed to do was continue channel surfing until I landed on Beverly Cleverly Live. I actually wanted to watch that show, I mean, not regularly, but this particular show was important. Plus, I promised to tune in. What I ended up doing was flipping back to the news report by a bunch of bigots with fake smiles because I was clearly masochistic.

"Look, the Global Guild rankings used to mean something…" one of the reporters said, explaining it poorly to his audience, with so-called bullshit facts about policies that never once existed, but no one watching this show with intent would bother fact-checking anything that didn't match their perception.

He acted as if the shakeup in the rankings had less to do with talent and everything to do with performative promotions. And honestly, most of this industry was based on popularity over skill, but the Global Guild didn't play. In order to be among their best, their witches had to possess talent and fame.

"You know, Chris, I get Enchanter Stone stepping down," Reporter Johnson said. The same prick from the press conference Gladiatrix held a few months back. The guy who had the audacity to question Gladiatrix's choices, the merit of her interns, and blatantly spoke with prejudice. "The guy's old and has been hanging onto that number two ranking for years."

After the top ten Global Guild members were possessed and transformed into devils, it caused quite a stir. Some members faced long-standing physical side effects from the possession, like Enchanter Stone. While Gladiatrix was able to properly exorcise the vampire inside the man, his age made it difficult for him to fully recover.

The same could be said for Wadsworth, but since that old bastard walked around in constant chronic pain, I doubted anything truly fazed him anymore. Still, both men stepped down from their positions in the top ten of the Global Guild.

Chances were, Wadsworth would use the newfound freedom to move more freely in his pursuit of The True Witch and her Celestial Coven. As for Enchanter Stone, I had no idea. He'd probably spend his retirement serving as a spokesperson for some vile oil corporation while claiming fracking was somehow good for the environment, and as a witch who controlled plants, idiots would buy into the bullshit.

"What I don't understand," Reporter Johnson continued, "is Enchanter Kingston stepping down?"

That was huge news. Epic. The man who held the number one rank in the Global Guild for more than a decade had decided to step away from enchanter work and reflect on the events that led to his possession. He was a powerful man, possibly the most powerful man, but his confidence had been shaken, rattled, and he needed time to heal from the emotional devastation that came with possession.

Flashes of Jamie Novak hit me. The young teen possessed by a wicked chimera left hollowed out and emotionally distraught from the events. While the top ten didn't suffer a long possession dragged out over months like Jamie had, I was certain they each held similar scars to the boy I failed to save.

"He's stepping down because he's a coward," Reporter Chris blurted, holding up a picture of Enchanter Kingston before ripping it in half. Quite the declaration, considering Kingston had a worldwide audience. And I hoped those obsessed fans ruined this reporter's whole fucking month. "Wah, I got possessed, and now I need to take a break from guild work. Talk about pathetic."

"It does raise a lot of questions," Reporter Johnson said. "I mean, how can anyone call themselves a top-ranked enchanter if they got possessed in the first place? Everyone knows only a weak mind succumbs to possession."

Lies. Utterly unfact-checked garbage spouted as truth. Possession couldn't be prevented. The only way to stop a demon from forcing its way inside your body would be to successfully banish it before the assault began. But many demons ambush their prey, their victims, offering them little to no opportunity to resist.

What was next? Were these fuckers going to claim one could pray away a demon? There were plenty of fools who believed such things, and that always led to the death of the host, and often the deaths of many more.

"Exactly," Reporter Chris said, his voice grating on my ears. "Claiming to be America's Champion, he should be able to at least bounce back from this little possession."

"Enchanter Barlowe hasn't let it slow him down," Reporter Johnson said, cutting to a clip of the devout Christian enchanter holding a vigil while casting his Heavenly Ice—quite the name he picked for his unique branch magic.

Not everyone got the opportunity to name their branch, since the Department of Magical Records would dictate one's official branch. However, if the witch in question was deemed the first on record with the licensing facility, then they got to name it. As such, this extremely religious witch chose a name to reflect his faith.

"But see, this is what I'm talking about," Reporter Chris said. "Enchanter

Barlowe should've moved up to the number one ranked enchanter in the Global Guild. He was ranked third. With Kingston and Stone, the former number one and two enchanters, stepping down, it only makes sense that Barlowe would move to number one. Yet this new rearrangement of the top ten feels very fake."

"Yup, the math isn't mathing, that's for sure," Reporter Johnson said. "But we all know it's part of a political stunt. A woke agenda meant to cater to the witches who cast more PC policies than actual magic. Honestly, the top ten seems to be aiming for some type of diversity Olympics—"

"Oh, fuck this." I flipped the station, unable to bear another second of these assholes.

I landed on Beverly Cleverly Live just in time to catch Gladiatrix mid-interview. Good, I hadn't missed it yet.

Beverly was a big woman, tall and wide, with most of her height in her torso. It made her tower over Gladiatrix as the women sat on the couch. Just looking at her, she didn't seem like the girl next door. Still, Beverly had this captivating demeanor, charming audiences for years as a singer-songwriter, filling stadiums and hitting notes even the best magics couldn't hit. I wasn't a fan, but even I enjoyed her bigger singles from time to time. Now, she used that charm to captivate American audiences from the comfort of their home.

"So, how do you address the rumors that your rank change had to do with politics over talent?"

"Rankings are an extremely complicated matter," Gladiatrix answered with a smile. "It doesn't help that every state, every city, honestly, has their own qualifiers when it comes to ranking their guild members."

"Plus, the schools," Beverly chimed in. "My daughters attend two different academies, each focused on different specialties, and let me say, the ranking systems at their schools don't add up the same way."

I scoffed. Specialty academies didn't exist. They were merely titles of elitism to ensure that a particular academy wasn't forced to cater to unsavory students. Basically, the specialty allowed them to discriminate without being called out for it, keeping their wealthiest witch families in a coveted private education.

"Precisely," Gladiatrix replied to Beverly's anecdote. "As for my ranking, it's often being reevaluated, as any member of the Global Guild, especially the top ten. After the incident in Chicago, it was deemed that my actions pushed me over Enchanter Barlowe's placement."

"You mean where you single-handedly fought him, Kingston, and Stone?" Beverly paused for the audience's applause. "Then safely exorcised the demons possessing them."

"Not single-handedly," Gladiatrix corrected. "There was plenty of help on the field before and after I stepped in. But I did face off against those three. It's important to note that the demons possessing them weren't able to harness the full extent of their magical capabilities."

"Yes, but they were still devils. Three devils. And you yourself had also just shaken off a possession."

Gladiatrix laughed. "I'd hardly call passing out from sheer exhaustion 'shaking it off.' But yes, I did manage to collect myself enough to help purge the devils from the area."

"Humble and all powerful," Beverly said, gesturing to Gladiatrix. "Can we just all take another moment to applaud the spectacular Gladiatrix?"

The audience roared, cheering louder and longer than before. Some even stood up, practically on cue, for the cameras that panned through the crowd of overly excited audience members.

Beverly Cleverly waited for her audience to settle before moving back into her interview. "Your top ranking might be the biggest news in the Global Guild, but it's certainly not the only change happening, is it?"

Gladiatrix beamed. "Yes, there are many things happening that I'm so proud of. For years, I've been advocating that the Global Guild can only truly call itself a guild of the world if we open our membership rankings up to other nations."

"And you've done just that." Beverly pointed to the big screen behind her, showing pictures of masked vigilantes from the UK. "Several of these witches assisted in bringing a bit of order back to the streets of Chicago."

Milo and Gladiatrix had wrangled nearly twenty of the masked witches, but I only spotted two of them, King Liberty and Queen of Jesters, when they fought off the other possessed top ten enchanters.

"I'm thrilled we're making room for other highly qualified witches," Gladiatrix said.

"Now, I heard this will open complications," Beverly said. "Many nations don't use the enchanter ranking system."

"Yes, they won't be Global Guild enchanters," Gladiatrix said with a coy smile. "But as we addressed earlier, the ranking system differs everywhere, by everyone. It's subjective and objective, outdated and rigorous, and many more things. These are still highly capable witches, though. Perhaps the Global Guild needs new terminology suited just for us, to represent every witch from every nation."

"Hmmm." Beverly made an inquisitively playful expression. "More rumblings planned by our number one enchanter? I can't wait to hear all about it. But first, let's break for a commercial."

During the commercial break, I scrolled through my phone, checking socials, and noticing a few articles relating to Gladiatrix's new ranking, the shakeup in the Global Guild, and other countries being approached. So far, fifteen different countries were rumored to be in negotiations to officially join the Global Guild. This would completely change the face of the magical industry. It might even open exchange programs on the academy level. That'd be quite a sight, allowing students the opportunity to learn how magical policy worked in another nation.

Beverly Cleverly Live returned with her and Gladiatrix doing a little dance with the audience before making their way back to the couch.

"Okay, so the biggest curiosity I have about the recent changes involve a certain psychic witch who played a role in holding off the top ten enchanters," Beverly said, showing snippets of Milo's battle.

Some of the footage was shaky, grainy, and choppy, but it seemed lots of people recorded the attack. My chest warmed, partly from pride in Milo's valor, and partly in aggravation from the dumbasses who stayed in striking distance so they could film the fight. Seriously, those fucking morons should've run away. They could've gotten Milo injured protecting them.

"Now, I know what he did was amazing," Beverly said with a wistful edge in her voice. "But I have to ask the obvious question. If he predicted this happening, why didn't he just stop the vampires before they possessed anyone?"

"That's not how clairvoyance works," Gladiatrix explained. "You saw the snippets of that battle. Now imagine cutting those seconds down even more. Chop them up and rearrange them. Heck, add a couple unrelated images to other visions in the mix."

"Wow." Beverly's expression tightened to something more serious. "I'm getting a headache just thinking about it."

She had no fucking clue. Hell, I had more insight into Milo's branch than any other person in the world, and I still struggled to make sense of how he kept it organized.

"Okay, so what he did was clearly impressive." Beverly conceded with a shrug to her audience. "But is his new ranking really appropriate?"

I glared. Just when I was starting to not hate this woman, she had the audacity to question Milo's capabilities.

"Not many people make a ranking jump from one-hundredth to fifth, but I assure you, Enchanter Evergreen is more than qualified for this leap."

Gladiatrix's statement sent a shiver of excitement through me. Milo had joined the top ten Global Guild members. I knew it already, since he received the news privately before the public announcements. Still, it hadn't truly sunk in that Milo was now recognized as one of the best-ranked witches in the world.

He was officially an international rock star. Milo would soar higher than any of us ever dreamed of as children. My heart fluttered. I wondered how Finn would feel about this. What would he think? Would he be surprised? Unlikely. All I knew was that Finn would be proud of where Milo had risen.

I was proud of him, too. But I still worried. After his battle with the top ten enchanters, I imagined he'd enter into more battles with even more dangerous foes. But what else could I expect from Milo? He sought to offer everyone the best possible outcome, which often meant facing off against insurmountable odds.

"Okay, let's meet this mysterious Enchanter Evergreen," Beverly announced, making way for the music cue as Milo stepped out onto the talk show.

Ugh. He wore the silliest orange suit. It was bright and cheery and made him pop out as he took a seat on the couch beside Gladiatrix.

"It's an honor to have you here," Beverly said.

"My first official interview now that I'm sitting among the top ten," Milo said. "I should be the one who's honored. Beverly Cleverly wanted to have me here. That's something to write home about."

Beverly smiled, pausing for a moment, and making sure she didn't blush or lose her composure from a little flattery. After all, this was a woman who interviewed thousands of celebrities. Whether they were enchanters, musicians, actors, pop stars, or divas, anyone who was anyone appeared on Beverly Cleverly Live.

"How are you feeling since your battle?" she asked.

"Sore," Milo jested. "Have you seen my face?"

He pointed to the scars running along his face, smiling so proudly that it practically washed away the injuries. Seriously, his joy was enigmatic. I could see it in Beverly's eyes, the way Milo's infectious happiness reeled her in. It pulled at the hearts of the audience, too. Their expressions said as much.

Minds all across Chicago soared with delight as they locked in on the show to watch their enchanter, too. Milo belonged to this city first and foremost. He'd always remain a hero of Chicago, a beacon of pride. Even if now, he'd stepped onto a global platform.

"But I'll wear these with honor," Milo said. "I went a round with one of America's best enchanters and have lived to tell the tale. Enchanter Kingston has been an idol of mine for years, so it was an absolute honor to play a role in helping him. Even a small one like mine."

"Well, I'd hardly call your role small." How quickly Beverly's tune had shifted. "What I find most astounding about this incident is you managed to hold your own with just your roots."

"They're the most important part of any witch's repertoire." Milo smirked. "Anyone who says otherwise doesn't have respect or understanding for their fundamentals, and that's just a pity."

"Yes, but your roots are above and beyond. Perfected, they say."

"True, but that doesn't mean I can use perfected roots all the time. It's something to keep in the reserves. It expels a lot of energy. Plus, just because the roots are perfected, doesn't mean the witch using them is perfect. I'm just as flawed as the next person."

With that, he'd won over everyone. God, how people loved a humble, charming man.

I sank into the couch, watching Milo's interview continue. He was funny and sweet and silly. A total goofball. The three of them ended up doing some cooking bit after the next commercial, then they played some guessing game where Milo and Gladiatrix had to name magics based on ingredient clues.

For the life of me, I would never understand the joy people got in silly little talk shows like this, but seeing Milo beam ear to ear made my heart patter. He'd grown into an amazing man over the years, and to see his star shine so high and bright…

I was absolutely honored to have him in my life, and more than anything, grateful he never gave up on me being in his life.

CHAPTER THIRTY-FOUR

BY the time Milo's interview had ended, a manifestation of my making had flown through the psychic plane to reach him. Of course I couldn't simply wait for his return. Well, it certainly didn't help that I anxiously worried he'd injure himself again. But in truth, I was clingy, so my subconscious magic had to assuage my concerns by stretching across state lines until it reached Milo in New York.

Milo and Gladiatrix exited the studio and leisurely walked through the busy streets. While the pair should've simply basked in their accomplishments, taken a minute to really enjoy themselves, they spent the time brainstorming potential changes to the Global Guild, ways to improve it for everyone, to expand the initiatives meant to help people.

Somewhere along the way, they found themselves in Times Square. The bustle alone was enough to put my mind on the fritz, but the added attention their presence brought only made it worse.

Suddenly, Milo's late flight made even more sense. He'd scheduled a casual PR meet and greet out in the wild. It seemed mostly tourists stopped and gawked at Milo and Gladiatrix, but a few locals also stood in the makeshift line that formed. Everyone wanted autographs, selfies, and a chance to ask their absolute most pressing questions.

As the crowd thinned, Milo and Gladiatrix said their farewells and continued exploring. The rumbles of a hungry belly guided Milo's steps, leading the way.

"You two are quite the sensation," a familiar voice called out.

The British accent sent a wave of enticement coursing through Gladiatrix. As she turned to greet King Liberty, she tried her best to hide her joy and shock at his surprise visit. Milo, on the other hand, did a poor job pretending to be stunned by the arrival.

"What are you doing here?" Milo asked, flabbergasted.

"Did you tell him we'd be here?" Gladiatrix squinted at Milo.

"What? Me? Why would I do that?"

"Because your heartbeat says you knew he'd show up."

"My heart is a notorious liar," Milo said, making a crossing gesture. "I swear, I didn't have a part in this."

"He didn't," King Liberty confirmed. "Though, I would be curious how you may have become aware."

"Damn clairvoyants." Milo shrugged playfully. "I know, I know. You're telling yourself you have the best cloaking wards in the world. That's what they all say. I still usually glimpse a possibility here or there or anywhere."

"Fascinating." King Liberty nodded politely, making his way toward Gladiatrix. "I was hoping to have a word."

"About?"

"About us."

"We already had this discussion."

"And you made it quite clear that a secret relationship wasn't what you wanted." King Liberty reached for a clip on his mask, one of the fasteners that held it in place during combat. "I couldn't agree more with such sentiment."

"What?" Gladiatrix reached out, stopping King Liberty's hand mid-motion. "What are you doing?"

"Revealing myself." He eyed the busy crowds of people making their way up and down the streets, the large screens broadcasting commercials and news.

"Not here," Gladiatrix protested. "Not now. Not for…"

The word got stuck in her throat. *Me.* She didn't see herself as worthy enough for King Liberty to reveal his identity, to subsequently end his career.

"You would never be able to cast again, not professionally, not the way you work to help others," she continued. "It'd be over for you. Hell, you might even face sanctions."

"I was a law-abiding vigilante—no worries for penalty there."

"Yeah, they say that, but that's because none of y'all reveal yourselves," Gladiatrix retorted.

"Some reveal their identities," Milo added, revealing his obvious eavesdropping and his eagerness to know who was under the mask. "Granted, most of them had already retired and were one foot in the grave, but still. I really don't think the Crown will retaliate."

"Oh, they most definitely will," King Liberty said with a chuckle. "But I was thinking of becoming a professional caster over here. What are they called again? Enchanters."

"That is a big move," Gladiatrix replied. "Too big."

"No such thing." King Liberty smirked. "Besides, it's already a done deal. I already found the next King Liberty."

"What?"

"I'm handing over the title," King Liberty declared, slowly lifting his mask off his face. "Giving up the mantle, the mask, and the masquerade."

Milo's eyes bulged at the sudden reveal of King Liberty, who now stood unmasked in front of Gladiatrix.

"Alicia, I've never met a woman who makes me so happy." He removed the top hat next, revealing his ruffled black hair as a glamour washed away the chestnut illusion he kept. "It's time for another to carry the torch of this title."

"Are you certain?" she asked, lip trembling, and pulse pounding as she awaited the answer.

"Yes, absolutely." King Liberty smiled. "I've never been so certain of anything in my life."

"I fucking knew it," Milo blurted, ruining the moment as he levitated like some child lacking control of his roots.

In this moment, he did lose control, floating in the giddy realization that King Liberty was none other than the second son of the royal family, Henrik.

"There's a thousand theories surrounding King Liberty, most of which suspect that the third son or that Duke from what's-it-ma-called," Milo continued. "But I always knew Prince Henrik seemed suss."

"How astute." Henrik nodded.

"You have no idea," Milo said, ready to divulge his every potential theory.

The biggest being how Henrik likely possessed two branches to throw off suspicion. The public branch he used was a primal magic, controlling ice, but King Liberty only ever utilized his powerful warding barrier magics.

Now that Henrik had removed his mask and top hat, the protective sigils blocking his thoughts fell away too. His guard also dropped while in the company of Gladiatrix, making it easy for me to discover the truth. Henrik didn't possess two branches. He only ever had one, but he used secret enchantments to show off the ice magic. According to his surface thoughts, his family believed he was born branchless, and creating discreet enchantments for him was a way for them to hide that fact from the public.

I scoffed. Of course, they wouldn't want to announce a royal branchless child. Bad for their image. Kudos to him for hiding his real branch from his family, associates, security, and literally the entire nosy world. Though I couldn't help but wonder how the royal family image would look with him stepping out from the shadows, announcing himself publicly, and dating an American trans woman.

"You know," Milo continued. "I actually have a few ques—"

"Later." Gladiatrix flicked her fingers, hurling Milo through the air with a delicate wave of telekinesis, carrying him across the street. "I'd like to speak with just you."

"As would I, love." Henrik smiled.

Prince Henrik stepped closer, removing the gap between him and Gladiatrix. Her body trembled, thoughts flashing with images of their last intimate encounter. The memories moved by so quickly, I didn't have time to block them but also didn't glimpse much in the sudden flutter.

The only thing that I clung to from those memories was the fact that Gladiatrix had seen King Liberty without his mask those nights together. She'd experienced the pleasure of Henrik's company. The man behind the mask, the man without the royal title. She loved talking with him without the secret identity or air of royal pretense.

Still, she never believed she'd experience such a thing outside the darkness of a bedroom.

Henrik leaned in, his lips almost brushing against hers.

"Wait." Gladiatrix surveyed the street, finding a mostly unaware public but spotting a few reporters lurking nearby. "Are you sure about this? It's a big statement. One you can't take back."

"Let them enjoy the show, love." Henrik kissed Gladiatrix. Their lust oozed through the air, mixing with my psychic energy and giving me a tiny taste of the passion they held for one another.

Reporters snapped photos from across the street, landing the scoop of the century no doubt. England's second son, a royal rockstar of impish behavior, was actually none other than the most infamous masked witch in the United Kingdom. Not only that, but he was making out with America's number one enchanter, Gladiatrix.

Chapter Thirty-Five

MILO read Ben his seventh story for the night, declaring this would be the final story. It would. But not because of Milo's adamant declarations. He made that same statement every time, and somehow, Ben still managed to con Milo into picking up another book.

Fortunately, Ben's eyes weighed heavy, and I knew his sleepy expression better than anyone else. He was seconds from dozing off.

I stood in the doorway, quietly observing.

Ben preferred Milo's storytelling over mine, mainly because he did all the silly voices. As Milo read, Ben rolled onto his side, using the light of his lamp to keep his focus. All it did was force his eyes to shut tighter. Still, he tried to listen intently.

Meanwhile, as Ben's thoughts drifted into a dreamland, his dog lay at the foot of the bed, pretending to be asleep. We all knew the dog would end up next to Ben the moment we closed his door.

Seeing them all together brought me joy, and I couldn't help but smile. Milo's terrible impressions nearly made me laugh. But the more I stayed, the more a twinge of guilt stabbed at me. It came with pressure against my chest, making it harder to breathe.

I couldn't stay and watch them any longer. It hurt too much to smile. I walked down the hallway, each step becoming heavier and heavier as my legs filled with lead.

I wasn't sure if it was having Milo home and safe for the last few days, if it was the lingering sadness of the funerals, or if I finally had enough time to sit with my sorrow. But it hit me like a fucking avalanche, crushing me beneath the weight of guilt I carried. Guilt for failing Tara and Caleb.

Every happy moment I shared… It haunted me. They were out there, petrified, trapped. And I had the audacity to enjoy small family moments.

Milo met me at the end of the hallway, kindness in his thoughts, and a calm sincerity in his expression. "Are you okay?"

My lip trembled, making it impossible to speak without breaking, so I nodded. Hopefully that'd suffice.

"It's okay not to be okay." Milo placed his hands on my shoulders, a gentle embrace coupled with a soft touch as he ran his hands along my neck and cradled my head. "Don't push me away."

"I'm not…" My voice cracked. "I just feel so responsible for everything."

"You feel responsible? You put in more work than anyone at the Global Guild. We were the ones who were supposed to—"

"I don't even care that the Celestial Coven got away," I said, knowing where this conversation led. "I care that they took Tara. They took Caleb. They hijacked Katherine's mind. They nearly killed several of my students. They did kill…"

Tears spilled down my cheeks, and my face burned. Each breath I took carried a thick phlegm in my throat, making it difficult to speak.

"We'll get them back, I promise."

"How?"

"I don't know…yet, but I can see pathways leading to possibilities. They're faint."

"They're always faint, always changing," I said, pulling away from him. "Those possibilities could be gone in a week, in a day, in minutes. Admit it."

"True, under normal circumstances, but these possibilities are cemented by bonds of fate."

"What?"

"Your connection to your homeroom coven, their connection to each other, it has created this continuous spark," Milo said. "Sometimes, when lives interact with each other, they're bonded. Sometimes, when a clairvoyant interferes with the future, it can create some semblance of those bonds."

"Meaning?"

"Meaning they were always going to be connected in one form or another, as classmates, as peers, perhaps as survivors to a terrible event," Milo explained. "But then that horrible event, that awful fate, was averted, and all their futures were set on a different path."

"The day I saved Caleb from the void vision." I didn't even need to read Milo's thoughts to know that. "Well, the day they saved themselves, really."

Looking back on that assault, each of my students carried themselves with grace.

"Your interference saved Caleb's life. It painted a new future, and little by little, I began to realize your students' lives, possibilities, and potentials were all syncing up together."

"What does that mean exactly?"

"As a psychic, as a clairvoyant, I don't put much stock in Fate or Destiny," Milo said with a coy smile. "They're both rather fickle."

"And yet, here you are speaking of fate."

"I've seen her work." Milo's mind flitted with flashes of him, Finn, and me all together; memories of Milo and I finding our way back to each other; images of Ben entering our lives after I liberated him from an impossible magical trap. "Fate might be fickle, but she has rules. I just haven't learned them all yet."

Milo spoke of this Fate as an actual being, something he'd never really expressed with me, but there was a reverence he held for her in his mind. Like some kind of psychic deity floating in the abyss of possible futures. Perhaps a side effect of his branch magic, some mythical oddity.

Hell, maybe Fate was merely a projection of Milo's inner thoughts, perceiving his magic with consciousness to some degree.

I didn't need him to elaborate on this being of Fate so much as what he meant by my students' role in this.

"Your students' futures are tangled together, walking down the same roads," Milo continued. "Twelve bound by fate, so to speak."

"Meaning?"

"Meaning their connection to each other can solidify possibilities," Milo explained. "I can steer things, navigate paths, and ensure Caleb and Tara aren't swept away by some horrible ploy The True Witch has planned."

I took a shaky breath, trying and failing to exhale my anxiety.

"I do believe it's going to rely on your students, though."

"No," I said firmly. Not that I had much say in their lives. I wasn't even their teacher anymore. "Don't drag them into this."

"Dorian, they have a right to take control of their futures, too." Milo stared with soft, pleading eyes. "Don't you think they'll want the best possibility?"

"And if the best possibility puts their entire future at risk?"

"It wouldn't be the first time all their lives were at risk in order to rescue one of them."

Oh, that hit fucking hard. Yes, I unintentionally endangered my entire homeroom coven to rescue Caleb from his fate, from that horrible void vision. But I had no idea I was walking them all into a battle for survival.

"I didn't know I'd be dragging them all into this the last time," I said. "It wouldn't be fair to do that again, to put them in unknowing danger."

"Who said it'd be unknowing?"

"Does knowing a possibility prevent it?"

"Not always. Sometimes knowing a possibility makes it happen. Self-fulfilling and all that," Milo said. "Besides, the details aren't important, merely understanding their role in stepping down that path."

"A path that would put them in direct conflict with the Celestial Coven, with Theodore Whitlock, again."

"A path that would ensure Caleb and Tara survive, escape whatever destiny The True Witch has prophesied for them."

I reflected on Milo's words, on the spinning visions obscured by his magic, by the confidence of his thoughts, a working mind planning the best outcome for everyone.

"So, what do you propose?"

"Let's talk to your homeroom, explain the situation."

"Fine." I released my first calm breath of the night. "But if we're telling them, I want them to know it all. Know how their fates became intertwined."

Milo stared at me, stunned.

"I should've told them years ago how I meddled with their fate." I sighed. "If I'm going to drag them into danger yet again, I owe them that much."

CHAPTER THIRTY-SIX

CHANELLE let me borrow an empty classroom to meet with all my students. They didn't spend much time on the new Gemini Academy campus. This was technically my first time here.

Not exactly how I expected my first visit to go. I sort of expected to return to Gemini after resolving the Celestial Coven problem, yet here I was instead bringing my students into this.

One by one, they trickled into the classroom, reminding me of so many homeroom mornings. Right down to the fact that Kenzo and Gael showed up first. Even attending an impromptu evening meeting regarding Caleb and Tara, Kenzo fought for punctuality.

Though that might have had to do more with the fact that Kenzo's heart ached with Caleb's absence. He still blamed himself for his best friend's abduction. Soon, he would blame me. Perhaps they all would.

"Still a puppet?" Kenzo asked, glaring with hatred as Katherine shamefully walked past him. "What? No witty retort, know-it-all?"

"Stop, Kenzo." Gael nudged his boyfriend, deliberately bumping him with a few spikes. "She feels bad enough."

Kenzo growled. "Good."

I didn't know how much Katherine had divulged, but it was clear she'd shared the possession with others. Kenzo had more acute awareness than he should, based on what he'd seen the day Moire struck while holding Katherine's body captive.

"Just wondering if she can share where Caleb went." Kenzo pressed on, ready to tear Katherine down with cruel words.

"Fuck off, prick," Layla hissed, claws drawn as she sauntered by Kenzo.

She held no love for Katherine, but something about Campbell's loss had changed her. Not much, but it made her cherish the bonds she had with her fellow interns. Mostly, she hurt, realizing how unaware of Katherine's possession she'd been. It reminded her of Jamie's possession, and Layla began to wonder if her snide, self-absorbed attitude made her oblivious to the pain of others.

Who knew how she'd grow from this event, but she held Campbell close in her heart, opening herself up to the feelings of those around her in a way I never anticipated from Layla.

"What are we all doing here, Frost?" Kenzo asked, leaning against a student desk.

"I think I can explain that," Milo said, taking on the initial burden of discussion for me.

I needed to step up and speak, but despite making this choice, I hadn't fully figured out how to explain this truth to them. A truth they all deserved.

"Fate is funny. Sometimes, without realizing it, our lives become intertwined with the people around us." Milo led the discussion, giving me a chance to work up the nerve to speak. "You twelve have been through so many harrowing events, it's bonded you all."

"How unfortunate." Layla eyed Gael up and down.

"This bond could be the very thing that helps us in recovering Caleb and Tara," Milo continued.

"But this connection you all share is partly my fault," I blurted.

"What?" Gael's sharklike teeth formed into his trademark smile. "Not at all."

"It is," I continued. "My interference has dragged you all into danger."

"It's not like you made our schedules," Gael said, smile not wavering.

"Yeah, that's on our guidance counselor," Gael added.

"Ba-bawk."

"Exactly." Gael slammed a fist into his palm. "Damn her."

"I've been interfering with your lives since your first day at Gemini Academy."

No one knew what to make of that. Even their thoughts whispered with quiet rationalizations. Obviously, I interfered with their lives, as any teacher did. But they didn't realize the full extent of my role. My part in changing their fates.

"The first semester you all arrived at Gemini, Milo had a vision of Caleb's death," I explained. "There was almost no information surrounding the event. Not a cause, a time, a method. All I knew was that at some point, Caleb Huxley was going to die."

"And you think this is that vision coming to fruition?" Kenzo blurted, standing to his feet.

"No, I already prevented the vision," I clarified. "Theodore's first attack on our homeroom was when that vision was meant to unfold."

Kenzo trembled. It took everything he had not to explode with anger. Theodore had slain Kenzo's parents, had mocked their deaths, had slaughtered countless more, all in the name of fun. Now, he had Caleb. Kenzo wondered if things would be different right now if he'd killed Theodore the first time he attacked Gemini Academy.

I also wondered the same thing. But changing the past was impossible. I had a Finn-shaped hole in my heart offering proof enough of that.

"When I set out to prevent Milo's vision…" I paused, looking at Milo. "When we set out to change events, it had many unforeseen ramifications. For starters, I inadvertently bound each of you to each other."

Minds percolated over that comment, faces scrunched, and a few eyebrows raised suspiciously.

"Fates are often overlapped by our decisions," Milo elaborated, giving them a similar explanation to how futures and fortunes intertwined, especially when someone meddled with potential outcomes.

"So, saving Caleb bound our lives together?" Jennifer asked, genuinely curious.

"How lucky for you." Gael blew a sassy kiss her way.

Jennifer rolled her eyes and flipped him off.

"It's complicated and cosmic," Milo said. "Sometimes the connections remain subtle, almost six degrees of separation. Other times, whole lives are linked."

"Which is ours?" Carter asked.

"I believe the latter," Milo said. "I'm certain that the choices you all make will play a role in the outcome of Caleb and Tara's future."

"Leave it to branchless to require additional rescue," Kenzo said, thoughts calming. "So, that's your big speech, Frost? You saved Caleb once upon a time, and now we all have to play a part in saving him. Fine by me."

"Yeah," Gael added, raising a spiked hand. "I would've been down for a rescue even if we weren't bound by fate or whatever."

"A fated rescue," Jamius said with a nod.

"Think we can add that to our intern resumes?" Melanie asked, completely oblivious to the stakes at play.

"Rude." Yaritza nudged her, then turned to whisper. "But we should ask Enchanter Ortiz just in case."

"It's more than that," I said. "The fallout of rescuing Caleb from the vision… It lured the chimera to Chicago."

That confused my students. They didn't know anything about the chimera. The specifics of the devil attacking Chicago had never been publicly released.

"The demon that possessed Jamie Novak," I clarified. "It came to the city because of my actions."

That shocked them all. Some thought back to Jamie's antagonistic nature, the way he—or the devil—assaulted Tara during the Spring Showcase, the demons that stalked witches and warlocks alike on the streets of Chicago.

"There's more," I continued.

"Dorian, you don't have to explain everything." Milo pressed his hand against my shoulder.

"I do, I owe them the truth," I said softly, turning my gaze onto them.

"I owe you all answers."

I went on to explain how the chimera sought to possess me and how he only found me after my actions during Theodore's attack alerted the demon to my presence. It hurt, explaining even vaguely the role Finn played in shielding my magic from the chimera. Explaining how I lost Finn years earlier.

It wasn't just the arrival of the chimera I had to confess, I divulged how a piece of my magic broke free and acted of its own accord. How it stalked students and tried to kill some of them.

"Wait…it attacked us?" Gael asked, mind spiraling with the same fear he had the night he almost died at Peter Graham's hands. Only now, he knew it wasn't Peter at all, but in fact, a demon possessing the warlock.

"I'm so sorry," I said. "I never intended to interfere with your lives in such a way. I only wanted to help."

"I mean, you kind of did." Gael shrugged as his familiar nodded.

"Always knew you were playing favorites," Layla said, examining her clawed hand with an expression of disinterest. "Though, I suppose the whole saving his life part makes it somewhat valid."

"You guys have been looking out for us since we started Gemini?" Gael smiled at me and his mentor, his idol, more awed by Milo's role in matters than myself.

"Did you know how things would unfold?" Carter asked, mind flashing to my bloody body, the life he had to stitch together.

"No." The word barely escaped my lips, still haunted by the trauma my actions put Carter through.

"None of this matters," Kenzo stepped in, no longer caring to process. "Are we really surprised the world's most annoying telepath is also overbearing?"

"And super protective," Gael added.

"In a mother hen way." Gael and King Clucks cluckled in unison.

"All I care about is that you did your part to save Caleb," Kenzo said. "Now, it's up to us to save him this time around."

"Potentially," Milo elaborated. "The possibility is higher with everyone playing their role."

"And what exactly are our roles?" Layla asked, hands on her hips.

"To be determined." Milo winked, wasting his efforts because Layla found his charm as nauseating as Gael's voice.

"Why Caleb, though?" Jamius asked. "Like, is this just a wrong time, wrong place kind of thing?"

"No, because The True Witch sent Katherine back," Carter added. "Wouldn't she have just sent Caleb, too?"

"Why does she want Caleb?" Kenzo asked, eyes locked onto me.

I hesitated. There was so much I'd divulged about my secrets to prepare them…I hadn't realized how many of Caleb's secrets I'd have to reveal, too.

"She needs Caleb to open Hell," Katherine said quite plainly, letting the secret pour out like poison that'd kept her paralyzed for weeks.

"Whoa, what?" both Gaels blurted with wide eyes.

"It's all part of her plan to help Tara ascend to godhood," Milo elaborated.

"What?" everyone asked in shock, except for Gael and King Clucks, who were apparently in the know since Tara shared everything with them.

"There's a Gate to Hell?" Jennifer asked. "Like a real one or metaphoric?"

"Who cares?" Layla replied. "The bitch is psychotic. Fanatics don't care about facts."

"It is real," Katherine said. "I've seen it, through Moire's eyes."

"The witch possessing you?" Jennifer asked.

"Sort of," Katherine said, not explaining she didn't mean sort of like possession, when she meant sort of like a witch. After all, Moire was sentient magic.

"She wants to sacrifice Caleb to help Tara ascend?" Kenzo clamped his jaw. "So, how do we stop her?"

"The True Witch doesn't just want to open the Gate of Hell to sacrifice Caleb," Katherine said with a shaky stance. It took everything she had to breathe, to think, to speak. "She wants to unleash an army of demons big enough to slaughter everyone she deems unworthy of living in the new world order she's planning."

I trembled, drawn into Katherine's fear, and realized with Theodore, she could control hundreds, thousands, maybe even millions of demons.

"Okay, I get why Tara was taken," Carter said, mind puzzling together the jigsaw pieces of information much like the others did. "She's, like, special because of all her branches."

"She's not special because of her branches," Gael said, ready to explain in thorough detail how Tara was so much more than her magics.

"Anyway," Carter continued. "What I don't get is why Caleb's been taken."

That was a difficult thing to explain. They had a right to know, to understand, especially if they had a role to play in rescuing him. That said, Caleb and Tara had only recently learned the truth. Who even knew how they processed this family secret?

"Caleb's related to Tara," Katherine said.

"What?"

"They're siblings," Katherine continued.

"But they're like the same age," Gael said. "Aren't they? So, how are they siblings?"

"Twins."

"Oooooh, duh." Gael slapped his forehead. "But, like, not the identical kind."

"Who cares about the why?" Kenzo snapped, burying the confusion he had for this revelation. "When is The True Witch planning this deranged sacrifice?"

Katherine shrugged, still trying to piece together many of the memories left behind from Moire.

"I don't know when Amara will attempt to sacrifice Caleb," I chimed in, "but I believe it'll involve a celestial event."

"What's that?" Gael quirked a brow while King Clucks bawked at him. "Oh, those silly little star alignments."

"Cl-cl-cluck."

"I do pay attention in class," Gael scoffed. "It's just they're rare."

"They're more common than most people realize," Jennifer said with a glum sigh. "The levels of magic offered for rituals and spells vary. The bigger the cosmic event, the more people it draws, thus more witches attempting to harness the energy of the celestial event. The smaller ones might go unnoticed by most and offer less magic to draw upon."

"I didn't realize people still channeled celestial events," Jamius said, thinking to some of the texts we'd covered in history. "Thought that stuff was super old school."

"The True Witch is very old school," I said. "Ancient, in fact."

"Right," he sighed.

"And a lot of witches still practice the old ways," Layla added, thinking of the celebrations her grandmother had dragged her to every New Year's, every All Hallow's Eve, and a few other holidays. "They just don't do them much here."

Right. Globally, witches in other nations had stronger connections to their history of magic—even though they lost access to it for centuries, they didn't lose their customs or traditions. America, however, didn't have the same reverence for rituals.

"So, we just gotta track these celestial events, make sure we find Tara and Caleb before one of them happens," Gael said.

"But which one will she use?" Gael asked, spikes shrinking sheepishly. "What if there's like one tomorrow? Or next week?"

"We'll cross-reference possible dates, find the soonest event, and aim for rescuing Caleb by then." Kenzo practically snarled.

"And Tara." Gael and his familiar squinted.

"She's not at risk of being thrown into Hell," Kenzo growled.

"She's still in danger," I said.

Kenzo scoffed. "Yeah, from her family."

"She didn't choose her family," I said.

"Neither did Caleb," Gael added. "Seeing as he's part of Tara's family, too."

That quieted Kenzo. Much of his disdain for the Whitlocks became all the more complicated, now knowing Caleb was one of them.

"How are we even going to track them down?" Melanie asked.

"My family has connections with the state divination unit," Layla replied.

"Yeah, because some lost and found witches can do what the Global Guild never managed," Kenzo countered.

He wasn't wrong. Divination units usually focused on stolen items or people skipping bail. They had great successes with simpler tasks, but pinpointing someone or something that hid itself with wards or enchantments… They wouldn't be much use.

"Then tell the Global Guild witches to get off their asses." Layla folded her arms, then shot Milo a glare. "Maybe if we knew someone who ranked among them."

"Hey, hey, hey." Gael pointed a judgy finger. "Watch that attitude. You don't talk to Enchanter Evergreen that way."

Oh, Christ. Gael was about one bawk away from starting a full-blown argument with Layla because she insulted his hero.

"Well, do you have a better idea?" Layla snapped her teeth.

"Ba-bawk."

"Riiiiiight." Gael's apprehension washed away, and he smirked. "I grabbed Tara's familiar."

What?

"I didn't want the butterfly or whatever to like suffocate or starve, so I went to her place and grabbed it."

Right, Gael had retrieved it from the Whitlock Estate after Tara's abduction.

"So?" Layla rolled her eyes.

"So, familiars share a bond that no magic can hide," Gael explained. "King Clucks always knows where I am, and the same goes for me. Our magic is linked no matter the distance, the location, the whatever. Tara's familiar will be able to give us a precise location, no problem."

"That's fantastic," I said, almost smiling. "But how are we going to talk to Tara's familiar?"

None of us exactly shared the telepathic connection with the animal.

"Ba-ba-bawk."

"*Right? What an idiot.*" Gael grinned, then pointed a thumb at his rooster. "King Clucks will just translate. Duh."

"Then it's settled," I replied.

"Go get her familiar," Kenzo demanded. "The sooner we do this, the sooner—"

"Well, wait." I raised my hands. "We need to find them, yes, but we need a plan, before rushing into—"

"I have a plan," Kenzo snapped. "Kill The Bitch Witch and her psycho cunt son, then save Caleb."

"And Tara," Gael added, smiling with his sharklike teeth.

"Whatever, if there's time." Kenzo shrugged.

"I mean, we got time for a plan." Gael shrugged, kicking his foot against the floor as his rooster puffed his chest.

"What do you mean?" I asked.

"Tara's familiar is still cocooned," Gael answered. "Until it evolves or whatever, we can't really communicate."

"How long until it turns into a butterfly?" Layla asked.

"It usually takes one to three weeks," Jennifer answered.

"Not the case here," Gael said, to which King Clucks bawked. "Tara's familiar has been cocooned for months now. Plus, King Clucks here spent much longer in his chick state and the whole molting phase than most birds. The familiar bond warps timelines."

Right, because animals who bonded to a witch ended up with altered lifespans to match that of their witch partner.

"So, back to fucking square one," Kenzo grumbled.

"We're not at square one," Milo replied, stepping back into the conversation. "We have a plan, we have ideas, we are making contingencies. Finding Tara and Caleb through the familiar bond is one plan. The Global Guild is a second. Dorian's manifestations are a third. We have options."

Everyone nodded, a few minds wandered with weird thoughts of hearing my first name—only really thinking of me as Mr. Frost. Most minds focused on their concern for Caleb and Tara.

"Now, let's brainstorm," Milo said, taking a seat. "Stuff the arguments. We don't have time for them."

A consensus was met mentally, and everyone did their best planning for ways to help bring an end to the Celestial Coven once and for all.

Something about their fates being intertwined brought relief and dread in equal measures. While working with them would ensure we located Tara and Caleb, it also all but guaranteed they'd be thrust into the most dangerous fight of their lives. Every fiber of my being didn't wish to drag my students into a battle with the Celestial Coven, with Theodore Whitlock—again.

I'd follow these bounds that linked us together, I'd believe in Milo when he said he'd help create the best outcome for everyone, but I'd still hunt alone. If I got lucky, I'd track down Amara independently and finally put an end to the vile witch.

CHAPTER THIRTY-SEVEN

AFTER a few days of decompressing from the meeting with my students, I decided to take a little time for just Milo and me. Vanessa agreed to let Ben spend the night with the twins. Chanelle helped arrange a reservation at Milo's favorite restaurant. Milo's former acolytes even pushed their mentor out of the Cerberus office in a timely manner.

The world was on the brink of destruction with a psychotic witch attempting to open the Gate of Hell and usher in a new era of magic while slaughtering millions in the process. Even with such a catastrophe looming near, with the terror of losing my students, I couldn't ignore the feelings that'd been building inside me since I opened my heart to Milo again.

I waited impatiently, craving a cigarette in a way I hadn't in quite some time. Every second that ticked, I anticipated a text from Milo, some important task that'd called him away. Maybe it was for the best. Tonight was planned well enough but rushed. Too rushed. I never put enough thought into things.

"No," I hissed under my breath.

I'd thought long and hard on tonight. Everything was perfect.

Our server escorted Milo onto the private balcony where we could enjoy a night all to ourselves.

His suit made mine look all the frumpier. But I sucked in a breath and puffed my chest out a bit to fill my dark shirt. Milo's bright pink silk shirt appeared all the brighter with a backdrop of the city lights.

This restaurant was so many stories up, it had a lovely view of Chicago while still capturing a bit of the moon's light and the starry sky.

"Nice suit," I said, taking a seat across from Milo at our private balcony table.

"What can I say? I felt like matching."

I quirked a brow, staring at his simple black tie, then his jewelry accessories, and finding no hint of pink.

"If you're lucky, you might get to see what matches the shirt." Milo winked.

And suddenly, I found myself eager to skip dinner and get right to dessert.

A bitter breeze came in but couldn't spoil our night out. The nearby enchanted lantern released tiny embers that kept us warm in this winter weather, adding an elegant atmosphere to our dining experience.

Milo's eyes shimmered as he studied the fluttering embers like fireflies dancing in the wind.

"I'm glad you arranged this lovely little dinner," Milo said, perusing the menu.

This was the type of decadent spot that didn't label the prices of dishes or drinks. Most of their clientele didn't mind spending a mortgage payment on a night out. Truthfully, since moving in with Milo, I didn't really have many expenses.

Most of my money went to Ben, either for things he needed or the savings I started for his future. That left me with a lot of playing-around cash, so treating Milo seemed fitting.

Our server returned with a bottle of wine I'd preselected, poured our glasses, and offered us privacy while we looked over the menu.

"I'll be honest, I'm surprised you picked tonight of all nights."

"Seemed fitting." I gave a half smile. "Besides, we haven't had much time to breathe, let alone enjoy a little time together."

"Just the two of us."

"Three," I said, offering a silent pause to Finn. "In spirit."

"I wasn't sure if you realized…" Milo tiptoed around his thoughts as he took a seat.

"I could never forget Finn's birthday." I gave a bitter smile, still unable to find full solace in knowing Finn was at peace. At least, I hoped as much. "I figured it was the best night to go out and celebrate."

"What on earth are we celebrating?"

"Enjoying the small things."

Milo eyed me suspiciously, a playful squint and teasing thoughts of judgment.

"Okay, okay, maybe I just realized it's important to celebrate the small joys." I raised my glass of wine, inviting Milo to join me. "We both know I'm brilliant at panic and stress and guilt and sulking and…well, I'm not much of a crier, but I can be a baby."

"I'm not saying anything." Milo chuckled, raising his glass to meet mine.

"It's taken time, but I've learned to accept the things I can't control—work with others to change them because we all know I'm far too neurotic to simply accept them as is. However, I know how to be happy."

"Never thought I'd hear you say that."

"Never thought I'd make the time to be happy." I shrugged. "Guess the world's most annoying and persistent witch whittled me down."

"Really?" Milo gasped, feigning surprise. "Someone should get that witch a trophy, a sash, something to commemorate such a spectacular accomplishment."

"I couldn't agree more." I dug into my pocket and retrieved a small box, placing it on the table between Milo and me.

The action happened so swiftly, so nonchalantly, I didn't even have the chance to second-guess myself.

There were a hundred different ways I'd planned on sharing this. Find the right time. Right words.

All that need for perfection crumbled away as I stared into Milo's wide blue eyes.

I'd left him speechless, thoughtless too. A first for everything. The man who prepared for every possibility in the world never predicted this outcome.

"What is that?"

"Exactly what you think it is." I opened the box, showing two golden bands. "Will you?"

"I…" Milo swallowed, trying to comprehend what he saw before his eyes.

His thoughts flitted in and out of his visions, obscuring his mind from my telepathy.

"Are you telling me I really have never once proposed as a possibility?"

"If you did, I clearly didn't pay attention." Milo stared at the rings. "I've planned this a hundred times over and already had narrowed it down to eight perfect places and twenty-seven potential dates."

"All taking place after we deal with the threat of the Celestial Coven, I'm guessing?"

"After the pressing dangers are resolved, yes."

"I don't want to wait until things are perfect, until everything is fine." I grabbed one of the rings from the box. "You're a Global Guild member. Among the top ten, in fact."

"What can I say? I aim to be the best." Milo shot me a boyish grin, somewhat cocky, but mostly attempting to hide his still flabbergasted mind.

"There will always be another case, a reason to postpone happiness. I don't want to fall for that trap."

I slid the ring on my finger, letting Milo's vision flow through my mind. The mere sight of the ring on my hand warped his perception, flooding his thoughts with so many endorphins.

"I want to marry you."

Milo sucked in a shaky breath.

"I want to spend the rest of my life with you."

Milo's eyes watered.

"I want to build a family together."

Milo's mind wandered to the potential of more children, a bigger home, lots of ridiculous pets, and so many other fantasies, I couldn't help but let the thoughts and possibilities envelop my mind too.

"I want that too." Milo grabbed his ring and slid it on his finger like the most natural thing in the world.

Here we were, engaged. One step closer to our happiest ever after that ever aftered.

Our server returned, making Milo laugh with this sheepish, flustered excitement. He didn't know if we were in the bragging state or not. A night like tonight was meant to be for us, but that also meant celebrating with whoever we wanted and flaunting our happiness just a little.

"Looks like I'm finally making an honest man out of Enchanter Evergreen." I cupped Milo's hand in mine, raising them up to show our server.

"How lovely." The server smiled, focused on niceties, but genuinely not surprised since this location apparently led to quite a few engagements.

I frowned, realizing how predictable I was, but it didn't matter. It wasn't the moment itself that mattered so much as the life we'd build after this moment.

"Alrighty," Milo said, holding up the menu with his free hand. "I know what I want, but I'm about to butcher the pronunciation of everything."

I lightly laughed, following Milo's lead, and ordering the simplest-seeming dish I could. Milo went for extravagance. Which, to be fair, was pretty much everything on the menu, but I wanted something without a thousand different flavor palettes. I also wanted something I could sort of pronounce. Steak was universal, though the additions that came with it…not so much.

Still good food. Probably the best I'd ever had in my life. Seriously, one bite of this steak and I was ready to propose to the chef next.

"Not a fucking chance," Milo said, practically reading my mind.

"How do you do that?" I tilted my head, wondering how Milo glimpsed my thoughts with such ease.

"I see potentials, sometimes mid-conversation. The possibility of a funny joke or a bad joke flutters in my mind." Milo shrugged. "If I'm lucky, I can line it up with what I think someone else is thinking."

"So, there was a possibility in some version of the future where I made a joke about proposing to the chef because of this dish?"

"Yep."

"Well, is there a future where I put out for the chef?" I teased. "Because this steak is pretty damn good."

"Watch yourself." Milo pointed with his utensils. "Or I won't put out."

His mind flashed with images of all the things he planned on doing to me once we left this restaurant. It took everything I had not to convince him that the private balcony might make for a nice enough place for a little after-hours celebration.

The fact that our server arrived again with a dessert menu was probably the only reason I kept my hands to myself.

"I think we're going to skip dessert," Milo replied, retrieving his card.

"I don't think so." I slapped mine on the table. "My treat."

Milo smirked as our server left.

"Well, how will I ever repay you for such a generous night out?" Milo pursed his lips playfully, running his foot up my leg from under the table.

"I'm sure you'll think of something," I said with a slight chatter in my teeth.

I wanted to blame the cold, but the embers kept us nice and toasty on the balcony.

It didn't take long for us to leave. I went to retrieve my car when Milo grabbed me and pulled me back.

"Pick it up tomorrow," he whispered in my ear, wrapping an arm around the small of my back. "I don't want to wait any longer than I have to."

I growled in response, unable to form words, but eagerly holding tight as Milo lifted off into the night sky.

The flight home was made easy by Milo's magics. I allowed him to carry me while I focused my attention elsewhere. It was impossible to keep my hands off him, my lips. Wind chill hit hard, so I buried my face in the crook of Milo's neck, kissing him, licking him, tasting him.

I unfastened his belt, unzipped his slacks, and gripped his cock mid-flight, nearly sending us off course. As his attention rose, his levitation floundered.

"What happened to those perfected roots?" I whispered in his ear, teasing him, nibbling on his lobe too.

"The roots are perfect, the witch using them—not so much." Milo grinned, bucking and letting his hard shaft rub against my hip. "But the witch I'm with is quite perfect."

"Careful." I kissed his collarbone. "Flattery will get you everywhere."

It took everything I had to hold myself back once we landed on the balcony. A much easier route to return home than passing through the door attendants, the lobby, the elevator ride. Still, I had to practice patience as Milo punched in the security code. After all, anyone could fly through the balcony route, so the alarm dinged the second our feet reached the mat in front of the sliding glass doors.

Milo slid open the door, and I pushed him inside, practically riding his ass with each step. No way would I make it to the bedroom at this rate.

"Dorian," Milo groaned as I pushed him against the couch.

"Yes." I kissed his neck, running my fingers down his back, lightly clawing at his silk shirt.

"I need to get ready," Milo said, making it clear he wanted a moment to breathe, to prepare, to probably find a more comfortable spot in the penthouse, too.

It'd be so easy to bend him over right here, to plow him, to savor every second, every thrust into him.

"Okay," I said with a raspy breath, a hungry need for him.

We pulled apart long enough for Milo to make his way into our bedroom and the master bath.

I closed our door and took a few seconds to collect myself. His arousal intermingled with my own, making it difficult to control myself, contain my urges, but I settled enough. The heat of passion simmered just below the surface, and I knew the moment he stepped back out, I would boil over from anticipation.

I plopped onto the bed, slowly stripping off my clothes, taking my erection into my hand, and stroking as I thought of Milo.

The ring on my finger was cool to the touch. I took a moment to examine it, to study every detail on my hand. It looked so foreign. A seemingly impossible detail had become a reality. I'd gone from this isolated, broken man unable and unwilling to accept love. Yet here I was now, engaged to the most perfect man in the world. We were building a family together, a life together, a future.

"Penny for your thoughts?" Milo asked, swaggering out of the bathroom in nothing but a pair of pink boxer briefs.

"In this economy?" I scoffed. "It'll cost you way more."

"Can I get a lover's discount?" Milo strutted over to the bed, dropping to his knees the second he reached the edge.

He placed his hands on either side of me, running his knuckles against my hip bones, and without missing a beat, he went to work sucking my dick.

I groaned, growing harder in his mouth with every bob of his head. "Fuck."

Milo gagged, taking in as much as he could again and again until he worked his way to the base. He repeated this motion over and over, enveloping me as he swallowed my entire shaft.

Then he lifted off me, panting a bit. Drool spilled from his lips. His eyes watered. His breathing hastened. But Milo wasn't finished. He returned to my dick, stroking his hand up and down while he used his mouth to tease the head of my cock. Every nerve ignited, propelling me into euphoric ecstasy.

As Milo continued, I slowly started pumping upward, meeting his mouth and pushing in a bit deeper each time. Eventually, Milo released his hand, running it along my thigh to brace himself as I bucked against him, ramming my cock deeper into his mouth each time.

I ran my fingers through his blond hair, grabbing a fistful, and controlling his head as I face fucked him faster.

The gurgles and gasps he let out only further fueled me. Fuck, if I kept this up, I'd cum any second.

"I need to stop," I said, continuing to thrust into him. "I can't... Oh, you feel so fucking good."

Before I knew it, I was on the precipice of climaxing. Each time my cock head pushed into the tight warmth of Milo's throat. Each time Milo gagged on my dick. Each time I panted in sync with my own motion.

"I'm gonna cum." More an announcement than a warning because the second those words escaped my lips, so did a long, dragged-out moan as I burst into Milo's mouth.

I took twitchy thrusts, sliding in and out of Milo's mouth as I shot off my load. It was sticky and sweet, and Milo greedily lapped it up, swallowing every drop and slowly licking my cock clean.

A semi-erection kept me eager for another round, for a chance to fuck Milo, but I needed a second to recover, to prepare.

"Get over here." I pulled Milo up with a touch of telekinesis.

I didn't just call Milo to me, but also the lube in our nightstand.

He climbed up the bed, straddling me, and then lay atop me with his full weight. We kissed and cuddled and grinded against one another. I savored the taste of his mouth, the softness of his skin, the firmness of his muscles.

Pushing him off me, I rolled on top. I tugged at his pink undies, kissing his hip bone, and relishing how hot he looked, revealing almost everything. Pulling down his boxer briefs entirely, I blew Milo, taking in all of him.

Soon, Milo rolled onto his side, thrusting into my mouth and panting as he pushed deeper down my throat. A little whimper of excitement escaped his lips as I stuck a lubed finger inside him, then a second.

Milo was getting close to finishing, to releasing. The deeper I prodded him, the more he explored my throat, the closer he came.

"Wait." I pulled away, growing harder each second I had Milo's cock into my mouth. "I want to finish together this time."

Milo turned over, laying on his stomach, but that wouldn't do. God, I loved staring at his beautiful bubble butt, but I wanted to feel him entirely. I wanted to take in all of him as he took me.

I rolled Milo onto his back, spreading his legs, and slid my dick into his lubed hole. As my head pressed into him, I squeezed a bit more lube onto my cock, making it easier.

Every thrust into Milo made him moan. I kept a steady pace, stroking his cock in rhythm with my motion. I held his gaze, taking in his every expression, the twitch of his body, the panting of his breathing.

I wanted to hold onto this forever, to fuck him all night, but Milo's eyes rolled back, and I knew he was close. Part of me wanted to stop stroking him, to edge him longer, but I'd already made him wait once.

Putting in more effort, I pumped faster in and out of Milo, bringing myself closer, keeping a steady grip on Milo's cock.

"I'm gonna…" Milo whimpered, body convulsing as I railed into him.

Milo came right as I did. While my load filled him up, his load sprayed between us. I collapsed on top of him, our skin sticky with sweat and cum. We panted in unison, and I lay there with all my weight on Milo until we both dozed off.

CHAPTER THIRTY-EIGHT

THE following days, I planned for Christmas, decorating the penthouse because Ben begged and pleaded and bargained to be extra good for Santa Claus. Holidays were never my thing. Overrated, expensive, and tedious. But Ben and Milo enjoyed the cheer, so I rolled my eyes and trudged along to make our home a festive wonderland of horrors.

With Ben out of school for a break, I decided to take some time away from Cerberus. My guild work was lighter than most, since I never had much casework. Plus, the office remained a mourning ground, as many of the enchanters continued grieving Campbell's loss. They all reported to duty with smiles on their faces, but beneath it, their thoughts carved away at me.

"Let's go with this tree," Ben said, dragging me through the field of fresh pine trees. "No, this one. That one. Wait. That one. No. Yes. No. That one."

I huffed. Even Sheamus grumbled as he trudged alongside Ben, who walked up and down each row, picking over the same damn trees, indecisively choosing them based on which was greener or bigger or happier.

"None of these trees are happy."

"Outta my head, rude."

"Sorry about that," I said. "Habit."

Ben squeezed my hand tighter, then pointed to another tree. "This one's happy. It's smiling, see?"

He traced his small fingers along the pine needles at the curvature of some branches around the middle of the tree. His imagination amplified his thoughts, making the tree appear like a slight smiley face if one really stretched to see it that way. For a tiny child, an easy feat. Even the darker patches above helped add to the smiley image, appearing like oval eyes.

"What do you think?"

"I think—"

Sheamus barked, indicating Ben was speaking to him and seeking the dog's opinion over mine.

"I like it, too." Ben giggled.

Finally. I didn't even care if the damn dog was placating Ben. All I cared about was asking an attendant to chop the tree down.

"We're not taking it with us?" Ben asked, watching me pay extra for the company to deliver the tree.

Ben's mind fluttered with memories of his daddy arguing with a previous Christmas tree, demanding it obey him as he struggled to tie the thing to the roof of his SUV. Ben had fond memories of watching his father fight with the tree. It usually led to him being exhausted by the time they got home and cuddling up to watch whatever holiday movies Ben picked.

"I don't have anything to tie it down with," I said. "Plus, my car's not exactly built for it."

"Oh." Ben kicked his feet.

"It'll give us more time to decorate," I said, leading him to the car.

"Okay." Ben sulked.

"Then we can watch a movie." I opened the car door, letting him climb into his seat before I secured his seatbelt. "You can even pick them."

"Christmas movies?"

I groaned. "Sure."

"The Grinch," Ben said with a mischievous smile because he already planned on calling me a Grinch.

"Can't wait." I frowned, giving my grinchiest expression.

Ben laughed, smiling the entire ride home and all night while decorating. I had to redo the strings three times because *Benjiman* said I kept covering the tree's smile. I spent more time telekinetically levitating Ben than I did actually decorating the tree. If it were up to me, the tree would've been good after one box of ornaments, but Ben insisted we shower the tree with joy.

It was pretty morbid, decorating the corpse of a tree we chose to have killed and displayed at home. I grinned a little. That was probably the only part of this holiday I enjoyed. Very goth in its way.

"Stop sitting around." Ben pointed to the top of the tree. "It needs a star."

"Okay, okay." I lifted Ben up, raising him high enough to place the final touch on the tree.

We basked in his hard work. We weren't the only ones. Carlie and Charlie came over, sniffing the tree and curiously eyeing the ornaments.

"Don't even think about it." I pointed to Charlie, whose eyes had turned into giant saucers. He was a moment from pouncing on the smiling tree.

After a moment, I returned to studying the tree, finding a photo taped to the star at the top. It was a silly selfie Milo had taken of the three of us. Ben making a goofy face, Milo grinning from ear to ear, and me frowning. They were probably being annoying right before the photo, but I honestly couldn't recall.

Still, I couldn't help but smile now, loving how Ben chose to celebrate with his new family, his extended family. We'd never replace his parents, but I was glad he was finding joy with us despite all the losses he'd suffered.

"Not done yet. We gotta decorate the rest of the house now," Ben insisted, retrieving some stockings Milo and him had designed the other day.

"Ugh," I groaned, dragging my feet to follow *Benjiman*, the Christmas enforcer.

They were hideous stockings, covered in sparkly sequins and glitter and splotchy paint and random cutout pictures glued to the sock. But Ben had fun making them. Milo did, too. He was basically an overgrown child himself.

"All right, all right, I'm on my way."

By the time Ben and I finished decorating the living room, I collapsed onto the couch. He continued working on things, placing shiny stars in the dining room along with reindeer and snowman cutouts.

I was starting to think his father wasn't exhausted from his battle with the tree he would tie to the car but more drained from the grueling labor of meeting Benjiman's decorative expectations. Seriously, he was a little perfectionist when it came to Christmas. Thank goodness he didn't care this much about the other holidays.

Halloween, he was a bit picky when it came to landing the costume he wanted, but mostly he just wanted a bunch of candy so he could spend all of November crashing out from sugar comas.

By the time Ben finished, I handed him the controller and let him deal with the movie setup. All I wanted was to lie on the couch. Admittedly, watching the Grinch torment those annoying little whothingies was entertaining. They absolutely deserved it.

Unfortunately, Ben's thoughts twisted into a sulk the more we watched. The jokes made him giggle, and the plot kept him entertained even if he'd seen it a dozen times before. The problem came with the snow. It taunted him, teased him, and reminded him he still hadn't had a snowy Christmas despite all his wishes.

The problem was snow required just the right temperature and Chicago remained unseasonably warm this winter or would drop to below freezing with no in between. As such, it remained outside the perfect temperature bubble for a snow day.

Sheamus barked.

I ignored it, same as Ben.

He continued yapping, scratching at the sliding door.

Goddammit. Did he want to go on another walk?

I sighed.

"If you have to use the bathroom, just open the door," I shouted, sinking into the couch.

Milo bought Sheamus those potty grass pads and put them out on the balcony. The whole benefit of adopting an untethered familiar was that they were clever enough to use their magic and open the sliding door.

Still, he continued barking, running over to the couch and whining.

"What's wrong?" Ben paused the movie.

When he sat up, his eyes practically popped out of his head, and his thoughts whirled with excitement.

He bolted to the balcony faster than I could follow his mind. I sat up and saw him standing in frozen awe at the glass door.

"It's snowing!" Ben stared at the white clumps that fell all around the building, landing on the balcony.

Not only was it snowing, but it was sticking awfully fast. I checked my phone, expecting to see some random cold front alert of an unexpected storm rolling in. Instead, my weather app said it was 48 degrees.

What the hell?

"Can I see it?" Ben asked, feet dancing with antsy anticipation as he held the sliding door handle.

Every cell in his body wanted to touch the snow, taste it on his tongue, feel it between his fingers, but he knew the rules. Ben needed permission before stepping out onto the balcony, and only if one of us was home. Sheamus never counted as a chaperone, no matter how protective the dog was.

I nodded to Ben's request, and he rushed outside, shivering immediately at the snowflakes landing on his skin. Sheamus joined him, biting at the air to catch snowflakes. Charlie meowed and ran to the back of the penthouse to escape the chill that entered the house. Carlie, on the other hand, held her ground, laying on the top of the couch and thumping her tail with annoyance.

"I know, I know," I said to her, grabbing one of the throw blankets for her to bundle up with. "How dare we humans make this home less accommodating to your delicate needs."

Carlie let out a groaning meow, then kneaded the blanket before cuddling up for warmth.

I joined Ben on the balcony, folding my arms to stay warm and standing under an awning to avoid the snowflakes. It was odd. The weather seemed far too warm, and I swore there was a sliver of sunlight cutting through the nearby clouds.

My pocket buzzed, and I retrieved my phone.

"Hey, guess who got off work just in time for a snow day?" Milo's voice was particularly cheery. "Bring Ben to the park."

"Ugh, it's probably not going to last that long," I said. "By the time we're dressed and ready and downstairs, then walk to the park, it'll all be melted."

"Not a chance. Consider it a clairvoyant guarantee."

Milo hung up before I could further protest.

Reluctantly, I got ready. It didn't take much to convince Ben or Sheamus. Ben held my hand, skipping through the snow while Sheamus pranced beside him, imitating the human joy.

Thankfully, we had a nice park a few blocks away, perfect to bring kids and play at.

By the time we got to the park, the snow was sticking everywhere. Milo stood on a nearby hill, waving a hand and calling us over. He had sleds.

"How the hell did you manage to get sleds this quickly?"

Milo smiled. "I had a hunch."

"It's a big hill." Ben's eyes widened as he watched other children plunge down the kiddie hill.

"Me and Sheamus will keep you safe." Milo slapped his face against the dog's, showing off their matching scars, and somehow soothing Ben with the reminder.

Milo and Sheamus were twins now. They were strong, and they'd always be there to protect Ben. He didn't have to fear the world with Milo nearby, he didn't have to worry about being alone with Sheamus at his side, and he didn't have to miss his family with me around.

I turned away, eyes watering slightly as those thoughts filled Ben's mind. I took a lot of pride in how much Ben had grown to trust us, love us, but I still worried for him so much. Every little thing needed to be perfect. I didn't want to fail him any more than the world already had.

Milo and Sheamus took turns riding down the hill with Ben. Each of them helped steady the sled so it'd go faster than the others and jump ever so but always land with ease. Ben laughed and screamed and ran up the hill again and again. It wore Milo out pretty quickly.

By his tenth trip, Milo tapped out and took a break while Ben and Sheamus continued.

I let my mind wander as I took in the snowy park, cheering children, and serendipitous snow day.

The thoughts of a nearby woman called out, her mind fixated on the perfect temperature as she channeled her magic.

"Did you seriously hire a Weather Witch?" I turned to Milo, who had the goofiest grin, then tried to blink away his surprise.

Weather Witches were rare and almost exclusively hired by the government. It was one of the most useful cosmic magics in the world, and with their sophisticated skillset, they helped avert many natural disasters by taming the weather. They'd push hurricanes back out to sea, rain down thunderstorms on out-of-control fires, and bring the sun to carve through deadly blizzards.

Still, there were only a handful in the US as far as I knew, and they had limitations.

"How the hell did you hire out some government official?"

"Called in a favor." Milo shrugged, hiding painful thoughts before drifting back to optimism. "She was here for Campbell's funeral. We chatted during the wake."

Every horror held a silver lining in Milo's mind. Campbell's death was a tragedy that'd haunt him for years, yet he considered the blessing of stumbling onto a Weather Witch he was friends with.

"It'd been years since she just conjured a little snow globe of fun for folks."

"And you told her Ben had never experienced a snow day."

"Her only condition is she wants to meet our kiddo."

I sighed. "Fine by me. But I'm not engaging in conversation."

"I already warned her you're a sourpuss."

I scoffed, playfully shoving Milo.

It didn't take long for Milo to abandon me, joining Ben and Sheamus as they ran around in the snow. Milo showed Ben how to make snow angels, they had a telekinetic snowball fight, then they built a snowman with the most deranged pinecone face.

I really liked watching my family have fun. Ben had quickly become the glue that held our family together. It was nice to see him find joy again after suffering such tremendous loss.

Chapter Thirty-Nine

I CONTINUED chasing holiday festivities during the break, anything to distract myself from Caleb and Tara's abduction. There was nothing to be done, not yet. The Global Guild had no leads, Milo had no leads, I had no leads.

All the same, I continued sending manifestations out into the world in hopes one would stumble onto the Celestial Coven. It merely made my day-to-day activities exhausting. I walked in a fog, exerting more magic than usual. I doubled the number of projections searching the world, each returning without the faintest trace.

Ben proved very distracting during these long days, wanting to try something new and holiday themed every day. When I wasn't taking him to see Santa or some Christmas-themed land, I was meeting Vanessa for a playdate with her twins.

Whenever I was home, I was burning baked cookies, poorly decorating them, or doing something not on theme. Usually, I let Milo take the lead on the cooking side of things, but Ben could be insistent.

I also got stuck with cleaning up a lot around the house—especially when it came to the tree itself. It turned into a disaster zone for Charlie and Carlie to terrorize. They each managed to break at least one ornament a day.

Still, it made for a strong distraction from the absence of Caleb and Tara. They were out there, lost somewhere in Amara's clutches. Who knew what hell she had planned? Sadly, I did know. Literal Hell.

I researched celestial and cosmic events coming up. From constellation alignments to passing comets, all the way to magical symphonies planned with the ebb and flow of magical planes.

We had months to plan, according to online searches. And that was if Amara could make use of the nearest comet scheduled to fly by. It'd be years before a bigger event came to pass. Something told me Amara wouldn't wait that long. For a woman who'd patiently plotted for millennia, she seemed pressed to reach the end of her plan, which meant she'd ensure Tara ascended into this divine goddess soon.

And I wasn't comfortable leaving Caleb and Tara in Amara's care for months on end. I'd seen how she treated Theodore, how she broke him until he behaved. My students wouldn't suffer under her deranged plots.

The more I dwelled, the longer the days lasted.

As the night rolled around, I tucked Ben into bed and prepared to join Milo on the couch. Watch a few episodes of something dreadful and pass out.

A haunting hum echoed in my ears, like a faint ringing. I knew this sound, this voice. Pausing in the hall, I focused on the whisper. Words were impossible to catch, but I knew someone was speaking, calling out.

This link held strong like something I shared with Milo. Only foreign and foul.

"Theodore," I whispered.

I channeled my telepathy, reaching out to link with all my roaming manifestations. None of them had found him, nor had a trace or trail led to the wicked warlock.

Still, he reached out, contacting me in the faintest way. A desperate plea for help or a devious ploy? If I had to guess—both. It was Theodore Whitlock, after all.

Following the hum, I trailed the edges of the psychic plane, knowing somewhere out there I had a literal beacon with Theodore's location.

"What's going on?" Milo asked, staring at me from the couch.

I must've looked ridiculous, taking odd steps, pacing in circles, and craning my neck ever so slightly to catch a glimpse of Theodore's voice.

"I think I know how to find the Celestial Coven."

Milo quirked a brow. "How?"

"Through Theodore."

"Absolutely not, that psychopath will—"

"Will lead me to Caleb and Tara."

"And how exactly will you track him?"

"I'll follow the breadcrumbs he's left me."

Milo's expression turned pensive. For Theodore's mind to call out to me from literally anywhere in the world, it meant we shared a connection. I didn't need to explain the bond between Theodore and me, though it was nothing like what I shared with Milo. My bond to Theodore was through trauma, pain, and suffering.

Since diving into his mind during the kidnapping, his connection to me had only amplified. Honestly, I didn't believe I'd rid myself of Theodore's sadistic thoughts until he'd finally died. One could only hope.

"You don't have to do this."

"I know I don't. I want to."

"We have months to track them," Milo said. "You don't have to take on this burden of scouring the globe on your own."

"I don't want to wait months. I've been sick to my stomach with the days and weeks that've already passed. Leaving Caleb and Tara locked away in Amara's clutches for… I can't."

"Okay, I understand, but you need to be on your guard." Milo's thoughts twisted to the trap I'd mentioned, the one which Amara used to immobilize me during her attack on Chicago.

"I won't interact."

"All the same, Theodore could be luring you simply for Amara to spring some new trap on you."

"Doubtful," I replied. "He'd never help her with anything. Their mutual disgust for each other is one thing we can count to our advantage."

Milo didn't respond, merely kept his worries buried beneath his surface thoughts.

"My only goal would be to find a location; I'll leave putting a stop to the Celestial Coven and all the glorious rescue plans to you and the Global Guild."

Part of me hoped that if I followed this thread, we could resolve things without involving my homeroom coven. But another part knew the fates of lives had become cemented. We were all bound, and something told me this wouldn't come to a conclusion until my students and I all faced off against Theodore Whitlock again in a final showdown.

Still, that didn't mean those vile witches could keep Caleb and Tara.

"So, how are we doing this?" Milo asked, running his thumb along the golden band of his engagement ring.

Damn, that little gesture practically took the air out of my lungs.

We.

We were a we. We'd always be a we moving forward.

"We're not doing anything," I said, attempting and failing to lighten the mood. "I'm not even doing much."

"Meaning?"

"I'm calling back all my manifestations, and creating one manifestation," I explained. "It'll be infused with a bit more strength simply to defend against any possible traps or tricks."

"Plus, the added benefit of a quicker search with one enhanced manifestation over a pack."

"Precisely."

Not that it'd do much good if I didn't have a trail to follow.

"I'm going to contact the Global Guild," Milo said. "Let them know we might get a location soon."

"One can hope."

I summoned a manifestation, an extension of my mind, and broke him off from my core self. He followed the tune of Theodore's soft hum and disappeared into the psychic plane. With any luck, we'd find and retrieve Caleb and Tara before the new year.

CHAPTER FORTY

I FOLLOWED the tiniest thread of psychotic energy. Theodore's thoughts held a chaotic frequency, one of which I understood all too well now that I'd embraced his mind. The wicked musings called out with a soft echo, guiding my manifested self through the psychic plane until I reached a dark cavern.

This was where Tara and Caleb had been dragged weeks ago. I didn't know this location. Was it underground? Was it some archaic temple? Was this ancient mystique merely an illusion meant to deceive those who entered this cave?

It didn't matter. I needed to pinpoint this location, give Milo the destination, and then prepare for a war where I'd have no choice but to drag my other students into it in order to ensure all my students survived.

Twelve bound by fate, all because I had to change the life of one student. My interference in Caleb's life that semester now linked all of them together on a mystical level I'd never comprehend. I wasn't even sure Milo fully gleaned it, but he knew their futures held stronger together than apart. My homeroom coven was intertwined, and I had to make sure it stayed that way.

I wouldn't lose Caleb to Hell. I wouldn't lose Tara to her mother's deranged obsession. I wouldn't lose anyone to The True Witch or her Celestial Coven.

Skirting around the pillars, I carefully studied them. I only made a little sense out of the sigils, mainly from knowledge I shared with Katherine. My students had opened their minds to me, offering intel and insight where they possessed it. Katherine's comprehension of enchantments far superseded the average witch. Hell, she excelled beyond most of the expert witches across the globe.

Most of that talent came from years of dedicated study, but part of her strength came from the memories of Moire she absorbed. While the vile grimoire controlled her body like a puppet, Katherine did her part to learn the wealth of knowledge that book contained. It helped ensure I didn't trigger any of these traps.

The pillars and walls were soaked in protective magics that'd easily ignite even when met with the psychic projection. Carefully, I weaved around them, searching for an exit, for a distinguishable landmark, for a concrete location.

"*I know you're here, friend.*" Theodore's thoughts shuddered, filled with quaking anticipation.

I ignored him, making my way through this horrifying lair. Bones lay strewn throughout the cave floor. Were these victims of Grim? Former Celestial Coven members? Foolish witches who challenged The True Witch? Or perhaps sacrifices in some ancient blood magic ritual when witches still believed in such perverse forms of casting.

"*Better hurry,*" Theodore teased, his teeth chattering alongside his whispering thoughts. "*Mommy's casting a ritual to ship off my baby bro. I'd hate for you to miss the best part.*"

The suddenness of his voice startled me, but I wouldn't let his wicked words deceive me.

He was lying. There was no way Amara had opened the Gate of Hell already. Right? She mentioned requiring a celestial event, something to harness.

But if Theodore was telling the truth…

I couldn't chance it. I had to know. On the off-chance Theodore planned on tricking me, I kept my guard up. Not that he could do too much to a manifestation, but I didn't want to lose this opportunity to gain intel on their location.

Drifting through the halls of this ancient ruin, I followed the vibrations of Theodore's guiding thoughts.

In the deepest depths of this place stood a ritual chamber with a large arched doorway. Like two pillars outstretched and twisted together at the tip. The top where they met held a flame. Many built-in torches lined the arch all the way to the bottom, but none were lit except for the flickering fire at the top.

Amara stood before the archway, chanting a spell.

Theodore's mind opened to me, revealing this location, the meaning of the symbols on the pillar, the purpose of Amara's ancient words.

This was the Gate of Hell. She was…she was opening it. But how?

Surrounding her were all three of her children. Tara was placed the furthest out, still within Amara's sight, but far enough from any immediate danger that came with opening the literal Gate of Hell. A white barrier held Tara in place, blocking her magic despite the constant bombardment of strikes.

Tara shouted, screaming with a soft echo. I barely heard her behind the barrier containing her. Shadows and ice and crackling screeches did nothing to break the white barrier holding her in place.

Directly behind Amara, Caleb sat on his knees, hands bound behind his back, and a chain around his neck keeping him completely centered with the warded pentagram he was bound within.

On Amara's other side, opposite Tara, but nearly as far away, lay Theodore. He was bound with heavy shackles on his back within a similar pentagram to Caleb's. Though Theodore's held more binding sigils.

"*How is she doing this?*" I trembled in the presence of Hell opening before my eyes. "*She needed a celestial event.*"

Theodore quietly chuckled. "*I am a celestial event. All of her children are. She's used our births to move her plans forward for thousands of years.*"

"*What?*" I cocked my head, locking onto Theodore's hollow blue eyes.

"*She's birthed heroes and villains for centuries, bringing legends into this world all in some pathetic ploy to attain her dream, her vision, of ruling the universe alongside the perfect child."* Theodore flicked his eyes toward the barrier containing his sister. *"Tragic Tara was the best she managed."*

Amara continued performing her ritual, retrieving a blade and turning to face Caleb.

The fear lodged in his throat passed to me, locking me in place as I trembled.

With a wicked smile, Amara held the blade out, then turned it back on herself and sliced open her palm. Taking strong strides, her heels clicked against the stone floor as she approached Theodore.

Amara spoke in some twisted language; the words carried a dark echo with them.

When she finished her chant, she slapped her bloody hand against Theodore's forehead and sent a surge of energy hurling toward the sleeping Gate.

Amara channeled Theodore's magic as she chanted her ritual. She was really going to do it. Amara was about to open the Gate of Hell itself.

No!

I couldn't allow this. I couldn't let her throw Caleb into Hell itself. But I didn't have the strength to beat her. Not as a manifestation. Even if I left now, no one would get here in time. Not even Gladiatrix or Milo could fly who-the-fuck-even-knew where in a matter of minutes. Seconds, really.

Maybe I could free Caleb, free Tara. Give them a chance to fight back.

No.

Amara had defeated them once before. Now, she'd have demons ushered through the Gate, come to claim their sacrificial prize.

Flames ignited one by one on the rounded pillar of the arch that formed the Gate of Hell. The empty space turned black and murky like a pool of tar. Not like…literally just that. The Gate was made of fiendish demonic energy.

Beasts of all kinds stepped through, twelve in total. They were made of tar, mere silhouettes of demon shapes. Some humanoid, some arachnid-like, others slithering, and one even fluttered a bit as it found its footing on the ground.

"What kind of demons are these?"

"Demon lords," Theodore whispered, staring inquisitively at their presence. "They're too powerful to step into this reality. They either need to possess a host immediately or walk in this world as a proxy of themselves."

The tar bodies. It was the demon equivalent of a manifestation, like how I broke apart my overpowering telepathy.

"Welcome." Amara curtsied.

The demons knelt or bowed, absorbing the magic in Amara's words. Their blank faces twisted in on themselves as the tar of their silhouette bodies bubbled.

"It is long overdue, but I have acquired the sacrifice you desire." Amara pointed at Caleb, who trembled at the sight and power of the demons surrounding him.

This couldn't happen. I had to stop it. Caleb and Tara's minds made me shake uncontrollably, barely able to think rationally with their fear consuming me.

"*I could help,*" Theodore taunted, always screwing with me since the day we met. "*If you do the tiniest of favors for me.*"

"*You can't stop her,*" I snarled. "*She's had you under her control since the day she liberated you.*"

"*Biding my time, friend.*" Theodore smiled, blood trickling down his face, making his expression all the more menacing. "*I can spare my siblings Mommy's fate, but I require something first.*"

"*What?*"

"*You.*" Theodore's blue eyes widened. "*I want your psychic touch. I want the gentle embrace of another mind against mine.*"

The toxic, hollowed-out soul of Theodore's every exposed thought revealed no deceit. He longed for companionship, craved acceptance beyond everything else. His crew had died, but even when they lived, they only offered a portion of fulfillment. The doctor who groomed him left Theodore longing and lusting for a telepath's touch.

"*I'm not him,*" I attempted to explain. "*I'm not Dorian. I mean, I am, but only a fraction of myself. I'm a manifestation of my mind. Just a piece broken off from the whole.*"

"That's fine." Theodore smirked. *"I can settle for a taste and devour the rest of you later."*

I hovered near him, eyeing the spelled shackles which held him in place.

"Don't worry. Mommy's bindings are a lot looser now that she doesn't have her residential enchantment witch to reinforce the wards." Theodore batted his long lashes, playfully, excited, and entertained. *"Guess I owe you for that one, huh, friend?"*

There wasn't another way. Caleb was seconds away from being dragged into the pits of Hell itself. I couldn't, wouldn't allow such a fate to befall him.

With little time and no alternative, I delved into Theodore's mind. I sank deeper into his thoughts, reaching the gnarled tree of his inner core. Broken branches twitched and rattled, crackling as they stretched out far and wide, searching for me.

One by one, the twisted branches snatched at me, clawing at my flesh, digging beneath my skin, binding me in place, and dragging me closer to the core of the tree.

I resisted out on instinct, a futile effort. Still, I couldn't help but shudder in Theodore's grasp.

Once I reached the trunk, the bark dripped with an oozy black tar, smelling of rot and burning on contact. Tar bubbled and popped, sizzling against my skin, and pulling me closer to the tree.

It pulled me into itself, carving space between the bark and locking me in the deepest depths of Theodore's mind.

"Gotta keep you nice and safe." Theodore stood tall, stretching with cat-like aloofness. *"Wouldn't want you running off after I fulfill my end of the deal."*

Theodore locked his eyes on the etched bindings of his chains. He shook his head back and forth, channeling telekinesis in the same fluid motion. A seemingly random move, but it held precision. The casting pulled at the blood dripping down his face, his mother's blood.

Now, he held it before him, split apart into hundreds of droplets. Theodore muttered something in a foreign language and sent the blood drops splashing against the carvings that spelled his shackles.

They crackled and hissed from the acidic touch. Smoke wafted from his chains and skin in equal measure, and suddenly, Theodore leapt from the pentagram which contained him.

"My glory can't be contained." He cocked his head, studying the demons surrounding Amara and Caleb.

"Think before you act, my sweet." Amara turned to Theodore, the calmest expression with the coldest green eyes.

I used to believe Theodore inherited his icy stare from his father, but all they shared were the same baby blues. No, the heartless gaze he gained from his mother.

"Thinking is for chumps," Theodore said with a cackle. "It's all about chaos, Mommy."

Amara waved a hand at Theodore, locking him in an ocean instantaneously. He floated in his dark mind, lost in the sea of his mother's wrath. This whirlpool force dragged him deeper and deeper until he reached the gnarled tree at the bottom.

Until he reached me.

Theodore struggled against the current, resisted the pull, gasped for breath, but despite it all, he couldn't free himself.

I resisted the prison of the tree, clawing at the water between Theodore and me. If I could reach him, I could help.

Theodore choked, drowning on the water he swallowed.

He wouldn't last much longer. I needed to reach him. Help him. Break him free of Amara's Oceanic Collapse magic. If I were my core self, filled with my full branch magic, I could snap my fingers and shatter this ocean to nothingness.

Theodore fought the current, grasping a stray branch, and pulled himself closer. Soon, his lips reached mine, a breath apart, and his thoughts begged for oxygen.

"Then snap out of it." I slapped a hand over his face, blocking his lips from pressing to mine, and hit him with all the psychic energy at my disposal.

Theodore gasped, choking on the air as he snapped out of the trap his mother had bound him within. He collapsed, falling to his knees, and panted as many breaths as he could fill his lungs with.

"How did you…" Amara furrowed her brow. "That goddamn telepath. I need to kill that one."

"He's mine," Theodore wheezed. "Same as my brother. You can't have him."

"This thing isn't your brother." Amara flicked a hand in Caleb's direction, gesturing to him like he really was an abomination in her eyes. "It's a tool. Nothing more."

"Well, all the same, I'm keeping Tater Tot." Theodore forced himself up, struggling to stand at his feet. Despite breaking him free from the watery prison, he still stood like a man who'd just stepped out of a pool, heavy and wobbly.

"I don't have time for this." Amara turned back to the demons, speaking some foul demonic language as she no doubt instructed them to retrieve Caleb.

Each of these horrendous creatures crept toward Caleb, each stretching their clawed hands out to snatch him away.

Panic consumed me. There was nothing I could do, nothing Theodore would do. It was too late. They were going to drag Caleb to Hell.

"Stop," Theodore roared, carrying a powerful command in his voice.

Every demon froze.

"They will never stop," Amara snapped. "They require a ruler, a servant. A sacrificial prisoner offering them a taste of magic."

Perhaps due to the Gate itself or the close proximity to so many demons, Amara's mind was left unguarded. Her protective magics no longer shielded her thoughts, and I gained a glimmer of her goal for Caleb.

Caleb was meant to be a glass of water in Hell. Not nearly enough to satiate the thirst of billions, but enough for them all to fight over. They'd devour Caleb, drinking down his magical energy until they consumed him entirely. Once dead and gone, he'd restore himself, bound eternally to Hell as its king, but meant to serve forever as substance for the magic-hungry demons.

He'd die a million deaths, suffer a billion agonies, and serve a trillion years. He'd never know peace, freedom, anything.

"*Stop her,*" I begged.

"Take The True Witch," Theodore commanded. "Take her to Hell, make her your queen, and ravish her until your world crumbles to ashes."

In that instance, the demons sprang on Amara, ripping at her flesh, stabbing deep into her body. She thrashed and screeched and cast countless spells.

It made no difference. These demons were the elite lords of Hell. They resisted her magic, tearing into her, biting and beating her.

They dragged Amara toward the Gate. She screamed and wailed and reached out for Theodore, for Tara, for anyone.

"You will regret this, Theodore!" Amara bellowed, fighting against the demons who pulled her through the black pit of tar. "You think Hell can hold me? Nothing can contain my glory! I will drag myself back and break you into a thousand pieces! I will make you beg for death! You will be an obedient boy. When I'm done with—"

With that, Amara sank through the tar entirely. In a matter of seconds, that bubbling liquid hardened, and the Gate of Hell sealed again.

Caleb quaked, staring at the flames on the rounded pillars flicker out one by one as the Gate closed entirely. "Is she…is she dead?"

"Lord, I hope not." Theodore knelt beside Caleb. "Wouldn't be any fun if she got off that easily, right, Tater Tot?"

Caleb cringed at Theodore's gentle touch. He brushed the back of his hand against Caleb's cheek, running his knuckles along his collarbone.

"I remember trying to kill you once." Theodore smiled. "You know what they say, if at first you don't succeed."

Theodore wrapped his hands around Caleb's throat and squeezed.

"*Stop,*" I shouted to no avail.

"What makes you so special, Tate Whitlock?" Theodore straddled Caleb, sitting on top of the boy as he thrashed in place, unable to fight back with his hands bound. "Huh, Tater Tot? Why did Father go out of his way to make sure you were shielded from Mommy's wrath? He never protected me from my destiny. Never protected Tragic Tara. Why you?"

Caleb gasped, struggling to breathe as his face turned red. His thoughts blurred, dizzying as he lost consciousness.

Tara slammed against her barrier even harder, begging and screaming for Theodore to stop.

"*I said stop,*" I screamed, rattling the trunk of the gnarled tree containing me.

The bark splintered and cracked. Not enough to escape, but enough to draw Theodore's attention.

He released Caleb, who wheezed and panted beneath Theodore.

Tara calmed herself, staring at Caleb with concern.

"*Well, well, well…*" Theodore ran his hands through his hair, smiling. "*I do so love an assertive psychic.*"

"*Let them go,*" I pleaded.

"*I think you and I are gonna have a lot of fun together, friend.*" Theodore ran his fingers along his stomach, almost like he was caressing himself.

"*You have everything you want. Your father is dead. Your mother is in Hell. You're free. You have me.*"

"*A piece.*" Theodore rocked his head side to side, contemplating. "*No, I still have so much more to do.*"

He stood up, casting telekinesis to unbind Caleb. It didn't release Caleb entirely, still bound by the pentagram, but now he wouldn't be defenseless if Theodore had another psychotic tantrum.

"I think I should summon a real army of demons," Theodore said, approaching the dormant Gate of Hell. "Then I can level more than just a simple, stupid city. I can slaughter the world, bathe it in blood."

Theodore's mind reveled in the chaos, the craving, the carnage he sought to unleash upon the world. The gnarled tree of his inner core swelled bigger and stronger, more branches stretched out wide as his mind buzzed with a thousand thoughts, possibilities of destroying the entire world.

All he needed to do was figure out how to open the Gate of Hell without his mother.

"I wonder what the world would look like if every demon returned again," Theodore mused, studying the symbols lining the Gate. "Under my rule, nonetheless."

Theodore turned his gaze to Caleb, then to Tara. His heart pounded, thrumming loudly as he considered his siblings, his blood, his family.

"Who needs the blessing of the old gods?" He glared down at Caleb, then flicked his attention to Tara. "Or the divine leadership of a new goddess? I'll make a much better god than you ever would, dearest Tragic Tara."

He wouldn't be a god, merely a beast bent on destroying everything with an army of demons under his thrall.

I had to find a way to break loose from his inner core. I had to find a way to free Caleb and Tara, communicate with my core self, and somehow, stop Theodore Whitlock from ending all life.

THE END

...UNTIL THE CONCLUSION
NEXT SEMESTER.

BRANCHES
OF PAST
AND
FUTURE
CODEX

For unknown reasons, a little over two hundred years ago, magic returned to the world. When everyone gained access to magic, people were referred to by two different titles.

Witch – Law abiding citizens using their magic for good.

Warlock – Corrupted people who cast their magic selfishly.

THERE ARE TWO TYPES OF MAGIC:
Root magic – Standard magic that all witches have access to.

Branch magic – Unique magic that differs person to person.

ROOT MAGIC

There are four root magics. Every witch in the world has access to these same four root magics; however, the amount of control is based on training and skill.

Telekinesis – The ability to move things with one's mind.

Levitation – Harnessing gravitational polarity in the core of one's body to float.

Sensory – The ability to track and pinpoint demonic energy.

Banishment – The ability to repel demonic energy from the mortal world, exorcising the unnatural presence.

BRANCH MAGIC

There are twelve types of branches. Each branch has their own unique attributes. Most witches are born with only one branch magic. Some people are born branchless, meaning they have no unique magic. In rare cases, some people are born with multiple branches.

Alteration – This branch focuses on altering a witch's physical limits. This can involve enhancing strength or senses. It can also involve manipulating and altering what a body can do such as invisibility or duplication.

Arcane – Unique and rare unclassified magic. Witches who possess arcane magic are often coveted because of their power. Arcane magic is usually a mix of two or three types of branches in such a way that it becomes impossible to classify the magic into any other branch.

Augmentation – Altering the physical nature of a witch's body. This can include added appendages such as tails or wings. It can also include the removal or replacement of certain limbs or organs. There are many varieties to augmentation magic, some major or minor, but it's important to understand this differs from standard physical anomalies. Most augmentations are interwoven in such a way that they link the nervous system and the magic of the witch together.

Bestial – This branch connects a witch to the animal kingdom in one form or another. There are dozens of different varieties to this branch, all revolving around animals. Some witches are born as therianthropes, which allows them to take on the physical attributes of an animal. Others can shift entirely into an animal form. Some can communicate with animals. Many witches with a bestial branch are born linked to one animal in particular that becomes their familiar. These familiars share the magic with their witch.

Cosmic – Magical energy that is drawn from the stars and astral plane of existence. This can include things such as manipulating light or darkness. It can also involve moving through the astral plane through things such as teleportation or portal doorways.

Enchantment – A written and spoken form of magic. This is where the traditionally known form of spellbooks comes from. Channeling magic into symbols is a common form of enchantment magic that allows anyone access to the spell so long as the witch who created the spell freely shares it. Enchantments can come in the form of words on parchment, reciting key phrases, combining ingredients into a potion, and storing magic into sigils.

Entropy – Often regarded as the most shameful branch in existence. This magic deals with things like poison, venom, toxins, and other diseased aspects of necrotic rot. Because of the deadly nature of this branch, entropy witches are shunned by most of society and blamed for the sickness in the world.

Hex – A darker magic that allows a witch to manipulate probability around them. Hexes can counter or weaken other magics. They can warp the senses of another person. Some hexes can breathe life to curses, striking down foes with in simple or severe ways.

Primal – Elemental control. This can come in the form of controlling or creating an element through magic. Most witches can harness either control or creation, but some can do both. Common elements include fire, water, earth, air, electricity, ice, and steel. There are many others including unique minerals, types of florals, and combinations of elements.

Psychic – This type of magic delves in mental control beyond normal limitations. Psychic magics have the widest array of types. There are lots of mental magics from reading minds, sensing emotions, predicting the future, observing the past, manipulating thoughts, conjuring illusions, and countless others. It is often said, if a person can think it, the psychic magic is likely out there somewhere.

Rejuvenation – This is a healing type magic. While rejuvenation can be used by a witch to heal themselves or others, there are often limitations. Many healing magics are only temporary as the magic is a shortcut. Most of the time, when the magical effects wear off, the injury returns even in a mild form. Severe wounds must be looked at by medical professionals before the rejuvenation magic fades away.

Ward – This is typically a binding or barrier type magic. In most cases this is used to protect individuals or entire areas. Schools, hospitals, and government facilities are often covered in warding magic.

TYPES OF DEMONIC ENERGY

This type of energy is unnatural to the mortal world. Demons claw their way through dimensional barriers so they can feast upon the magic in the world. When demons break into the dimension, they often shatter into pieces.

Wisps – fractured droplets of demonic energy usually in the form of small white lights. They act on instinct alone, seeking out magic.

Fiends – Tarlike creatures made from a collection of wisps. They are feral, low level demonic beasts that crave magic. If they absorb enough magic, they'll ascend to demons.

Demons – Otherworldly creatures that crave magic to sustain their existence in the mortal world. They must constantly consume magic as they will perish without a steady supply. Demon bodies leak magic quickly, making them regularly hunt witches for more substance. There are tens of thousands of types of demons. Most monster lore is inspired by actual demons such as gorgons, vampires, sirens, hydras, and so much more.

Devils – When a demon possesses a human host, they transcend to something far stronger and harder to kill. They don't leak magic, and they become almost impossible to detect. However, hosts can't contain a demon for very long and most possessions end in the body rotting inside and out.

PROFESSIONAL WITCH RANKINGS

There are many types of government and private sector jobs that require magic. The most aspired to position is a guild witch.

In order to legally cast magic, a witch requires a license, waiver, or fledgling permit. Without official government documentation and approval a witch can face fines or even jail time for illegally casting their magic.

Guilds – Private companies that work to protect citizens within a particular territory. Many guilds compete for popularity and work to be the most successful in an area. Some take on jobs by the city, picking up the slack. Many work for private citizens. Others specialize in particular magics.

Acolytes – These are young witches who are recently licensed and seeking to become professional enchanters. They usually work for free as assistants and sidekicks to gain experience in the industry.

Enchanters – Professional witches who are deemed the best in their field. They keep the streets clean of demonic energy, dangerous warlocks, and anything deemed a threat to society.

Guild Masters – The leading witch of a particular guild. They oversee all the enchanters and acolytes of a particular guild. While proficiency in magic is significant to claim this title, it is important to note that guild masters are not always the strongest witch in an area, but simply the most calculating. To become a guild master a witch requires approval from the enchanters working there and from the board that funds the guild.

ACKNOWLEDGMENTS

I want to give a huge thank you to everyone who has continued returning to the Branches of Past and Future series. When I originally plotted this out for six books, I never thought I'd see it all the way through. Part of me wrote book one with a solid conclusion as a way to close the door on the massive world and the many characters within it. But I wanted to make sure to leave that door cracked just a bit so I could explore them for the semesters that followed just like I envisioned. Dedicating so much time and energy to a series can really take it out of you—in the best way, of course. Still, I always struggled with this series because my goal is to offer all the characters their moment to shine.

Since writing book one, there have been characters I've known about since the beginning who weren't introduced right away. There have been characters I've had to cut because there just wasn't enough time plot wise to explore. And there are scenes that I never really wrote out fully because I couldn't fit them into the story organically. All and all though, it's been a really exciting ride. I've loved sharing Dorian's growth with readers. I've loved exploring the many facets of Milo. I've loved grieving Finn. Honestly, it's been such a fun journey with all the students, staff, professional enchanters, and villains.

I can't believe we're one book away from the very end. I'm not ready to say farewell to this world. *Three Meant To Be* was a big part of my launch during my first year of publication and I've put out another book to this series every year since deciding to enter the world of indie writing. It's bizarre knowing this beautiful series is almost to the conclusion. I hope you'll join me for one final book as we say farewell to everyone and wish them a wonderful ending.

Thank you for diving into this world with me. It really means a lot.

AUTHOR BIO

MN Bennet is a former high school teacher, writer, and reader. He lives in the mountains of Arizona.

He enjoys writing paranormal and fantasy stories with huge worlds (sometimes too big), loveable romances (with so much angst and banter), and Happily Ever Afters (once he's dragged his characters through some emotional turmoil).

When he's not balancing classes, writing, or reading, he can be found binge watching anime or replaying Baldur's Gate 3 for the millionth time.

Author website:

https://www.mnbennet.com

Amazon page:

https://www.amazon.com/stores/MN-Bennet/author/B0BLJJK5NF

Goodreads page:

https://www.goodreads.com/author/show/23017668.M_N_Bennet

Patreon:

patreon.com/MNBennet

Find All My Stuff:

https://linktr.ee/mnbennet